Death
in the
Silent Places

Death
in the
Silent Places

PETER HATHAWAY CAPSTICK

St. Martin's Press • New York

For information, write: St. Martin's Press,
175 Fifth Avenue, New York, N.Y. 10010
Manufactured in the United States of America

Library of Congress Cataloging in Publication Data

Capstick, Peter Hathaway.
Death in the silent places.

1. Big game hunting.   I. Title.
SK33.C34   799.2′6′0922   80-29284
ISBN 0-312-18618-5

Design by Dennis J. Grastorf

10 9 8 7 6 5 4 3

For Mary Catharine—*Nkosikazi gamina.*

Author's Note

MANY OF THE MORE REMOTE PLACE names in this book
were, at the times of the various actions, improperly spelled
by the characters in the light of modern usage. Normally,
the reason for this was the fact that they were interpreted
phonetically from a wide variety of unwritten native languages. Further, the names of some individuals mentioned
peripherally are spelled according to the most common
modern custom. For example, Frederick Courteney Selous
is insisted to be Frederick Courtenay Selous by his biographer, Millais. Both William Cornwallis Harris and Roualeyn
Gordon Cumming, pioneer hunters, are commonly given
hyphenated names. To further confuse the issue, a good
many sources maintain that Cumming's first name was, in
fact, Ronaleyn. Take your choice.

"But there are no words that can tell the hidden spirit of the wilderness, that can reveal its mystery, its melancholy and its charm. There is delight in the hardy life of the open, in long rides rifle in hand, in the thrill of the fight with dangerous game. Apart from this, yet mingled with it, is the strong attraction of the silent places, of the large tropic moons, and the splendor of the new stars; where the wanderer sees the awful glory of sunrise and sunset in the wide waste spaces of the earth, unworn of man, and changed only by the slow changes of the ages through time everlasting."

THEODORE ROOSEVELT
Khartoum, March 15, 1910

Death
in the
Silent Places

Contents

Illustrations appear between pages 114 and 115.

Foreword

IT HAS BEEN SAID that romantic adventure is violence in retrospect. I am a retrospective man and this, although possibly not romantic, is a book about violent adventure. To what would be the sincere regret of most of the characters portrayed, it is also a work of nonfiction.

This is not a book about heroes, although some of the people spoken of were unquestionably heroic. It is a collection of extraordinary events and often ordinary men under circumstances of primitive and savage stress. If bravery is the performance of an act despite great personal fear and risk, then we may certainly say that they were all brave. A few may even have been noble, but I'll let you pass on that.

As I am a veteran of the silent places through my career as a professional hunter in central Africa and South America, you will understand that the men I have chosen were hunters, either of dangerous animals or the most deadly prey, man. I have shared their way of life to some degree and in many cases spent time where they had years before. I know the terror a man-eating cat can generate, and I know what it feels like to stalk an armed enemy through the long grass and rocky hills. To be privileged to tell these men's stories in my own words, however, is the closest association I can claim to their deeds.

Today, in a culture where real physical risk is largely limited to changing lanes on a freeway or being bludgeoned in your bed by some overenthusiastic hophead in dire need of whatever the latest chemical escape from reality may be, the contemplation of a life-style in which you may be pulled down and dragged off at any dark moment by a man-eating lion, tiger or leopard is almost beyond comprehension. But it still happens every day in Africa and Asia, and may be taking place as you read these words. Capsulized as we are in a world in which our electronically vicarious thrills and

Hollywoodized "nature" shows are served up over the flash-frozen, microwave-revived, mass-prepared corpse of some long-dead chicken in its disposable aluminum coffin, segmented by insipid feminine-hygiene-product commercials, it's not all that easy to remember—let alone relate to—the fact that we once were, and still are, hunters. As in predators.

Because of our largely urbanized existence, I suspect that some readers may find this book "gory." If this is so, then it is because the truth is gory. In our carefully insulated world of the West, genuinely violent death and its aftermath are visual rarities, although even a few hours of any evening on any network will provide an almost unbelievable casualty list of shooting, explosion, strangling, poisoning, drowning and more thoughtfully disposed-of victims. But not *real* death. In our society that inevitability is neatly and sanitarily packaged in obituaries, memorial services and checks to charities which seem to vie for evermore unpronounceable and dreaded diseases to stamp out.

Alas, death is not so neat in the silent places.

Peter Hathaway Capstick
Naples, Florida
August 1980

Lt. Colonel John Henry Patterson

IT'S A WARM March night in the East African Protectorate in 1898, the smooth, black air around the compound of Indian workmen soft with the promise of the coming rainy season. If there were more of a moon, the half-completed skeleton of the Tsavo Bridge would jut darkly some hundreds of yards away from the field of tents, which loom like strange, pointed khaki mushrooms clustered loosely about the dying eyes of scores of untended campfires. It has been a hard day of work for the more than 2,000 imported laborers, and now, at midnight, nearly all are asleep.

One tent, much like the rest, contains seven men: six laborers and one supervisor, *Jemadar* Ungan Singh, whose title denotes a rank of lieutenant in the Indian Army. He is nearest the open fly of the tent, snoring enough to awaken one of the coolies of his team. Irritated, the man sits up and rubs his eyes, glancing about the murk, over the sleeping forms of his fellows and out the door into the shadowy expanse of the open compound. Wiping away a film of sweat from the close night, he is about to lie back. One does not complain about the snoring of a superior, let alone a *Jemadar*. But something catches his eye, something darker than the pale shadows, creeping slowly toward the open tent. He blinks as fear hooks his stomach with long claws, his eyes growing wider. In rising terror he stares as the form ghosts nearer, a tawny wraith flattened against the ground. It pauses for a heartbeat at the door, then instantly lunges at the sleeping Ungan Singh. Thick white fangs audibly clash against each other as they meet through the flesh of the *Jemadar*'s neck, yet he manages to give a strangled shout of *"Choro!"*—"Let go!"—before, with an irresistible lurch, he is pulled from the tent. At the last instant he is seen to wrap his

1

arm around the giant lion's neck as he disappears into the night.

Ungan Singh does not die easily. Helpless in the lion's jaws, he is dragged struggling through the thorns, futilely flailing the man-eater with his fists. It's likely that the *Jemadar's* unusual personal size and strength give the Sikh quite a few extra moments of unwelcome life as the cat continues to pull and carry him away from the growing clamor of shouts from the camp. The men back in the tent can clearly hear his repeated gargled attempts to scream, and the sounds of his struggle are terrible. After a hundred yards, fate shows some dark mercy in the shape of another huge lion, which charges forward and bites him deeply in the chest, killing the Indian. Irritated by the poor table manners of his partner, the first lion growls loudly, struggling to keep hold of his prey, tugging with all the steel-muscled power of his 500-pound body. As the long fangs tear and the pressure is increased, the man's head is torn completely off, rolling away to land, by chance, balanced on the stump of neck, the eyes still open wide and staring, dead pools of dread. Ignoring the head, the big cat snarls and leaps to grasp the decapitated corpse, fighting briefly with the second lion before both settle down to feed hungrily until the body is consumed but for scattered red scraps of flesh and a few bones. The Tsavo Man-eaters have just killed their third official victim, although quite probably Ungan Singh is actually number ten or eleven. This, however, is just a warm-up, a canapé before the main course. Over the next nine months these two incredibly deadly animals will actually stall the largest colonial power in the world, that of Victorian Britain, bringing one of its most important construction projects to a complete halt and one of its less likely citizens to the status of an international hero.

It was known at home, back in Blighty, as the "Lunatic Line," so dubbed by the London press and generally considered the screwiest exploit of an age not shy of sensationalism. Technically and officially called the Mombasa-Victoria-Uganda Railway, it was planned to run from damn near nowhere, the sweltering east coast port of Mombasa, to virtually the middle of nowhere, which in those days was a pretty fair description of Lake Victoria. On the face of it, especially in the light of today's technology, such an undertaking might not seem very unusual. But in the 1890s, things were a mite different. Most work was done by great gangs of hand labor over some of the toughest terrain south of Abyssinia. If the cost in pounds sterling was virtually obscene, it was downright cheap compared to the price in lives paid by the hordes of Indian coolies whose imported skills and experience were required as the only labor pool before the local WaJamousi, WaKikuyu and Masai started going to Yale and Oxford. Of the more than 35,000 Indians imported, nearly 9,000 were killed, died or were permanently maimed. More than 25,000 additional laborers of the same force were injured or taken ill, but recovered. The dark, coy virgin called Africa had a very hard bosom.

In itself, the "Lunatic Line" was a master stroke of nineteenth-century engineering and execution. Started at the coast in 1896, it was not completed until December 19, 1901. Ostensibly, it was created to help combat the slave trade, although the commercial advantages of a wilderness railroad running deep into the heart of Africa's lake country are also obvious. In all, it twisted snakelike for 580 miles through the most indescribable *nyika,* or wilderness, north-east from Mombasa, across plains and over highlands, spanning rivers and gorges, passing through exotic stops such as Voi, Nairobi and the lakes of Naivasha, ending at last at Kisumu on Lake Victoria. To carve and burrow the "Lunatic Line" through the swamps and highlands by hand labor was an awful undertaking, but, despite the price, it struggled inexorably farther inland every day, foot by foot, rail by rail, mile by murderous mile until, in March of 1898, it touched the Tsavo River, 132 miles up the line. But of the 162 bridges that would have to be built, none would ever bear a name so synonymous with terror and abject human misery as Tsavo.

It doesn't look like much if you care to climb the steep

N'dungu escarpment and gaze over the savage wasteland below. Your vista is a rock-studded desert of pale, leafless thorn and snaggled wait-a-bit bushes making a lousy living from the thick red soil, the only hint of green life the winding crest of feathery hardwoods along the river. Over there, away to the south where the frosty glow of Kiliman-jaro's snows catches the equatorial sun in the distance, you will still see the bridge across the twinkle of cool running water and the glitter of smooth-worn iron flashing off into the bush. The old rails and weather-beaten bridge certainly don't appear very imposing now, hardly worth the horror their building caused. But there was a time when these few square miles were the center of the greatest animal ring of terror in all of Africa.

Obviously, where a railway meets a river, there must be a bridge. The man whose responsibility it became to see the project through turned out to be a Lt. Colonel John Henry Patterson, some years later adding the Distinguished Service Order to his moniker. He arrived at Tsavo from Mombasa on March 1, 1898, blissfully oblivious to the lurking panic about to descend upon the site over the next nine months. Although he later wrote a smashing best-seller about his misadventures with the Tsavo Man-eaters, published by Macmillan in 1907, J. H. was very casual about his own life and career, to the extent that it took me several months to determine what his initials stood for.

An Englishman raised in India who spoke fluent Hindustani, he looks from contemporary photographs to have been somewhere in his thirties at the time of the man-eating outbreak; a perfect *pukka Sahib* in white pith helmet, jodphurs and riding boots, slenderly built and with a most proper mustache. His style of writing, bearing in mind that he was an engineer by trade and not a journalist, is classically Victorian, often charmingly stilted. It's hard to find two paragraphs in a row that don't have some reference to the lions as "the savage brutes." Yet, with the story he had to tell from what was frequently on an uncomfortably first-hand basis, he could hardly have written less than a best-seller.

Considering the importance of the Tsavo Bridge and the necessity of its completion within weather-dictated schedules, Patterson must have been a well-qualified engineer to have been placed in charge of the whole project. Also, from the way in which he attempted to handle the man-eaters, it's almost certain that he had hunted tiger or leopard while in India, as did most British officers when there. In 1909, well after the events of Tsavo, he wrote another book called *In the Grip of the Nyika* (also Macmillan), which deals with some reminiscences of the Tsavo episode as well as hunting experiences of a later trip to East Africa, during which he killed a new species of eland, that continent's largest antelope. It still bears his name as Patterson's Eland. The point is that he was not inexperienced in big-game hunting, although the difficulties he was to have in trying to kill the lions and the number of times he very nearly became a blue-plate special on their menu seem to indicate he was not possessed of any uncanny skill at the hunting arts besides great persistence.

So much for the times and the man. What about the lions?

If we want to second-guess more than eighty years after the events, the Man-eaters of Tsavo were probably rank amateurs, only learning the specialized skill of hunting and killing man through trial and error. The whole area along the track as it passed through southeast Kenya had long been notorious for man-eaters before anybody dreamed of building a railroad there, so their depredations were certainly not without precedent, or later sequel. It would be impossible to surmise what the total number of victims of the Tsavo Man-eaters aggregated; however, they were mature animals when they began giving the railroad problems, and the fact that their den was found, sometime after their deaths, littered with human remains from Africans would indicate that they may have been responsible for nearly one hundred killings. Because outbreaks of man-eating often follow war, plague or slaving caravans, all of which litter the bush with dead bodies, there is no reason to believe that these particular man-eaters did not begin their career by feeding on the coolies dead of disease or injury, who were not buried as ordered but dumped in the heavy bush along the right-of-way. This practice would be the same as teaching lions to eat people and seems to have done precisely this. If a lion happens to eat people and seems to have a healthy streak of free enterprise, he learns quickly that man-eating for fun and profit isn't as easy as it looks. To develop a really first-class reputation takes patience and perseverance; one inherent occupational hazard being that the prey has a disturbing tendency to throw spears and shoot once a good shopping route has been established. However, if he works hard, sacrifices, learns from his mistakes and really pays attention, he may become the subject of a best-selling book, provided he doesn't actually eat the author in his enthusiasm.

When Patterson arrived by train at Tsavo, then the end of the line, he found between 2,000 and 3,000 coolies ganged at the railhead, ready to start work. From the record, it seems that the lions got there about the same time and began the festivities quietly and fumblingly at first, but clearly recognizing the setup as a literally movable feast. The railroad laborers still had no idea of the peril to which they were now exposed.

Within his first few days there, Patterson had been told that two men had been carried off by man-eaters, but, since both were known to be excellent workmen and to have accumulated decent savings, he decided that they had much more likely been murdered for their money. Since such skullduggery was common, he gave the matter little more thought. He didn't know it then, but he was soon to begin thinking of nothing but the lions.

An embarrassed blush of dawn was creeping through the bush when Patterson was shaken awake and told of the snatching of Ungan Singh. Taking another officer who happened to be at the railroad, a Captain Haslem (who shortly thereafter was murdered by the Kikuyu and his body savagely mutilated), the two men found the pug marks of the killer lion with no difficulty in the sand and followed them bloodily to the point where the second lion had entered, stage right. A few more yards and they were feeling fortunate not to have had breakfast. I can personally assure you that what is left of a human being after a pair of man-eaters have done their act would give a garbage grinder the gags. The presence of the *Jemadar*'s head, untouched but for the ragged stump of neck, the open eyes staring at them with a horrified expression, was a touch that undid them both to the core, even though, with Indian service, they would not have been naive to the more unsettling aspects of violent death. With a few coolies, they gathered up the chewed bones and overlooked scraps of the lieutenant and buried them under a cairn of rocks, carrying the surprisingly heavy head back to camp for identification by the medical officer. Realizing the degree of potential disaster the lions represented to the project as well as to the personnel, the shaken Patterson swore to "rid the neighborhood of the brutes." This was to be one hell of a lot more easily vowed than accomplished.

This same evening marked the beginning of one of the most incredible extended episodes ever to occur between man and beast as adversaries. Patterson, with few options open, climbed a tree near the tent where the *Jemadar* had been taken and began a vigil, waiting for the killer to return to the place where he had last found food. After several uncomfortable hours, in company of his .303 service rifle and a 12-gauge shotgun loaded with one barrel of slug and the other ball, he heard the lions begin to roar some distance away, the blood-chilling thunder slowly coming closer and closer. If there's anything more courage-draining than listening to a pair of man-eaters advertising as they close on your position, then it is the sudden stop of the roaring, leaving you no idea of their location, although their silence means they have begun to hunt. Minutes crawled to a half hour as Patterson stared with aching, unseeing eyes into the darkness, body screaming from the torture of the hard tree-limb perch. Silence. Not even a murmur came from the terrified men below in their closed tents. Then, from half a mile away, unearthly screams and shouts razored the night

as the man-eaters broke into another tent in a different
section of the railhead camp and dragged off a laborer.
Frustration welling up, Patterson realized that there was
nothing to be done but wait until dawn to investigate. Surely,
there would be no sign of the lions around this area tonight,
now that they had made a kill. Disgusted and discouraged,
he climbed back down and returned to his tent, which he
was sharing with Dr. Rose, a medical officer.

Considering that a man had been killed close by the night
before and another just taken within a half mile an hour
ago, Patterson doesn't precisely tend to stun one with his
smarts. His own tent was light canvas, as lion-proof as damp
tissue paper, pitched in the open without any sort of barrier,
an easy mark for even a dim-witted *simba*. In the wee hours,
both Patterson and Dr. Rose were awakened by something
stumbling over the tent ropes. With an even greater display
of folly, they went outside with a lantern, but they saw
nothing and returned to bed. The next morning revealed
that it had indeed been one of the lions who had stopped by
for a late snack, probably changing his mind about attacking
when confused by getting tangled up in the ropes. Patterson
got the hint and moved to quarters in a hut surrounded by a
then-presumed-safe thorn enclosure with a fire burning all
night, his roommate another medical officer named Dr.
Brock.

The next evening, Patterson decided to try his luck again
at the tent where the last coolie had been nailed. As he
would find later, he took quite a chance walking the half
mile to the place in the dark, followed by a man carrying a
lantern and another leading a goat, which he tied to the base
of his tree in hope of the lions getting bored with their
steady diet of coolie laborer. As further experience proved,
light or fire was of absolutely no effect as a deterrent to the
man-eaters' attacks; they seemed to regard even a bonfire as
a rather romantic touch of candlelight to a good dinner.
Patterson *Sahib,* however, lucked out, and he and his men
made the trip without any surprises with big teeth. Soon he
was up the chosen tree, praying for a shot at his savage
brutes. As the evening wore on, the rainy season chanced to

begin, and the colonel had to sit through a chilling, steady drizzle until midnight, when, as if the lions had made a reservation, the usual terrified uproar of Indians sounded from yet another camp. Guess who had come to dinner?

At this point, let's take a harder look at the layout of the large camp and the pattern of the lion attacks. The bridge was, at the time, the end of the track, or railhead camp, so most of the personnel were concentrated over about a square mile around it, on the far side of the river. Patterson reckoned them at about 3,000, spread out into some eight subcamps. Since the lions had never been hunted before, the uncanny way in which they always managed to strike a camp while Patterson was waiting in another can only be attributed to luck rather than cunning. Unfortunately, as they were able to avoid the armed man for months on end, they quickly achieved the reputation of supernatural "demons" or devils in the minds of the Indians. This, of course, was at first considered by Patterson and his cohorts as ignorance typical of the coolie laborer. But, after a while, even the colonel had to be wondering deep in the back of his mind.

The early "learning" period of the Tsavo lions is in itself a fascinating exercise in animal behavior and psychology. For much of this pattern-forming stage, only one lion would do the actual stalking and, normally, killing, while the second would wait for him in the nearby cover and join him in feeding. Later on, as their confidence and skill grew, they hunted together, showing a complete disdain for the densest, highest barriers, loud noise, rifle fire, campfires and anything else meant to keep them at bay, literally killing any time and place they damned well felt like and eating their prey casually in a sleet of bullets without ever being touched. No wonder the Hindus had them pegged as spooks! Yet, while they were still beginners, the Tsavo Man-eaters were far from invincible and pulled a series of boneheaded stunts that, viewed from the distance of years, actually seem humorous, at least in a graveyard sense.

One night, when Patterson was undoubtedly numbing his bum on some tree branch, waiting for a shot or sitting over a half-eaten body, the killer lion came across a *bunniah,* or

Indian trader, who was riding his donkey in apparent ignorance of the lions' presence at Tsavo. As he picked his way along a black path, the lion sprang at him, knocking both the man and the donkey flat. The donkey was very badly hurt, and the lion, who clearly was not in the mood for a piece of—uumm, err—donkey, jumped again at the Indian. As he did, his claws somehow got tangled up in the rope by which a pair of oilcans were hung around the donkey's neck. The metallic commotion these caused as he dragged them behind upset him enough to break off the attack and retire, clattering into the bush. The trader spent the rest of what had to be a very long night up a tree and was rescued the following morning. The ass died.

A few nights after this episode, a Greek contractor by name of Themistocles Pappadimitrini was sleeping in his hut when the lion broke in. Not yet having this people-grabbing thing down to a science, the lion must have been overexcited at the prospect of a change from coolie because he sank his fangs into the mattress on which the Greek was lying and, with presumed triumph, carried it off into the night. I wish I could have heard the comments in Lionese when he and his pal tried to eat it!

There's an interesting aside on Pappadimitrini worth mentioning here, if only to show that when the bell tolls, brother, there's no place to hide. Certainly, he considered himself lucky beyond belief that night; in point of fact, it might have gone easier with him had the lion killed him in light of his fate shortly thereafter. He went down to Mt. Kilima N'jaro—that big frosty lump that we call Kilimanjaro—to buy some cattle and on his way back decided to take a shortcut cross-country to the rail line. His water ran out, and he died the terrible, lingering death of thirst. If Africa doesn't get you one way, it will another.

As is so frequently the attitude of African natives, it was also the case with the Indian laborers that they, while the railhead camp was still at Tsavo, were not especially frightened or apprehensive about being the lions' next victims. The attitude reported by Patterson was apparently based upon the odds being slim, with so many men around to choose from, of getting converted into a sand-box deposit. Whatever, man-eaters or not, the weeks passed into a month, and the temporary works for crossing the Tsavo River were completed, enabling the laying of track on the far side. The main labor force moved with the track, farther and farther from Tsavo, leaving only a few hundred workers with Patterson and his medical staff to finish the permanent bridge. All this greatly changed the dynamics of the situation.

Up to this time, Patterson had dutifully and unsuccessfully hunted the lions, using every tactic he could think of; waiting up all night, even resorting to suicidal daylight forays into the unimaginably thick thorn *nyika* on both sides of the tracks for miles. This was really a very brave gesture, if futile, as he knew only too well that all the odds were with the lions seeing or hearing the hunter first and perhaps having an early dinner that particular day. Unfortunately— or perhaps fortunately—he saw nothing despite his efforts, and, even after dark, the lions continued to kill and eat people just about everywhere the colonel wasn't, with the demoralizing habit of hitting north if he was south, east if he was waiting west. Even so, if matters had been maddening previously with a widespread camp, they reached full-blown panic when the main labor force moved up the line, and the Indians assigned to work on the permanent bridge realized that the chances of being chopped had increased tenfold.

Patterson *Sahib* must have been quite persuasive with the remainder to get them to stay, even though now clustered in one camp to the presumed shopping convenience of the lions. Only by permitting the men to knock off all work to build towering, thick *bomas*—ferociously spiked high fences of thorn—around every group of tents and huts would they even consider staying on. The results of this measure illustrate well what many of us professional hunters and game officers have found out over the years since Patterson's Peril—that it is for all practical purposes impossible to build a *boma*, or *zareba*, as it's called in up-country Kenya, high and strong enough to keep out a determined man-eating lion. I know it doesn't make much sense, but, as Patterson was to

discover, lions, even with their relatively thin skins and
sensitive paws, have some Houdini-like method of penetrating incredibly thick and dense thorn barriers soundlessly
with little more than a few scratches. Adding insult, they
then normally pull their kill back through the barrier on the
way out. In all the man-killings at Tsavo, only once was a
body left stuck in the thorns, the cat apparently unable to
force his way out with the corpse. Even when the *bomas* were
built, despite all-night fires and the constant clatter of a
bunch of empty oil tins being rattled steadily by the night
watchman, men continued to be taken from their tents
almost every night. One terrified Indian was dragged from a
goods wagon, a type of freight car, with another man trying
to hold onto his legs until sheer force tore him loose. He was
eaten within grisly hearing of the other laborers in the
wagon. Another night, five *Sikh* carpenters had built a
platform upon which to pitch their tent in the very er-
roneous belief that the eight-foot height would place them
out of reach. How they decided on this distance from the
ground is unfathomable, as a lion can easily reach twelve feet
into the air without even jumping. Questioned as to the
safety of their perch by Patterson, they assured him that
God would protect them.

Maybe they were right. A few nights after the platform
was built, one of the man-eaters stalked it and easily jumped
up to the opening. To the Indians' great good luck, or
perhaps some overtime on God's part, the lion threw his full
weight onto the end of a ladder protruding from the
entrance, used to climb up to the tent. It tipped like a
teeterboard under his great bulk, tore through the top of
the tent and swatted him a solid thump on the head as it
came down. The cat ran off into the night, although the
raised tent suddenly lost popularity, God Almighty or not.

Near the main campground stood the hospital compound
tent of the departed main force, left behind under the care
of the bridge builders. Surrounded as it was by a very heavy
and high *boma* presumed to be lion-proof, it was somewhat
isolated. It was here, early one evening, that a hospital
assistant heard a small noise and opened his adjoining tent

front to see what it was. To his understandable horror, a tremendous lion was standing a few yards away, looking right at him. As he froze, paralyzed with fear, the lion started to spring at him, which shook him out of his stupor and sent him reeling into a box of glass medical supplies. This fell with a shattering crash and startled the cat, which ran off to another part of the compound and immediately jumped onto and through the walls of a tent containing eight sick and injured Indians. Two of them were badly lacerated by claw wounds, a third killed on the spot and pulled through the ice-pick thorn *boma,* probably looking like a sack of bloody cole slaw from the spikes when he reached the other side. The two wounded coolies lay where they fell all night long under a piece of torn canvas, which must have been something less than a dull experience.

Not illogically, Patterson ordered the survivors moved to a new hospital closer to the main camp and had an even heavier enclosure built around it. All the patients were "safe" inside before nightfall. I find it interesting that John Henry had gotten the idea from somebody that lions tend to visit recently abandoned camps and, therefore, decided to sit up all night in the vacated hospital where the lions had struck the night before. Armed to the molars, he was halfway through the night when—what else?—the *new* hospital exploded into a high babble of terrified human voices. The lions had won the deadly shell game again.

Smart enough by this time to stay put for the rest of the night, he hurried over to the new hospital at daylight. This latest onslaught of the lions had been a real humdinger, the events of which were witnessed in the big circle of firelight by some other Indian patients. A water carrier had been lying asleep with his head toward the center of the tent, his feet radiating outward until they almost touched the canvas wall. Somehow, the more enthusiastic of the lions had actually jumped over the high *boma* and managed to get his head under the edge of the tent wall. He grabbed the water carrier's foot in his teeth, tugging on it viciously to pull him out of the tent. Awakening to a real nightmare, the man desperately caught hold of a heavy box in an effort to keep from being dragged away, but his grip was broken when the box got hung up at the bottom of the tent. Still fighting for his life, the terrified coolie got his hands on a strong tent rope, which he clutched with insane strength until the lion jerked so hard that the rope broke in the man's hands. Outside now, the lion instantly bit the Indian in the throat, shaking him like a cat with a mouse. With the body gripped across the middle, the man-eater was seen to run up and down the thick hedge until he chose a spot, plunged through and disappeared into the blackness, leaving chunks of the man's flesh and shreds of his clothing all along his passage through the *boma*.

Patterson and Dr. Brock followed the track after listening to the witnesses, finding that it only ran some 400 yards into the bush. The end of the trail held the inevitable horror, a well-chewed skull and jaws, some larger bones and part of the palm of one hand with a couple of fingers still remaining. Encircling one finger was a silver ring which, along with the teeth, Patterson arranged to have shipped back to the man's widow in India.

Well, what now? What else? Move the hospital again, and build a thicker and higher barrier. This being done and the enclosure finished by dark after much hard work by the men, Patterson and Brock decided their next round of strategy. Still hooked on the notion that lions love to visit deserted camps rather than those filled with nice juicy people, they left a couple of tents standing in the old—one-day old—hospital compound and tied a trio of cows in them for bait, despite the fact that the lions had thus far shown a clear disinterest in anything but human flesh. This night, however, rather than sitting up in a tree or hiding in a tent, the two white men had a goods wagon pulled up on a nearby track siding close to the hospital where they would set their ambush. It would seem that the water carrier must have left them hungry, as the man-eaters were reported all over the place that day, April 23. Four miles from Tsavo Bridge, they had tried to catch a coolie walking along the tracks in bright daylight, but he made it up a tree just in time. He was rescued, half dead with fright, after being sighted by a passing train some hours later. Then, the lions were reported seen together, right at Tsavo Station, and again, at dusk, actually stalking Dr. Brock as he was on his way back from the hospital to his compound.

It was surprisingly late by the time the two men finished dinner and, with astonishing lack of caution, walked the entire mile through the dark to the goods wagon, getting set up at ten o'clock. The railroad car had a "Dutch" door design, and Patterson and Brock kept their vigil outside the thorn corral with the bottom half of the door closed and the top half open for a shooting port, facing the second abandoned hospital which they could not even see due to the darkness of the night.

A few hours passed with oppressive, stygian silence, the hunters becoming restless. Then, with bone-chilling crispness, a dry stick cracked somewhere outside. Instantly, nobody was bored. A few minutes later, a dull thud could be heard, just the sort of sound a lion would make on landing after jumping over the *boma,* as he had done the night previously. Even the cattle were stirring nervously but then settled down again. Silence crept back like an invisible fog through the blackness, but it was not the silence of emptiness. Patterson, who was half-mad with frustration for a shot at the killers, suddenly got another one of his bright ideas. He proposed to Brock that the doctor stay there while he got out and lay on the ground below, in hopes of seeing the lion better if he came in their direction with his kill. Brock, fortunately, was still mentally firing on all cylinders and dissuaded Patterson from leaving the shelter of the goods wagon. As they would find out in just a few seconds, it was superb advice, for, at that very instant, at least one of the lions had spotted them and was oozing up for a quick, decisive charge.

What neither man realized, besides the fact that *they* were now the bait, was that the hospital *boma,* ordered carefully locked, was in fact wide open! So, while they were expecting the sound of a lion bulling his way out through the wall of the fence with a dead cow, in actuality the lion or lions were never inside the enclosure at all but had been prowling around the goods wagon all this time.

As they continued to stare out the top of the door, Patterson suddenly felt a mixed thrill of fear and excitement, fancying he saw something dark edging with lethal stealth toward them. However, his eyes were so strained by prolonged staring that he was afraid to trust them, concerned that if he fired and the blob turned out to be only a shadow or his imagination, any chance to kill the real lions would be missed. Under his breath he asked Brock if he saw it too, but the doctor was careful enough not to answer. Or maybe he never had time.

The silence throbbed on for the space of a few more seconds, and then the dark shape was in the air, launched straight at the open door. "The lion!" Patterson shouted involuntarily as both men fired, blinding themselves with the muzzle flashes, their ears deafened as the twin crash of shots reverberated beneath the sheet-iron roof of the wagon. In the confusion, neither man saw what had become of the lion, which must have sheered away at the shots. For certain, had they not been so alert one or the other would have been killed. As it was, the big cat was long gone, and first light showed that Brock's bullet had struck the sand close by a pug mark, while Patterson's was never found. The bullet had, however, not touched the charmed "demon" lion, as no blood or other damage showed on the spoor. It was back to the old drawing board for Patterson *Sahib*.

By simple mathematical interpolation, it's a fair guess that the Tsavo Man-eaters may have killed and eaten between thirty and thirty-five railroad personnel between the beginning of March and the twenty-third of April; additionally, there were bound to have been some African victims, which would possibly raise the fatality total to forty. Yet, from Patterson's records of dates and events, it became clear that the ambush that he and Brock had laid in the goods wagon had at least succeeded in throwing a scare into the lions, as they left the Tsavo Bridge area and proceeded up the line to

the advanced railhead, where two men were carried off on
successive nights shortly after the twenty-third, and another
at a place called Engomani, some ten miles away. The man-
eaters liked Engomani, as they hit it twice more the same
week, killing and eating one man and tearing up another so
badly that he died in a couple of days. Tsavo remained
unmolested, for the moment. . . .

The weeks trickled past and pooled into months. The
coolies at the bridgehead gradually began to lose their fear
of the man-eaters, sleeping outside again as if their "demon"
lions had never existed. Constant reports reached Patterson
of continued terrorization of other places, but the lions had
kept their distance from Tsavo since the big surprise back in
April. On the other hand, the colonel realized that they
could return at any moment and take up where they had left
off, and so he decided to have an appropriate reception
catered for their homecoming.

Patterson launched himself into the design and construction of an elaborate lion trap. It was really quite a slick
affair, made out of available materials of railway ties and
sleepers, tram rails, telegraph wire and heavy chain, divided
into two compartments. One section was to hold the lion and
the other to accommodate the human bait that would have
to be used. The idea was to utilize a sliding door in the rear
of the trap to admit the men who, once inside, would be
completely safe, as the compartment was separated from the
front one by a grid of heavy iron rails only three inches
apart, their ends deeply embedded in thick wooden sleepers.
The front door, which would be open to admit the lion
trying to reach the bait in the rear, was a powerful and
flexible curtain of short lengths of iron rail, wired to logging
chain that hung down on either side of the entrance when in
the closed position. A trip release was rigged by means of a
spring concealed in the dirt of the floor, which, when
touched, triggered a lever holding the folding door open
over the trap's mouth. Upon touching the hidden spring,
which he would be bound to do, the lion would cause the
heavy door to come crashing down and lock into immovable

position by wedging its lower edge between two carefully secured iron rails sunk into the ground of the mouth. Pretty tricky, old Patterson.

The lion trap took a lot of time and ingenuity, one of the biggest headaches being the boring of holes through the many lengths of tough iron rail for the door so that they could be wired into position. Patterson finally solved this by firing hard-nosed bullets from his .303 rifle, the metal-jacketed slugs boring through the iron as neatly as if they were punched by a hydraulic press. When the great creation was at last ready, the colonel prepared the finishing touches by pitching a tent over the whole contraption and building a *boma* around it strong enough to stall a rhino, save for an entrance in front of the mouth and a removable gap at the rear, which was to be sealed by the human bait pulling a spiky bundle of thorns behind them. Patterson had to put up with a good deal of ribbing by other officers who inspected the unlikely trap, but he persevered, even sleeping in it as bait the first few nights himself. Unfortunately, he attracted nothing more of the man-eating tribe than a horrendous cloud of mosquitoes, which chewed him with nearly all the enthusiasm of the lions. During this period, while the lions were operating elsewhere, Patterson almost gave the impression that he wished they would return to give him another crack at them. Obligingly, they did.

One particularly dark night several months later, the Tsavo Bridgehead was again aroused by the all-too-familiar screams of terror as one of the lions was discovered breaking through the *boma* of a compound. One thing was immediately apparent: they had gained in boldness and daring to a degree far beyond their previous behavior. On this first night of their return engagement, it was odd that the lions even bothered breaking into a *boma;* there were many men ripe for the picking, sleeping outside. They must have been overlooked, or the man-eaters had fallen into the habit of finding food inside the thorn enclosures and didn't want to lose their touch. Although the alarm was given and sticks, stones and firebrands thrown at the lion, he remained undeterred, charging into the panicked coolies and killing one, whom he methodically carried and dragged back through the thorn. Gone now was the nicety of removing the corpses several hundred yards into the night before feeding. As soon as he was clear of the fence, the lion was joined by his companion, and together they completely ate the body within thirty yards of the spot where the victim had been caught. So brazen were they that they paid not the slightest attention to the shots fired at them by a *Jemadar*, who, at least so far, had enjoyed better luck than the late, lamented Ungan Singh.

Although there was a very little left of the coolie's body, Patterson elected not to bury the scraps, in the desperate hope that the lions would return the next night to the same spot. One can realize his need to take any opportunity, but it would be thought that he would by now understand that these lions did not, at least by pattern, normally return to the same place where they had killed the night before, a fact that had kept them alive so long. As usual, halfway through the long night Patterson heard an uproar in the distance that made it clear the lions had struck a camp two miles away.

By this time, the Man-eaters of Tsavo had become genuine celebrities, rather in the same sense that Jack the Ripper had been; the fact that they had killed more than five times the number of Jack's victims was not hurting their international notoriety. As such, they attracted many fame-seeking outsiders—mostly civil and military officers who came to hunt them—but all met the failure that Patterson had gotten to know so well. How the lions could continue to take a man every night without catching a bullet, even by chance, seemed almost beyond the laws of possibility. The sense of black-hearted frustration Patterson felt is clarified when he speaks of one evening when the lions chose to eat their man-kill within easy hearing of his tent, almost trying to taunt him:

"I could plainly hear them crunching the bones, the sound of their dreadful purring filled the air and rang in my ears for days afterward. The terrible thing was to feel so helpless;

it was useless to attempt to go out, as of course the poor fellow was dead, and in addition it was so pitch dark as to make it impossible to see anything."

As Patterson lay impotently listening to the lions feeding, a half-dozen workmen who were living in a small *boma* near his also heard the gruesome symphony and lost their nerve, pleading to be let into the *Sahib*'s enclosure. Of course, he admitted them, realizing a few minutes later that one of them who had been sick appeared to be missing. Patterson asked what had become of him and discovered that the other men had callously abandoned him, too ill to move, back in their tent. Infuriated, Patterson got up a small rescue team and went out to bring him back. In the light of a lantern, he approached the still-open tent front and looked inside. The poor devil was beyond need of help. Deserted by his friends with the lions within hearing, he had died of fear and shock.

It hardly seems possible, but things began to get even worse. Heretofore, only one lion had been the actual killer while the other kept back, merely joining in the feeding. Not any more. Now both lions began to attack together, each catching its own separate meal. Thus, instead of one man being taken a night, two were now often slaughtered. The more shy lion, who had not been killing until now, was still inexperienced, as is evidenced by the killing of two Swahili porters at the end of November. One was immediately carried off through the thorns and eaten, but the second continued to moan for a long time. When the men finally got up enough courage to investigate, they found him suspended in the *boma,* the only failure of the lions to escape with a victim through the thick thorn barriers. He was still alive—for all practical purposes crucified—in the morning when Patterson saw him, but he was so horribly mangled by teeth, claws and thorns that he died before he could reach the hospital.

Several nights later, the pair of cats smoothly pulled some poor beggar right out of the middle of the largest camp, which was quite close to the iron hut of a permanent right-of-way inspector. While the victim was being eaten right outside the main camp, the inspector, named Dalgairns, fired more than *fifty shots* at the sound of the feeding lions. They paid not the least attention as bullets whined all around them. Finally finishing the man, they casually got up and wandered off a short distance, probably burping demurely. Patterson met with Dalgairns the next morning, learning that the inspector felt he had hit at least one of the killers, not a very consistent conclusion according to his description of the lions staying where they were under fire. But perhaps there was some chance that Dalgairns had scored; along the spoor was an odd, trailing mark that looked like a broken leg being dragged. After some mighty careful sneaking through the scrub brush, the two men were frozen in their tracks by a sudden growling from a nearby thicket. Rifles ready, they picked their way forward until spotting what Patterson thought was a lion cub crouched in a clump of bush. As they got closer, it turned out to be what was left of the body of the coolie, the legs, one arm and half the body eaten. The stiff fingers of the remaining arm trailing in the sand as the corpse was carried had made the strange drag mark, but by the time this was figured out, the lions had disappeared into the heavy bush beyond, where tracking was impossible.

That did it. If the "demon" theory had had its adherents before, the firing of fifty rounds of ammo without a hit was enough to convince anybody that they were dealing with a lot more than lions. The same day, December 1, 1898, the entire labor force had packed it in and were waiting to speak to Patterson on his return with the shreds of the dead coolie. The meeting didn't last long, the men simply stating that they had come to work for the government, not to be a delicatessen for a couple of devils. That was all, no discussion. They stampeded off to pick up their belongings and stopped the next train by lying down on the tracks. Swarming over the cars for any handhold, they chugged off, and the Tsavo Bridge project was shut down cold for the next three weeks.

Of course, not all the Indians left, and a good deal of courage has to be recognized in those who decided to stick around, despite the very good chance of becoming a coolie on rye. From Patterson's description, over one hundred laborers stayed, their whole time being spent constructing "lion-proof" shelters practically anywhere out of reach, such as on the tops of water tanks, roofs, girders, trees, anyplace that seemed safe. Some of the men decided to go down rather than up, digging deep pits in the floors of their tents where they would sleep at night with heavy logs pulled over for protection. Some of this got a bit overdone, especially the trees, as some very frightened Indians found out one night. One particular tree was so overloaded with beds lashed on to each substantial branch that it actually toppled over from the weight just as the lions were killing a man beneath it. Coolies were scattered everywhere around and almost on the cats. To their extraordinary good luck, the lions couldn't have cared less, ignoring the panic-stricken men for the one they had already killed.

In the early days of December, the most improbable and incredible incidents of the whole reign of terror occurred, the first of these centering around a district officer by name of Whitehead, who had been asked by Patterson to come up to Tsavo and lend a hand with his lions. Whitehead's note of acceptance advised that he should be expected about dinner time on December 2, his train being due at Tsavo Station at six o'clock. Accordingly, the colonel sent a servant to meet him and help with luggage. No sooner was the man gone on his errand but he was back, shaking with terror, reporting that there was no sign of the train or anybody else, with the notable exception of a tremendous lion standing on the station platform.

At the time, Patterson dismissed the tale as absurd on the basis that everybody was so tense they would imagine even a hyena to be one of the man-eaters. But the next day he found that the servant had been absolutely right, the stationmaster and signalman both having locked themselves in the station when they saw the lion stalking up. The colonel waited dinner for some time, in hopes of the arrival of the district commissioner, but finally decided that, for some reason, Whitehead had postponed his trip until the following day. During his late meal, Patterson heard several shots fired but paid them no mind; gunfire was no rarity in an area of man-eating activity. Finishing his dinner, he proceeded to take his position for the night in a structure he had had built atop an elevated girder, a heavy cage of crossed ties offering a good field of fire. Only a few minutes after he settled down, he was startled to hear the clear and now unmistakable sound of the lions eating a man, crushing bones and purring only about seventy yards away. It made no sense to him; there had been no outcry as was usual when the lions attacked a party of Indians, so he mentally marked the kill down to some native traveler whose luck had run out.

After some minutes of listening to the awful sounds, Patterson wrote that, despite the darkness, he was able to make out the lions' eyes glowing through the blackness. He mentioned no nearby fire or other illumination, so this was clearly an impossibility, although he referred, on several occasions in his two books, to seeing animals' eyes glowing in the dark. Sorry, J.H. No way. Shine is from reflection, and without an outside source of light to be reflected there can be no glow. To be fair, his nerves were in a state that would permit his believing he could see the eyes. In any case, he took careful aim and opened fire. The lions, as usual, ignored him but to move a few yards away, over a slight rise, where they were hidden from the line of fire. Not disturbed further, they leisurely finished the unidentified corpse.

When daylight started to bloom, Patterson climbed stiffly down from his fortress and started toward the place where he had last heard the lions. On the way, he was completely nonplussed to run into none other than his missing guest, District Commissioner Whitehead, who looked as if he'd spent quite an interesting evening. Astonished, Patterson asked where on earth he'd come from and why he hadn't turned up the night before.

"Nice reception you give a fellow when you invite him to dinner," replied Whitehead laconically.

The colonel asked him what he was talking about, and Whitehead allowed that the lions had just about nabbed him the previous night. Still incredulous, Patterson told him that he must have been dreaming. Without another word, the commissioner turned his back and asked Patterson if what he saw looked like a dream. The engineer shut up at the sight of Whitehead's back—a mass of shredded cloth and clotted blood from four long claw marks that had scored the skin and meat. While having his wounds dressed at Patterson's quarters, Whitehead recounted what had happened in the earlier darkness.

The train had been very late, arriving well after sundown. Whitehead, along with his sergeant of native troops, a man called Abdullah, had elected to walk to Patterson's camp along a track spur which ran through a rise that was cut some four or five feet deep to reduce the grade, leaving a lip of earth on each side. Abdullah walking behind with a lantern, all went well until they were in the middle of the cut when, without warning, a lion sprang off the embankment, smashing Whitehead to the ground and tearing his back with a paw stroke while trying to grip the man. More by good luck than planning, the impact caused Whitehead's carbine to fire, startling the lion enough that it left him and swarmed over the native sergeant. Abdullah had time only to say, *"Eh, Bwana, simba,"* or "Hey, boss, lion," a wonderfully distilled observation. In the same moment, although Whitehead was able to get off another shot from a few yards and miss cleanly, the lion and Abdullah were gone over the embankment. Of course it had been the body of Abdullah that Patterson had heard being eaten while in the fortress, which solved the mystery of the kill, although darkly. Just what Whitehead had been doing since the attack was never recorded, but it's probable he spent the night up a tree. The district commissioner had come about as close to death by lion as you're likely to hear of, but his wounds healed well and without septic complications.

Confirming the African version of it never raining but that it pours, the same day, December 3, reinforcements arrived under a Mr. Farquhar, the superintendent of police, who had in tow some twenty sepoys (native troops of the Indian Army), armed with Martini rifles. Together with

Patterson, Whitehead, Farquhar, the sepoys and other sportsmen officers, there was now quite a reasonable army arrayed against the lions. Not only that, the lion trap was given a fine tuning and set with two sepoys, armed to the eyeballs, as bait. We may presume they accepted their assignment with understandable reluctance. Patterson had taken plenty of ribbing from what he calls "wise-acre officers" about the trap, but he finally prevailed to have it at least tried out. With riflemen hanging from every tree and elevated position in sight, darkness fell with a tangible feeling of expectancy. Nothing happened until about nine o'clock, when, with a wild surge of satisfaction, Patterson heard the rumbling clank of the lion trap being sprung, the heavy door falling into place, echoing over the bridgehead. At last, one of the man-eaters was as good as dead.

Wasn't he?

Hunting big, dangerous game is an excellent method of culturing one's sense of fatalism. People die from the slightest error, while others survive without a scratch the most mind-boggling acts of idiocy. Who knows why? In the Xingu Basin of Brazil, a remote southern Amazon tributary where I was a jaguar hunter years ago, the Indians had developed this philosophy almost into a religion. If we failed to connect with what had looked like virtually a sure kill at the last moment through some quirk of fate, they would merely shrug and observe that "it was not the jaguar's day to die." That was that.

But how could this possibly not be the man-eater's night to die? Look at the facts: He is trapped in a cage strong enough to restrain King Kong and three of his closest associates; two armed men are near enough, although completely protected, actually to touch the lion with the muzzles of their rifles. Even after he is dead, it will take six strong men ten minutes even to free the heavy door from its locking slot with pry bars and drag him out. Ah, friend, but never underestimate Africa, the hoary motherland that spawned and nurtured Murphy's Law.

Strangely, nothing happened at all for the first several minutes, but the night was filled with the frenzy of roars from the lion, who was lashing himself against the bars. Despite their orders to open fire immediately if a lion should enter the trap, the sepoys were huddled in the rear of the bait compartment, paralyzed with terror. After some time, the voice of Superintendent Farquhar reached them, shouting for them to shoot, godammit! Shoot they did. As fast as they could load and fire they blindly opened up with the Martinis, .450 caliber bullets whipping and whining off in every direction but the right one. At complete right angles, Patterson and Whitehead hugged the floor of their wooden shelter as slugs lashed around them and thumped into the ties. Branches fell and dirt blossomed as the score or more shots erupted until an impossible, completely insane thing happened. A bullet *blanged* into one of the door's rails where it was secured with telegraph wire and cut it, the end of the rail fell free and the lion squeezed out to evaporate into the night. It *couldn't* have happened. But it did. From a range of inches, with two soldiers firing more than twenty rounds, the lion was merely lightly creased by a ricochet and was freed to kill again. Only in Africa . . .

As if Patterson hadn't learned by then, bad luck has a way of rubbing it in. Six days later, on the ninth, after the main party of hunters had left in disgust, he was leaving his *boma* just after dawn when a screaming Swahili popped up, running toward him, yelling, *"Simba! Simba!"* and looking back over his shoulder. Patterson stopped him and found out that both lions had tried to nab a man from the camp nearest the river but had missed and killed a donkey instead, which they were at this moment eating a short distance away. The colonel dashed back into his tent for the double-barreled express rifle lent him by Farquhar, in case just such a chance might turn up. Loading it, he prevailed upon the African to return and show him where the lions were dining on the donkey. (They must have been very hungry, as this is the first recorded case of their taking other than human food.) All went just peachy with the stalk, Patterson even able to discern the outline of one of the cats through the heavy bush, but he held his fire for a more open chance. Naturally, the native stepped on a rotten branch, and the lion melted quickly back into heavier cover. Practically hysterical at the idea of missing yet another chance, Patterson ran back to camp to round up a crew of coolie beaters and all the cans, drums and other noisemakers they could lay their hands on.

As quickly as possible, he arranged them around the far side of the thicket the lion had entered, with instructions to give him time to cover the down side of the thicket before starting the beat to drive the lion out. Patterson sneaked back to the other side, finding a termite hill near a well-worn game trail which it seemed reasonable the lion would use. Hiding behind it, he got ready just before the first clatter of metal and blare of horns began. Almost immediately, to his excited joy, a gigantic, maneless lion swaggered out onto the trail and, with looks behind him, started toward Patterson. The angle was such that the man was not completely concealed by the termite mound, but the big cat didn't notice him until they were only fifteen yards apart and the hunter made a slow movement of raising the double-barrel to lock the sights on the man-eater's brain. The lion recoiled in surprise back onto his haunches. But too late. Patterson nestled the front bead into the wide vee of the rear sight and started to squeeze off the shot. At that range he couldn't miss, and the heavy Nitro Express bullet would take off the cat's head as if he'd had a stick of dynamite jammed up his nose. But it didn't.

Should you be under the impression that the most terrifying sounds of the world of big-game hunting are the close snarl of a man-eater and the shrieking trumpet of a bull elephant right over your head, you're wrong. It is the cold, dead, metallic *click!* of the firing pin falling on a defective cartridge primer. There is no sound quite like it— trust me; unimaginably clear and crisp, yet at the same time slightly hollow and muffled by the barrel's chamber. It is one of the true sounds of death.

As the British might say it, up Patterson had screwed. He was used to a shotgun, but there are differences between a double-barreled rifle and a smoothbore. His bolt-action .303 Enfield bore not the slightest resemblance to the borrowed express rifle, and in times when one needs a rifle, he tends to need it very badly. It may have been the cartridge that was defective; perhaps the firing-pin mechanism itself was broken. No matter. To take an unfamiliar and, even worse, untried weapon against man-eaters is looking for even more trouble than is already at hand. To the good luck of his future readership and his creditors, the beaters were now close enough that the lion was forced to run, almost vanishing into the heavy bush before Patterson even realized that he had a second barrel, loaded and ready to fire with a mechanism independent from the first. At last he shot again and was finally rewarded by an answering snarl from the lion, indicating a hit. But the blood soon stopped, and the track was lost on rocky ground. It just didn't seem fated that Patterson was to kill the lions. Maybe the stars were trying to tell him something.

But there's one thing you have to give John Henry: He doesn't dazzle you with footwork, but he sure hangs in there! Heading back to camp, his spirits badly needing garters, he was somewhat cheered to find that there was quite a bit left of the donkey, perhaps enough that the lion would return for the rest that night. Despite earlier experiences, he had a *machan*, or raised shooting platform, erected a few yards from the carcass, as there were no handy trees. It wasn't much, just four poles sunk into the earth, inclined toward each other at the tops, with a plank lashed into place as a seat. It was hardly the sort of affair that *I* would pick from which to display my sweet young body to a couple of man-eaters, but Patterson appeared to have thought it just dandy, although it was only twelve feet high. Nonetheless, the colonel wired the defunct burro to a nearby stump so it couldn't be dragged away and, at sundown, climbed up to face a night of utter, moonless dark and the savage silence of creeping death. If this sounds melodramatic, try sitting up some night until dawn in your own living-room easy chair, motionless in the dark, even knowing there aren't any man-eating lions around. As the hours wore on, mental exhaustion lulled him into almost a drugged state, somehow feeling he was drifting weightless in the quiet shroud of night.

Crack! The snapping of a twig sounded like a sonic boom in the stillness; Patterson lurched out of his reverie. His ears hollow with the rush of his own blood, he could hear the tiniest rustling of a large body picking its way through the dry grass and bushes. "The man-eater," he thought to himself; "surely tonight my luck will change, and I shall bag one of the brutes." It is somehow doubtful, even in pristine Victorian times, that this was the precise syntax that rushed through Patterson's hackle-bristled skull. Silence again, so quiet it was loud. Then, a long, deep, drawn-out sigh from very close, followed by another creep of movement and a nasty snarl. The lion had spotted the man, just a few feet above him.

Patterson was to have considerable time to reconsider his stupidity in building the *machan* in the first place, because, as soon as J.H. was seen, the lion ignored the donkey and resolutely began to stalk the man. It was a war of nerves in the classic sense, and it's also clear that the lion probably had a lot more nerve than the worn-out colonel. For a terrifying two hours, the lion sneaked round and round the tree platform, searching for a weak point, Patterson trying to keep absolutely still, expecting a charge any second. The man was afraid even to blink his eyes, yet unable to make out the dim form of the cat below in the darkness and fire. By midnight, he was almost stupefied by nervous exhaustion, every muscle jumping as he tried to anticipate the lion's coming spring. A second of cardiac-arrest terror raced through him as something struck him a sharp blow on the back of the head. The man-eater! His involuntary start was answered by a harsh snarl from below. His heart coming through the buttons of his shirt, he realized that it was an owl that had tried to light on his head, mistaking him in his silence for part of a tree. Good garden peas! Of all times to be taken for a knothead!

When an equally startled owl flew off, the game resumed, with the lion circling the *machan* platform, but now so closely that Patterson could actually hear the feet padding softly as the lion readied himself for the leap. At last, the man could barely make out the foggy form against the whitish thorn bushes and raised the rifle as the big cat gathered himself, stationary, mere feet below. At the shot, there was a roar that seemed to rock the platform, followed by the sounds of the cat thrashing and jumping in all directions. Although the lion was now invisible, Patterson continued to fire as fast as he could at the noise, which finally subsided into a series of deep groans and sighs. At last, all sound stopped. Could it be?

A chorus of shouted questions in Hindustani carried from the camp a quarter mile away, to which Patterson called back that he was unhurt and believed the lion was dead. Instantly, the greatest cheer which may have been heard to that date in east Africa went up, fireflies of light from torches darting through the bush as the coolies ran to the *machan*. Amid the bedlam of drums and horns played by the insanely happy Indians, each man prostrated himself before the engineer, shouting, *"Mabarak! Mabarak!"* or "Saviour."

Patterson still could not quite believe his luck and did not permit a search for the lion's body in case it wasn't yet dead. Back at camp, first light was awaited with a wild party, the African contingent particularly uninhibited with a leaping dance of triumph. At last, dawn crept in tie-dyed majesty through the shadows, and, with a group of men, Patterson returned to the scene of the shooting.

Over the hours of waiting, he had convinced himself that somehow the cat had escaped again—he could hardly be blamed in light of his previous experiences—so his shock at rounding a bush and seeing the lion crouched as if ready to spring can be imagined. Before he fired again, he noticed that it was as dead as virginity. The festivities began all over again, Patterson being carried around on the shoulders of the men until he was dizzy. When things settled down a bit, he had an opportunity to examine the body. As lions go, this was no ninety-pound weakling, but a tremendous animal, nine feet, eight inches from tail-tip to nose, forty-five inches at the shoulder, and requiring eight men to carry him back to camp to be skinned. Like most man-eaters, because human flesh is much more fat-marbled than that of game, the cat was in superb condition and extremely heavy. Two bullets had been effective—one in the hind leg, and the killer, behind the left shoulder and through the heart.

The news of the man-eater's death spread like a grass fire through the bush and along the rail line until hundreds of congratulatory telegrams and scores of fascinated visitors poured into the bridgehead. But for the moment everybody seemed to have forgotten a not very minor item: There were *two* Man-eaters of Tsavo.

It was only a couple of nights later that the surviving lion cleared up any hopeful speculation that he might have retired. A permanent-way inspector was awakened by the sound of something prowling around his bungalow and veranda. Thinking it just a drunken coolie, he shouted angrily through the door for him to go away but luckily did not open up. Quite probably because the remaining coolies were by now well enough protected to be difficult to catch and the man-eater certainly hungry, the lion vented his frustration and appetite by killing and eating two of the inspector's goats then and there. Hearing of the incident the next morning, Patterson decided to sit up near the hut that evening, waiting in a vacant iron shanty that had a rifle loophole in the side. Just outside, he tied three goats as bait to a heavy length of iron rail. All was quiet through the night until, just at dawn, the lion finally made an appearance, killed one of the goats and dragged the others away, rail and all. We have no idea why Patterson didn't fire, nor does he offer an excuse.

When the sun was fully up, Patterson and a small party followed the drag mark of the rail some 400 yards into the bush and smack into the lion, who was still having breakfast. This time, however, he did not slink away but suddenly charged. With a remarkable demonstration of good sense, all native personnel quickly disappeared up the nearest tree, while the colonel and one of his white assistants, a Mr. Winkler, stayed put. The lion, for some reason, broke off the charge, although the question again arises as to why neither Patterson nor Winkler fired a shot. After throwing some stones into the bushes where the lion had run, the men came on the dead goats, two of them hardly touched. Back to the graveyard shift for Patterson.

Having learned a lasting lesson from the earlier night in the rickety *machan,* he had a very strong platform erected a few feet from the dead goats and, as he was thoroughly exhausted, brought along his Indian gunbearer, Mahina, to help keep watch. Several hours into the vigil, when Patterson was just dozing off, he felt Mahina grab his arm and point in the direction of the goats. *"Sher!"* (Literally "tiger," although clearly meant to mean "lion," as there is a terrible shortage of tigers in Africa.) John Henry grabbed the double-barreled shotgun loaded with solid slugs and waited, eyes peeled for movement. In a few moments the lion appeared between some bushes and passed almost directly beneath the platform. The colonel fired both barrels almost at once into the lion's shoulder and was overjoyed to knock the big cat down. As Patterson switched to the .303 magazine rifle, the lion bounced back up and evaporated into the bush in a hail of random bullets. Certain he would be found dead in the morning, Patterson left Mahina to keep watching and went happily to sleep.

When at last dawn came, the two men followed the blood spoor with drooping spirits. At first, there was quite a lot of blood, but it ran out shortly, and the track was lost on rocky ground.

The next ten days were filled with increasing hope that, even though no *corpus delecti* had been located, the lion might have died of the effect of his wounds. Although nobody had been attacked, neither did anyone let down his guard. This was just as well. On the night of December 27, the old horror started again, an eruption of shouts coming from a crew of trolleymen who slept in a tree near Patterson's *boma.* It being a densely cloudy night with the moon hidden, the most the *Sahib* could do was send a few slugs in the lion's direction, which drove him off without a kill. In the morning, tracks showed that he had hung around for a long time, entering every single tent (all were unoccupied) and leaving a thick band of tracks in a circle around the trolleymen's tree.

As darkness fell, Patterson was again aloft, in the same tree in which the trolleymen had roosted. It was a perfect night, for a change, the moon full and flooding the bush with a strong silver glow that gave excellent visibility. Again, Mahina was in tow and slept while his boss took first watch. At midnight, they changed, and Patterson fell soundly asleep until about two A.M., when he was awakened by a strange, uncanny feeling that something was wrong. This is a peculiar and most discomfiting sensation difficult to describe to someone who has never experienced it, as I have. It has only happened to me while in the bush and is rarely, if ever, wrong. It's almost as if danger gives off a psychic aura. As something of an offshoot, consider the feeling of someone staring at you across a theater lobby and the real sensation of eyes touching you. This, incidentally, is often the case with animals, and I think many professional hunters will agree with me that game is sometimes spooked by being stared at for long periods during a stalk. I try to keep my eyes off any animal I am stalking, lest it sense me through this weird mechanism.

Mahina was awake and alert but had detected nothing. Patterson carefully looked all about the tree and saw nothing either, although the feeling was still with him. About to shrug it off, he suddenly thought he saw something move a way off, among some low bushes, silver-plated in the moonlight. As he continued to stare, he was startled to find that the strange sensation was quite correct: The man-eater was carefully stalking the men.

Fascinated in a crawly way, Patterson marveled at the flowing, soundless skill of the lion stealing stealthily toward him, a clear demonstration of his experiences as he took advantage of the smallest particle of cover. Using his head and determined to wait until the lion was as close as possible, J.H. remained still until the great cat was a mere twenty yards away, a tawny moon-washed form flattened against the sandy earth. Slipping the .303 into position, the colonel sent a hot whiplash of lead into the lion's chest, hearing the meaty impact of the bullet over the muzzle report. A terrific growl blew over the hunters as the killer turned in a blink and ran off with a series of great, smooth bounds. In the thin cover he was in sight long enough for Patterson to get off three more shots, the last of which brought another snarl. Then he was gone. It was another long wait until dawn.

As soon as it was light enough to see the trail, Patterson, Mahina and an African tracker immediately gave chase to the wounded lion, the Indian carrying a Martini carbine, which, in his hands, was as useful as a martini cocktail. With a good blood spoor, the men were able to cover ground quickly as the bush became more and more dense. After no more than a quarter of a mile, they were stopped by a ferocious growl right in front of them. Peering carefully through the cover, Patterson could make out the lion clearly, lips drawn back to expose thick, long fangs in warning. At Patterson's shot, the lion began a determined, flat-out charge, catching another bullet as he got going, which knocked him down, but he regained his feet and kept on coming, like a nightmare. Another aimed shot had no effect whatever. The .303 is no cannon; then, neither is it a popgun, but Patterson dropped it and reached behind him for the heavier-caliber Martini, which should have been immediately passed to him by Mahina. If he was already half-panicked at not being able to stop the lion with accurately placed shots, the empty air his fist closed around must not have added greatly to his confidence. Mahina, who had reached the immediate conclusion that discretion is the better part of chasing down wounded, charging, man-eating lions, was by now well up a tree. So was the carbine. Unarmed, Patterson, demonstrating an amazing under-standing of the concept, was not far behind. At the moment the lion reached the tree, Patterson was just out of reach. Had one of his bullets not chanced to break the lion's hind leg, apparently one of his favorite lion shots, the colonel might well have gained fame as the highest-ranking meal the

Tsavo lions had eaten. Seeing that he was too late, the lion limped back toward the thicket from which he had come.

As he retired, Patterson had time to pry the carbine out of Mahina's hands and get off another shot. To what must have been his surprise, the cat fell in a heap and appeared to be dead. Appearances can be deceiving. Patterson jumped from the tree and, like the greenest *Bwana* in Nairobi's growing cemetery, ran up to the lion. To his consternation, it jumped back up at very close range and came for him again. This time, however, the ninth bullet Patterson had put into the man-eater coincided with the last of his lives, a carbine slug in the boiler room putting him back down while a final tenth shot kept him there as he chewed a stick to shreds, thrashing out his last moments. At bloody, long last, the Man-eaters of Tsavo were dead.

Of course it was hero time again, with a definite sense of finality now. The second lion was even bigger than the first; although two inches less in length, it was two and a half inches taller at the shoulder and much heavier. The much-scarred hide, cut by the thorn *bomas,* was full of bullet holes, as well as the double dose of shotgun slug from the platform ten days before. For some odd reason, the slugs had not penetrated deeply enough to kill, even though they had knocked the cat down.

One of the most practical immediate dividends to accrue from the death of the second man-eater, besides the fact that people weren't getting eaten any more, was the return of the deserted coolie force and resumption of the bridge work that had been stopped three weeks before. If Patterson's timing, with general respect to the lions, hadn't exactly been unerring, at least he did get lucky now. The bridge was finished just before the first heavy rains, and, as the river rose in angry flood, all the temporary spanning was carried away within a few days of the bridge's completion. Had the schedule been even a bit behind, the whole project might have been ruined and all the lives taken by the lions for nothing.

Although the actual number of kills of the Tsavo Man-eaters was relatively modest compared with such heavy hitters as the Njombe Lions, the impact of the depredations of these two incredible animals was certainly not limited to Africa. In fact, at least to that date, they are believed to hold the distinction of being the only wild animals ever considered worthy of recognition by the British House of Lords. Speaking of the Tsavo Lions and their effect upon the Uganda Railroad, Lord Salisbury, then prime minister, made the following statement:

"The whole of the works were put a stop to for three weeks because a party of man-eating lions appeared and conceived a most unfortunate taste for our porters. At last the laborers entirely declined to go on unless they were guarded by an iron entrenchment. Of course it is difficult to work a railway under these conditions, and until we found an enthusiastic sportsman to get rid of these lions our enterprise was seriously hindered."

As for Patterson, the "enthusiastic sportsman," he stayed on in Africa until April of 1900, returning in 1907 to make several safaris into the Kenyan *nyika,* where he discovered the Patterson's Eland. He also had the misfortune to have one of his companions commit suicide by blowing his brains out with a pistol while suffering from a bout of malaria. Before leaving for England in 1900, Patterson was to find that his association with lions was not quite over. Although he had killed the two most famous *simbas* in the Tsavo area, that by no means meant that there were not others. One in particular caused an unforgettable night of tragedy just twenty miles down the track from Tsavo, at Voi, in 1899, when Patterson was visiting his old buddy, Dr. Rose, the medical officer. At dinner one evening, Rose told J.H. of the building of a new branch line through the Kilima N'jaro District under the charge of an engineer named O'Hara.

The very next morning, while out for a few *francolin,* or guinea fowl, with his shotgun, Patterson noticed four Swahili bearers carrying a makeshift stretcher along the new road from the line under construction. He shouted, asking who was being carried, and the Swahilis yelled back, *"Bwana."* Patterson asked again which *Bwana* and was told that it was

O'Hara. Some distance behind the porters staggered the saddest little group imaginable, the grief-stricken Mrs. O'Hara with a small child in her tired arms and another tiny girl so exhausted that she hung onto her mother's skirt to keep up. Patterson helped them to Rose's tent, where the doctor did what he could and sedated Mrs. O'Hara. The most they had been able to learn from the Swahilis was that her husband had been killed by a lion the night before. Late in the afternoon, when the new widow was able to speak coherently, she told the following story. These are her own words as recorded by Patterson:

"We were all asleep in the tent, my husband and I in one bed and my two children in another. The baby was feverish and restless, so I got up to give her something to drink; and as I was doing so, I heard what I thought was a lion walking around the tent. I at once woke my husband and told him I felt sure there was a lion about. He jumped up and went out, taking his gun with him. He looked round the outside of the tent and spoke to the Swahili *askari* [a native guard or armed soldier] who was on sentry by the camp fire a little distance off. The *askari* said he had seen nothing except a donkey, so my husband came in again, telling me not to worry as it was only a donkey that I had heard.

"The night being very hot, my husband threw back the tent door and lay down again beside me. After a while I dozed off, but was suddenly roused by a feeling as if the pillow were being pulled away from under my head. On looking round I found that my husband was gone. I jumped up and called him loudly, but got no answer. Just then I heard a noise among the boxes outside the door and saw my poor husband lying between the boxes. I ran up to him and tried to lift him, but found I could not do so. I then called to the *askari* to come and help me, but he refused, saying that there was a lion standing beside me. I looked up and saw the huge beast glowering at me, not more than two yards away. At this moment the *askari* fired his rifle, and this fortunately frightened the lion, for it at once jumped off into the bush.

"All four *askaris* then came forward and lifted my husband back on to the bed. He was quite dead. We had hardly got back into the tent before the lion returned and prowled about in front of the door, showing every intention of springing in to recover his prey. The *askaris* fired at him, but did no damage beyond frightening him away again for a moment or two. He soon came back and continued to walk round the tent until daylight, growling and purring, and it was only by firing through the tent every now and then that we kept him out. At daybreak he disappeared and I had my husband's body carried here, while I followed with the children until I met you."

The most comfort Patterson and Rose were able to give the distracted Mrs. O'Hara was the assurance, after the postmortem by Rose, that her husband had not suffered. Rose determined that O'Hara had been lying on his back at the time of the lion's attack and had been bitten once through the temples, the teeth actually meeting in the brain. This is classic killing behavior for a man-eating lion, silent, instantly fatal, no chance of a struggle. This particular cat had undoubtedly been active for some time, but the sketchy records of the period, in especial relationship to Africans eaten, give us no more information, except to say that the Voi Man-eater was killed a few weeks later by a poisoned arrow shot from a treetop by a WaTaita tribesman.

It's a long time now since Patterson spent his nine months of terror, and almost as much of that clear water has passed beneath the fateful bridge since O'Hara was nailed at Voi. But don't get the idea that lions have quit eating people along the Uganda Railroad. Hunter Robert Foran killed an incredible four man-eaters in a single day after they had run up a score of more than fifty kills in only three months in the late 1940s, right in this same area. In 1955, a telegram was sent from Tsavo to Nairobi with all the nostalgia of the bad old days:

"Odeke narrowly escaped being caught by lion. . . . All staff unwilling to do night duty. Afford protection."

The last reference I can find handily to a man-eater operating in the Tsavo range is the one describing a lion killed in 1965 by the well-known professional hunter, John Kingsley-Heath. It was emaciated and weighed only 380 pounds. Kingsley-Heath discovered a porcupine quill festering in one of its nostrils, a good probability of why it turned man-eater.

The two Man-eaters of Tsavo were subsequently mounted by Rowland Ward of London and were presented to the Chicago Field Museum of Natural History, where they reside to this day in Hall Twenty-two. An interesting sidelight between the Tsavo Bridge and the Field Museum is found in the fact that John Henry Patterson's son, Bryan Patterson, served on the staff of the museum as a distinguished paleontologist from 1926 to 1955. Aware that he was scheduled to return in 1979 as a visiting curator, I attempted to contact him to verify some personal details of his father's life. Telephoning in the spring of 1980, I was too late. Bryan Patterson had died the previous autumn.

BIBLIOGRAPHY

Patterson, J. H., Lieutenant Colonel, D.S.O. *The Man-eaters of Tsavo.* London: Macmillan and Company, Ltd., 1907.

————. *In the Grip of the Nyika.* London: Macmillan and Company, Ltd., 1910.

————. "The Lions That Stopped a Railroad," The World's Work, three parts, pp. 10897–11158, privately bound article, circa 1907.

C. H. Stigand

I T'S VERY EARLY FOR VULTURES to be flying, the dew still glimmering in the low sun on emerald stalks of long Nile grass, dense as an endless, towering hedge and resilient from last month's short rains. Through it, in classic British Army box formation, weaves the Equatorial Battalion, the khaki column two miles west of Kor Raby, a place of remarkable remoteness, even for Sudan's southernmost province. The heat is building, swelling in the oppressive stillness even at this hour, 7:10 A.M. on December 8, 1919, the silence tainted only by the slither of grass across puttees and the muffled metallic clink of weapons, the furtive marching song of war in savage lands. The porters of the punitive expedition, protected by troops on both flanks as well as by an advance and rear guard, sweat freely under their loads of food, tentage and ammunition, while dark splotches begin to seep through the dull, cotton uniforms of the soldiers. Ahead, and off to their right, members of the right flank catch an occasional glimpse of an officer through the few gaps in the grass and shake their heads at the deadly risk of his lone exposure in this thick cover. They glance upward to where the big griffon vultures hang and slide against the bleached denim sky. *They* know. The bloody birds always know. Death is out there this fine morning. Perhaps to the front, maybe the sides. Behind? Only the birds know, the birds and the enemy. But this morning he's there, all right, maybe thousands of him. Warriors of the Aliab branch of the Dinka tribe—tough, utterly wild and fearless, mostly naked but for a coating of wood ash, a thick, strong shield and, blimey, those great long spears sharp as the regimental surgeon's scalpel.

But the officer hasn't missed the vultures or anything else

41

around him, although he looks to be a suicidal, green fool so far from the main body, making notes and sketches and taking bearings for a future map of the area, which has never been charted. He damned well *ought* to know what he's doing. He's been out here frying and freezing, fever-racked and footsore, for the better part of twenty years, quietly doing things that would give Tarzan second thoughts. He's written a trunkful of papers and nine full books on African matters as diverse as the protective coloration of insects, to how to govern your own province, to updated and revised KiSwahili dictionaries. He speaks a dozen languages, several of them well enough to be a certified translator. He's killed a hell of a lot of people and captured many more. He is one of the most talented hunters, scouts and administrators of his day, unquestionably a genius with a multifaceted intellect that makes him appear one moment a cross between John Wayne and the Scarlet Pimpernel, the next a mixture of Margaret Mead and a zoo curator. He is Major Chauncey Hugh Stigand, Order of the British Empire, Order of the Nile, War Medal, Victory Medal. He is a Fellow of both the Royal Geographical and Zoological Societies. He is Stigand *Bey*, Governor of the Anglo-Sudanese Province of Mongalla. He is also the most important man on the African continent.

Perhaps the birds know that he has approximately seven more minutes to live, although these last few moments of sparring with death will be as extraordinary as the rest of his career in Africa has been. He was forty-two years old the previous October.

How C. H. Stigand ever managed to reach the age of forty-two is in itself a minor miracle, considering how close he came to getting his terminal leave at least three times before his big day in the long grass of Kor Raby. Yet, an even more amazing aspect of Stigand and his deeds is that he never reached the household-word status of some of his contemporaries, such as T. E. "Lawrence of Arabia" whom, in an uncanny number of ways, Stigand resembled in breadth and depth of talent. Both British officers were linguists, able to immerse themselves into cultures almost totally dissimilar to their own. So, too, were they both adventurer-philosophers, capable of the gentlest thought and the bloodiest deed, if the latter needed doing in the call of duty. The big difference and probable cause of Stigand's relative anonymity is directly connected to his colossal over-modesty. Despite the wealth of information his books have left us, he constantly and consistently refused to refer to any of his hair-raising adventures in any but the mildest of terms; he often omitted them entirely! Most of his more interesting episodes—and Stigand attracted danger the way a dead horse draws flies—are best reconstructed with the help of his fellow officers, in particular a Colonel Thorp, who was Stigand's good friend, and General Sir Reginald Wingate, Governor-General of Sudan, the man who assembled Stigand's material for his posthumous book. When Stigand was dead and not able to object, Wingate and Thorp wrote a memoir of Stigand and included it in *Equatoria,* the book published in 1923 which throws a good deal of welcome light on the modest major, without which people like me, trying to research Stigand, would have years ago thrown up their hands in despair and wandered off to open an artery.

Before I turn the incredible Chauncey loose on you, you ought to know a *little* about his background. Born in 1877, the son of the British consul in France at a city that doesn't make the slightest difference, he was locked into a liberal arts education despite a mighty yearning for the blood-and-thunder of the army. After he almost destroyed the chemistry lab at one school in an attempt to make explosives—apparently he succeeded—his family relented and permitted him to study for a commission. At this point, around age sixteen, some 200-pound bully must have kicked sand in his face at Brighton Beach because, picturing himself as a "lank, overgrown youth," he dove headlong into physical fitness. For two solid years he boxed, tumbled, lifted weights and especially studied the then-famous Sandow exercises, named for the Charles Atlas of his day. The Great Sandow must have known what he was doing; by Stigand's eighteenth birthday, he was no longer a gawky kid but 182 pounds of chiseled muscle sought after for charity events, at which he would tear packs of playing cards in half, bend iron bars and perform other feats of strength. Even Sandow personally presented him with a medal as being one of his best students.

His military career began with the receipt of his commission as a lieutenant in the Queen's Own Royal West Kent Regiment early in January of 1899. He shipped out for Burma and his first dose of lifelong malaria. Still, he was fit and continued to wow the chaps with his strength until it was conceded that he was probably the strongest man in the British Army. Burma was also his first chance to foray into the jungles, and the regimental gazette of his outfit calls his quarters a veritable museum of dead and live critters. His prize specimen was a huge hamadryad, or king cobra, which he would force-feed with a penholder across the jaws as his mates looked on from a very prudent distance. It was also in Burma that he began studying "native" languages, hiring a tutor to learn Burmese. An officer pal of his reports visiting his bungalow at the hottest hour of the day, to find him hard at work with his Burmese instructor while surrounded with the four baskets of his "tame" cobras.

When, shortly thereafter, his regiment was transferred to Aden, British territory on the coast of southern Arabia, just across the mouth of the Red Sea from potentially cantankerous Somaliland, Stigand decided that he wouldn't be speaking much Burmese and switched to Somali and Arabic, shortly mastering them both despite their dissimilarity to the English tongue. (He might as well have chosen Sanskrit and Quechua for degree of difficulty.) Within a year, Colonel Thorp recalls that a walk through the native bazaar with Chauncey conclusively proved that he knew the native name, value, place of origin and use of every item he saw. Very different sort, this guy Stigand, especially if you remember that in 1901, British colonial powers were largely of the mentality that, rather than learn native customs and languages, the way to communicate with the "wogs" was to shout loudly and clearly in English.

While in Aden, we begin to get an idea of Stigand's sense of adventure. Just after he got settled, he bought a first-class riding camel named Tari. When he had enough Arabic under his belt to be able to brazen out any possible situations that might eventuate a collection of blue-edged rifle bullet holes through his new Arab robes, he began a personal and highly unofficial series of after-dark reconnaissances of the area around Aden, incredibly not yet explored by the British. Stigand isn't very helpful with the escapades, but he did discuss his one-man forays with Thorp the following year during long marches together.

When parade was over for the day and the rest of the regiment had turned in, Stigand would saddle Tari, having changed into his ersatz robes, place a service rifle in the camel's voluminous saddlebags and sneak past the guard into the night. We may be pretty certain that southern Arabia then was nearly as dangerous to wander in alone by night as New York's Central Park is today, and the fate of a lone, young English officer, obviously a spy and an infidel dressed in believers' clothing to boot, would likely have had an especially nasty last few hours of life had he been captured by Arabian authorities, or even common bandits.

But he did it, night after night, reaching well beyond Lahej (now spelled Lahij), mapping out the land. That he had iron nerves is very clear, as he dared to sleep on his way back aboard Tari, counting on being awakened by the swish of grain against his legs as he re-entered the cultivated area around the city of Aden. He then had to sneak past the guard again (ever try to sneak a camel past anybody?) and be back in uniform, trying to stay awake during morning parade. We don't know if he was ever confronted or if there might be a few old bones still moldering under a lonely desert bush with a British bullet through them. But then, Stigand never spoke about killing people in his own books. Poor form, probably. There is, however, no question that in one of his first actions he showed the initiative and deadliness welded into his professor's brain and strong man's body. . . .

If you happened to be born in Somaliland sometime late in the last century, you would have learned in short order that what you should aim for was the title *Mullah,* the Somali term for a powerful combination of political/religious leader. A certain Mrs. Hassan's boy made the grade, one Muhamed Abdulla, and was causing quite a few upper-echelon British headaches, what with raiding and fomenting revolution as if he was getting a volume discount. The nice part of the job of being *Mullah* was that you got all the dervishes you needed, a very effective mounted fighting force of ascetic Muslims who, between working themselves up into a religious lather by chanting and dancing, spent the rest of their time chopping up just about anybody handy. The British, after little consideration, decided to cut Muhamed Abdulla bin Hassan and his chaps down a few notches, and an expedition was mounted in January 1901 under a Colonel Swayne, Indian Army, who was at the time in command of the Somali Coast Protectorate. Stigand was ordered, perched swaying on Tari, to hold the town of Hargaisa, about 105 miles from the *Mullah* and somewhat out on a tactical limb, with only a small force. It would seem that nobody was all *that* mad at anybody else, because it wasn't until May 22 that the main expedition finally got moving from its assembly point at Burao. Stigand was given command of A Company, First Corps, under Captain G. E. Phillips. (Incidentally, a lot of these place-names are still left on modern maps; just look in the very northwest corner of Somalia on Africa's northeast coast.)

At long last, on July 17, the armies finally clashed at a desolate place you won't find, Fardiddin, a rocky, hilly battlefield assaulted by Phillips' force on the right, which put the British in a position to place a hornet's nest of .303 caliber fire into the *Mullah*'s dervishes, forcing them to take cover and return fire from behind bushes and boulders. Chauncey saw his chance. Taking a single "tame" Somali in tow, he broke further to the right on his own initiative and outflanked the dervishes, pouring fire into them until they broke and ran for their lives. Stigand was singled out for gallantry in dispatches by Phillips; his action forced the whole dervish line to break and take a bad beating. Among the others of the enemy that Stigand surely shot during the flanking movement were two of the *Mullah*'s personal bodyguards, distinct in their white turbans.

That's the story from official records, but, like the night forays at Aden, Stigand never even mentioned them.

Although a professional soldier, Stigand was at heart a hunter; in fact, it was largely his skills at bushcraft and tracking that made him so effective in combat. Certainly, he was a grand shot and killed without compunction in action, but his idea of a really big time was to go out and capture somebody—or even a couple of dozen somebodies. As he put it, after commenting that most organized expeditions against the natives were dull, ". . . if there is nothing to rejoice the heart of the soldier, the sportsman can often amuse himself, if he can escape from the crowd and get away by himself." Stigand loved the sport of people-hunting much as a small boy gets a kick out of hide-and-seek. The only difference in Stigand's case is that the men he was seeking were invariably armed and experienced warriors, trained from earliest childhood.

During the First Somali Campaign, Stigand and another officer, a Captain Fredericks, were off on their own, trying to nab a prisoner from whom to extract information about the *Mullah*'s retreat. Spotting four enemy horsemen obviously on an espionage mission, they sat tight until the dervishes rode into a box canyon to leave their horses. At the narrowest point between the walls, Stigand killed the last horse with a single shot, sealing off the enemy, who immediately abandoned their mounts and scampered up the rock walls, with Chauncey firing over their heads to get them to stop. Of course, he could easily have killed them on the wall—they were completely exposed—but he let them go, joking that the last one disappeared over the lip with his shield across his back, as if he believed it was bulletproof. One of the horses captured was a famous steed among the Somalis called *Godir Hore,* or Swifter than the Lesser Kudu, a mount that Stigand rode for the remainder of the campaign.

Within a few days of this episode, he took a small force and personally tracked down and so perfectly anticipated the movements of a dervish patrol in rocky country that the whole lot were surprised and captured.

Stigand did recount a few of the more humorous turns of events of his man-hunting experiences, one taking place in Kenya in 1908. He was off on his own with a very small force of porters and various bush staff, erecting surveyors' beacons, when a runner reached him with a telegram ordering him to join an expedition against the Kisii tribe, some distance up-country. After quite a few days' hard walk through heavy jungle, he managed to get within sight of villages burning in the distance. In the lead of his men, as he always was (a habit that finally got him killed), he topped a rise and spotted a lone Kisii warrior coming up from the bottom of the valley. He signed his men to stop, which to them usually meant he had seen game and, therefore, fresh meat.

Silent as a cat, he began to stalk the native, slipping from bush to bush until he was within twenty yards of the unsuspecting spearman. At this moment, there was the blast of a rifle close behind him, startling both Stigand and the Kisii half to death. One of his porters, who couldn't resist investigating what Chauncey was after, had crawled up and, seeing the enemy warrior so close, fired an old watchman's carbine to frighten him away. It sure worked! Instantly, the man was off down the hill with Stigand flat-out on his heels, the native dropping his spear and shield as he fled. At the bottom of the hill was a stream into which the Kisii immediately plunged, Stigand waiting on the bank for him to reappear. Some time went by without a ripple, so Chauncey sent men up- and downstream to look for him, but without a hint of where he had gone. Deciding to examine more closely the place where he had disappeared, Stigand heard a slight breathing sound and made for the exact spot. The Kisii came out from under a small tuft of grass where he had been hiding and stood up in midstream.

At this moment, with the white man standing a few feet away, a strange native who had attached himself to Stigand's party came running up with the Kisii's dropped spear and tried to earn a quick reputation for bravery by stabbing the defenseless prisoner to death in the water. As he thrust, Stigand knocked the butt aside; at the same second, the Kisii, a big, strong man, grabbed the spear away. Frightened out of his skull by the attempted murder, the captive exploded into a frenzy of terror, waving the spear around in huge circles with one hand and throwing chunks of grass at the Englishman with the other, an ancient African peace gesture.

All of Stigand's staff were now assembled and babbling so that he could not make himself heard over their rumpus and the shrieks of the prisoner. Chauncey pushed through them, accepted a tuft of the grass and pulled the Kisii out of the water by his hand. Personally, this seems a bit dicey to me, as the frightened man still had unquestioned possession of that spear and might have used it in desperation. Apparently, Stigand's native staff would have agreed with me as there was a general shout of, "Look out! He will kill our white man!" at which point a dozen hands grabbed for the spear. With all these bloodthirsty people about, Stigand observed, ". . . the Kisii thought his only safety lay in my immediate proximity so, wet, dripping, and covered with mud as he was, he threw himself on my neck."

As if there was not enough confusion, the cook rushed forward and made the howling observance that the warrior still had a knife at his belt—which, indeed, he did—and grabbed it by the hilt to take it away. Naturally, the poor Kisii made the immediate assumption that it was required to cut his throat and struggled with his free hand, one being wrapped around Stigand's neck for protection, to keep the knife from being freed. The cook, however, was equally determined, and the strange tableau continued for some minutes, the weird waltz so ridiculous that Stigand was reduced to laughter as his men tried to separate the knot of struggling, screeching people.

At long last, the prisoner was calmed down and roped by the neck, led along with the column. Realizing that he wasn't to be killed in cold blood, Stigand wrote that he assumed the haughty air of an honored guest. It was decided to give him a load to carry, which was half a tent, but after a few minutes

the Kisii dropped it and demanded that the rope about his
neck also be released! If I know Chauncey, I'll bet the
African picked that half-tent back up in one very big hurry.

This book could be filled with stories of Stigand's favorite
sport of people-catching, yet there's one more that proves
conclusively that not only was he foolhardily brave, but he
knew the African mind with an insight few whites ever gain.
On an unrecorded date in Somaliland, surprising a tribe of
rebels at dawn, Chauncey gave chase to a couple of men
driving camels away and bumped into two more on foot who
were trying to reach cover. He captured them and took their
spears, ordering them to come along with him. A few
minutes later, he spotted a horseman and, hiding behind a
large bush, ordered his prisoners to step into the open and
tell the rider to come over and dismount. Innocently, he did,
and Stigand came around the bush and added him to the
bag. Stigand just has to tell you this himself:

"By this time, I had got six spears and another pony
beside my own pony and rifle to look after, *so I gave their
spears back to the men and told them they must carry them for
themselves as I could not be bored with them.*" [Author's italics.]
Can you imagine the nerve it took to rearm six of your
enemy prisoners? Stigand was pretty clearly not suffering
from a self-confidence crisis! He then casually continues,
"The mounted man I told to lead his pony and then we set
off back to find the column. On the way I made a few more
prisoners till we were quite a large party."

Everything had gone so smoothly until then that Stigand
was a bit off his guard and let the man leading the pony get
behind him, to the left, where he would have no way to
swing around the saddle to fire. The man jumped into his
own saddle and started off, but Chauncey fired at him with
his rifle resting over his thigh, missing him but scaring him
so badly that he fell from his horse, absolutely convinced he
was dead. By the time he found his column, Stigand was so
surrounded by armed prisoners that, "To anyone observing
the procession approach, it must have appeared that I was
the prisoner and that they were guarding me on every side."

There's no need to follow Stigand's military career to

every bush and rock in East and Central Africa; the high points should be enough. At the end of the First Somali Campaign, he was so ill with malaria he had to be shipped back to Britain. Upon his recovery, he was seconded from his own regiment to the First (Central Africa) Battalion of the famous King's African Rifles at Zomba, then Nyasaland and now Malawi, and promoted to captain on March 21, 1904. Over the next few years, he had much more opportunity to hunt and travel, shooting from Nyasaland to as far as the swamps of Lake Bangweulu in modern Zambia, where he was one of the earlier sportsmen to hunt the rare aquatic antelope, the sitatunga. He hunted my old haunts on the Luangwa River and, on one of these trips, killed a greater kudu, that marvelous spiral-horned antelope in banker's chalk-stripe gray; his first, but also a probable world record for the time. It's not listed in Rowland Ward's *Records* because another taxidermist mounted it, but the longest horn measured 63⅝ inches on the flat of the curve, a real whopper by any standard.

Poor Chauncey seemed to have been jinxed as far as his luck with big game went. Oh, sure, he was a great elephant hunter and took a full complement of other dangerous game. The trouble was, he had an unfortunate habit of zigging when he should have been zagging. In fact, of the "Big Five" dangerous, large African man-killers, only two of them *didn't* catch up with Chauncey—the buffalo and the leopard. The rhino, lion and elephant all, however, managed to knock one hell of a lot of bark off Stigand. The first to make direct and everlastingly unforgettable contact was a rhino, when he was stationed at Fort Manning in 1905.

Stigand, in his writings, makes one of the points I pounded to a pulp in *Death in the Long Grass:* that the degrees of danger and difficulty in hunting a particular species such as rhino depends to a great extent upon local conditions of terrain and vegetation. He had shot quite a few rhino on the open plains of the north and admitted it to have been a fairly uninteresting business. *But* in the thick grass and *miombo* scrub of central Africa, where the rhino is not so common and often encountered at uncomfortably close range by mutual surprise, the game is a very different one. Rhino met at short distances in the really thick crud where there is little room to evade them will charge more often than not. If a turning or killing shot isn't made fast, you're most likely to regret mightily that you took up big-game hunting instead of interior design.

The morning that Stigand got a good, solid hint that he was not immortal found him some thirty miles out from Fort Manning, following an oldish elephant spoor across a wide *dambo,* or flat, covered with growth of twelve feet of grass and offering a visibility of two yards. About halfway across the flat, he noticed another track crossing the elephant trail at right angles, so fresh that the crushed grass was still springing back up, yet covering the tracks of the animal that made it. Curious, Stigand turned onto it for a couple of yards, bending down to try to see what had passed. The Angoni carriers he had with him—members of a northern branch of the Zulu—were still back on the elephant trail behind him. After a few steps, Chauncey's curiosity was unhappily satisfied as the locomotivelike snorts of a pair of rhino charging from the gloom of the grass cleared up the mystery. The first sight he had was of a great, double-spiked head tearing into view straight at him from no more than six feet away. There was nothing to do but stick the muzzle of his Mannlicher sporting rifle (he never tells us the caliber, but traditionally it would have been fairly light—for that matter, anything smaller than a howitzer is light for stopping rhinos from two yards!) into its face and pull the trigger. Still, it was enough to force the first animal to swerve slightly, and Stigand never knew what became of it. At the same moment, he became aware of the second rhino, a big bull, almost on him from a bit to the left. There was, of course, no time to work the bolt action and reload, so Stigand desperately tried to leap aside.

He tripped.

On the initial charge, Stigand said that the rhino "kicked him," although I think that what he meant was that he probably caught a blow from a foreleg; a rhino actually kicking out like a zebra or mule would be most unusual and perhaps anatomically impossible. Also, let's admit that he had quite a bit on his mind at that moment—a couple of tons, in fact—for the recollection of the finest detail. Whatever the case, displaying the astounding agility of an animal that appears so unwieldy to anybody who has never been chased by one, the rhino swapped ends with the speed of a Spanish fighting bull and charged thundering and snorting back. The next thing Stigand knew, he was flying like a bird. (With his usual classic understatement, he interrupted his own story to observe that, although his men saw him clear the top of the grass, "they are so unreliable in their statements that it would be quite enough for them, if they heard what had happened, to imagine that they had seen it.")

Despite the terrific shock of the toss, Stigand had the presence of mind to give some thought to his landing and attempted to control his fall. All those years of tumbling in the gym seem to have paid off; he managed to land heavily on his shoulder blades, thus not breaking any assorted arms, legs or his neck. Although partially stunned, he remembered giving a great mental sigh of relief when he saw the rhino's wrinkled rear disappearing into the grass. Later, he could recall actually being tossed only once, figuring that the "kick" might have given him the idea of having been on the horn more than one time. From this, it seems pretty safe to conclude that the first thump must have been like a glancing blow from a garbage truck, although Stigand played it down.

Undaunted, and with a growing sense of relief, he automatically began to look around for his rifle, spotting it on the ground some yards away now that the grass had been so nicely trampled. He got up and walked over to see if it had been damaged. While inspecting it, he noticed that a fingernail had somehow been torn completely off and was bleeding strongly. Even he admits that, after discovering this, it became intensely painful.

As he was checking out his finger, the Angonis came up and began to howl in horror at the sight of him, which made no sense to Stigand until he followed their stares down to his chest; he must have gotten quite a start himself. He saw that his shirt was torn wide open, sopping in blood, and that there was a god-awful rip of a wound on the upper left side of his chest, ". . . just over the spot in which the heart is popularly supposed to be situated." Chunks of flesh and muscle—he called them "mincemeat"—were scattered all over his shirt and skin from the presumed tearing loose of the rhino's horn from the gore wound.

At this point, I can't resist a bit of literary forensic diagnosis. As usual, Stigand made as little as possible of the terrible injury, although he was plainly concerned and probably scared motherless (and with every right). He was casual enough to say that the chest wound had taken his mind off the missing fingernail, yet added that he felt nothing but a numb sensation in his chest. (This tends to confirm some reports of many badly mauled hunters: that large and severe wounds usually do not hurt until sometime after the event takes place.) The next comment, and a key one as to the severity of the tear, was his statement that, "It struck me that it must have pierced my lungs." Well, I submit that this means that he could clearly see his ribs and possibly a hole between them or, with his hunter's and soldier's knowledge of chest wounds, would not have been worried that a lung had been pierced. He even sat down on the ground for a few minutes to see whether or not he would begin to spit up blood, so it must have been mighty close.

Stigand located the wound for us almost exactly where the heart is traditionally supposed to be, close to the area of the left nipple, the same spot where one would place the right hand to pledge allegiance to the flag. It follows, therefore, that the left breast muscle or pectoral (pectoralis major) must have been pierced through by the horn and then torn free of the chest and rib cage. This would be severe enough for an ordinary man, but let's not forget that Stigand was built like a goddam gorilla; those Sandow exercises especially developed the upper body, the most prominent muscles of which are the pectorals.

About the time that Stigand determined that his lungs

were not, after all, full of horn holes, there was another rustling in the grass which scared the loincloths practically off the Angonis. The rhinos were coming back. One of the carriers helped Chauncey back up and got his rifle into his hands. Anticlimax. The rhinos got wind of them and trotted off without charging.

Stigand, still dazed, sat down again to consider the situation, rather closely, I suppose, because what he did now would likely determine if he was going to live or die. He was bleeding heavily, by his own estimates thirty miles from home, only too aware of the probability of complications— such as death—setting in. Now, after a while, the shock was wearing off, and the pain must have been ripping him in half. At last he decided to send one of his men back to Fort Manning to advise the other resident officer of his predica- ment while he tried to make it to the nearest village, the distance to which, damn his eyes, he didn't tell us. However, by interpretation of his estimates (as a scout he was trained to estimate mileage accurately), it could not possibly have been less than six to ten miles, even if the village happened to lie in a straight line between the site of the accident and Fort Manning, presuming that we may exclude the pos- sibility that he would walk to a village farther away from help. Stigand did not mention it, but he must have forced potassium permanganate crystals into the wound to try to prevent infection, as Colonel Thorp reported that Chauncey was greatly bothered by the crystals being forced out with the blood flow. After "some time" Stigand began to feel very faint and weak (small wonder, considering the blood loss, shock and stumbling along rugged *miombo* trails with the upper left quadrant of his chest torn off!) and contrived to have a pole cut and himself lashed to it with his puttees. For a man of Stigand's strength and stamina to order himself trussed to a pole like a fresh-killed wart hog gives some idea of how much pain he was in. This, however, hurt him so terribly that he had himself unwrapped and somehow managed to walk the rest of the agonizing way under his own power.

Arriving at last in the village, he sat down and sent for his camp kit, which was at another village some distance away. When it pitched up hours later, he did what little he could to bandage himself and then lay down, figuring that there was no way that the other officer from Fort Manning, Captain J. C. L. Mostyn, could reach him before noon the next day.

When Stigand's runner made it to Fort Manning in good time, there was a case of "something being lost in the translation." The Angoni carrier found Mostyn, and, whether the captain misunderstood or the Angoni misspoke, the message that the officer understood was that the white man had killed a rhino, to which he replied, "Good." The information was repeated, Mostyn not understanding the native's growing agitation until it finally came through that it was the reverse of the situation: A rhino had killed the white man. The Angoni was apparently too shaken to explain what had happened to Mostyn's satisfaction, but it was clear that there had been a bad accident. Very much to his credit, Mostyn grabbed an Indian hospital attendant by the name of Ghulam Mohamed and was off on the forced march to help Stigand by seven in the evening.

Chauncey was awake, in too much pain to sleep, when Mostyn and Mohamed arrived at two in the morning. Stigand thought it an excellent feat to cover the twenty to twenty-four miles in such quick time, in the dark and over bad trails, not even knowing for sure where Chauncey had decided to go. (Since Stigand reported the accident to have happened thirty miles from the fort, his reference to his rescuers having come twenty to twenty-four miles is the basis for our deduction that he himself walked six to ten miles after the goring, not exactly a stroll in his condition.) In fact, the Indian was so exhausted that, despite his own wounds, Stigand suggested the man rest until morning before attempting to doctor his injuries. The Indian gallantly refused, sewing him up by lamplight, doing such a fine job of disinfecting and stitching that, after a mere three weeks' rest, Stigand set off on a 240-mile march, still in bandages, and made it in ten days!

If 1905 was not exactly a vintage year for luck, it's just as well that Stigand didn't know what was in his stars for the following season.

I know you haven't forgotten that macabre little Toonerville Trolley, the Uganda Railroad and its environs, that gave Patterson *Sahib* such a wonderful release from boredom a bit earlier in this report. Well, about seventy-five miles up the line from Tsavo is a small stop named, with uncanny perception, Simba Station. You will also remember that *"simba"* is KiSwahili for "lion." The place didn't get its name on an arbitrary basis, either, the whole area being famous for large numbers of lion, and it was to this spot in 1906 that the battered, tattered Stigand came to collect a few of the species.

The significant feline attraction of Simba Station was, in the dry season, the spillage of the main water tank used to replenish steam locomotives that collected in a pool or trough next to the tracks, this being the only handy surface water for a considerable distance. Accordingly, one moonlit night found Chauncey sitting on one of the iron beams of the tank's frame about seven feet in the air, which wasn't exactly prudent, considering how high a lion can reach.

After a short wait, Stigand saw a lioness padding casually up to drink, stopping directly beneath him. Although only a few feet away, the angle made the shot impossible. (At this juncture, it must be iterated that both lion and leopard of either sex were considered vermin in eastern Africa at the time, indeed, for many years afterward. As a matter of general practice, if a group of lions of both sexes was met, the normal procedure was to take the female first, as she would be faster and more inclined to charge.) Stigand shifted slightly to clear the shot, and the lioness must have heard him as she gave a bound of about four yards to one side and stood, listening. Chauncey nailed her in the chest, with a probable heart shot, as she ran like mad 200 yards up the line and fell dead across the tracks.

The moon must have been very bright because, just as Stigand was thinking of hopping off his perch, he was able to see clearly two male lions walk out of the bush and come up to the body of the lioness. They inspected her, scratching and pawing, for about a half hour—lions will eat other dead lions with no compunctions—and then slowly began to approach the water. The captain waited patiently until the lead cat was almost on him before firing. As he squeezed the trigger, the lion collapsed into the water trough below him, and Chauncey swung the sights on the second *simba*. It had stopped at the shot but then continued on without the least concern. Stigand placed a slug precisely into the dark mass of his chest. He thrashed around for a few moments, then dashed into the heavy cover and grass nearby where he was found the next morning, dead as stale beer.

Sounds like a pretty simple situation, right? Three shots, three dead lions. Not quite, chaps. Just as Stigand was again about to bail off the girder, the lion lying "dead" in the water trough revived and took off through the night into the high grass, barely catching a late snapshot from Stigand, who, we may be sure, was muttering some very specific comments. It would have been extremely interesting had he landed, off balance from his jump from the girder, just as the lion came to.

If you've spent any time in Africa, you know for a certainty that this was the precise moment the moon chose to duck behind some heavy clouds, reducing visibility drastically just when you needed it the most, such as while wandering around high grass in the middle of the night, looking for wounded lions which may or may not be dead.

Chauncey decided to go up to the station and get his orderly to bring a lamp. They passed the spot where the last lion had fallen—Stigand had heard him pile up at his last shot—but could see nothing and elected to check out the lioness up the track before hyenas or a train came along and reduced his trophy to lion hash. By this time, a small knot of station hands had gathered about fifty yards from the place where the third lion had disappeared, interested in the proceedings, and Stigand passed them on his way back to have another try at spotting the lion's body in the grass. Finally, he was just able to make out a dim lump in the darkness but was unaware whether it was dead or alive.

Darkness has a curious way of distorting distances and angles, and so it was with Stigand that night. The body seemed to be quite a way down the line, and he imagined he was standing on an embankment with the lion well below him. Reckoning that he would have an easy shot if the lion was not dead and tried to charge uphill, he decided to have a closer look over the nonexistent "edge."

Big mistake.

In a flash of dark fury, the lion was on him in a single bound, the orderly behind him disappearing as if teleported. As the lion sprang over the embankment, which proved to be only a foot high, the man managed to get off a shot into its chest the instant before the big cat hit him, the right paw, studded with two-inch pruning hooks, over the man's left shoulder, digging into meat, Stigand's left arm firmly in the lion's jaws. Extended along the forestock of the rifle, it was the first part of the captain's anatomy to come within reach of the fangs.

The tremendous impact leveled Stigand, and he now found himself flat on his back, the arm being very thoroughly chewed, although the rifle was still clenched in his fist, pinned under his body. Stigand tried to break free, scrambling around with his arm still between the massive teeth until he was kneeling beside the shaggy, rumbling head.

Okay, what else would you expect Chauncey Hugh Stigand to do? He wound up with his free right hand and began to punch the lion as hard as he could in the back of the neck. As powerful a man as Stigand was, I can hardly believe that such blows would faze a furious, wounded 450-pound cat. Maybe the punches, directed from behind, confused the lion into thinking that there was another attacker. Whatever the reason, the lion gave him one more terrible shake and dropped him, running back into the grass between the man and the station house.

You've got to hand it to old C.H., at least for his presence of mind. He carefully reloaded and eased past the spot where the lion was presumably lying, although without enough visibility for a shot. Classic Stigand fare: "I could not see him in the grass, and thinking him well left alone [this with his own arm almost torn off] continued toward the station, meeting the admiring audience who had witnessed the scene just past the water tank."

When he reached the station house, after deciding not to give the lion any more trouble, he took stock of his own condition with a paraffin light. His clothes looked as if they'd been passed through a shredding machine, he had eight big holes in his left arm leaking blood and three marvelously macho-looking claw marks on his back. By now, we automatically suspect these are just the highlights; he must have accumulated more damage, especially since he reported that his pants were also torn and bloody. The gravest part of the wound, besides blood loss, was an almost-severed nerve and the loss of the use of his left wrist. He recalled, however, that he had no difficulty in reloading the rifle and coming to the firing position on his way back to the station.

He sat up in the waiting room for six hours, until the Nairobi train was due, a wire having been sent to the stop at Makindu to bring some dressings. Under his direction, the stationmaster syringed out as best he could the worst fang holes and scratches with good old potassium permanganate solution to prevent the horrible infections caused by the layer of septic filth in the grooves of lions' claws, a layer of decaying meat from earlier meals. At last the train arrived, and the guard bandaged him up; he was finally able to board at 5 A.M. Of course, all the white passengers were asleep at this hour, and, in a colony where inebriation was not exactly unknown, one glimpse of the tattered, staggering figure was enough almost to get him bodily thrown back onto the tracks until he was able to explain what had happened. In the end, the passengers were most helpful.

Even the iron-willed Stigand conceded that the lurching journey to Nairobi was a solid whirl of agony, now that his wounds had stiffened, especially the torn nerve in his mangled arm. He made it to Nairobi Hospital, though, but over the next few days it was a very, very close thing that he did not lose the arm, which "swelled to enormous proportions and assumed every color of the rainbow, but owing to the assiduous attention of the nurses it was just saved."

Although the arm was spared probable amputation—which would almost surely have been required had he not been mauled right at a railroad station instead of out in the bush, where the infection would probably have killed him without hospitalization within twelve hours—it would be a long road before he finally recovered fully. It was seven months before he could use his wrist at all and a full two years until he felt steady at shooting. It's interesting to note that he literally forced himself on another lion hunt just nine months after the mauling at Simba Station, being genuinely concerned that he might have lost his nerve from the horrible experience. For Stigand to admit this gives some insight into how much the whole episode affected him, not just physically but mentally. After all, I sometimes wake up with the wee-hour cold sweats, and I never really got nailed, let alone creamed by two of Africa's heavies in the space of about a year!

Thorp reports that Stigand was sent back to Britain for further work on the arm nerve, and it is unclear from the surviving records whether Thorp was with him there or if Stigand was still undergoing treatment upon his return to British East Africa. Wherever it was, Colonel Thorp gives us some idea of the extended, excruciating ordeal that Stigand went through during the period the nerve was regenerating: "The pluck with which he withstood the cruel but necessary pain of the treatment for the restoration of nerve power [and God can only imagine what process *that* might have been in 1906!] was characteristic of the man. Often I saw great beads of cold sweat gather on his brow while undergoing the treatment, yet he continued to converse in a perfectly natural manner the while."

This statement of Thorp's reminds me of the similarity on another point between Lawrence of Arabia and Stigand. Lawrence, on one occasion, reportedly extinguished a lighted lucifer match with his bare fingers without a blink. His orderly, suspecting some sleight-of-hand parlor trick, tried the same thing, obviously burning himself painfully.

"Eh, Gawd! It 'urts!" exclaimed the orderly in surprise, dropping the match. "Wot's the secret, then?"

"The secret," intoned Lawrence in his mystical way, "is not *minding* that it hurts."

Ah, but whatever happened to the lion that had subdivided Stigand?

Before he left Simba Station, Stigand gave explicit instructions to his orderly, the man who had bolted at the lion's charge, repeating himself three times, as Chauncey refers to the man as being a "rather dense person." Nothing was very involved; the orderly was to climb the water tower at first light, where he would be able to perceive the lion without danger and fire at it to see if it was dead. Clearly, nobody was to go anywhere near the place in the grass where it had last been seen until the cat had been accounted for.

Oh, yes. Africa wins again. As might be expected, precisely the opposite to Stigand's instructions was carried out. A foot procession set out in the morning, led by an unarmed boy, with the rifle-toting orderly bringing up the rear where he could do the least possible good. The boy saw the lion lying in the grass and ran up to it, presuming it to be dead. Wrong. The kid was savagely clawed, while the orderly, who was even a member of the same tribe, did nothing. The boy was finally able to draw away because (it was later discovered) Stigand's first bullet of the night before had damaged the lower jaw of the lion, and, although it was demonstrably able to give a ferocious account of itself to Stigand when the wound was fresh, its jaws had probably stiffened during the night and it was unable to bite. A guard from the next train finally killed the die-hard lion with his service rifle, firing from the train's guard van.

Stigand stayed out of additional trouble with dangerous game until about 1912, despite the fact that he had by now established himself as one of the top elephant hunters in Africa. His military exploits during—and after—this period were so diverse as to make their description impossible, except to say that he was the first white man to undertake a fantastic journey through unknown Abyssinia on his way back to England, let alone complete the trip. Arriving back at his regiment in Britain, he discovered he was several months overdue on his leave. This was not funny in the British Army. However, when the investigatory board, convened to determine his fate, discovered what he had done and where he had been, he was exonerated fully and even given a special grant of fifty pounds by the Geographical Section of the General Staff to help defray his expenses. In 1910, when the Lado Enclave, a boot-shaped piece of Belgian territory, was ceded to Sudan by prior agreement upon the death of Leopold II, it was Stigand, a mere captain, who was selected to do the actual "taking-over." Following this, he was placed in charge of Kajo Kaji District in Mongalla, the Upper Nile Province, a post he held for some time until, in 1915, he made major and, four years later, became governor, or *bey,* of the whole of Mongalla Province.

One of the great mysteries of Stigand's hunting adventures is his near-fatal brush with an elephant, somewhere in southern Sudan in 1912. General Wingate merely says that "Stigand had had a contest at very close quarters with an elephant, which had trampled on him and nearly killed him; he was brought to Khartoum seriously ill and spent his convalescence under the *Sirdar*'s [Wingate's title] roof."

In Theodore Roosevelt's foreword to Stigand's classic *Hunting the Elephant in Africa* (see bibliography), even Teddy brings up the fact that it was generally unknown what had happened in the elephant incident except that Stigand was badly injured, although we have no details. To quote Roosevelt in his exasperation: "But it is as difficult to get Captain Stigand to tell what he has himself done as it was to get General Grant to talk about his battles. After this manuscript was in my hands [late 1911 or early 1912], Captain Stigand was nearly killed by an elephant. It was in the Lado and he was taken down to Khartoum; but his letters to his friends at home touched so lightly on the subject that they had to obtain all real information from outside sources." This "outside" information has not, to my knowledge, survived. What a shame.

While languishing in Wingate's garden one day, recovering from the mysterious elephant incident, Stigand confided to the governor-general that he was smitten with a lady and wished to marry. The usual consequence of such a decision was to offer the resignation of one's commission, which Stigand did. Although Wingate tried to talk Chauncey out of bringing a wife to the severe living conditions of Sudan, neither was he unaware of Stigand's value. He relented and granted an exception to regulations. The captain (at that time) took the hand of Miss Nancy Yulee Neff of Washington, D.C., on January 4, 1913, in England. He brought her back to his duties at Kajo Kaji, and they began to build a home there. Then Stigand went down with blood poisoning, and, by the time he had recovered, she was half-dead of blackwater fever and had to return to a healthier climate.

As the years went on, despite problems of health and primitive conditions, they managed quite a lot of time together, even if sporadically. During his ten years in Sudan proper, he was constantly on the go, mostly putting down native risings and rebellions, in the course of which he was twice again mentioned in dispatches in the *London Gazette,* in time earning his Order of the British Empire, as well as the other decorations already mentioned. In 1917, his daughter, Florida, was born. Late May of 1919 saw Stigand on leave in America with his wife, daughter and parents-in-law, until ordered to return to Mongalla on July 20, reaching his post on September 12. Neither he nor Nancy had the faintest notion that they had had their last sight of each other.. . . .

It took a few weeks for Stigand *Bey* to sort out what was really going on, not so simple in a place where communications are difficult even today. The problem came down to the fact that the Aliab Dinkas were having a wonderful time raising general hell and had gone so far as to attack and burn Minkammon Station on the White Nile, scaring the native authorities thoroughly and, based upon their successes, encouraging their own kind to rise.

The company of troops Stigand sent to reconnoiter reported 3,000 Dinkas and Minkammon in ashes. Worse, this force had effected no retribution (somewhat understandable, considering a mere company against 3,000 wild men!), and Stigand knew very well that unless somebody slapped the Aliab fingers, there could be a general revolt savage beyond belief. Aliab Dinkas were not the sort of chaps one fooled around with.

On the sixth of November, he sent another company from Tombe, a few miles upriver from Minkammon, under Victoria Cross winner Major F. C. Roberts and a Major White, White actually commanding the movement. When White and Roberts learned that the first force had, indeed, done nothing, they advised Stigand, as governor, that, even though their own force was but 200 men, it was imperative they attack the Dinkas immediately before the rest of the tribe joined them.

Stigand agreed. All of the Dinkas were not Aliabs, and he was anxious that those "sitting on the fence" be shown a display of force so they would not go over to the enemy. Therefore, he took sixty men and a Captain Wynne-Finch from his position at Tombe down to the village of Jongley and from there on a two-day forced march inland, east to Kongor where the uncommitted Dinkas were. He noted that things "look rather nasty and the whole countryside long grass."

Twelve days later, Chauncey wrote his wife that the Dinka chiefs claimed to be loyal and seemed sufficiently cowed that he recrossed the White Nile and marched back to near Minkammon, running into the column of White and Roberts. This force had been attacked in heavy numbers at three o'clock in the morning by the Aliab Dinkas and only beat off the enemy in fierce hand-to-hand fighting in a very hairy engagement. They had sustained seven killed and nine wounded, plus some porters lost. The enemy had managed to sneak up to the edge of the *zareba,* or protective thorn stockade, and broken through. It must have been a terrifying experience for the British; the Dinkas poured through the gap in the hundreds, each warrior making a weird whistling sound by which they could recognize each other in the dark. At dawn, the British were astounded that they had gotten off so lightly; two officers reported that spearmen even ran between their beds and woke them! At length, the Dinkas retired, and more than one hundred spears were picked up next morning, indicating a good number of enemy dead, as the Dinkas always tried to carry away their casualties and were determined not to leave behind fine, valuable spears.

A week later, Stigand again wrote Nancy that, despite his dislike of patrols and punitive expeditions, this one had been forced on him. To paraphrase: "Any failure . . . to give them a good hammering . . . will only lead to future trouble or encourage other tribes to do the same. . . ."

In his final letter, December 3, five days before his death, he said that he planned a two-week sortie against the Dinkas, having received intelligence that enemy losses at Minkammon and in the night attack against White and Roberts were more costly in dead and wounded than expected. He complained of a sore throat, from the smoke of grass fires, and a touch of fever. He expressed his hopes to be home early in the new year and closed with all his love. It was signed "C."

Stigand never realized it, but in his writings, somewhere between 1908 and 1911, he described his own death almost perfectly. He detailed the typical expedition getting started after some white was murdered or a tribe under British jurisdiction got mauled by one that wasn't. What then happened was the arrival of the punishing force, before which the natives scattered, trying to hide their stock; some huts were burned and a few men shot down until the miniwar was over. Messengers of peace were sent out, and the natives promised to be good boys. If they were, they might even have gotten some of their cattle back after a year or two. Perhaps a soldier or two became separated and skewered, but losses on both sides were usually very light. This was the case, said Stigand, ninety-nine times out of a hundred.

There is, however, that hundredth time. It all starts as the other ninety-nine, but either the enemy is unfamiliar with the effectiveness of firearms or enjoys a particular superiority of men, position or both. Then, as Stigand related with eerily accurate foresight, "Nothing is seen of the assailants except a few flying men. Suddenly, there is a rush in thick grass or bush and the little column gets massacred." How right he was.

For Stigand, the hundredth time was here, this morning, in the long grass of Kor Raby where a thousand stark-naked, six-and-a-half-foot-tall Aliab Dinkas lay silent in the thick cover, watching the British column advance. Sharp eyes noted the lone officer on the far right front, and a dozen dusky tribesmen wriggled through the grass to cut him off. Waiting until the troops closed to within a few yards, where their rifles would not be so effective, there was a sudden shout, and with a wild screaming the spearmen washed like a wave onto the staggering soldiers, startling the advance guard and the carriers into a backward rush that threatened to break the all-important defensive square.

The air was thick with gleaming spears which fluttered and hummed with a sharp, *whickering* sound, some ending their flight with a solid *thug!* as they sliced into flesh. A mist grew from the dust of running feet and the smoke of return rifle fire, crackling like popcorn. From the right, Stigand was seen firing as fast as he could into the charging mass of whooping warriors, his empty cartridges catching the early sun in flashing arches of brass as they were ejected from the repeater. Across the formation, a tough campaigner, Sergeant Macalister, dropped under a sleet of steel, and Commanding Officer White also fell, three spears through him, a strange, khaki butterfly pinned for mounting. He was dead in a few minutes of hemorrhage.

Stigand had to break for the main column at once if he was not to be overwhelmed. But a glance at the situation showed that only pressure from his position could stem the retreat of the advance guard back into the bearers, collapsing the box. He knew exactly what he was about to do. Without a thought to his own safety, the Governor of Mongalla Province set his jaw and rammed home another ten-round clip into his .303 rifle.

Nobody saw Stigand killed, the last sight of him recorded

as pouring fire into the enemy as fast as he could load. It is almost certain that he was rushed by a group of the enemy from point-blank range and speared to death before he could cut them down. About a dozen of his empty cartridge cases were picked up from about his body, although he must have fired quite a few more shots than this, the empty cases of which were missed in the long grass. Also, even though he is thought to have been killed in the first two minutes of fighting, his position was surely not static; he would have been moving about to avoid thrown spears as well as to present himself with better angles on targets of opportunity. As a master rifleman, firing as rapidly as possible at a more or less massed enemy, it would seem on the low side to presume that he did not take at least twenty of the enemy with him. Most important, he did save the square by spending his life, knowingly and willingly, to throw back the impetus of the Dinkas' first rush, quite possibly saving the entire column before the formation and firepower based upon it was crushed.

Stigand, White and Macalister were temporarily buried at Kor Raby, where the detachment had spent the night before. Later, the bodies were recovered and permanently interred at Tombe, under a solidly built cairn of stones brought from the Stigand home at Kajo Kaji, at the special request of Mrs. Stigand.

One of the most fascinating and touching documents I have ever read is the letter of condolence from Major Roberts, V.C., to Mrs. Stigand, describing the action that day and the death of her husband. It's worth reading:

Dear Mrs. Stigand,
   It is with great sorrow that I am writing to give you the details of Stigand Bey's death. I am sure that you will wish me to tell you everything. In the beginning of November the Aliab Dinkas on the western bank of the Nile round Tombe rose. Stigand Bey did his utmost to settle matters peaceably, but to no purpose. The Equatorial Battalion was ordered out, and up to the 5th December had a certain amount of fighting.

On this latter date the column again commenced operations with Stigand Bey as Political Officer. I own that it was not right for the "Governor" to come with us, but unfortunately no one else was available owing to sickness. Stigand Bey had also by this time made up his mind that half measures were of no use, and that the Dinkas required severe handling. He himself showed the greatest keenness in all the arrangements; and I am afraid from the start took unnecessary risks, always being well in front or on the flanks of the column reconnoitering, and taking bearings for a future sketch of the country marched through. At 7.15 a.m. on the 8th December the head and flanks of the column were rushed in very thick grass, by what I estimated to be a thousand of the enemy (in order to explain things better I am enclosing a rough plan of our formation, and where Stigand Bey was at the moment the rush came). Personally I was at the head of the left flank guard, and did not see Stigand Bey fall, but Bimbashi Kent-Lemon, who was at the head of the right flank guard, saw him with his rifle to his shoulder firing as hard as he could and attempting to stop the backward rush of the advance guard and the carriers, which threatened to break up our square formation. No one I can find in the battalion saw him killed, but it must have happened within the first two minutes. His end I know was an extremely gallant and a happy one, by the smile on his face when we picked him up. From the spear wound through his chest he must have died instantaneously and have suffered no pain. All of us know that he gave his life to save the column from utter destruction, which would have been certain unless he had stopped the first rush before too many of the enemy got inside the square. We afterwards picked up about a dozen of his empty cartridge cases, which I think speaks for itself. At dusk the same day we buried him and Major White, our Commanding Officer, who was also killed, fifty yards to the N.W. of a small clump of trees at a place named Kor Raby, where we had spent the night of the 7th/8th December; this spot will be well remembered by all on the patrol, and you must not worry about the exact position not being found in the future.

It is impossible for me to tell you how all, British and Native officers, non-commissioned and men, feel for you in your great loss; your consolation is that he was one of the most gallant officers and the finest man the Sudan or Africa has ever known, and I feel certain that his death was the one he would have chosen above all things—giving his life for others.

With deepest sympathy,
Yours very sincerely,
F. C. Roberts, Bimbashi, *a.* O. C. Equat. Bn.

Mongalla, 21st December, 1919

A caveat here: Anybody who knows anything about armies and dead soldiers is aware that there are some common devices employed; i.e., to assure the family of the deceased that he met his end painlessly, no matter what horror of lingering agony he may really have suffered, very frequently "with a smile on his face." I have seen people bayoneted to death and can assure you none was smiling. All cutting instruments, be they spear, arrowhead or bayonet, kill by ultimate loss of oxygen to the brain by bleeding, unless they happen to pierce the brain itself or the upper spinal cord. To look down and see a couple of feet of spear shaft jutting from *your* ribs, covered with *your* blood, would not tend to put a smile on your face. In actuality, the expression is usually one of unbelievable surprise, Hollywood be damned.

On the other hand, if you've gotten to know old Chauncey as well as I have, I'll bet you two hangovers and next month's mortgage payment that Stigand really *did* have a smile on his face! He had that much class.

BIBLIOGRAPHY

Stigand, C. H., *Central African Game and Its Spoor* (In collaboration with D. D. Lyell) (The *Field,* London, 1906).

———. *Scouting and Reconnaissance in Savage Countries* (Hugh Rees, 1906).

———. *The Game of British East Africa* (The *Field,* London, 1909).

———. *Hunting the Elephant in Africa* (And Other Recollections of Thirteen Years' Wandering) (New York: The Macmillan Company, 1913).

———. *The Land of Zinj* (London, Bombay, Sydney: Constable & Co., Ltd., 1913).

———. *To Abyssinia Through an Unknown Land* (London: Seeley & Co., 1910).

———. *Administration in Tropical Africa* (London: Constable & Co., Ltd., 1914).

———. *Dialect in Swahili* (or, A Grammar of Dialectic Changes in the Kiswahili Language) (London: The Cambridge University Press, 1915).

———. *Equatoria, The Lado Enclave* (including a Memoir by General Sir Reginald Wingate, Br., G.C.B., Etc. and comments by Colonel Thorp) (London, Bombay, Sydney: Constable & Co., 1923) (Posthumous work).

Major P. J. Pretorius

SHE SLIDES THROUGH the southern sea in sinuous silence, her silhouette no more than a black blot on the horizon where the stars are missing. The thrumming of her engines is barely audible, even on her bridge where blue eyes probe the sepia African waters through crisp Zeiss lenses. Her stealth is not out of fear, but caution. There is nothing in these vast hunting grounds but prey—the British enemy. Already she has left a spoor of bloated bodies from the dozens of merchantmen she has slaughtered, and now, miles astern, even the burning debris of her latest kill is no longer visible off Zanzibar—the noble (and undergunned) H.M.S. *Pegasus,* now firmly settling into the bottom mud with her two loyal guard ships. It had been a quick, decisive victory for the Imperial German Navy, but her commander realizes he may have jeopardized his mission by its very success: When *Pegasus*—who surely got off a wireless message—is discovered to have been sunk, the British will be forced to come after the German raider or lose all ability to supply her East African colonies.

The engines slow in response to bridge signals, the faint bow wake a slender, dully glowing feather as the mass of the German East African shoreline looms off the starboard bow. She knows the way to her lair. In the years before *Der Tag,* her intelligence had carefully charted the great Rufiji River to a distance of nearly twenty miles inland and found it navigable even for a light cruiser of her class. Cautiously, battle cruiser *Königsberg* noses her steel snout into the main channel and churns slowly out of sight into the heavy jungled river inland. At this moment, in 1914, she has the distinction of being the biggest and most dangerous game in Africa.

The first years of the Great War in the colonies, especially in eastern Africa, presented an inconclusive set of affairs from either side's point of view. The British had led with a haymaker of a naval bombardment on August 8, 1914, at Bagamoyo and Dar es Salaam in German East Africa (later Tanganyika, literally "Where One Walks in the Wilderness," and now Tanzania). But they were badly mauled in an attempted invasion the following November by a far smaller force of defenders under the brilliant German General von Lettow-Vorbeck, who bloodied the Allies' collective nose at the Battle of Tanga, between Dar es Salaam and Mombasa. After this action, the campaign broke down into limited skirmishing on a small but ferociously bloody scale through the 1914–1915 period, neither side gaining any decisive advantage. In fact, the hunt for the *Königsberg*, besides being one of the most colorful operations of the war, was also one of the first Allied successes in Africa on a tactical basis. Its inception and ultimate execution constitute one of the most outrageous one-man exploits in the history of warfare. As so often is the case when Fate gets involved, that man was also one of the most unlikely chaps available.

He was P. J. Pretorius, later Major, with C.M.G., D.S.O. and Bar. A descendant of the famous Boer *Voortrekker* general who gave his name to Pretoria, South Africa, and the son of a man who had twice fought against the British, he was nonetheless loyal to the Crown, which turned out eventually to be some of the best news since Waterloo for the British and the Allies. But let's not get too far ahead of ourselves; there's far more to the story of P. J. Pretorius than his hunt for the *Königsberg*, both before and after that incredible adventure.

A small, lean, dark-complected man whom Prime Minister Jan Smuts thought looked more like a Somali or an Arab than a European, Pretorius was just sixteen when sent by his father to ride transport for the British South Africa Company in 1893, during the war with King Lobengula of the AmaNdebele Zulu. The B.S.A. Company, as it was called, was a quasi-military land conquest and development company put together by Cecil Rhodes. The company had its own troops, who put down the uprising, Pretorius arriving in Lobengula's captured capital of Bulawayo only two days after the great Rhodes himself. As things simmered down, P.J. was called home to his parents' farm in the Transvaal and told to remain there. But he'd seen the local equivalent of *Paree* and, determined to make his fortune in the interior, pulled up stakes and left. It would be twenty-five years before he saw the farm or his parents again. Becoming a member of the B.S.A. forces, he soon demonstrated his phenomenal eyesight during a fight with the MaShona people and was elected guide to his company, commanded by Rhodes's own brother.

Over the years that seemed to flow by like rapids, Pretorius wandered over much of the Zambezi region, even penetrating as far as "King Khama's Country," modern Botswana. He lived in the Congo with Pygmies, fought cannibals, dug for gold and, most critically for his future as a soldier, became an ivory hunter and later poacher in German East Africa. These latest extralegal activities were centered around the Rufiji—where the *Königsberg* was to hide—and the Ruvuma River, which now forms the border between Tanzania and Mozambique, then Portuguese territory.

That Pretorius held no fondness for Germans is historically not open to speculation. From his first brushes with various colonial officers, it seemed a case of hate at first sight. Early incidents were minor, but a full ten years before the Great War, there came a confrontation with the Huns which would cost the young South African two years of his life, much of his health and almost all of his worldly chattels which, by 1904, were not insubstantial. Here's what happened. . . .

Pretorius, after years of wandering, found himself in the Ituri Forest of the Congo, living with Pygmies as he hunted ivory and, as abominable as the idea seems today, was one of the first to kill a huge male gorilla. Deciding to take his large party of hired porters on a route out of the country which would bring him to Ruanda-Burundi, land of the towering, fabled WaTutsi, he had to pass through the eastern Congo region, infamous for its cannibal tribes. As he had been supplying plenty of meat, a couple of dozen Pygmies had come along with his safari, to accompany their windfall meal ticket as far as possible.

Well into cannibal country, Pretorius' safari came across the freshly butchered carcasses of sixteen natives, the choicer cuts of their mutilated bodies having been carried off to be prepared as food. Later in the day, the party was confronted by a cannibal force of several hundred men, led by a witch doctor. The two groups shouted abuse at each other for several minutes and, when neither would back down, the witch doctor incited his men to charge. P.J. shot him deader than easy credit, the rest of the attackers turning tail like the proverbial pin-striped primate. Where the cannibals had been gathered upon discovering Pretorius' safari were found the half-eaten bodies of three more captives.

Not anxious to hang around to get a *real* inside look at cannibal culture, the safari pushed on, Pygmies in tow, reaching a large village that did not seem overinclined to eat them. Pretorius bartered for a pair of oxen in exchange for calico, to forestall any potential barbecues in which he or his men might play a starring role. He told his head man to give one ox to the Pygmies to eat and the other back to the locals. Tired, P.J. then lay down to rest but was awakened by loud peals of laughter from the center of the village. Arriving there, he found the Pygmies cutting off and eating chunks of bloody meat from the still-living ox, a performance the locals seemed to think about the most humorous they had ever seen. Having one of his men kill the agonized ox, he went back to bed, only to be routed out again by war cries and shouts. Grabbing his pistol, he ran to see what was going on and found the Pygmies and the villagers beginning a pitched battle. The little people had found the communal pea patch and raided it, pulling up the plants, roots and all. Pretorius, exasperated by the antics of his fearless little friends from the forest, was just able to make peace before anybody got speared or arrowed by offering more calico. Finally back to sleep, he was once more awakened by terrible groans of pain. It was the Pygmies, so gorged on the peas that by dawn, five had died. As they clearly could not cope with this unfamiliar world outside their dark Ituri Forest, Pretorius sent them back with the provision that he would provide an armed guard as far as the forest. The guard was back with the safari two nights later, the trip having been made without incident.

Continuing the march, Pretorius' party pitched camp one night at a deserted village near a small lake. While his tent was being erected, a porter ran up to P.J. to report that a party of men sent to carry water from the lake had been attacked by cannibals, and that the cook and four other men had been killed on the spot. Pretorius immediately sent his head man to investigate but never saw him again, as the moment the unfortunate Swahili left, hundreds of screaming warriors poured down on the camp in a mass attack.

Although he fired into them as fast as he could load his shotgun, Pretorius' tent was shredded and the safari stripped of everything the savages could lay hands on. Pretorius must have been killing many of the horde of attackers, numb in their bloodlust, because the volume of shells he put through the shotgun made it so hot that the solder holding the barrels together actually melted, leaving the gun useless! It was painfully clear to Pretorius that his only chance was to run for it. Many of his men had been scattered and killed by now, but he broke back the way the party had come, with five survivors, and reached heavy bamboo cover. Running as fast as they could, they disappeared into the shadows with more than one hundred cannibals whooping triumphantly on their flying heels.

Through a fluke of luck, they hit an elephant path a short distance into the bamboo and turned off onto it, dropping flat. It was the ultimate chance. Trying to restrain their heaving lungs from giving away their position, they watched and listened as the mob of cannibals streamed past them a few yards away. They had managed to give them the slip! P.J.'s relief was tremendous until he took stock of the situation: He and his five men had among them only Pretorius' remaining Mauser pistol, down to seven car-

tridges, and were deep in dangerous country aswarm with
cannibals. Waiting in the bamboo until full dark, they
scrambled down a mountain and floundered through an
especially nasty swamp to temporary safety. One of the main
problems among the charming assortment from which they
had to choose was that they had been forced back into the
territory they had come through and were now hiding on
the edge of the valley where they had found the sixteen
mutilated bodies. Surely there was nothing for it but to wait;
travel by daylight would be suicide. With nothing else to do,
Pretorius was watching the cannibal stronghold below at
noon when, before his unbelieving eyes, twenty of his
surviving porters who had gathered together walked calmly
into the enemy village. His heart sank. How could they be so
stupid? His hopes rose when, at first, they were nicely
received and seated in the shade for a palaver with the
cannibals. Then Pretorius noticed that more and more
spearmen began gathering around the unarmed porters. At
some unseen signal, the sun gleamed on upraised spears,
and the twenty were slaughtered, stabbed and skewered to
death. Not one was even able to break for freedom.

In despair, there was nothing Pretorius and his men could
do but watch and, at dark, sneak past the village feast to
begin the 400-mile escape route that would take an agonizing, starving eight days—an unbelievable fifty miles per
night on virtually no rations.

When, sick and half-dead of disease and exhaustion, he
and his men finally reached the WaTutsi country, he found
that a German warrant had been issued for his arrest for
killing forty-seven natives.

Certain he could explain his actions as self-defense, he
marched for several more days to give himself up. Upon
doing so, he found he saw things a bit differently from the
colonial officials. The Germans placed him under detention
and shipped him down to the coast at Dar es Salaam, where
he spent most of the next year in the local cooler while
inquiries were made back into the bush. At last, still without
a trial, he was released on bail when evidence clearly
established that he had acted in his own and his men's

defense. However, red tape and sheer maliciousness denied him his full freedom until a total of two full years had passed in the stinking, steaming "Haven of Peace." When he was finally released from bond, he'd lost more than two prime years of his life; during his confinement, the German authorities had sold off his entire cattle herd of 774 head to favored politicians for the unthinkable pittance of the equivalent of 150 English pounds. The affair left the twenty-nine-year-old Pretorius bankrupt, with only enough to start life all over, including a used 8mm rifle, a few blankets, an ability to speak fluent German and a glowing hatred of the Huns that would cost them thousands of men killed and captured when the war broke out, not to mention the only effective ship they had in the Indian Ocean. No, Pretorius did not like Germans. Not at all.

Several years later, when he had ivory-hunted his way back to prosperity and had acquired a beautiful farm on the upper Rufiji, Pretorius received a letter from the German authorities *ordering* him to sell the farm to a certain *Hauptmann* (Captain) Blake, a German officer. Blake offered 400 pounds for the place, an insanely low bid as the house alone had cost 800 pounds to build, not including the land or cost of clearing it. The letter further stated that, as a foreigner, if Pretorius did not sell to Blake, the place would be confiscated and *given* to the officer! Something less than pleased, Pretorius sent a sizzling note back to the powers-that-were by native runner which read to the effect that if this happened, he would happily poach German ivory in their territory until a considerably higher price—plus interest and expenses—had been repaid.

Nobody was bluffing. The Germans confiscated the farm and gave it to Blake, and Pretorius began professional ivory poaching in German territory, crossing the river on extended raids and making damned fools on any and all occasions of the German *askari* police sent against him. Over the months and years, Pretorius recovered the cost of his farm and considerably more, becoming a very long, sharp thorn in Hun flesh that worked ever deeper. The Germans did not realize how firmly the barb was embedded until the guns started booming and the war came on in August of '14.

It was late in the afternoon of August 14, 1914, on the Ruvuma River, the lowering sun gilding the comfortable camp shared by Pretorius and his two friends, Captain Hemming and another wanderer named Mare, a fellow Afrikaaner. The three white men and their staff had been loafing for months after a last deep strike into German territory for ivory, now shooting only for food while they planned a grand lark of a trip across the breadth of Africa to Liberia. Having sent their porters out with ivory to exchange for extensive supplies for the journey, the men were relaxed and expectant that the supply safari would be along any day. The three were sitting, smoking in the twilight, when the sweating form of a post runner dashing madly into camp broke their easy conversation. The runner was incoherent with excitement and, at being asked what was going on, blurted out that the English and the Germans were fighting. Astonished, the hunters managed to gather from the details that this was not some sort of skirmish, but a major confrontation which had caused the Germans to remove all the native plantation labor from along the coast, many thousands of Africans. Realizing the meaning of the news, they were exultant at the prospect of war with their hated enemies, until Pretorius soberly suggested that they had to remember that they were at that moment on German soil. They had to get to the nearest British post to enlist, and, although it lay deeper into the enemy regions than they were on the marginal Ruvuma, they decided to reach the town of Lindi, where fighting had been reported and the British Navy most likely in charge by this time.

Breaking camp and setting off the next morning, their first objective was the mission station at a tiny bush village called Masasi. On the way, they were warned by fleeing natives that all the missionaries had been picked up and sent to Lindi. Obviously, the British Navy wasn't in control *there*. With no alternative, the party then turned back for the Ruvuma with the idea of marching all the way to Nyasaland (British Central Africa of the time), a full 1,500 miles away.

Upon returning to their old camp on the Ruvuma, the party was warned of the approach of a German column some 200 men strong that had left nearby Newala and was heading in their direction. The poachers' camp was well known to the Germans through informers, and, on the chance he hadn't heard about the formal declaration of unpleasantries, they hoped to nab Pretorius and cut off a potential source of Allied intelligence on their doorstep. Realizing the column's probable intentions, Pretorius moved camp to an island in the river located in such a position that any approaching force would be visible for at least 1,000 yards, while Pretorius' men were hidden in heavy cover. With sentries carefully posted, the night was quiet until ten o'clock, when a guard came up to P.J. to report a big campfire on the enemy bank. Looking closely, Pretorius saw, from the smaller individual fires, that there was no doubt that the Germans had arrived in full strength. Although it was Hemming's turn on sentry duty, Pretorius decided to lay awake with his rifle, plenty of extra cartridges and his shooting clothes laid out next to his bed.

By two in the morning, Hemming had been replaced by Mare, and Pretorius and Hemming sat up talking about the next day's tactics. The porters were sleeping in a dry water cut with small fires to keep down the mosquitoes, while Mare went on his first tour of inspection. He was apparently no feather-foot, as Pretorius complained that he could be heard 200 yards away stumbling over his own big feet. Mare stopped good-naturedly to chat for a moment when he passed, and at that instant the night tore apart with a terrific yell from the porters that the Germans were in camp!

The three hunters immediately grabbed for their equipment, Pretorius able only to dress partially and arm himself by the time the enemy was ashore and shooting up the place; he was forced to leave his socks, boots and belt. Running forward, Hemming and Pretorius returned fire from as close as five yards, but, despite the deadly barrage, there were too many, and the German *askaris* swept onward. Loading and firing, the little force was pressed to retreat back to the camp dining table on which a paraffin lamp was burning. Hemming tried to smash it so they would not be outlined as targets, but the fool thing only set its own fuel reservoir afire, showing the defenders up even better. Forced by the increased enemy firing to break and scuttle from shadow to shadow in a swarm of Mauser bullets, Pretorius suddenly found himself alone, separated from his friends in the confusion of the fight. Ridiculously outnumbered at more than fifty to one in terms of armed men, P.J. recalled that it had been agreed that if overrun, those who could would meet at a rock outcrop up the island some 400 yards away for a final stand. Running, dodging, Pretorius now broke for this cover, bullets churning up the dirt around him and whining through the bush as the sonic boom of their passage buffeted his ears. (Bullets do not whistle past one's ears, despite what the pulps say; they crack like a bullwhip.) It was a terrifying, desperate run. Once he almost knocked himself unconscious crashing full-speed into a tree; a few seconds later falling over a branch and jarring his rifle loose. He scrabbled for precious seconds in the blackness, trying to find it as enemy feet swarmed toward him, the attackers firing as fast as they could. He couldn't believe he hadn't been hit yet but realized that, in trying to find the rifle, he had lost the time needed to reach the rocks. Gasping, he was suddenly aware that the only place from which enemy fire wasn't pouring was the river. With the clarity of horrified realization, he knew that it must be the river—or death. He was not in uniform and would be shot as a spy if captured; as if the Germans needed an excuse, anyway.

He rose to dash for the water, legs tensing under him as he burst from cover, hammering toward the dark beach. His hopes were nearly shattered when, short of the river's safety, he felt the tearing tug of a bullet piercing both legs and a German voice screaming: "Get him at all costs!" Pretorius personally knew the man who shouted the order, a *Leutnant* Wack, and saw him in the shadows only yards away. As the Germans rushed him, despite the numbing shock of the bullet wound, Pretorius lunged for the water and threw himself into its black embrace.

The current was, happily, very swift, carrying the wounded man quickly behind a reed bed, where he was hidden from the still wildly firing enemy soldiers only thirty yards away. Encouraged to be momentarily out of the line of water-whipping slugs, he almost forgot his leg wounds in his struggle to keep from drowning, dragged down by the weight of his bandoliers of ammunition. Twice he hit bottom before being able to shrug off the load which weighed him down like a diver's belt. The pain in his legs came back in a blinding burst of agony as he found a shallow bar and tried to stand up. The right shin was smashed by the bullet, which had passed through the muscle of the left and gone on, completely through both legs.

Gagging down waves of nausea, he paddled softly into a shallower place, sitting still for an hour, the water up to his neck, as German lead continued randomly to comb the reeds. With the growing legion of red pain devils in his legs and skull, he had no time to worry about the crocodiles that infested the Ruvuma, every moment consumed in trying to keep away a school of minnows that were torturing him by darting up to his wounds and eating the raw, live flesh from the edges of the bullet holes.

Throughout the next day he remained in the reeds, always within ninety feet of the enemy, listening to them talk about him. Finally, he overheard somebody say in German that he had surely drowned or died of his wounds, and that it wouldn't be worthwhile to conduct a further search. Whew!

That night the German force broke camp on the island, and at last, the voices faded away into the blackness back to their own side. So far, so good, thought P.J. At least he was alive. But what a spot to be in: crippled and unable to walk, without food or arms, well over a thousand miles from the nearest friendly lines. Even if there had been survivors of his party who had not been captured, they would draw the same conclusion as the Germans—that he was dead.

Pretorius' desperation mounted as he considered his position. Losing strength through hunger and continually oozing blood, he had decided at least to attempt the suicidal swim across the Ruvuma to the Portuguese side, when, at first to his shock and then exhilaration, he heard voices in the local native dialect of KiSwahili, accompanied by the perfect rhythm of the dip of paddles. As river natives who knew him well and had no love for the Hun, they picked him up and ferried him to the southern Portuguese side of the river. Here began one of the most remarkable journeys ever even contemplated by a half-dead man a thousand miles behind enemy lines, wounded, alone and with some of the most hostile terrain in Africa between him and his goal. He was to endure capture, engineer an escape, suffer extended, awful pain and even be forced to self-mutilation. Nonetheless, one thought continued to burn in the brain of P.J. Pretorius: revenge. And he would have it.

On the third day after his arrival on the Portuguese bank of the Ruvuma, Pretorius awoke from a delirious sleep in great pain to find himself alone, lying in a sandy *spruit* near a village. Stubbornly refusing to give up hope of completing his journey, and only too bloody aware of the death sentence placed on his head by the Germans, he somehow fashioned a simple bamboo crutch and started hobbling toward Nyasaland. Unarmed and too sick to hide, he was almost immediately captured by a pair of Portuguese native soldiers, who had orders to turn him over to the Germans. In itself this doesn't make much sense, as the Portuguese were fighting with the British and South Africans *against* the Germans. Perhaps these chaps and their officers hadn't gotten the word. With the possibility of some medical treatment, Pretorius put up no fuss, hoping that on the trip down to Palma he would have a chance to escape. His heart sank, though, on reaching the post at Ngomano, at the confluence of the Ruvuma and Lujenda Rivers. There was neither a doctor nor medial supplies. In a stretcher carried by porters and flanked by armed guards, the Portuguese commandant sent him along to his appointment with a blindfold and a wall.

Two more days of agony crawled by, every moment spent with the shriveling chance of escape. And then, while resting at a village in the shade of a hut while his captors ate thirty yards away under a tree, Lady Luck appeared in a most unusual form. Pretorius looked up and saw his old gun-bearer, Saidi, walking straight across the compound to him, his face charcoal gray with fright. He came up to the white man and told his story of having survived the fight on the island and being captured with Hemming and Mare, both of whom had been sent down to the coast for formal execution three days ago. When he had heard a rumor that his *Bwana* was alive, he had escaped at the first opportunity and come to find him.

"Have you any weapons?" P.J. asked hopefully.

"I have the old Lee-Metford, *Bwana,*" announced Saidi, "and twenty cartridges." (This was an antiquated rifle for which Pretorius had made a bad trade when short of ammo for his .303 rifle.)

Excitement poured through Pretorius like an injection of adrenalin. *"Wapi?"* he asked in KiSwahili. "Where?"

"Hidden in the corn, five hundred yards over there," said Saidi, starting to gesture. Pretorius snapped at him not to point; his guards would get suspicious. Telling the frightened but loyal man that if he could get the rifle and cartridges to him, P.J. could get out of this, the *Bwana* sent him off into the corn.

Fifteen minutes later, incredible as it sounds, Saidi walked brazenly right through the village with the loaded rifle against his leg and handed it to Pretorius. None of the guards had even noticed him. Getting the drop on his captors, Pretorius told the guards to clear out, leaving the porters who were carrying his stretcher, or hammocklike *machila*. Knowing Pretorius' reputation with a rifle, nobody argued.

Back on his escape route, Pretorius had himself carried until it was too dark to see and then made camp. In the morning, despite both his and Saidi's vigilance, all but two of the porters had slipped away, again leaving him in a spot. After some consideration and consultation with his gunbearer, it was decided to return to a village they had passed through the previous afternoon to "enlist" some new labor. Arriving there, Pretorius found the place empty of all men, only women and children in sight. Asking where the men were—knowing full well they had seen his approach and had scattered into the bush, rather than be conscripted as porters—he was told by the oldest woman that they were all at a beer-drink sixteen miles away. Ever practical, and with enough years of applied African psychology to open a clinic, Pretorius promptly comandeered twenty of the strongest-looking females to carry his *machila* and the supplies he "requisitioned" at the village. Sure enough, after a half hour on the trail, Saidi reported that they were being followed by a man whom Pretorius let come up and demand the return of his wife, who was one of the ladies carrying the *machila.*

"Take her place and she may go," said P.J. The man did so, and the woman returned to her village. Within an hour, all the women had been reclaimed and replaced by their husbands!

By midday, they were back at the Lujenda River, where Pretorius washed off his wounds and had the men plait strong bark fiber ropes with which he had them tied together. In a blood-and-thunder speech, he firmly planted the idea that anybody trying for a bit of unauthorized leave would catch a bullet from the Lee-Metford before they were out of sight. Pretorius wasn't fooling around. As he was to put it: "It was a matter of life and death to me; why shouldn't it be the same for them?"

After six days of unspeakable pain while being carried over the rough terrain, Pretorius' leg became so stiff, swollen and infected that he instinctively knew he would never live to reach Nyasaland on a direct route; he decided to chance a trip up to a Portuguese fort at Mazewa, on the Ruvuma, where an old friend named Dr. Da Costa ran the show. However, after the distance had been covered to within a mile, Saidi, who had scouted ahead, returned with the disheartening news that the Germans had raided the place and murdered both Da Costa and his wife when they opened the door.

Not a very nice little war.

Pretorius continued on to the fort to see for himself. Both Dr. and Mrs. Da Costa had been buried inside the walls, and anything of any use had been carried across the river to German soil. Horrified and furious at the atrocity, Pretorius turned his safari back south along the Chulesi River for three days, then branched off for the headwaters of the Emtapiri and across the semidesert *nyika* to the Luwatezi. At this point, despite some apprehension, hunger forced the party to head directly for the villages of the infamous Chief Mwembe.

Chief Mwembe was not reputed to be the most genial of hosts. Fort Valentine, which was in this district (although apparently deserted at this time, or Pretorius would have made for it), had been named for a Lieutenant Valentine, who had been one of the vanguard British officers into the area. Valentine had been taken prisoner at the first village, where Mwembe had ordered his hands cut off. He had been placed at the head of a parade through the rest of the villages to demonstrate how ineffective the whites were, compared to Mwembe's might. It had probably been his good fortune to be stabbed to death only, at the end of the grisly tour. P.J., his party having been without food for two days, had no choice but to try to obtain supplies here. Once more his luck held as his safari blundered into a hunting party of which the chief himself was a member. The chief was captured and stocked Pretorius with food in exchange for his freedom.

More searing, endless days. Sleepless nights of throbbing agony. Fainting and delirium. Then, at last, the low, mottled profile of the Livingstone Mountains, on the eastern shore of Lake Nyasa. They were a welcome sight; beyond them lay British territory and safety. But Pretorius knew he would never live through the last of the ordeal unless something was done about his right leg. Another day or two, and gangrene or blood poisoning would unquestionably squeeze the last life from his fevered, emaciated body. The left leg, with no more than a flesh wound, had healed nicely, but the other was in a nauseating condition. The entrance and exit holes of the wound had healed over, but with the smashed, fractured bone and horridly swollen and festering flesh, his entire leg from toe to knee was a deadly black. P.J. knew that only if this was opened and drained would he have even a small chance to live. Dreading what he knew he had to do, he prepared to open the wound.

Choosing the sharpest of the party's knives, he probably filled his head with thoughts of his time in prison, his dead friends—Hemming, Mare, Da Costa—and his stolen farm. Placing the point of the knife on the tremendous lump between the two bullet holes, the mere weight of the cutting tool was enough to make him reel. Saidi held his foot, and, with sweat pouring down his face, Pretorius made the first cut.

Almagtig! God! Even the years of privation and pain of a bushvelt life could not prepare him for this. He fainted dead away, falling on his back and waking in a few seconds with screaming agony rocketing throughout his body. So terrific was the self-torture that he forced himself to sit up and grip the leg around the knee, squeezing the mangled flesh as hard as he could.

As he looked down, he almost gave up. Despite a long, deep gash in the leg, only a little black, smelly blood was oozing out.

He would have to do it all over again.

It took Pretorius a full five minutes to steel himself for the new torment he was forced to inflict upon himself. Rather than chance another ineffective slash, he bound the blade of the knife in cloth so it would not slip out of his hands as it had the first time, leaving an inch of the sharp tip exposed. With a deep breath and clenched teeth, he inserted the point into the top of the last cut and slammed the hilt with the heel of his right hand. Once more, waves of gagging agony slapped him back into blackness, yet, when he awoke, he could see thick rivulets of foul pus running from the wound. Too weak to do it for himself, he ordered Saidi and another man to grip the leg and squeeze hard to force out as much of the putrefied matter as they could. This caused even more pain, if possible, than the two cuts. When they were finished, he washed the leg in water despite the unceasing, excruciating torture, and, two hours later, the pressure much relieved, he fell into a sound sleep, the first since he was wounded.

After more weeks of traveling, what had seemed impossible began to come close to hand. Behind them were the Livingstones, and, on a bright, clear morning, suddenly they were at Malindi on Lake Nyasa, British Central Africa. As they collapsed to rest and drink, a priest from the mission station happened by on his bicycle, stopped and walked over to Pretorius, who certainly must have been an interesting-looking person after his ordeal. *"Jambo,"* said the priest. "Greetings." Pretorius felt the first niggle of humor for a long, long time. The priest didn't recognize him, although they were, in fact, old friends. Not until being told who the dark, painfully thin man was did the father dream it might be his old pal. At the mission station, when Pretorius looked into a mirror, the humor faded. He didn't recognize his own reflection, either. Small wonder. It had been a full twenty-six days since he had been shot and had jumped into the river.

After a short rest, Pretorius made his way down the lake to Fort Johnson, where he was finally able to get medical attention for his smashed leg. An operation was performed by the post doctor, who concluded that had the awful bit of bush surgery not been done, Pretorius would not have lived another day. As it was, he spent the next forty days completely immobile, there being no feeling in the leg at all (probably a relief after the past sensations), until it began to regenerate. After another three weeks, he was strong enough to be moved to Blantyre, where, after a final two weeks of recuperation, he was able to hobble.

All together, almost four months had gone by from the night of the fight on the island until he was able to reach Pretoria, South Africa, the nearest British recruiting post, to join up.

When he presented himself at the recruiting office, he was flatly refused!

After telling the story of his fight, wounding, capture and escape, the army decided that the entire affair was just too convenient, and that Pretorius must be a German agent. As he discovered after the war, counterspies were set on him for several weeks until things were straightened out. Completely frustrated, he boiled off and traveled to his old home at Nylstroom, which he had not seen in a quarter of a century, unaware that within a matter of weeks his life was to reverse itself completely. In the street one day, he was grabbed by a policeman who asked if he was Pretorius. Admitting that he was, he was ordered by the officer to come along to the Charge Office. Wondering if this spy business had reached the prosecution point, he was taken reluctantly into tow and delivered at the station. Ready for trouble, he was astonished to find not a sheaf of formal charges against him, but—of all things—a telegram asking if he would consider accepting service with the Imperial Government and taking the train to Durban!

Dumbfounded, he complied. From that day on, the change in his status from suspected spy to V.I.P. was absolutely diametric. He was given special coaches, attended meetings with cloak-and-dagger intelligence types and was even met, still bewildered, by a special train outside the port of Durban so that a telegram could be hand delivered. It read:

WITH COMPLIMENTS FROM ADMIRAL KING-HALL ON YOUR ARRIVAL IN DURBAN PROCEED IMMEDIATELY TO C SHED POINT.

As nobody seemed to know what or where C Shed Point was, there was some discussion as to the mystery with the military personnel on the special train. While this was going on, another telegram came over the wire, saying that upon arrival in Durban, a second special train would be waiting for Pretorius. It was, and before he knew what the whole thing was about, he was whisked aboard the great British battleship *Goliath* by the captain himself. Fed, given a private stateroom, he was left to ponder why on earth he had been chosen to meet personally with the famous Admiral King-Hall the next morning. As he lay in his bed, listening to the throb of engines as the ship got underway, he reflected on the incongruity of his being an honored guest of the Royal Navy. It was sure as hell a long way from hunting ivory in the Congo.

The following morning, P.J. was summoned to his meeting with the admiral, whom he liked immediately for his wit and way of getting down to cases. At last Pretorius was told that it was the *Königsberg* the British wanted, and they had a pretty fair idea where she might be found. Fascinated, Pretorius listened to the redfaced, bushy-browed King-Hall brief him on all that they knew. It was thought by Intelligence that the German battle cruiser was up the Rufiji, this being confirmed in rather a negative manner, as everybody dispatched to look for her had developed a disconcerting habit of never being seen again. Two seaplanes had been sent over the delta, and neither had returned. Of a pair of armed whalers ordered to scout, the one which went up the river had also disappeared. Even an ordinary boatload of loyal local natives had vanished into oblivion on the way upriver.

As Pretorius was the only man available to the Allies known to have spent time hunting the Rufiji area, his experience would be invaluable in scouting for the *Königsberg* and figuring out a way to bring her under fire by the British. King-Hall had a private scheme of constructing a sort of superraft, capable of carrying heavy guns and men, but Pretorius quickly dissuaded him from this idea; from the terrain, he knew it would be the equivalent of suicide. The Salali, as the main channel of the Rufiji is called, is deep and some sixteen miles long, threading through swamps and studded with small islands perfect for ambush. There being no reason to doubt that *Königsberg* still had all her big guns and torpedoes, such an attack would be completely impractical. The logical approach, suggested a thoughtful Pretorius, would be to scout her out, pinpoint her location and then decide how best to blast her to hell.

King-Hall just smiled quietly and pressed a buzzer.

Some twenty-two miles off the mouth of the Rufiji lies the

island of Mafia, an old Arab slaving center, only a rough 160 square miles of coconut groves. Previously a German base, it had been shelled and overrun by the British in January of 1915 and now became the nerve center of Pretorius' hunt for the cruiser. Landing with his staff of one man—a wireless operator—the brand-new Major Pretorius quickly set about selecting a native crew to assist him. He was assured by the resident commissioner of the island that he had unerringly picked the six biggest rogues on Mafia, yet he grudgingly observed that what they might lack in morality, they made up for in toughness. After a short chat with his new chaps in which Pretorius promised them faithfully in KiSwahili that loose tongues would be removed by him personally, he got the lot well whipped into shape and chose another smaller island called Koma, only a few miles from the delta, as a forward observation post and jumping-off point for his scouting forays. Before leaving Mafia for Koma, he received a wireless from Whitehall, asking how long he thought it would take to determine the *Königsberg's* location if she, indeed, was up the Rufiji. Pretorius thought eight days should do it. He was right on the button.

To capsulize those eight days considerably, P.J. and his men spent most of the time rooting around the mainland after dark, trying to capture somebody who knew where the *Königsberg* was. Fortunately, the rainy season was in full force, and, although movement was not comfortable, it was at least safer. At last, having pushed inland from the deserted coastal villages—a German tactic that effectively advertised the presence of the warship by the very lack of people—the perfect "snatch" came along, two dawdling locals whom the spy party silently overpowered and dragged far enough off into the bush, so that their interrogation would not be overheard.

With the willing prisoners as guides, Pretorius and his men spent a whole day within 300 yards of the ship, studying her closely with binoculars. No wonder she had not been spotted; her decks were covered with live trees, her guns entwined with leafy vines and her sides camouflaged to blend perfectly with the surrounding jungle banks. Sneaking back to Koma in a dugout, Pretorius signaled to be picked up and arrived back at Mafia on schedule.

Advising King-Hall by coded message that the *Königsberg* had been found, Pretorius met with the admiral the next day on his arrival at Mafia. The mere location was not nearly enough for the Royal Navy, certain details being crucial to the assault operation. Back went Pretorius and his merry band to check on the enemy guns, the location of her torpedoes and the exact distance the ship lay from the coast. Also, a hydrographic chart would have to be made of the Rufiji channel and adjoining flowages.

After a few days to work out his plans, he had his wireless operator call up another naval "taxi" to get him back to his forward position at Koma. To give some idea of the importance of P.J.'s mission as far as the Admiralty was concerned, the "taxi" turned out to be the tremendous Cunard Line *Laconia,* converted to wartime use. All this to move one officer, six *askaris* and two prisoners of war twenty miles. Under the veil of darkness and with strictest security, she safely deposited Pretorius and his men on Koma, lowering the dugout so they could paddle ashore. The following night, they again were guided by the now enthusiastic prisoners to the vantage point in the trees above the *Königsberg.* Careful to avoid any lens reflection, Pretorius was able to study the finest detail of the man o' war through powerful binoculars. Point one: Her eight big guns were apparently in perfect condition and undamaged. Somehow, he had determined that the distance to the ship from the coast was seventeen miles, but how this was calculated is not known. Next, he had to find out if the torpedoes were aboard and if any mines had been laid, and start measurements to compute the navigable channel of the Rufiji and its tide pattern. The Allies had no charts of the river's hydrography, and the prospect of an attacking force being left stranded by the tide in the face of German fire created visions of the naval equivalent of another Balaclava for the British. Pretorius sweated over the implications of his assignments.

Pretorius knew that the Germans had conscripted native

labor and also knew that a certain chief from a nearby village would be bound to have a pretty good idea of what was going on. Consequently, he sent one of his prisoners to ask the chief to meet with him outside the village in the bush, where he waited in the rain. With some embarrassment at the chief's lack of guile, Pretorius placed him under arrest and told him that, although he would not be permitted to return to his village, he would be paid five pounds per month and given all rations, a captivity much better than his liberty among the Germans. The chief was so delighted with the idea that he swore complete cooperation and even begged a half hour to go back to his *kraal* to kill five Germans who were making life generally and specifically unpleasant at his village.

When Pretorius explained his purposes, the chief excitedly announced that his own son was a stoker aboard the *Königsberg,* and that, with the gift of a basket of live chickens, one would be permitted to visit a relative who was conscripted. On the spot, Pretorius decided to go with him.

A lifetime of African sun and malaria provided Pretorius with a disguise requiring nothing but some rather seedy-looking Arab robes to pass as the genuine article. The chief was carefully coached in his role as Pretorius' "servant" and many rehearsals held as to exactly what the chief should ask his son, as it might appear suspicious for the "Arab" to be directing questions at the boy while ostensibly on a social visit with his father. All finally straight between them, a day was chosen for the visit to the *Königsberg.*

As they approached the lair of the warship very casually, they were stopped by a picket. Past him, Pretorius was able to see the tents where the sailors made their quarters, the crew living ashore. Fortunately, the German *askari* sentry was not a local man and did not recognize the chief. Pretorius explained in a very humble manner that his "boy" wanted to meet with his son for a few minutes, as they were passing by on their way to Mahoro. Accepting the basket of scrawny chickens, the *askari* went off to get permission from an officer and quickly returned with word that the chief's son would be along shortly. In about fifteen very nervous minutes, the boy came from the ship and sat down with Pretorius and his father.

Following the careful instructions P.J. had given the father, the question was asked: "Where are the long bullets that swim in the water?"

The son replied that he was sure the torpedoes had been removed from the ship and thought they had been transferred to boats at the mouth of the Rufiji, in ambush for any British shipping that might come within range. This turned out to be very accurate and valuable intelligence, the leak of which confused all hell out of the Huns. When Pretorius immediately got word off to King-Hall, the admiral ordered all Allied ship traffic to keep well wide of the river mouth. Totally unaware of Pretorius' reconnaissance, the Germans were furious when, just as the torpedo boats became operational, all British targets disappeared. In fact, so frustrated were the Germans that they actually arrested one of the *Königsberg*'s own officers and charged him with being a traitor! This was confirmed in the enemy press later in the war, so it's safe to assume that some poor Hun officer had a mighty hot time for quite a while.

In contacting King-Hall with his scoop on the "long bullets," Pretorius received more instructions, this time for the most tedious part of his work, if any part of the business of sneaking around enemy lines could be considered tedious. The next step in the destruction of the cruiser was to select a channel that would permit close enough approach to the marauder without grounding. After several weeks of taking soundings with a wooden push-pole, often risking broad daylight to map his observations accurately, Pretorius concluded that the most northerly channel was the best choice. For seven miles, there was no obstacle, the depth running between six and seven feet. And then a solid ridge of unpredictable reef cut the passage as effectively as a submerged dike. It would be the end of the line, but close enough for the right craft. And the British had them: monitors, squat gunships, heavily armed and armored. With a draft of only four feet and packing six-inch guns, they could smash the German cruiser if only they could manage to get this far. At that moment, however, they were halfway around the world, off Belgium.

Belgium be damned. When he received Pretorius' findings, King-Hall immediately cut orders for two of the monitors to make for the Rufiji with all speed, while Allied forces did what they could to prevent a potential breakout of the raider. At this time, the dullest possible duty fell to the Afrikaaner and his men. They drove a pole into the sea floor some distance from shore and, for a full month, recorded the hourly changes of the tide. It was with a mighty sigh of relief that Pretorius finally handed the completed chart into the well-manicured hands of the admiral.

At long last, the monitors arrived from Belgium, a pair of squat, ugly aquatic adders named *Mersey* and *Severn*. P.J. was ordered aboard the flagship of the fleet for a series of conferences, with the eventual end that he was chosen to command a pair of armed Arab-style *dhows,* or coastal sailboats, which, based upon retrospection, were supposed to draw the barracuda cruiser from its lair by acting as live bait. Why the *Königsberg* would be expected to spring into the open just to eviscerate a couple of native sailing boats has never been made exactly lucid. But, in any case, both boats were separated in the darkness, and the craft carrying Pretorius splintered on one of the many reefs between Mafia and the Rufiji. The boat was hung up on the reef a mile offshore and some three miles from a known German outpost, which would spot the wreck at dawn like a large beetle on a white plate. Not knowing what to do, Pretorius decided to vacate the premises posthaste upon the appearance of a small steam launch from the German shore, containing armed and presumably displeased German naval personnel. The crew of the *dhow* bailed out into neck-deep water and made for Koma Island, a good mile and a half away. After 600 yards of floundering, they were mightily relieved to see an armed whaler under a Captain Wood coming to pick them up. The enemy steamer realized the practical side of the relationship between discretion and valor, and showed her tail.

Nobody knew what had become of the second, missing

dhow, but it was no longer much of a secret that the Limeys were out to tear a strip off that floating chunk of *Deutschland* hiding back in the boondocks. If there was any question of this, it was soon dispelled by Pretorius, who again scouted the *Königsberg* and discovered the lost *dhow* neatly trussed to the side of the cruiser. Hiding in the bush all day, P.J. overheard Germans speaking of defenses as he sneaked out to the coast with darkness. Certainly, the enemy would have some less than subtle methods of inducing enlightened conversation from the survivors of the sailboat, but how much his men actually knew of the British plans and how much they would spill was unknown. Certainly, the African prisoners were not in on the full strategy of the operation; actually, it hadn't been completely formed yet. Thus, the enemy could learn little more than the obvious: The British lion was stalking the *Königsberg.* The German reaction to this knowledge would be of importance if their own plans were to be countered. Time to go man-hunting again.

Returning to Koma, Pretorius gathered the rest of his cutthroats and organized another scouting raid to pick up somebody who would know what countermeasures the enemy was planning, hopefully a genuine German officer. Aware that the enemy was alert to the probability that he was being scouted, Pretorius instructed his two boatmen to remain where they landed on the mainland for one hour and, if no firing was heard by that time, to return in eight days to pick up his scouts and himself. On the chance that the raiding party was attacked or ambushed, he distributed small German change to his chaps to buy local food should they become separated. If the little *kommando* (an Afrikaans word coined in the Boer War) was hit, the men were to scatter and find their way back to the coast. Here, provided they weren't full of Mauser bullets, they were to steal a boat of any kind and get offshore, where, with luck, a patrolling British ship would pick them up.

It was nine o'clock on an especially filthy, rain-swept evening when the German-hunters left Koma, the paddles silently dipping and swirling soft kaleidoscopes of disturbed phosphorescent plankton. With a muffled crunch of wet, scraping sand, the dugout was beached and pulled a few feet up the shore. Pretorius, with three men, began to pick his way inland, covering some 500 yards, when he realized that even he and his catpawed henchmen had little chance of passing undetected through an alerted enemy picket line. There were shouts from every direction ordering them to halt, and the bright tongues of muzzle flashes flared in the blackness like savage, giant fireflies. It was flame and dark insanity. An officer screamed to concentrate fire on those running back to the beach—Pretorius and one of his men— the crashing they made through the thick bush betraying their position. Was it all to be for nothing? P.J. wondered wildly. The brutal agony of his escape all wasted? Full-jacketed slugs *chwiped* and *chwinged* through the branches, clawing like blind fingers for flesh. As they reached the water, they saw that the dugout had already pulled out but bobbed forty yards offshore. It stopped and backed up as they swam hard to it, bullets blowing columns of water into the air around them in a spurting, lashing torrent. The boatmen pulled them aboard and struck out for the dark waters through the misting rain. By the most improbable turn of luck, not one of the men was hit, although the entire enemy force stood on the beach, emptying their weapons in a random sleet of lead. At last back at Koma, Pretorius had the oil-soaked sacks fired, and Captain Wood soon arrived to pick them up in the whaler.

Of the two other men with Pretorius who did not run for the boat, nothing was known. He prayed that they had not been captured and, knowing of their resourcefulness, con-tinued a four-day vigil on a rescue craft, up and down the coast. At long last, a small object was spotted in the distant swells; it proved to be the missing men, unwounded, but almost dead from exposure, thirst and hunger in a small native boat. With no paddles, they were steering with a piece of wood from a broken box, their power supplied by a tattered sail made from their loincloths.

Although the last "snatching" raid had been spectacularly unsuccessful, it was mutually clear that the "cute" part of the sparring was over. The British knew where the *Königsberg* was to within a few hundred yards, and the Germans knew that the British knew. Would the cruiser break out for the open sea, seizing the initiative, or could the Royal Navy position herself quickly enough to fight the coming action on her own terms? Although he must have been understandably weary of getting shot at by most of the German East African forces, Pretorius and Captain Wood opened sealed orders at midnight a few nights later and found instructions for the whaler to come to anchor, acting as a living marker buoy, in a position smack in front of the shore batteries Pretorius knew to have been moved to the coast. It could not have been a pleasant sensation.

As the sea behind them began to glow with the carmine promise of an April dawn, the little whaler's men were relieved to note sixteen columns of smoke from warships on the horizon, gathering tight the steel net meant to snare the *Königsberg*. The flagship anchored right alongside the whaler, and Pretorius was called aboard by King-Hall. From his vantage point on the bridge, he watched the two squat monitors steam into the northern channel—the one with the reef selected by Pretorius—led by a pair of minesweepers. Suddenly, right between them, the sea erupted into a tremendous explosion of foaming water and whining shrapnel, as a heavy German gun opened the fight with a probing shot. It was frighteningly close, coming from the *Königsberg*, which was using the shore batteries as forward observers of her shell strikes. Within moments, more enemy shells began falling, both from the cruiser and now from the artillery near the beaches.

The monitors stuck to their course like the bulldogs they resembled, guns silent. Not so the flagship, which began to belch broadsides with a thunder and concussion never dreamed of by Pretorius. As the fire from both sides rose in intensity, Pretorius, ever the hunter, was able to spot and point out several tree platforms of snipers and artillery observers to *Hyacinth*'s officers, who were unable to make them out at first, even with powerful naval binoculars.

Pretorius needed no binoculars. The fleet's big guns obliterated the platforms, trees and all, the lyddite of the high-explosive shells blasting the nests to scraps.

Before the sun was an hour old, the northern channel had begun to echo with the quaking crunch of the monitors, which had reached the reef, lobbing six-inch incendiary rounds in high arcs over the jungle. After a few corrections, they were dead on the mark, confirmed by a pair of spotter aircraft repeatedly signaling: "FIRE AGAIN AT THE SAME MARK." Count on it, they did.

The battle boomed and raged from dawn until two in the afternoon, the British pouring on all the firepower they could muster for as long as they dared stay in position. The damage to the *Königsberg* was impossible to assay, as she was completely hidden from the sea, and even the spotter aircraft could determine little through the pall of smoke from the incendiaries, although it was clear that where there was smoke there was fire. Pretorius watched the greasy smudge over the jungle, standing behind King-Hall, who was pouring over the tidal chart that was the product of the awful month of boredom. His fingers crossed in hope that he had made no miscalculation, he listened to the admiral order, "Cease fire," as he prepared to get underway. Bells clanged and gargantuan engines thumped. *Hyacinth* shuddered. So did Pretorius. She did not move, her hull on the bottom, her screws blowing maelstroms of dirty water. The scout's heart seemed to stop in his chest as the big propellers raced, pushing and pulling for an interminable five minutes. Had he fouled up the tide chart? Would it cost the lives of a great warship and her crew? Had King-Hall simply waited too long to run for deeper water? With an audible metallic groan of release, the flagship lurched sluggishly forward, then slid free.

"Enter in the log book," remarked Admiral King-Hall quietly, "that the flagship grounded for five minutes."

As the attackers steamed out to sea, the action stopped as quickly as it had started. Rain began to darken the sky, and evil-looking gray-flannel clouds raced over the choppy surface of the Indian Ocean. When the short squall had passed, an impenetrable fog crept in on leopard's pads, settling as obstinately as an anvil for the next six days. *Königsberg?* Who knew? Was she crippled? Dead? Wait and see.

It cleared. A British landing party cautiously approached the shell-shattered shoreline, bypassing scattered bodies of enemy snipers and artillery observers. Those land batteries not caught by British gunfire had been moved inland by the enemy. A good sign, thought Pretorius; perhaps there was nothing left to defend. As the party penetrated farther upriver, bristling in anticipation of an ambush, the tortured and twisted corpse of the once-carnivorous *Königsberg,* Prince of the Southern Fleet, came into sight, a fire-blackened tangle of Krupp steel, torn and eviscerated, covered with the burned and explosive-mutilated, fly-covered bodies of her crew. *Königsberg* the Raider was dead, tracked, stalked and hunted to her den by a lean, quiet, dark-faced man who had learned not to like Germans.

Pretorius, it would seem, was not the forgiving sort. Although he had spent months risking his life hounding down the *Königsberg,* the exploit for which he would be most remembered, her destruction, only seemed to fan the fires that drove him against the Huns. Over the remainder of the war—the cruiser having brought him fame with both the Allies and the enemy—Pretorius acted mostly behind German lines in the capacity of chief scout to General Jan Smuts, commander of the South African Allied force and later prime minister of that country. If there was a more dangerous job in the African theater, it doesn't come immediately to mind.

At his first meeting with General Smuts, Pretorius was asked the best way to take strategic Salaita Hill, along the railway line and in possession of a powerful German force. At first, he thought Smuts was joking, asking *him* how to take a hill in the presence of a half-dozen other generals. However, General Japie van Deventer spoke with him in

Afrikaans and explained that they were very serious, his recommendation sought because he knew the country so well from his elephant-poaching days.

Pretorius thought the problem over for a few minutes and then proposed that the hill could be taken without firing a single shot. The assembled brass glanced sideways at each other. Perhaps this chap Pretorius had spent too much time wandering about without his pith helmet?

"Salaita," continued P.J., unruffled, "is in a little desert where there is not a drop of water to be found, and the Germans are getting their supply from Taveta, a town eight miles away. I would parade six hundred men in the afternoon so that the Germans could see them." Dead silence blanketed the room as Pretorius paused, then went on. "At the same time, I would leave with a column in a northerly direction until I got behind the skyline, and then I would turn back to the west, and by morning I would be at Taveta. Once our troops are in Taveta, thirst would beat the Germans."

Smuts thought the plan brilliant, yet inquired whether the enemy had any emplacements on Mt. Kilimanjaro which could attack the rear of the South African force. Pretorius didn't know, but since he was chief scout and the great, snow-crowned crag was only twenty miles away, he might as well go have a look. Within an hour, he and five men were on the way. It was one hell of a rough reconnoiter, but Pretorius found the slopes unoccupied by the enemy. There were, on the other hand, a few other problems—70,000 of them, actually. The powerful and warlike WaChaka tribe had recently declared war on the British Allies, and Taveta was in the center of their territory.

To simplify a rather involved maneuver, the two columns, one led by van Deventer and the other by General Coen Brits, ran into a very large and definitely unsociable *impi*, or regiment, of WaChaka. At loggerheads, Pretorius actually talked the warriors out of fighting for the Germans and bluffed the entire party into retiring! Taveta was occupied despite bloody hand-to-hand fighting in the covering hills of Reata and Latema, where the German General von Lettow-

Vorbeck staged a withdrawal action, badly mauling the South African infantry and the Second Rhodesians. Salaita Hill was taken, but the Germans had the forethought to destroy miles of the rail line so it was of no use to the Allies. Pretorius was in the bush eight days, following the Huns, and somehow was reported killed in action. When he showed up at Smuts's headquarters, he caused quite a stir, although he'd missed his own memorial service.

After the Salaita affair, Pretorius' war conformed much more closely to his old hunting style, ghosting through enemy territory so close to the Germans that one day, turning a corner of what he thought was a deserted trench, he was saluted by a pair of enemy *askaris* who thought he was one of their own officers.

To understand the pressure on Pretorius and his resiliency in the face of constant danger, it must be remembered that, ever since the *Königsberg*, there was not only a princely price on his head but the guarantee of summary execution of any native caught aiding him in any way.

Typical of the close calls he survived was a trap laid for his mounted scouting force one very hot day when, unaware that they had been seen by the enemy, they had to cross a clearing to the edge of a small river to let the horses drink. When they had taken water, the little patrol withdrew into the bush to light a small fire for a meal. Pretorius had just lit the flame when one of his sentries shouted, "Look out! Here come the Germans!" P.J. smothered the fire with his hand, and the scouts took off in a rain of German bullets, their luck again holding as nobody was hit. How close that escape really was became clear three months later when Pretorius personally captured two of his opposite numbers, a pair of German scouts named Schmidt and Linderkund. The architects of the ambush, they confirmed that the trap was almost ready to be sprung when the sentry spotted them. They even quoted some of the words written on the paper Pretorius had used to start the fire.

A week after this incident, Pretorius stumbled onto a seemingly contradictory bit of behavior on the part of the Germans. Watching a large camp he had found and was

studying with binoculars, he was amazed to see the troops
fall in at a command for target practice, using large amounts
of what the Allies had presumed to be very precious rifle
cartridges. Even Smuts himself had been under the impression that the enemy would soon be forced to surrender
through lack of ammunition. So, wondered Pretorius, why
were they wasting it in casual target practice? When the
enemy had finished firing and gone off to mess, Pretorius
crept down and collected several empty cartridge cases,
flabbergasted to find them head-stamped "Magdeburg—
1916." Brand-new. But where had they come from? And
how?

After the *Königsberg* operation, Pretorius knew that a
German steamer had been found near a small tidal creek
and had been sunk immediately by a British cruiser, so that
couldn't have been the source. Actually, it was. After
capturing Schmidt and Linderkund, Pretorius found that
the sunken steamer had crossed the British blockade under
a neutral flag with tons of supplies fresh from *Der Vaterland,*
especially artillery shells and rifle ammo. Realizing she was
bound to be sunk, all the cargo had been sealed in special
waterproof containers and sandbagged in the hold. Among
the crew were specially trained divers who, when the ship
went down and the British withdrew, returned the next day
and salvaged the entire cargo. Quite a slick operation, even
Pretorius had to admit.

Although a classic bushman and scout, known in later life
as "Jungle Man," so wary of his enemies that he never slept
twice in the same place while in the field, it would still have
been inevitable that one day he would just run low on luck
and be captured or killed. So why wasn't he ever caught or
even wounded again? Well, if you want to take his word for
it, he was psychic. "Slim Janie" Smuts believed him, and,
when we look at the record, perhaps he did have some sort
of sixth sense. . . .

Let's take a rainy night when Pretorius rode back to
friendly lines, leaving his twenty-man force (many of whom
had been converted from German service) a thousand yards
above a German camp with orders to watch for any move-

ments along the trails. Since it was six miles back to his position through the rain, the HQ staff suggested that he spend the night and return in the morning. He stayed for dinner gratefully but saddled up at nine o'clock, reaching his inconspicuous grass shelters two hours later.

His native troops reported no activity below, and, it being nearly midnight, Pretorius thought it safe enough to catch some sack time. He undressed, put on his pajamas and was about to get into his camp cot when the old, instinctive feeling of danger came over him. He knew better than to ignore it; redressing, he ordered his weary men to break camp and take a native path to the north, where a deserted village with fine, dry huts lay. His men, wet and half-frozen, were for staying over in the huts, but Pretorius' nagging sense of warning wouldn't quit. The party continued through the village to a low range of hills beyond. As they were laying out their mildewed blankets, they heard a fusillade of shots erupt at their old encampment above the enemy position. Perhaps his men had seen no Germans, but the opposite certainly wasn't true. They had left just before the jaws of the trap had clashed.

Realizing that the enemy would be bound to follow them, he warned his men to be ready, only to find that some of his *askaris* had straggled in the dark and had stayed behind in the deserted village. Up marched a large force of Germans and pounded on the door of a hut containing Pretorius' not overbright men, who were forced to surrender before the hut was burned down around them. Hiding in a stand of corn, P.J. watched with fifteen of his men as the Germans took the other five prisoner and then settled down for the night, taking off their boots and relaxing. As soon as they were quiet, the scouts opened fire, so startling the enemy that they left the prisoners and broke for the corn without returning a single shot.

Obviously, if Pretorius' "sixth sense" hadn't been working, he and his command would have been slaughtered in their first camp.

If Pretorius' sense of warning was effective for himself, it didn't seem to rub off easily on his men. In this same neighborhood, some time later, the Afrikaaner had a very close call in a German ambush set for him. He himself escaped, but the next morning he watched from hiding on a hill across a stream as seven of his men who had been captured were carefully hung from a big tree. They were not dropped to fracture the neck vertebrae—the instant death of a formal hanging—but strung up to choke and strangle their lives away over many minutes, eyeballs popping, tongues protruding. The Germans were making good on their promise of death for any black assisting that wraith, Major Pretorius.

On a later expedition, leading a column under a Colonel Morris, planning to cross the Rufiji River to attack the admittedly brilliant soldier General von Lettow-Vorbeck, Pretorius again heard the warning buzzer go off in his head. The party was within two miles of the crossing point, but, although he could not explain why, he insisted that they not continue as planned but march at right angles to the west, proceeding to a point some two miles from the original spot chosen. All went well, and the troops got across the river in collapsible boats, quickly entrenching themselves. Taking off on a personal scouting trip, Pretorius found a strong German force patiently waiting for the column at exactly where they had originally decided to cross. Caught in the water, that would have been the end of the Morris force.

If you question the premonitions of Pretorius, it's interesting to note that three times men who were acting as his replacement because of some last-minute change in plans were killed, mistaken for Pretorius himself. The first was one of the most gallant gentlemen, scholars, hunters and naturalists Africa ever produced, Frederick Courteney Selous. It had been Selous who had hunted Zambezia even before Pretorius, led Rhodes's pioneer column into what would become Rhodesia and was a close personal friend of Theodore Roosevelt, one of his highest-ranking admirers. Well over sixty years of age, Selous was a mere captain of the 25th Royal Fusiliers, but a scout of repute equal to that of Pretorius. Orders were changed, though, by Smuts, substituting Selous for Pretorius to guide an expedition to

Behobeho. Riding at the head of the force, he was killed by a sniper with a single bullet through the neck, dead before he hit the ground. He was buried on the spot, in later years a game reserve named for him. As of this writing, as Rhodesia has just become Zimbabwe, one of the most famous crack units of the army is called the Selous Scouts.

Another who took Pretorius' place in line at the pearly gates—or elsewhere—was an intelligence officer named van de Merwe, a well-trained twenty-four-year-old Afrikaaner. Again, a change of orders from Smuts, originally directing Pretorius to Makindu to check if von Lettow-Vorbeck (who, incidentally, was a good friend of Karen Blixen, the Danish noblewoman who wrote the hauntingly beautiful book *Out of Africa* under the pen name Isak Dinesen) had reoccupied the place, reversed the situation, and van de Merwe was sent on that mission; Pretorius' orders were changed to scout for General Beves in his attack on another German position. P.J. briefed van de Merwe, who was excited about being given the job, warning him to be extremely careful as the Germans had been keeping a sharp lookout for enemy scouting forces, and recent losses had been heavy. Pretorius suggested that he take his force up a rocky hill, or *kopje,* during the daytime near the main road, watch the enemy traffic and, above all, be sure to change to another position when night fell, even if he was positive that he hadn't been detected. Pretorius lent the young officer ten of his personal *askaris* and saw him off before leaving himself with Beves.

The next day, minutes after the force under Beves assaulted and took the trenches that were their objective (under the German commander Merensky), one of the *askaris* sent with van de Merwe showed up to speak with Pretorius. His report was not very cheerful. As Pretorius had advised, the scouting patrol had set up "shop" atop a convenient hill and monitored the German traffic below, which seemed light. Despite P.J.'s stiff warning to the young man to move at dark, he nonetheless determined to stay the night where he was, sure he and his men had not been seen by the enemy. At midnight, the scouts were jolted awake by the crack of a single rifle shot. Running to the huddled lump of blankets that wrapped van de Merwe, they found him thoroughly and instantly dead, shot squarely through the neck.

Of course the Afrikaaner's party *had* been spotted sometime during the day and a trap laid. As this area was known to be the haunt of Pretorius, the enemy sent a single sniper to pick him off, rather than risk detection by a sizable attack. Whoever was behind that Mauser was bloody good and had probably been following the white leader through the cross hairs for some time, smart enough to wait for the scouts to bed down and give himself time to make his escape after a single, precise shot. To make that shot in the dark at what must have been a reasonable distance—so sure of his target he didn't bother to fire an "insurance" shot—indicates a first-class bushman and marksman. There is nothing to substantiate the possibility, but it would seem the Germans might have assigned a crack sniper to the area who would be sent off any time Pretorius was reported sighted. Remember, it was a single neck shot that killed Selous, too, who was standing in for Pretorius.

Already, the *askari* reported, the German positions were celebrating the death of Major P. J. Pretorius, C.M.G., D.S.O. Not only did they believe him dead at last, but I wonder what they might have thought had they known then that the "Jungle Man" was still to do enough damage to earn a Bar to his Distinguished Service Order, and more.

The actions that added Pretorius' Bar to his D.S.O. comprise an interesting series of tales of immensely effective scouting and subterfuge behind the German lines, culminating in his persuading more than 2,000 German territorial natives to revolt and fight for the Allies. Armed with smuggled rifles, gun by gun, the revolt broke with perfect timing, smashing the German organization in the Makonde area, an enemy rear stronghold. In the letter of commendation which accompanied his second winning of the coveted decoration, General O'Grady wrote: "You are certainly a thorn in the side of von Lettow." Pretorius said that no compliment had ever given him such satisfaction.

The Makonde revolt was a telling blow to enemy personnel and morale, make no mistake. But for sheer drama, few of his military exploits approached the brilliance and personal resourcefulness of what we might refer to as the taking of the Tafel column. It was Pretorius' last campaign of the war and began when he was in the hospital as a result of the terrible beating he was giving his wiry body and the awful tension of living behind enemy lines. His strength had been slipping, but an Allied attack on von Lettow-Vorbeck's camp, in which he was involved, had brought him to the limit of his endurance. On that day, Pretorius had personally found an escape route for the South Africans who were being overwhelmed by the Germans, despite having killed over 800 of the enemy in the engagement. His horse was shot out from under him with two bullets, and he went without food for three days and four nights.

While in a field hospital, recuperating from fever, malnutrition and exhaustion, he still insisted that his scouts' reports on enemy movements be brought to him at his bedside. One morning, after only a few days of rest, a particularly juicy report arrived. Taken from a captured German messenger, it was addressed to General von Lettow-Vorbeck personally. It read:

"Yesterday I had to fight with the enemy. I vanquished them and managed to capture their food, but their supplies, together with mine, can last only three days. I am trekking to the top of the Bangala river [sic], from where I will follow it down to the crossroads at the river."

The signature was that of a Major Tafel.

Hmmmmm, thought Pretorius. The crossroads at the Bangala were only a couple of miles from his old poaching territory on the Ruvuma and seventy-five miles from the hospital. As he went over his mental map, it dawned on him that if he could get a force to the crossroads before Tafel got there, he could clear the district of natives, burn all supplies and put *Herr* Tafel's column into the position of watching their navels rapidly approach their spines. Starvation was as lethal as lead, and that "an army marches on its stomach" was a lot more than a stale, military platitude.

P.J. got off a note by special messenger to his old Boer pal,

General "Japie" van Deventer, proposing his interception and enclosing the captured dispatch. Two hours later, an orderly arrived at Pretorius' bed, saluted and handed him van Deventer's enthusiastic reply: "Herewith my car. Come immediately to headquarters." The doctors raised the canvas roof, promising Pretorius that he would be dead within a week even if his luck really held. But, then, a lot of people had been predicting Pretorius' death for some time without result.

Upon arrival at HQ, van Deventer had the details set up in accordance with the scout's plan as neatly as pins in a bowling alley. Although Pretorius looked and felt like death warmed over, he was instructed to send his forces into the bush to tell the native population of the area to head for Allied lines, where they would be fed and helped in every way; their own goods, which were to be torched, promised to be replaced.

Arriving at the Bangala River, at the appointed crossing, Pretorius was quick to note that the largest pool in the half-dry water course was undisturbed, certainly not used by the enemy and his animals as yet. They had beaten the un-suspecting Tafel! Pretorius sent word into the bush to comply with van Deventer's orders to the natives to carry as much food as possible and to burn the rest at once. The further advice that anybody caught in the area after five that afternoon would be arrested was probably unnecessary, but Pretorius was not about to permit a single kernel of corn to reach the starving Germans. Even as he was sending off the last of his messages, scouts came panting up to say that Tafel and his huge force were at that moment arriving at the pool. The Germans didn't know it then, but they might as well be landing on the moon with nothing but a pocketful of jelly beans, for all the supplies they would find here. All around him, tendrils of smoke advertised Pretorius' scorched-earth plan, but then, Tafel had no way of knowing that von Lettow-Vorbeck had not received his message requesting he be met here with supplies. There were no locals to give any information, having been moved out by Pretorius, but the scouts did capture two German *askaris*, who told of having been on half rations for many days. Under the camouflaged stare of the Afrikaaner, Tafel waited two critical and hungry days on the Bangala, until realizing that von Lettow was pretty clearly not on his way. He pushed downriver for ten miles, Pretorius and his men always ahead of him, watching the scraggly, straggling, starving Germans with what safely may be presumed to be little pity. Coursing well ahead of Tafel, Pretorius and a small scout force arrived at a gorge overlooking the river on the third day. As they looked the place over, it sounded, a noise that shook Pretorius to his shoes. It was a rifle shot, echoing and reverberating among the rocks. It had not come from Tafel's column, but from elsewhere. Yet where? Who had fired it? More important, had Tafel's men heard it?

"Good God!" whispered Pretorius aloud. He knew that von Lettow was somewhere in the district, loaded with enough supplies to save Tafel, even if only by accident. If that shot had come from von Lettow's men, knocking off a rare antelope for the pot, and if it led the two enemy forces to each other, not only would the plan to starve Tafel into surrender be lost, but Pretorius would be caught between two enemy armies. Ordering his men to lie low, Pretorius scrambled up the escarpment as fast as he could, his hands and knees bloody from his haste. At the top of the gorge, another ridge ran farther upward above the river trail like a stone spine. Reaching the crest, Pretorius lay flat on his stomach where he could see the suffering *askaris* and white soldiers of Major Tafel winding along. To his horror, on the other side, marching in the same direction, was von Lettow-Vorbeck's army! From his vantage pont, Pretorius saw that the two paths met not far ahead, and, although he had kept the knowledge of each force from the other, it looked as if fate was about to pitch a crowbar into the gears of his delicate plan.

Dying of suspense and frustration, Pretorius could do nothing but watch the two enemy columns plod blindly toward each other. At least, Tafel showed no sign of having heard the shot, although it didn't seem to matter much now. Then, as he watched with mushrooming despair, the Tafel column stopped, the officers knotting together in what seemed to be a heated discussion. The argument, lost in the sound of the river as it swept through the gorge, abruptly ended. Before Pretorius' unbelieving eyes, the Tafel force turned away from its rendezvous with von Lettow, making a turn onto another path that led away at a right angle. Pretorius' relief was so great that he almost gave himself away, trying to smother the half-insane laughter he was unable to contain. It was incredible. They had snatched starvation from the jaws of salvation only a half mile from safety. Across the bare, rocky Makonde plateau they marched, hunger chewing at their guts like rats.

Pretorius climbed back down the ridge, praying that nobody would find a reason to fire another shot. Assembling his men, he followed Tafel's trail and within a mile came on two German *askaris* dying of hunger, barely able to move. With them was one of the men's wives, also near death. The enemy troops told Pretorius that they had not eaten in days and that the whole force was about to drop.

Late in the afternoon, as the Germans were at the edge of a shallow, sandy river, they spotted some of the Allied force. Not knowing how many men opposed them, they dug in and camouflaged their positions against a possible attack. While they used up more precious energy, Pretorius and his men bedded down a mere 600 yards away, up at first light to watch Tafel continue his death march.

That morning, as the Germans crossed the Ruvuma, they came into contact with the first natives they had seen in four days, learning with growing horror of von Lettow-Vorbeck's route and how closely they must have missed him. The general was flush with food and supplies, captured from the Portuguese at Ngomano, an easy victory won when the Portuguese ran for their lives after their commander was killed. Too late. It was easy to figure out, even if hard to accept, that Tafel was much too far from von Lettow to attempt to reach him. With what must have been nearly the last of his own strength, he wrote to his commander: "Am ceasing hostilities at 6 P.M. Wish to surrender on best possible terms."

Guess who intercepted the message.

Pretorius sent a message by runner to General Hannyng-ton, commander of a brigade of King's African Rifles which was nearby. That afternoon, November 28, 1917, the entire Tafel command surrendered. By Pretorius' personal count there were 3,400 black *askaris,* 1,000 porters, 100 white noncommissioned officers and 19 German officers, a total of more than 4,500 enemy personnel out of the war. It wasn't the end of the war, but it was the end of German East Africa. It was also nearly the end of the man who had conceived the plan and executed it. Although a car was sent for him, it was needed for worse cases, and Pretorius was forced to ride thirty miles back to the hospital he had left so few days ago. In addition to his previous illnesses, he had contracted neuritis, developed acute gastritis and was even found to have burst an artery in his lung! None of the doctors gave him much of a chance to pull through, but he did; several months later actually dining with one of the officers on Tafel's staff, who was present when the fateful decision was made to turn away from von Lettow-Vorbeck. The officer, a Captain von Brandis, claimed he had been the only one for continuing straight but had been outvoted.

The East African war continued for another year, less three days. General von Lettow-Vorbeck continued to perform magnificently, outfoxing a vastly larger Allied force at almost every turn. He made it, in fact, all the way to the mouth of the Zambezi, then falling back on Lake Nyasa. Unbowed and not badly bloodied, he was just beginning the invasion of Rhodesia on November 2, 1918, and doing very well until halted by the Armistice, which was signed in Europe on the 12th of that month, and the war's end.

One might think that after such exploits as the hunt for the *Königsberg* and the destruction of the last enemy force in German East Africa, peacetime would be looming as some-thing of a bore to a man like Pretorius. It certainly was not; he returned to his adventurous life of big-game hunting as soon as his health permitted. One of his greatest exploits at arms was the shooting out of the stunted herd of *kali,* or rogue elephants, of the Addo District of South Africa. This particular herd was so savage that even the great Selous, considered one of the best hunters of his day, had refused the assignment, claiming it impossible to take on the Addo elephants and live. It was a hairy few months, but Pretorius did accomplish the bloody though necessary deed.

Later, he was a pioneer in filmmaking to record the charges of dangerous game, particularly lions, which he killed mere feet in front of the camera's lens.

By all accounts a very shy and modest man, Pretorius was only persuaded by a good friend, Mr. L. L. le Sueur of Johannesburg, to make notes of his fascinating life, which, although completed at the family farm at Nylstroom in July 1939, only saw print as *Jungle Man* in New York in 1948, nearly three years after his death in 1945 at the age of sixty-eight.

It's been a long time since that sixteen-year-old boy began riding transport during the Matabele War, and very little is left of the rusting carcass of the *Königsberg* in her watery, jungle grave on the Rufiji. But the spirit of Pretorius and the other Good Ones is still out there, alive in every blue-tongued lick of a lonely camp fire, enshrined in the distant trumpet of a big tusker or the grunt of a dark-maned lion in the night. Don't take my word for it; go out into the still-wild places of Africa and listen. Watch. He's there, all right. But if you do happen onto Pretorius' shade in person, do me a favor, will you?

Ask him what the hell P.J. stood for.

Patterson's extraordinary lion trap, which used human bait and from which one of the man-eaters of Tsavo made an incredible escape.

The last of the Tsavo man-eaters, dead after taking ten bullets, stood almost four feet at the shoulder.

A warrior of the Dinka tribe, who ambushed and nearly wiped out Major C. H. Stigand's force in 1919, spearing Stigand to death in the attack.

"Jungle Man" P. J. Pretorius, a one-man army fighting against the Germans in the First World War East African Campaign.

The legendary *Tigrero* Sasha Siemel received the charge of a jaguar on the blade of his *Zagaya* spear in Brazil's "Green Hell".

Sasha Siemel with two of his famous jaguar dogs. Left is Valente with whom he killed sixty-four *tigres* with spear, bow, and rifle.

Siemel with a male jaguar of about 300 pounds killed in a spear fight.

SKULL

LEVEL

Elephant in act of falling to brain shot from behind.

"Karamojo" Bell's diagram of the most difficult angle for the elephant hunter, the quartering rear brain shot. No one else has ever mastered it.

Colonel Jim Corbett with the huge man-eating leopard of Rudraprayag, who slaughtered and ate 125 human beings.

The extraordinary hunter of man-eaters, Jim Corbett, with a gigantic male tiger known as the Bachelor of Rowalgarh.

Harry Wolhuter—this frail-looking but ramrod-tough game ranger stabbed a man-eating lion to death with his knife while being dragged away by the cat.

Samuel Baker's own reconstruction of his terrifying encounter as a young man in Ceylon with a wounded Asian water buffalo.

The author after a hard day at the office.

Alexander "Sasha" Siemel

THE LONE HORSEMAN rode slowly through the afternoon heat, the first airborne waft of death fouling his nostrils from somewhere ahead in the towering grass of the *pantanal*. As he reined in, standing in the stirrups to see, the muffled, ghoulish croak of *urubi* vultures filtered through the stiff stalks, and one of the man's following mongrels gave a low whine of fear. Instinctively, he slid the old muzzle-loading gun from its scabbard and checked the percussion cap seated over the nipple. Drawing back the hammer, his brown face set into a hard, swarthy mask, José Ramos touched the horse's flanks. He knew what he would find.

By the sign, it had been early that morning, but by now the searing tropical sun of the western Brazilian Matto Grosso and the birds had nearly finished what the killer had begun. Lowering the gun, José Ramos watched the gorged vultures lumber off, their filth-smeared wings catching the air after a series of obscene hops. Dismounting, the *vaquero* inspected the gaping fang holes in the skull of the eyeless cow, recognizing them instantly. The heat of his fury chilled with the despair of realization. This was the thirteenth of the small herd to be slaughtered—and not even for food. It was a terrible loss for the little family trying to eke out a living in the vast and lonely Xarayes Marshes. If this devil cat was not killed, José Ramos knew that he and his wife and child would be ruined. If no one would help him, he would kill this demon himself. No matter that his gun was old and his dogs cowardly. Was he not a man? *Sí*, this thing would be necessary, and so he would do it.

Remounting, he carried the muzzle loader in his right hand and whistled the cringing dogs forward on the heavy-scent trail that led away through the thick grass toward a *capão,* an island of tall *buriti* palms and strangler figs that loomed in emerald solitude above the grass five hundred meters away. As he rode toward the grove, two hard yellow eyes watched from the shady limb of a fig. As smoothly as poured oil, a tremendous male jaguar rippled to the ground and was swallowed up by the grassy undergrowth. In less than ten minutes, Maria Ramos would be a widow.

A single yelp of mortal pain sliced the shimmering heat like a sliver of broken glass. Ahead, somewhere in the thick grass, one of the cur dogs lay disemboweled, eyes already glazing as flies swarmed the torn, pink-gray ropes of intestines protruding from the huge gash in its side. The other dog broke cover and shot past the horseman in a brindled flash of tuck-tailed panic, disappearing quickly on the path home. *Filho da puta,* thought José Ramos. It had been so easy for the *tigre.* As he had done so many times before, the cat had simply looped back on his own trail and with a lightning lunge ambushed the dog, raking it with a pawstroke that could spurt the brains from a steer's ears. Sweat beading on his sun-baked skin, the man gritted white teeth and urged the horse onward. If he went quickly he might get a shot, pray *São* Antonio will it.

The horse shied at the dog's mutilated body, nostrils flaring at the smell of blood and offal. Ramos gave only a glance downward, his eyes probing the grass ahead for movement. Beyond, the *capão* and shorter cover would give better visibility. The horse broke into a clearing.

José Ramos was only a few steps into the opening, eyes darting for a glimpse of the *tigre.* Halting the horse, he dropped the reins to steady the gun with both hands. "Come out, demon," his brain screamed, but he knew better than to shout aloud. He knew. It was watching him. He could feel the eyes, and a strange shiver scampered up his spine despite the awful heat.

And then it came. There was the smallest whisper of movement from his right rear, and a golden shape exploded out of the edge of the grass with terrifying speed. A numbing, stunning shock smashed José Ramos from the saddle, the gun, with its load of chopped nails, spinning away unfired. Dazed, on the ground, he started to raise himself to his knees, dully hearing the pounding of hooves as the horse hammered away in terror. Again, the impression of something huge and golden moving directly at him, very, very fast. There was no pain as the thick, hooked claws slashed through meat and sinew, red rivers welling in their wake. There was no pain as the big fangs drove deeply through the back of his skull.

There was nothing at all.

The body lay still, a huddled lump on its destroyed face. As the jaguar watched, fangs framed by bloodied black gums, the gore that had spurted from the ripped arteries ceased, thickening quickly in the hot sunshine. Cautiously, the big cat sniffed the corpse, unable to stifle a snarl of disgust at the familiar hated smell. Above, *urubi* were gathering, the first flapping noisily to light in the top of a *buriti* palm, others spiraling down to perch expectantly. With a soft series of grunts, the *tigre* stalked off to lie up in the shade. Assassino, the great cattle-marauding jaguar of the Xarayes Marshes, had become a man-killer.

It was full dawn before the terrified horse found its way back to the tiny *fazenda* (or ranch) of the Ramos family. Maria, haggard and emotionally exhausted from a night without sleep, ran outside to catch it, her heart turning to lead as she saw the dark bloodstains on the rough wooden saddle and the two long claw marks on the horse's flank. Swiftly, she mounted the tired horse and lashed him along the trail toward Ilha do Cara Cara and the camp of the famous *tigrero, Senhor* Siemel. He would not help before; perhaps he would now.

Of all the great hunter/adventurers of the recent past, none had a career in the wilderness that quite compared with that of Alexander "Sasha" Siemel. Every continent has had its great heroes of the hunt: Selous, Harris, Baker and dozens of others were the bright flames of Africa; Corbett of India; "Buffalo Bill" Cody, Jim Bridger and Hugh Glass of the American West; each in his time, place and company left indelible evidence of the magnificence of the human spirit under stress. But South America? Since the days of the *conquistadores,* there have been few men in the field of hunting prominent enough to hang your sombrero on. That, to be sure, doesn't mean they weren't there. Most of the reason these men did not achieve the worldwide recognition of their counterparts is that either they never published or their works were not translated from Portuguese or Spanish. Sasha Siemel is the notable exception for more reasons than one. He alone of all the famous bushmen made his name and reputation not with the rifle, but with the bow and spear, hunting the most dangerous New World big cat as the aborigines had done for untold millennia.

Of course, there was nothing new about bow hunting at the time that Sasha Siemel was taking jaguars; white pioneers such as Howard Hill and the classic twosome of Pope and Young had all killed the most dangerous of big game with bow and arrow. The difference is that they didn't do it as a steady diet for a living. One American cowboy, Buffalo Jones, even went to Africa to rope lions, which he managed successfully, but this cannot be considered as more than a sporting—although very brave and skillful—prank. It is the difference, however, between hunting with a bow and killing jaguars with a thrusting spear that set Sasha Siemel apart, in the opinion of many at the very top of the rank of the truly great hunters.

If you plan on being a professional spear hunter of jaguar, there are more convenient places to be born than Riga, Latvia, in 1890. Sasha solved this problem by following his brother Ernst to Argentina and, in 1914, to the backwaters of Brazil. His personal story is a dark reflection of the wild land and the ferocious individuality of a frontier people; a world of feudal honor, murder, intrigue and jealousy blended with the savagery of the tropical jungles and marshes, with their swarming, blood-feeding insects, ravenous *piranha* fish, fer-de-lance and bushmaster snakes and giant jaguars—*tigres*—the largest and most dangerous of the American cats.

Sasha Siemel was not an especially big man, in his prime a bit under six feet tall and weighing 180 pounds, with a red-

blond beard and blue eyes. But for his size, he was immensely strong and quick, a gifted wrestler and fighter. In his
earlier days in Brazil, he fought many times against professional strongmen and "Terrible Turk" types, usually winning the bouts and prize money handily. His physical
prowess had a dark aspect, though, that earned him the
blood enmity of such lesser men as one Ricardo Favelle, a
fellow employee of Siemel's at a silversmith's shop in the
little town of Passo Fundo. For months a deadly feud had
been building up between the men, which culminated with
Favelle trying to shoot Siemel, forcing the Latvian to take
away the revolver and rearrange the general contour of
Favelle's skull with the butt. Although the French-Brazilian
survived, Sasha thought he had killed him and lived much of
his life under the impression that he was a wanted mur-
derer. Actually, Favelle was to come to a far more exotic
death, as we'll see a bit farther on.

It was while this feud was warming up that Siemel first
heard stories of a legendary old Guató Indian some thousand miles away who possessed an ancient skill. He was a
tigrero, a master of the art of spearfighting the jaguar.

The revered title of *tigrero*, in its true Brazilian sense
meaning one who hunts jaguars professionally with a spear
(as opposed to the more common Spanish usage indicating
merely a hunter of *tigres*), had only been used with reference
to a very few Indians. Normally hunting in groups, some
tribes like the Guató did produce a real *tigrero* every few
generations, a solitary paladin who fought single-handed in
the jungles and marshes with his dogs, usually for hire to
ranch owners whose cattle were being killed by jaguars.
Mostly, aspiring *tigreros* never reached fame because of the
very nature of their calling. They died from their early
mistakes under the claws and fangs of their intended prey,
just more moldering bones in the *jungla*. With only a lance
blade between an infuriated 300-pound jaguar and sure
death, a single error in judgment or timing was fatal. Even a
bullfighter, a *torero*, could make mistakes and live. Who has
achieved fame in that profession without many *cornadas* and
hundreds of stitches after goofing? There are always others

to draw off the bull and an infirmary with expert medical help immediately available. Not so with the *tigrero*. Alone with his feline adversary, he had to kill or die. If a jaguar could get between the spear point and the man's body, there would be no help. No mistakes were allowed.

So why would anybody, white or Indian, with anything between his ears but solid bone want to hunt jaguars on foot, armed only with the *zagaya*, the Indian spear?

There are as many answers to that one as there are reasons men hunt, fight, skydive, gamble or take up with redheaded ladies. In the peculiar high, thick swamp grasses of the western Brazilian *pantanal*, or marshes, Siemel claimed that, incredibly, spear hunting was *safer* than using a rifle. It was his logic (certainly not without foundation, as he killed well over 300 jaguars in his career) that when visibility is down to a matter of a few feet and the gun misses or wounds, the jaguar will either charge instantly, before another shot is possible, or escape into the anonymous grass. If he charges, he will nearly always kill the hunter. With the *zagaya*, a man can continue to fight, keeping the cat off him so long as he has the strength to resist.

That, to be sure, is the technical side of the answer. Much more, as typified by Siemel's outlook, lies in the eternal mystique that has always existed between man and the deadly game animals. As we have examined in other works, the difference between shooting an elephant at one hundred yards through the chest and stalking a big tusker to within ten or so yards is the difference between simple animal assassination and real sport hunting. When you are within ten yards of a bull elephant, you, my friend, are in harm's way. With the long shot, one kills an elephant in a sterile, riskless and, in my opinion, cowardly manner. At halitosis range, you enter into the most ancient nonbiological passion of humanity: self-testing. And *on purpose*, which is the most important aspect of the implied morality of the act. Nobody stuck a .45 in your ear and forced you to get so close that you can smell the peanuts; quite the contrary, you probably paid the equivalent of a deposit on Westminster Abbey for the questionable privilege. Isn't it just peachy? What fun to stand there listening to the blood roar in your ears, your stomach flapping around like a startled bird, your hands so shaky and sweaty that the rifle feels like a freshly peeled sapling. A bystander would think it was you against the elephant. How wrong he would be. . . .

The point of big-game hunting is not just a matter of killing something that can bite back, but of how it is done and how much risk to which the hunter purposely exposes himself. It all comes down to that timeless moment between slamming heartbeats when you know for an absolute certainty that if you lose your nerve or blow the shot you are going to die. Dead. As in forever. No more pungent amber scotch, no more sea breezes over the malachite flats, no more charcoal-crusty, slab-sided steaks, no more mysterious girl aroma in the twilight. Not even any more taxes once the I.R.S. finishes mauling your bedraggled carcass for the last gold inlay. Like most things in life, you only get out of an experience what you put into it. There is no emotional free lunch, either.

This is acutely the case when hunting jaguar with a spear. A *tigre* that's been taking his vitamins will weigh twice as much as an average man and is probably five times stronger. As a cat, he's considerably quicker, forcing the hunter to fight a counterpunch game, reacting to the cat's tactics while controlling the overall strategy as much as possible. In all the world of hunting there could be little more satisfying than beating a big, mankilling cat on his own terms, alone and on foot, muscle against muscle, steel spear blade against ivory fang. I have hunted and killed African Cape buffalo with a thrown spear for much the same reasons Sasha Siemel fought his jaguars. But I promise you faithfully that I have no intention of trying my luck on any *tigres*. I guess I'm just not that emotionally starved.

The sixty-year-old Guató Indian known as Joaquim was a misty legend throughout the thousands of square miles of the upper Paraguay River's Xarayes and São Laurenço Pantanal when Sasha first heard of him from an old bounty hunter in Passo Fundo, *Dom* Carlos Roderigues. A very colorful sort—if he wasn't on your trail—the one-eyed

Roderigues kept a tally of his own human kills by stringing their dried ears on a length of cord that hung over the front door of his home, a most effective bit of advertising that served the same purpose as a cobbler displaying a large wooden boot over his shop.

At this time, just before his disagreement with Favelle erupted into violence, Sasha felt he was in a most awkward spot. To let Favelle kill him was pretty obviously not the answer, nor did he want to kill Favelle, because the little man's friends would hire either *Dom* Carlos or some other *pistolero* for revenge. Both Sasha and his brother Ernst had been considering a trip to look into business possibilities in the remote Mato Grosso, along the Bolivian and Paraguayan borders, and had decided to leave Passo Fundo. *Dom* Carlos Roderigues, who had years before seen Joaquim Guató (Indians took their tribal name as their surname, in many cases) spear-fight a jaguar, told the tale to Sasha, who became intrigued and determined to seek out the old man in the Mato Grosso Marshes, if possible. After his fight with Favelle accelerated his plans slightly, he left with his brother for this primitive land, along the way picking up a cowboy named Apparicio Pinheiro, whose badly infected *garapata* tick bites Sasha doctored. Taking odd jobs, particularly repairing simple machinery and guns, the three pushed sporadically north from ranch to ranch until finally reaching the *pantanal*. At last, Ernst having decided to stay in a town, Sasha found Joaquim Guató on the *fazenda* of *Senhor* Chico Pinto on the São Laurenço River.

It was an especially filthy and dilapidated mud and thatch hut along the river, containing one very drunken Indian, stoned out on *canha*, raw cane spirit that could strip paint or power a diesel engine. Although Joaquim could hardly speak, he did confirm that he was, indeed, the great *tigrero* of southern legend. With the unlikely spearman was his best dog, a slat-ribbed reddish mongrel called Dragão, whom Joaquim extolled as being the finest jaguar dog in all of Brazil. It was, he explained candidly, because of the insult of a rancher offering mere money for the dog that he had decided to assuage his injured sensibilities with *canha*. In any case, although Sasha thought he would need a week to sober up, the Indian offered to take Siemel hunting the following morning. To Sasha's surprise, Joaquim arrived, bright-eyed if not exactly bushy-tailed, with Dragão an hour before dawn.

After several miles of hard walking—Sasha carrying his Winchester and camera case (he had been anxious to photograph a jaguar), following the barechested Indian armed only with his *zagaya* spear—Dragão hit the trail of a puma, or mountain lion, the spoor still fresh. It wasn't a *tigre*, but it would do. Although Sasha was as tough and durable as dried boot leather, it was all he could do to keep up with the barefoot Indian, chasing after the howling dog. After a half hour, the puma came to bay in a *lapacho* tree, and the men came up with Dragão on guard below.

Pumas are odd animals, as large as big leopards but most inoffensive with regard to man. Although the species ranges from Alaska to Argentina and eastward as far as the Florida Everglades, there have been only one or possibly two documented cases of man-killing or eating in its long history. It's apparently a matter of species "personality" with this otherwise powerful, muscular and well-armed cat, which kills deer-sized animals with ease, that it is almost invariably shy and unaggressive toward man. In America's western states, pumas are regularly treed by dogs and captured with ropes, a performance which, if attempted with a leopard, would create a waiting list at any fair-sized hospital. Still, if cornered and pressed hard enough, even a field mouse will take the offensive sometimes.

After Siemel took a picture of the cat, the puma showed nervousness and leaped to a lower branch. Joaquim had indicated that Sasha should take the shot, which he did, hitting the chest. Mortally wounded, the puma leaped from the tree and fell over, but then recovered and jumped at Siemel. In the blink of an eye, fate threw a roundhouse low blow. At the same second that the cat was in midair, Joaquim and Dragão attacked simultaneously, the Indian with the spear and the dog with bared teeth. As he hurtled for the puma's throat, Dragão passed between the slashing *zagaya* blade and the cat, the point penetrating completely through the dog's neck and on into the puma's shoulder. The mountain lion was dead before he hit the ground; Dragão lived only a few seconds.

The old Indian deep in stunned grief, Sasha returned home to the hut where he was staying, leaving Joaquim Guató alone in his misery. The next morning, Joaquim came to Siemel's hut with two scraggy-looking dogs, the smaller of which was named Valente. As a gesture of friendship, the Indian presented Sasha with his choice, recommending Valente as a potential pack leader. Sasha was touched. He knew that *Senhor* Pinto, his host, had offered a great deal for the dog and had been refused. In return, Siemel gave Joaquim his Winchester (although Julian Duguid, Sasha's early biographer, says it was a double-barreled .32 pistol), not as payment for the dog but as a return gift between hunters. Joaquim had told the white man that he had decided not to hunt for the next two months, and Sasha headed north to the newly discovered diamond fields on the Rio Garça with Apparicio Pinheiro.

Ten weeks later, Siemel returned to find the Guató as drunk as usual, yet again ready to hunt the following day. The next morning, with Valente in the lead, a big male jaguar was cornered in a stand of *acuri* palms, and Siemel witnessed his first spear fight.

It was an incredible tableau that the novice came upon, a furious male *tigre* encircled by baiting dogs that dodged and lunged, staying clear of the flickering paw strokes as the cat, ears laid back and snarling, made short rushes at one dog, only to be nipped in the rear by another. Then the half-naked Indian stepped into the scene, his heavy spear pinned between his right elbow and his side. It was a completely different Joaquim Guató, on sure, bare feet, eyes clear, stare locked on the jaguar with terrible concentration. As he saw the man the *tigre* froze, ignoring the dogs, a rosetted statue with glowing yellow eyes wide with calculated hate, as the Indian moved slowly nearer. The distance between them shrank in ominous silence, each jungle killer measuring the other. At three yards the man stopped, the *zagaya* low and leveled. A puff of flying dirt erupted from Joaquim's feet as he kicked a clump of earth and leaves straight into the jaguar's twisted face, goading him into a charge. Confused and furious, the big male was just beginning his rush as the Indian feinted the spearhead at the cat's throat, drawing a lashing claw stroke. In a blink, he stabbed home as the charge began, the blade driving into meat up to the crossbar where it joins the shaft, slicing deeply into the neck.

It seemed impossible that the frail hunter could hold off the raging fury of the 300-pound jaguar as it fought the spear, sometimes lifting the little man clear off the ground as he clung to the shaft. Somehow he kept his balance, for to fall was to die. Suddenly the *tigre* backed up a few feet, trying to wriggle off the spear. Joaquim was with him, jerking the bloody blade free and, as fast as a closing steel trap, driving it full into the dappled chest. As the man turned on the shaft, the jaguar was now on its back, the chest matted with wet crimson. With all his strength, the Indian worked the spear in the wound, and the struggles of the stricken cat grew more feeble, at last stopping with a shudder that ran the length of the body. The dogs moved in to worry the carcass as Sasha expelled a breath he had been holding in petrified fascination throughout the fight.

He was hooked. What for the Latvian had been a smoldering desire burst into a wildfire of passion to match himself against a jaguar with the *zagaya*. He would become a *tigrero* or spend his life in the attempt.

Spear hunting, after throwing rocks or beating a prey animal's head into mush with a club, is probably the oldest form of hunting with a weapon. Before the *atl-atl*-type javelin or dart launcher was developed, and later the bow, the only way primitive man had to place a cutting edge into the body of his victim was to attach it to the shaft of a stick, which created the spear. In the very early days, passive hunting was likely the most productive way to kill bigger game, either with pitfalls or by driving herds over cliffs. Yet, as weaponry improved, active hunting, which involved stalking and killing, became the measure of our beetlebrowed forebears' prowess. In many parts of the world, it still is today. The vestigial heritage of this way of life may be seen very clearly, especially around modern Madison Avenue or Wall Street.

From the most elemental point of view, hunting with the spear falls into two main categories: throwing and thrusting. Obviously, the object in either case is to place the spearhead with its sharp cutting edges where it will do the greatest physiological harm. Like the arrowhead or swordpoint, the principle is to disrupt the circulatory system by hemorrhage, thereby cutting off the flow of oxygenated blood to the brain. When you think about it, a spear, an arrow or even a bullet through the heart actually causes death by asphyxiation, as the heart ceases to pump and the brain dies of oxygen starvation.

The greatest danger in hunting big game with the spear is that it forces the hunter into very close proximity to his quarry. The spear may be perfectly placed, but considerable time can elapse before the prey loses consciousness and dies, every moment of which it may spend tearing sirloins and rump roasts out of the hunter. In the case of the throwing spear or javelin, the advantages and disadvantages tend to offset one another. The problem lies in the fact that few people can throw a spear very far with any reliable accuracy, and precision placement in a vital area is all-important. Also, in the case of fast-reacting game or men in battle, the giveaway movement of the throw, as well as the slow flight time of the spear, can permit dodging, which negates the probability of a hit. The positive side of the matter is that of distance. Once thrown at something big and ugly, the hunter is free to run like hell with a head start. As one tribe in New Guinea (whose national sport is placing their neighboring warriors *en brochette*) tells their young men, the only thing more important than being a good spear thrower is being a very good spear dodger.

Where the spear is most in evidence today—Africa—the throwing type ranks about equally with the *assegai,* which is a short stabbing spear popular with the southern Bantu races, such as the Zulu. Far more game in Africa is killed with the arrow than the spear, but certain animals are hunted with the spear under local conditions that may vary widely. Among the Nilo-Hamites, such as the Masai, Nandi, Karamojong, Samburu and others, the spear is always used on lions and, in some blooding rituals, for elephants. The Bambuti Pygmies of the Ituri Forest in the Congo region regularly hunt elephants with a wide-bladed stabbing spear lent to them by their Bantu neighbors. In this unbelievably dangerous form of hunting, they stalk right up to the selected elephant and thrust from beneath for the kidney region and then dash away. Needless to say, elephants don't like this very much, and a great many Pygmies don't get a chance to try this more than once—their first and last time.

The great classical animal hunted with the thrusting spear has been the European wild boar *(Sus scrofa),* and hunting literature, from the Persian cylinder of 600 B.C. in the British Museum to the present day, varies little in awed appreciation of the savage ferocity of this grand animal. It was killed in most acceptable form on foot with a heavy spear incorporating one or another "stops," or crossbars, to prevent the animal from coming right up the shaft at the hunter. Gaston Phoebus, author of one of the earliest European books on hunting, published in Paris in the early 1500s, offers some advice on the spearing of a charging boar while on foot:

> Hold your spear about the middle, not too far forward lest he strike you with his tusks, and as soon as the point has entered the body, take the haft of the spear under your armpit, and press and push as hard as you can and never let go the haft, and if the beast be stronger than you then you must turn from side to side as best you can without letting go the haft, until God comes to your aid or other assistance reaches you.

Boar hunting may have had a lot to do with the popularity of religion in the Middle Ages. Certainly, during a large boar drive the woods must have been ringing with invocations of the Deity!

The so-called sport of "pig-sticking" became immensely

popular with the British cavalry units in India and developed into a real art form. Although done from horseback, an amazing number of men were killed by the boar, not to mention the slaughter of their mounts under the self-whetting ivory scissors of the boars' tusks.

A wild boar is a terrible opponent for a spearman, granted, but a cat is something else again. To appreciate the degree of risk involved with taking on a jaguar—alone, on foot, with but a *zagaya*—the animal itself has to be considered. *Panthera onca,* the jaguar, is one of the least studied of all the big cats, excepting, possibly, only the snow leopard of the remote Himalayas. The reason for this neglect is largely that jaguars thrive in some of the most difficult terrain on earth, the jungles of Central and South America, where sheer lack of visibility greatly hinders observation. This is not to say that jungle is their sole habitat; jaguars also live— in reduced numbers because of controlled hunting to keep them from killing cattle—in the grassland marshes typified by the Xarayes Pantanal where Siemel hunted them for more than thirty years.

Very recently, Dr. George B. Schaller, the well-known wildlife expert, tried to conduct a study of jaguars in this region. Nearly every time he located a *tigre* to tag with a radio collar, it was killed by ranch hands, despite the laws forbidding this. Illegal hide hunting also plays a major role in the *local* reduction of numbers of jaguars in the Great Marshes, although reasonable-to-good levels of population still exist in the more remote areas of the South American and Central American interiors.

Once again, it's the old problem of the poacher taking over when the sportsman is forced out by the creation of idealistic but hopelessly unrealistic laws, such as that forbidding the import of any spotted cat pelt into the United States, no matter how legally obtained in its country of origin. When a species such as a jaguar cannot pay its own way—through the generation of license fees, rural employment, government export taxes and the many other financial considerations that have so greatly contributed to the preservation of tens of thousands of square miles of virgin

Africa for hunting concessions, instead of being turned over to cattle and goats—it is consequently of no economic value except for its poached hide on the black market. Who will reasonably pay for the conservation and management of an animal whose only financial impact upon a backwoods economy such as the Mato Grosso is decidedly negative because it kills and eats cattle? The ranchers who own the cattle? Hardly. Of bloody *course,* they're going to order their *vaqueros* to shoot, poison or trap any jaguar they can, law or no law.

Back in 1977, when I wrote *Death in the Long Grass,* a collection of my experiences over a decade as a professional hunter and game control officer in Africa, I tried to make this same point about the supposedly "endangered" leopard. Now, almost four years later, it is with intense satisfaction that I find the sportsman's argument may have done some good. The U.S. Fish and Wildlife Service of the Department of the Interior proposed in the March 24, 1980, *Federal Register* "Reclassification for the Leopard." One of the paragraphs sounds as if I wrote it:

> . . . In addition, the Fish and Wildlife Service is proposing to ease its restrictions to allow the importation of sport hunting trophies as an economic incentive to encourage the leopard's conservation by landowners in Africa, where in some areas it is indiscriminately destroyed as a predator. Trophy hunting brings additional jobs and income to African citizens and landowners and added revenue to the governments from tourists and the sale of hunting licenses that may cost $500 or more. It is expected that reclassifying the leopard to give it some economic value will lead to measures to protect it as a valuable resource.

Hallelujah, brother!

Would it be unreasonable to suggest that the same economic dynamics might apply to some areas of the jaguar's status, too?

The jaguar, or *tigre*—literally "tiger" in Spanish or Portuguese—was once fairly well established in the United States, as well as in its more southern current home. If memory serves me right, Smith and Wesson ran some early dramatic ads for their revolvers featuring jaguars attacking cowboys, presumably in the American Southwest. Once prowling as far north as Arkansas, it is now an extremely rare animal north of Mexico, although some experts feel that it is again expanding its range toward the United States. It is by far the largest of the New World cats, ranking about third in size with the rest of the true panthers—the lion, tiger and leopard.

There has always been considerable discussion about the size of a "big" male jaguar. Appearing to the uninitiated as rather an overweight leopard, estimates vary from 250 pounds as the top weight all the way up to the whopper I saw a poor-quality photo of while hunting in Brazil, on cattle scales tipping in at 460 pounds (209 kilos on the metric scales). There's no doubt in my mind that, as the Brazilians claim, many localized races of jaguars may vary considerably in size because of particular genetic and/or dietary conditions. Therefore, a "big" jaguar in Mexico might weigh 200 pounds, and in the Mato Grosso as much as 350 or more pounds. One skin from a jaguar, killed by Siemel, was reported by the famous hunter and author, Russell B. Aitken, who photographed it, as bigger than a very large male African lion. No weight was given, if, indeed, the cat was ever weighed, but the size would indicate well over 400 pounds.

Few naturalists would argue that the largest race of jaguars is that of the Mato Grosso, although some very hefty specimens have come from Amazonia. In the Xingu Basin, a southern tributary of the Amazon where I hunted, the largest type was locally called the *canguçu,* so named for the peculiar "swallow wing" pattern of the rosette conformation on the hide. Three distinct types of jaguar were supposed to be recognized in the Xingu, although whether they were merely individual differences between single animals or truly disparate races I could not say.

Despite a cosmetic similarity to the leopard at first glance, jaguars are really quite different, beside being half-again heavier and stronger. Possibly they are not quite so agile as the unbelievably shifty leopard, yet are thoroughly aboreal, as well as aquatically adapted. For all practical purposes as strong as a lion or a fair-sized tiger—which is the largest of all the cats—the jaguar feeds on virtually any meat he can catch, including swamp deer, tapir, capybara, fish, birds, snakes, alligators and domestic cattle. Whereas the other big cats, especially lions, tend to kill by biting the windpipe and keeping it closed until their victim suffocates (despite the common belief that they pull down big game in a manner that breaks their neck in the fall, which happens only incidentally, in my experience), the jaguar usually bites through the top of the skull, driving the canines deep into the brain to cause instant death.

Tigres are highly territorial, the usual pattern being for the range of a male to overlap those of two or even three females. Solitary and highly jealous, jaguars will defend their stomping grounds ferociously from other males. A very big "black," or melanistic phase, male jaguar I killed in the Xingu back in the 1960s has an epidermis that looks as if it did its undergraduate work at Heidelberg. On the shoulders, neck and rump are more than sixty deep claw and fang marks, undoubtedly sustained in a lifetime of territorial battles. Since this particular tabby was pushing 300 pounds himself, I wonder what the opposition looked like after he got through with them. A pasting from this chap—which I very nearly got—must have had the same effect as an extended cold shower!

One curious aspect to this particular black jaguar, in addition to his rare color phase, is that he does not have the normal long tail of the ordinary *tigre*. It is more or less a stump, just thirteen inches in length. On first examination I thought it had been bitten off by a rival or perhaps even by *piranha*, but close inspection shows that unquestionably it is natural, being perfectly rounded and showing no sign of having been amputated. A photo I have of another skin from the same area, also black, obtained by a friend who traded for it with Indians, clearly shows the same stump tail. Now, there's been little enough work done on jaguars as a species, let alone black ones from a region still so nasty that prospectors and missionaries are found clubbed to death with unnerving frequency, so perhaps the Indians are correct that the black jaguar as found in the Xingu Basin has evolved into a separate subspecies. Additional to the stump tail as a distinguishing feature, the tribes claim that the pugmarks are slightly different, that the call is more highly pitched and that black jaguars will only mate with others of the same genetic mutation. I have no idea of the truth of the matter, but considering the frequency of such mutant traits as extra toes on domestic cats, perhaps the solidification of genetic errata in circumstances of relative confinement such as the Xingu region would be possible. On second thought, maybe I'd better cover all bets by suggesting with characteristic modesty that this elusive creature, should it be defined by science, might be handsomely labeled *Panthera onca capstickii!*

Animal behaviorists appear to be in rare agreement that the main factor determining the danger of the jaguar to man lies in its highly developed sense of territorialism. In comparison to the also territorial leopard, by way of example, it is far more likely to stand its ground in the face of real or imagined threat, even by man, and it is this characteristic that is the primary reason for the great majority of jaguar-caused deaths. This situation is at its most deadly when a jaguar, who has taken to preying on a herd of cattle, decides to include the cows as part of his territory, actually considering them possessions to be defended. Unlucky or careless cowboys are usually the victims of this behavior, charged from close quarters as they ride up to the herd. In fact, the death of José Ramos in the Xarayes Pantanal seems to have been a bloodily classic confirmation of these tactics.

In the same vein, individual jaguars are certainly man killers for other reasons, quite as diverse as those affecting the other great cats of the world who take up people pouncing for fun and profit. Oddly, though, actual man-eating is comparatively rare in jaguars, as opposed to simple homicide. There have been no recorded protracted plagues of man-eating by *tigres* that would in any way compare with the many reigns of terror of the lions, tigers and leopards of both Africa and Asia. Still, to the hunter or traveler who happens to get his check cashed by a man-killing jaguar, who, for reasons of hygiene or heartburn, does not eat the body, the point is somewhat moot. Siemel himself wrote that a jaguar that has once killed a man will turn man-eater as soon as he realizes what easy prey people are. Sasha once killed such an animal on the Terere River. This particular jaguar had stalked a *vaquero* with the obvious intention of making a meal of him and, cornering him in a hut, did just that. Siemel caught up with the cat two days later and killed it with his Winchester.

Over many weeks after Sasha Siemel watched gap-mouthed for the first time as Joaquim Guató battled the *tigre,* the two men of different worlds hunted together, the Latvian quickly learning the deft techniques that permitted a fast and strong man to challenge a charging jaguar with only the *zagaya* and emerge alive. Several times, as they fought the great cats together, student and teacher, Sasha nearly was caught by his undeveloped sense of timing the thrust, but always the old Indian saved him with his leaping, darting blade. Siemel learned not only the bushcraft of the unforgiving Mato Grosso, but the true elements of spear hunting. With each fight, he developed better the absolute concentration of the master *tigrero,* a pure serum that saturated the body and brain of the *zagayero,* welding confidence, balance and muscle action into a finely tuned killing machine, leaving the hunter fainting and exhausted, physically and mentally, after he had killed.

It was 1925 before Sasha was to hunt his first jaguar alone with the *zagaya.* Although Joaquim had forbidden him to attempt to spear a *tigre* by himself, when the old man went off on an assignment to settle a cattle raider, Siemel decided that his time had come. He felt he had developed the concentration and confidence as well as the technique, learning to watch and react only to the feet of the *tigre* before the charge, as all jaguars attack differently; some leaping up at the head and throat of the spearman, others charging in low to the ground with feinting movements.

Only at the last instant, after the cat had committed himself, could the decision be made to raise or lower the lance point, the decision that determined life or death.

Sasha Siemel spear-fought his first solo jaguar—a big male—in the thick marsh grass of the São Laurenço Pantanal, facing a double charge when the cat wrenched himself off the spear blade in his chest and launched himself at the man a second time. It died as the first of sixty-four *tigres* that his dog Valente would give him and the head of the list of the more than three hundred jaguars he would kill with various weapons. By 1948, twenty-three years after his first spear fight, he had taken 281, plus 22 more captured alive. Of his total at that time (which was at least seven years before he retired, although the last accounting of his kills is not, to my knowledge, recorded in print), 30 were taken with the *zagaya,* 111 with bow and arrow and the remainder with a rifle, the different weapons reflecting the fact that jaguars will not charge under all conditions, and, in some terrain, use of the spear is impossible.

It's interesting to note that some authorities claim it is unusual for a jaguar to "tree" when pursued by a man with dogs. My experience, and that of other hunters I have consulted on this, has largely been the opposite, as was Siemel's. The difference depends upon individual animals and circumstances, although the jaguar is far more likely to leave a tree where hounds have chased him and charge the man when he comes up than is the puma. It is the jaguar that does not "tree," however, that is the most dangerous, as it usually indicates that he has been hunted before and knows how to kill dogs. It was precisely this education that was so well used by the famous Assassino jaguar of the Xarayes, probably the best known and most feared jaguar in Brazil's history.

For three years from the day he became a true *tigrero,* Sasha hunted jaguar with his beloved pack of dogs—led by the great Valente and two others named Vinte and Pardo—working as a bounty hunter for cattle ranchers suffering severe losses from jaguar depredation. Except for a few months spent running a small zoo in São Paulo and a short trip to Germany, he was in the field. But for the hunting, it was a torturously sad period of Sasha's life. His brother, Ernst, was shot in the back and murdered. His best friend, Apparicio Pinheiro, swore to kill him and broke off their relationship over a woman. Near the banks of the São Laurenco, returning from the investigation of his brother's murder at Cuyaba, Sasha stumbled onto the badly crushed skeleton of a man in the grass. Nearby was a tooth-scarred *zagaya* shaft, broken in two, and the remains of a Guató canoe. Joaquim Guató had fought his last battle with a jaguar here, probably charged from behind as he dragged the canoe up onto the bank. Likely, he had seen the *tigre* from the water, possibly called it with a hollow gourd. From the spear shaft, he had gotten a thrust in but had been overwhelmed. Sasha buried his skull and some fragmented ribs close by where he fell. As if this wasn't enough, Valente was killed and eaten by a female jaguar with half-grown cubs, outnumbered at last. Possibly the only bright spot of these years was the death of Ricardo Favelle, who was eviscerated by the terrible *piranha* fish and blew his own brains out in his agony. Never a dull moment in the Mato Grosso . . .

The last in this chain of events had been the death of his dog, Valente. Whatever the facts of the matter, Sasha had had enough. He quit hunting and went to Europe for four months, then decided to return to the wilderness to resume his life as a *tigrero* and to make films of the Mato Grosso. Once more, he passed through the haunts of his old friend, *Dom* Carlos, the collector of dried human ears, then on to the Xarayes Marshes, where he set up a camp near Cara Cara Island. His surviving dogs, Vinte and Pardo, had been kept for him by a rancher, and now he added another untried but promising lead dog named Raivoso, as well as a small fox terrier he called Tupi, merely a house pet.

The huge cattle-killing jaguar that came to be called Assassino by the backwoodsmen of the Mato Grosso had long ravaged the *pantanal* before Sasha ever hunted him. A feline Jack-the-Ripper if ever one prowled the lonely morass of marsh, Assassino could certainly be considered a truly murderous maniac, a gigantic male that stalked and killed any animal that crossed his path for sheer fun, leaving the torn and disemboweled bodies where they lay, unless he chanced to be hungry at the moment. There were other reasons, too, why he was not your average, garden-variety jaguar. Once having been run by dogs and treed, he had been slightly wounded in the shoulder by a rifle bullet from a nervous *vaquero,* who panicked when he saw the size of the cat. The man ran, and Assassino killed the whole pack of dogs. No dog ever set on his trail from that day onward ever survived a meeting with this great *tigre.* Assassino's specialty was to stay carefully in the high grass and permit the dogs to follow his scent spoor for as long as it took the pack to become slightly strung out. When one bark seemed well ahead of the others, the jaguar would fishhook back on his own trail and lie in ambush, killing the first dog as it ran by, and then running ahead to repeat the performance until all the dogs were dead. He had also learned never to seek refuge in a tree, where the searing thundercrack of a bullet could ever hurt him again.

During the years that he had been on his crusade of slaughter, Assassino had earned the reputation as a "devil-tiger," much the same status successful man-eaters in Africa and Asia are awarded. It was generally believed that no bullet could harm him, nor could any man kill him in any way. Anybody who hunted him lost all his dogs and never got so much as a glimpse of his anthracite and amber hide. After killing an estimated 400 head of cattle to the south of the Xarayes, for some reason he became inactive for a period of time before resurfacing near the *Fazenda* Descalvados, a large ranch in the Xarayes Pantanal. It may have been that he was injured in a territorial battle or was sick for a while; the reason for his absence is unknown.

It compliments Siemel's believability and humility that he freely admits having refused to hunt Assassino, although begged to do so by ranchers on several occasions. He was only too aware, as a professional, that to try to hunt the big *tigre* with his hounds would be a death sentence for them, skilled though they were. And now, without his lead dog

Valente, who might have stood some chance, there was no hope for it. Yet this decision had been made before Assassino killed José Ramos.

It was Ramos himself who had ridden into Sasha's camp near Ilha do Cara Cara, his horse lathered and his clothes crusty with sweat. Not taking time to dismount, he implored Siemel to come with his dogs to hunt Assassino, who had killed twelve of his small herd.

Sasha turned him down flat. He would as soon send the fox terrier pup as his jaguar dogs for all the chance they would have. José Ramos, desperate, begged again, but the most Sasha could promise was that he would go after the cat if he saw him or knew he was close by. With a smoldering sense of resignation, Ramos swore to go after Assassino himself. He would kill or be killed. Little did he realize . . .

It was within two days of Ramos' visit that Sasha noticed a tall, dense column of vultures some miles off, over the marshes. Suspecting one of Assassino's calling cards, he investigated and soon found the mangled body of a marsh deer, the carcass badly ripped by claws and teeth but the meat uneaten. Incredibly, as he went on with the dogs in close control, five marsh deer in all were found executed by the assassin cat, the spoor of his huge pug marks unmistakable. Not one ounce of meat had been eaten from any of the bodies except by the *urubi*. Assassino was having a fine day of sport.

At the fifth kill, Raivoso lost control and ran off on the scent of the jaguar, Sasha quickly collaring the other dogs lest they take up the deadly trail, too. Clenching his teeth in impotent fury, Siemel listened to the bass bawling of the lead dog through the long grass, knowing what he would hear soon. It came as a piercing canine scream of agony that stopped abruptly as a slammed door. Assassino had won again.

Siemel was at a complete loss as to how to hunt this insane *tigre* through the dense cover of the marshes. Back at camp, having buried the tattered remains of Raivoso, he thought back over the jaguar's career, realizing the apparent impossibility of trying to run down the big cat without dogs, at the same time knowing that to expose his pack was as good as shooting them. For hours he pondered the problem. His rifle would be useless in the heavy grass; only the spear could draw the life blood of the *tigre* at such suicidally close quarters. But, he thought, even with the loss of Raivoso, possibly he could use the dogs to get close enough to the jaguar to deal with it. He was still wrestling with the problem the next morning when the thud of Maria Ramos' horse galloping into camp set little Tupi into a paroxysm of excited barking.

Maria was a wreck. Half-hysterical and bush-torn, she poured out all she knew; that José had gone after Assassino and only the claw-torn horse had returned with blood on the saddle. To the junglewise *tigrero,* it was like reading a newspaper headline. There was nothing to do but go now and try to find whatever might be left of José Ramos. He took four leashed dogs, two new ones called Amigo and Leon joining with Vinte and Pardo, and tied the fox terrier to one of the hut poles so he would not follow. Maria led the way along the river to the place where she said José had cut off the trail, refusing when Siemel tried to get her to ride home. She was a woman of the *pantanal* and insisted on coming.

A mile ahead, the green *capão* stood like a beacon over the ocean of grass, a strange, verdant projection like a lichen-covered rock in some tropic sea. Above it, small specks that were vultures volplaned and circled.

José Ramos lay as Assassino had left him, a mass of torn meat lying on its face. As Siemel rolled the corpse over in a loud whine of flies, Maria fainted and nearly fell from her horse. She did not now argue when sent back to the ranch.

The sign was as clear as neon. Deep scars marked the spot from which the jaguar had leaped, and blackening speckles of blood freckled the grass stems around the hoof marks. Some yards away lay the unfired percussion gun. Siemel looked around him. If Assassino had knocked a man from his horse once, he would do it again. Also, there was no way to spear-fight effectively from horseback. Dismounting, he tied the animal to a tree in a small clearing and took the protective sheath off his *zagaya* blade. A pistol, probably the ubiquitous Smith and Wesson .38 Special revolver, the Brazilian standard against which all other handguns were judged, was in a belt holster. Years later, Sasha would manage to shoot himself with it in the leg while spear-fighting a jaguar. In any case, the .38 Special cartridge is of little value against a charging jaguar and was carried for delivering the *coup de grace*. On a hunch, he also took his bow and two arrows, in case he had the opportunity of provoking a charge with them.

A very simple plan—Sasha decided that the cat was probably still quite close, and, by releasing the dogs and running after them as fast as he could, there was a possibility that he might throw the jaguar's ambush tactics off. Yes, if he could keep up, maybe there was a chance. He let slip the dogs.

Aften ten minutes of running through the marsh grass, the vocal bedlam of the dogs ever farther ahead, he knew that he had been wrong. The death shriek of Pardo, the leader, sounded over the plain and was followed in less than a minute by the screech of the disembowelled Vinte. Within 450 yards, Assassino killed all four of the dogs in his classic ambush pattern. His lungs of fire, Siemel was sick with fury at finding the last one, Leon, in an opening in the *capão*. And then another bark filtered through the bush and caught his ear. It was the fox terrier, Tupi, who had chewed through his tether and followed his master's scent.

As the little dog ran by, barking insanely at the cat smell, Sasha slammed his heel over the trailing end of the broken tether, flipping Tupi over as the line tautened in a full run. As the pet yelped in surprise, that same moment there was the rustle of heavy movement just across the clearing, then ominous silence. Carefully, Sasha laid his spear at his feet and nocked an arrow. Without a glance down, he stepped on the little dog's foot, making it shriek with startled pain.

It worked. Across the opening a few stalks of grass twitched. In a single fluid movement, Sasha came to full draw, and his arrow hissed blindly into the tangle as Tupi began to bark again. The *thug!* of the arrow told Siemel he had touched the jaguar, and there was a flurry of movement through the curtain of grass. Scant seconds ticked mutely by in time with his heaving chest as he sighted his last shaft and sent it whipping into the cover. Would the confusion of the barking dog and the flash of the arrows bring the charge he needed? The answer appeared in a blur of streaking motion as Assassino, a broken-off shaft protruding from the bunched muscles of his shoulder, ran for a low scrub tree out of pure instinct. He was nearly there when he saw Sasha.

The man gulped involuntarily when he saw the jaguar's tremendous size as the cat stopped and then stood glowering at Siemel across a thirty-yard open space. The *zagaya* in position, the spearman realized that he would never again have a fight like this one, very possibly because he would not be alive for the next one. He had none of the advantages of the dogs to break the concentration of the jaguar, to keep him off balance. Furious with the pain in his shoulder, the monster cat would be completely unpredictable in his next attack. It became a battle of nerve and will, the killer *tigre* measuring the man, stalking back and forth with guttural growls as if caged, punctuated with screaming roars that fluttered Sasha's guts. Every sense locked on the cat, he began to move slowly in, edging closer, pushing for the charge. Both man and jaguar were searching for an opening. The *tigre*'s came first.

It was just the airy flutter of wings, the flap of an *urubi* vulture settling into a tree above him. But it was enough. The terrible strain broke Siemel's all-important concentration, and he committed the fatal sin of glancing away from the jaguar. In that microsecond, it saw its chance and launched itself straight at the spearman. Off balance, Sasha lunged and pivoted at the same time, the foot-long forged-steel spearhead catching Assassino a lucky slice on the neck as the mottled mass of golden-sheathed muscle hurtled by. A giant, talon-studded paw glanced off Siemel's right shoulder, knocking him down like a flung doll. In that moment, he should have been a dead man.

Somehow, probably because of the shock of the neck wound, the cat was also thrown off balance. Siemel gained the second he needed to roll to the side and scramble to his knees, the spearblade once more leveled and weaving for a thrust. As lithe as any cat, Sasha regained his feet. He could feel his strength flowing away like sweat, but Assassino was also showing some effect of the heavily bleeding neck wound. Mere feet between them, the two fighters stood panting, eyes locked, for what seemed to Siemel a long time. He knew that if he could drive the blade home once more, he would win. The question was really whether he could stand up to the charge that would make that thrust possible. He did not have long to ponder the question. As if reading his mind, through the blue eyes, the jaguar gave a last terrific roar and exploded straight at Siemel.

It was so fast and from so close a range that Sasha nearly did not manage to lift the spear point in time. As the irresistible impact slammed through the thick shaft of *louro* wood, he saw that the blade had caught the throat too high, and a thrill of horror raced over him; so close were the raking claws that he was sure he had held the shaft too far forward. As he had seen Joaquim Guató do, he pushed forward hard, withdrawing the spear, and in the same motion plunged it deep into the chest. With the last of his draining strength, he pinned the jaguar down, the cutting steel buried near the heart. Assassino fought madly, the lashing of his claws deeply lacerating the spear shaft, scoring the wood as Sasha drove his full weight down. As the tip of the blade passed completely through the chest and grated against the ground on the far side despite the flesh-buried cross-stop, the paw strokes slowed and, with a great shudder, stopped. How long he leaned on the *zagaya* shaft, Sasha Siemel did not know. He did know that Assassino was dead, and he was alive.

For a long time he sat regaining his strength, as Tupi nipped bravely at the dead cat. Finally able to return to his horse, he rode back to the brush-covered body of José Ramos and returned the corpse to the widow, seeing that she and her child were moved down to the big *Fazenda* Descalvados. It was two days before Sasha was able to return to the lonely little clearing in the *capão* that had been the silent arena of one of the greatest known battles between man and beast. Assassino had been largely eaten by the eternal *urubi,* but Siemel was able to salvage the skull as a trophy and to measure the body. Assassino's maggot-crawling hulk was nine feet three inches long and estimated by Siemel—who knew his jaguars like nobody else—at something very near 400 pounds!

In many ways, the spear fight with the great assassin jaguar was a prominent marker along the trail that was Sasha Siemel's life. For a man of such daring and sense of adventure, he was wonderfully human to come to grips with the fact that he had very nearly been the loser of that battle. This seemed to shake him from an interesting angle, possibly influenced by the psychological impact left over from discovering the desolate end of his teacher, Joaquim Guató. No one could ever make the insinuation that Sasha Siemel was afraid of death or dying; that ran counter to every fact of his life. What he did seem worried about, though, was the idea of dying *alone,* food for birds somewhere in the marshes. With the humility to admit that should he come up against another such *tigre* as Assassino, he might indeed become the trophy, he never hunted jaguar as a lone *tigrero* again. He killed many more over his long career with the *zagaya* (the Assassino fight having taken place in the summer of 1928), yet always had someone nearby or with him who would know his fate, if not be of any help in the combat.

In September of 1928, Sasha joined forces with three amateur adventurers: Mamerto Urriolagoita, who later became president of Bolivia; a British photographer named Bee-Mason; and a writer, Julian Duguid, who later returned to Brazil to write Sasha's early biography. Their venture was a journey across the wilderness of the Bolivian *Grán Chaco,* following the route of a Spanish conquistador to the Andes. The trip produced the well-known book by Duguid, *Green Hell,* as well as the later work, *Tiger Man,* which sprang Sasha (Duguid spelled it "Sacha") Siemel into the world adventure spotlight.

Siemel married a talented woman, Edith Bray, a Philadelphian whom he met while giving a lecture in that city in 1938. Tying the knot in 1940 in Rio de Janeiro, they had three children, the youngest, "Sashino," becoming something of an adventurer and author in his own right. For years the Siemel family lived in the Mato Grosso on Sasha's houseboat, the *Adventureira;* Sasha ran hunting safaris and gave lectures in the United States. At one time, he was presented the "Adventurers' Medal" of the Adventurers' Club of New York. When he finally wrote his own story, *Tigrero,* the book did well and further established him as the giant of adventure he really was.

The *tigre* called Death finally slipped past Sasha's flashing blade in Green Lane, Pennsylvania, in February 1970 when he was nearly eighty years of age.

It was my honor to know him slightly, so perhaps you'll take my word for it that never again shall we see his like.

BIBLIOGRAPHY

Aitken, Russell Barnett. *Great Game Animals of the World.* New York: MacMillan Co., 1968.

Baillie-Grohman, W.A. and F. *The Master of Game—The Oldest English Book on Hunting.* London: 1904, translation of *Gaston Phoebus,* Paris: circa 1510.

Capstick, Peter Hathaway. *Death in the Long Grass.* New York: St. Martin's Press, 1977.

Clarke, James. *Man Is the Prey.* New York: Stein & Day, 1969.

Duguid, Julian. *Green Hell.* New York: The Century Co., 1931.

———. *Tiger-Man.* New York: The Century Co., 1932.

Schaller, George B. "Epitaph for a Jaguar," *Animal Kingdom,* New York Zoological Society: April/May 1980.

Siemel, Sasha (Alexander). *Tigrero.* New York: Prentice-Hall, 1953.

Stuart, Hans and Connor, Inez. "Reclassification Proposed for the Leopard," *News Release of U.S. Fish and Wildlife Service of the Department of the Interior,* March 31, 1980.

W. D. M. "Karamojo" Bell

I VORY HUNTER! Lord, what images the very term dredges up from the dark past of the old Africa: long, chanting, sweating lines of tusk-toting porters; sweat-rimed khaki; the delicious waft of cordite smoke on the hot breeze, mingled with that of drying blood and the whine of flies. And the man. Faceless, yet legend, with names like Sutherland, Taylor, Neumann, Stigand—and "Karamojo" Bell—the pure individualists who *did* what so many of us wish we could do: Live our lives on our own terms. Totally self-sufficient in savage and often unexplored lands with dozens of lives hanging on their judgment, the professional elephant hunter was the highest form of Man the Predator, each one as romantic and fearless, as resourceful and steadfast as any knight who ever opened the dragon season or went Holy Grailing. From one point of view, the only difference was that ivory hunting held no requirements of purity. . . .

Since 1661, when a Dutch hunter in South Africa named Pieter Roman achieved the somewhat negative distinction of being first on the very long list of whites killed by African elephants, the profession of ivory hunting has been considered one of the most dangerous and romantic vocations open to the adventure-minded of the recent past. Many were drawn to this tenuous way of life by the early classic writings of Captain Sir William Cornwallis-Harris and Roualeyn Gordon-Cumming, both of whom hunted southern Africa in the 1830s and 1840s and produced some very colorful tales of their exploits. By the 1870s, commercial elephant hunting in southern Africa was, from a practical standpoint, a thing of the past. Since East Africa had not opened up at that time, and would not do so to any great degree until the building of the Uganda Railroad near the turn of the century, things looked mighty bleak for would-be ivory hunters who had the bum luck not to be even born until 1880.

Through the entire fabric of legend that wraps the elite who comprised the ivory hunters, there is one name woven with a bolder thread than that of any other. Absolutely determined to succeed with unorthodox methods others thought insanely perilous; admired for his toughness, bravery and skill by some, while hated by competitors for the same reasons; that name is still guaranteed to provoke as much controversy today as it did in 1923, after the publication of his first book, *The Wanderings of an Elephant Hunter.* That name was Walter Dalrymple Maitland Bell, but the world would know him as "Karamojo" Bell, for the Karamojo region of northeast Uganda where he hunted for five years, ending in 1907.

Although any shooter with the most remote interest in big game can tell you that Bell was famous for his use of extremely light-caliber rifles to kill the largest land animal with precision bullet placement, rather than employing the shoulder artillery of the British "elephant guns" favored by the heavy majority of professionals, those who have not read his scarce books know little of the personal side of this amazing man. His story and his achievements have left a mark on the entire field of big-game hunting which is very unlikely to fade. Certainly, so long as there are elephants and men willing to risk their lives in what Bell himself called "the real classic of all big-game hunting," he will always be the standard against which others will be measured.

The second youngest of a family of ten children, Bell was born in Edinburgh twenty years short of the beginning of this century and orphaned at the age of six. Raised by older brothers whom he resented, Walter's earliest dream was to become a hunter; at first in America, and soon thereafter, in Africa. Shipped off to school, he became almost completely unmanageable, quitting at the age of twelve, when he was apprenticed to a shipping line and sailed to Tasmania. Here he jumped ship, exercising his "highly developed technique of wandering," and took work in a starch factory. Two years later, he was back in Scotland, only to be again sentenced to school, now in Germany. For two years he endured this, at last "escaping" down the Weser River to the sea in a homemade kayak. It foundered, forcing him to sell his beloved shotgun for passage across to Britain. Now sixteen, Bell again went home once more to beg his guardians to outfit him for his obsession of elephant hunting in Africa. The eight years of unrelenting nagging must have built up a cumulative effect on the family; to Bell's disbelief, permission was granted. He was actually going to Africa!

Despite the fact that Bell's brother was suffering from the classic Scottish syndrome of moths in the sporran, he at least provided second-class passage and a secondhand, single-shot Fraser rifle in .303 caliber. Along with a few clothes, some ammunition and precious little money, Bell took ship on a German freighter and passenger vessel for the fabled port of Mombasa, arriving there in 1897, not yet seventeen years old.

At that time, with the Uganda Railroad still far from completion, Mombasa was the jumping-off point for major caravans to the interior, usually under Arab or Swahili command. The trade circuit was to go inland with tobacco, beads, calico, wire and such, returning after an absence of what was often several years with ivory and, clandestinely, slaves. Because slaving was somewhat frowned upon by the Europeans, many captured men were circumcized and then "adopted" under the laws of Islam by their captors. Their "father" then put them to work or out to hire as obedient "sons," although the actual practice was, nonetheless, slavery. It was to one of these caravans that Bell hoped to attach himself, shooting for meat and ivory in exchange for the protection of the expedition. Probably to his good luck, no such arrangement could be made. In those days, modern rifles such as Bell's .303 were unappreciated by the muzzle-loader-armed slavers. Anyway, a white man anxious to join a trading caravan was looked on as the most obvious of spies. Bell's white friends were particularly against his joining up, as they knew the workings of these "black ivory" outfits. Settling temporarily in a remote area, the caravan would

team up with one tribe against another, adding the force of
their several hundred muskets to their new allies' spears in a
bloodbath raid which would provide them with a good haul
of human cargo. Anybody too young, old, ill or pregnant
was put to the sword. It was a life no Britisher could brook,
he was told emphatically. Disappointed, Bell looked
elsewhere for a start.

A short time later, living frugally off his tiny capital, he
ran into a man whom he had met on shipboard who turned
out to be the chap in charge of supplies for the embryo
railroad. According to this man, the company was hiring
white guards. To date, the hospitality of the *nyika* had
proved rather trying to the Indian surveying crews, who
went off on their remote missions in imported American
buckboard wagons drawn by mules from Cyprus, much to
the delight of wild native bloods looking for a bit of spear
practice. Lions, which may or may not have included the
actual pair that became known as the infamous Man-eaters
of Tsavo, had also killed several Indians and mules. The
Indian mule skinners and surveyors went on strike, de-
manding that an armed white man accompany each party.
To Bell, it was "a foresniff of Paradise." He was immediately
accepted for such a position upon it being determined that
he had his own rifle and ammunition, and was ordered up
the line to temporary headquarters at Voi.

For the young Bell, acting as bodyguard and meat hunter
to a survey party in the deep bush must have been a slice of
heaven, although he was shortly to discover that he had
some serious equipment problems. The falling-block action
of the Fraser rifle was of such design that when the .303
cartridge was fired in the chamber after it had been heated
by the sun, the increased pressures caused thereby, due to
the nature of the early cordite propellant (introduced for
the .303 in 1892), made the empty case stick in the rifle and
stubbornly refuse to be extracted. So not only was he
hindered by having a single-shot rifle in the first place, but
he could not reload without taking the time to punch out the
empty case with a ramrod shoved through the barrel from
the muzzle. It was a great handicap for a boy entrusted to

keep his party safe from war parties and lions by means of his rifle, but in reality may have contributed considerably to his later great artistry with a rifle. Knowing he would have no chance for a second shot in a pinch, he learned to make the first one count at all costs, placing his initial bullet with great precision. This was to become his trademark.

Despite the beautiful lines and workmanship of the Fraser, Bell knew that its failure to extract might well lead to somebody getting killed—very likely himself. Meeting a Greek trader at a railroad camp one day, the two men examined each other's rifle, the Greek falling in love with the classy little Fraser. It is not recorded whether Bell went so far as to point out the extraction problem of the .303, but a trade was effected, the Scot getting the Greek's Winchester .450 black-powder, single-shot, falling-block rifle, an older gun but accurate, powerful and a good extractor. With the .450 came a good supply of cartridges of a type Bell had never tried, the hollow copper-point, or "capped," Westley-Richards style. His experience with these bullets would greatly influence his ideas on hunting-bullet design and performance and, therefore, the preferences of unborn generations of riflemen.

Bell found the .450 bullets acceptable on light-skinned animals, such as antelope, but had great difficulty killing buffalo and rhino with them if bone was hit. Made to expand quickly, the bullets lacked penetration and stability, and were generally discontinued early in this century. This erratic performance of the hollow copper-points nearly got Bell lionized by the first big cat at which he ever fired.

One dawn, a bunch of his men came storming into camp with the news that a lion was drinking at a nearby waterhole. Bell grabbed the Winchester and went out immediately, in the company of an African carrying a "gas-pipe" muzzle-loading gun. Although it was the dry season and much grass had been burned off, there was still some left near water and also plenty of thick bush—excellent cover, if you happened to be a lion. As the two men approached, only thirty yards away they saw the lion's head in some grass. There was a deep growl of warning. Instantly, Bell fired at the head, expecting to blow it off with his new gun and heavy bullet. To his consternation, the grass patch seemed to explode, but he saw nothing to permit a finishing shot. Then, before Bell could get off another round, the cat streaked into a nearby clump of dense bush and quieted down.

With applied wishful thinking, the African told Bell that the lion must be dead. Hoping that it would prove to be a brilliant observation, the man who would become "Karamojo" nonetheless thought that a quick look from a tree might be prudent before entering the bush. Balancing his rifle across some branches, he was in the act of hauling himself up, when, out of the corner of his eye, he caught a streak of tawny motion shortly accompanied by a terrific roar. The lion was in full charge at him—his hands empty of the rifle, *simba* just two feet away. With incredible reflexes, Bell just had time to jerk his legs up and out of the way as the lion tore by beneath him. Turning on the African, who had started to run down the open slope, the lion gained rapidly. Bell dropped out of the tree with the rifle and drew a bead on the racing cat, but couldn't shoot as the line of fire included the speeding figure of the terrified black. Just as the lion was about to pounce, the tribesman tripped and fell flat, the lion soaring over his body to land a few yards past. As he swung around to catch the man, Bell stuck another of the .450 slugs into the shoulder, distracting the feline but not even knocking it off its feet. The African wasted no time in dashing off at an angle and soon joined Bell back at the foot of the tree, sweating buckets but grinning broadly. Bell thought he'd never heard such a liar when the man calmly told him he often dodged lions with that trick.

The nameless African may have done little previous lion dodging, but he certainly seemed to have pluck. As the wounded cat had again gone into cover, the black returned to camp, recruited a team of enthusiastic beaters and assembled them near the bush where the lion was lying up. They were carrying everything from torches to bush knives, loaded with various noisemakers to drive the cat out. Bell confides that as they went fearlessly into that heavy stuff, knowing a wounded lion was in residence, he was himself scared stiff that somebody was about to get the chop. The performance of his rifle on the shoulder shot did little to bolster his confidence in the weapon, either. However, the last bullet had taken a lot of moxie out of the big cat, and, although he was no wilting lily when the beaters put him up at a couple of yards, the excited mob incredibly swarmed over him with clubs and knives so ferociously that Bell had difficulty in placing a finishing shot without hitting somebody.

When the Scot had a chance to look over the carcass, he found that the copper-point bullets had completely blown up on impact, causing minor flesh wounds called "cratering." It had been damned good luck that the first head shot had broken the jaw, so that none of his men had been bitten. Combined with earlier experience with buffalo and rhino, Bell reached the conclusion (which I share with few reservations) that would guide the rest of his hunting career, although he had not yet seen his first elephant: A bullet that breaks up is worse than worthless. Penetration is what counts. A bullet that cannot reach the vitals it is aimed at, no matter what the intervening tissue and bone, not only does not kill quickly and reliably but vastly compounds the element of danger to the hunter. A wounded animal is ten times more likely to kill or injure the shooter than an unharmed one. The answer for dangerous game, especially thick-skinned, heavily boned species, is the "solid" bullet, precisely placed from a rifle of sufficient caliber to provide the power needed to penetrate, but not so heavy as to be awkward or overpowered.

For the nonhunter, a word of explanation is in order here. The great majority of both commercially produced rifle cartridges and those custom hand-loaded by shooters who demand specifications of finer tolerances than the mass-produced product, good though they are, are one form or another of the "expanding," or soft-point, bullet types. There are as many individual styles of this type as there are brands of deodorants, but the concept of their ideal performance is, upon entering animal tissue, to expand, or "mushroom," thus causing more damage in passage, up to the skin on the far side of the animal. The basis for this design and school of thought is the idea of so-called "hydrostatic shock," the notion that since meat is more than 90 percent water, the kinetic energy, or "shocking power," of the bullet—usually expressed in foot-pounds—will remain in the body, expending all its crushing *theoretical* knockdown power there.

At the risk of achieving literary overkill, permit a practical example of the invalidity of the topspin logic used by those shooters who worship at the shrine of massive foot-pounds and shocking power. Anybody who has ever shot an American woodchuck with one of the very high-velocity centerfire .22s, such as the .22-250, knows that a hit produces pretty violent damage. We won't go through the figures, but the ratio between the foot-pounds of energy and the six-pound weight of the animal is a hefty 216–to–1. Under these circumstances, "hydrostatic shock" is, without any question, a valid concept. *But* see what happens when the same principle is applied to, for example, a 12,000-pound bull elephant. If he is tagged with a big slug from a .458 Winchester Magnum (which produces 4,050 foot-pounds at 100 yards from the muzzle), the ratio here is 1–to–3, which is saying that the elephant's size gives him more than 600 *times* the resistance to each foot-pound of shock than the woodchuck has. Clearly, foot-pounds are of no more than theoretical worth under field conditions except on quite small game. Even on an animal as large as a white-tail deer there may be some value to "shock," but in Africa, where things have a tendency to bite you, reliance on the effectiveness of foot-pounds is best confined to the ballistics tables.

The other side of the concept is shared today by most professional hunters and game officers I know. "Shock," or impact, counts for little *per se*, whereas penetration in an undeviating line through obstructing tissue to a *vital organ* is paramount. Because soft-points, usually with a soft lead or alloy tip and a harder jacket covering the remainder of the bullet, are designed to change their shape and expand to a larger diameter, they also tend to act unpredictably in many cases, either "cratering" at high velocities (as Bell experienced), or otherwise rupturing—the separation of the core from the jacket—which may give unreliable performance.

The alternative is the "solid," or full metal-jacket, bullet, which is created to do just one thing: penetrate to and through the organ at which it is directed. It should not "rivet" on the heaviest bone, lose stability or expand. Many hunters who have not used the solid decry it on the supposition that it "just whisks through game without doing any damage." This is completely untrue, provided the shooter has a reasonable knowledge of his game's anatomy. Because of its cohesiveness, the solid, upon contact with bone, is very deadly, sending shards of that bone through the body at high velocities. Of course the primary advantage of the solid remains that, if aimed properly, it will *reach* the heart, brain or spine with instantly fatal consequences.

This whole solid/soft-point business may seem to be overblown, but it is the key to Bell's unmatched success and critical to his case. When Bell started hunting in Africa, and to a large degree even today, the accent was on the use of the heaviest possible rifle calibers for any dangerous game. Of course "heavy" is a relative term, but you'll get the drift from Arthur H. Neumann, who hunted ivory professionally for three years, beginning in 1893. "I was never in favor of big bores. . . ." said Neumann. "I had been laughed at by many for starting on such a hunting trip with no larger rifle, but I was always an advocate of small bores."

Small bores? Neumann used the ponderous and powerful .577 Nitro Express almost exclusively, this howitzer throwing a 750-grain bullet with over 7,000 foot-pounds of muzzle energy! To him and his fellows, this was a "small bore"! This double-barreled rifle weighed approximately sixteen pounds empty, an interesting comparison to Bell's .256, which tipped in at five and a quarter pounds. Yet, by the standards of the time, it *was* a small bore in comparison to the 10-, 8-, and 4-gauges (.935 caliber) favored by older hands on the ivory trail. A 4-gauge would weigh thirty-five pounds and fired a four-ounce bullet. Hard to believe; even these guns were of mild and sweet disposition, viewed in the light of Sir Samuel Baker's monster rifle called "Baby." This brute was, in effect, a 2-gauge, firing a one half-pound explosive shell too big to be called a bullet! Despite its obvious effectiveness, Baker was none too fond of it, as the recoil did roughly as much damage to the unfortunate behind the stock as to the target.

It was in the face of this big-bore concept that Walter Bell formed his own ideas. On the logic that correct solid-bullet design and a good knowledge of game anatomy was the best combination of attributes adding up to instant kills, Bell further deduced that, since precise placement of the shot was the key, the caliber size used shouldn't matter, so long as it was powerful enough to penetrate deeply. It wasn't the diameter of the bullet hole, but where it was located that mattered most. If a .303 solid, or, for that matter, a .275, or even the tiny .256 could reach the vital spots of a bull elephant, then why should a man carry an eighteen- or twenty-pound rifle around? The lighter guns were far faster, more comfortable, did not recoil nearly so much as the big bores. A man could also run a lot farther with a light rifle and not be out of breath when he got a chance for a shot. Of course, the shooting would have to be exact, but weren't the advantages worth it?

It has been said, and correctly, I think, that Bell was indirectly responsible for the deaths of perhaps as many as one hundred men who tried to imitate him and his small-bore methods without the benefit of his skill or luck. Most of these hunters were killed by big game, usually wounded, which they could not stop or turn in a charge with their light rifles. To be effective, the light guns actually had to hit the brain or spine of an animal to cause instant death, having no "stopping power" to stun with a near miss passing close to a vulnerable organ. A big bullet such as the .600 Nitro Express or the .577 could knock an elephant—in full charge—cold with a central head shot that missed the brain. A .303 wouldn't make him blink. They missed. Bell didn't.

After the lion fiasco with the copper-capped bullets, Bell switched to a Lee-Metford, the newest British Army service rifle in .303 caliber, firing a round-nose, solid, nickel-jacketed slug weighing 215 grains. All the while he worked as a bodyguard and meat hunter for the railroad, he kept trying to make native contacts to put together a safari into the interior at last to hunt elephant, his finances being far inferior to the cost of mounting his own expedition. Unfortunately, the natives were all wary of any white, and he stayed with the railroad until Nairobi and beyond were reached, one day hearing that an explorer was coming up the line. An excited Bell met with the man, an English-speaking German headed for the undefined but elephant-crammed Uganda-Abyssinia (Ethiopia) border. The explorer was reputed to have unquestioned references, and local traders offered him almost unlimited credit. Applying to the man for a position as a hunter for the expedition, Bell was hired on the provision that he give a month's notice to the railroad while the German crossed Lake Victoria to Entebbe, on the Uganda shore, where he would assemble the safari. The stranger seemed delighted to have the teenage wanderer, even saying that the ivory Bell would shoot would contribute nicely to help defray the costs of the expedition. Walter would be sent for in a month's time, after the trip had been organized. Itchy, he counted off the days, resigned from the railroad and settled down to await the message summoning him to Entebbe and glory.

He was still waiting weeks later, nearly broke and without any place to stay. Whereas the company had been feeding and housing him, now that he had quit he was on his own. In desperation, Bell made a deal with a native village on the lake shore, near Port Florence (Kisumu), getting the use of a hut and food in exchange for killing hippo for them. Bell says that the hut and the people, complete nudists, were clean, but the native fare was drab and tiresome. At night, mosquitoes swarmed the village, only kept down by ferocious clouds of smoke which made life as uncomfortable as the insects themselves did. With very little quinine to start with, malaria began to ravage the Scot, but he stuck to the village, awaiting the summons from across the lake. At last, word filtered over the water. The expedition had departed some time ago without any notification to Bell. Crushed with disappointment, with hardly a penny and burning with fever, he was defeated, at least for this round. Without sufficient capital, he would be forced to return to Scotland to try to pry some more funds out of his brother for a proper ivory safari. Traveling steerage back to Britain, he took heart that at least now he had some practical African experience. There *were* still elephants, and he knew roughly where to find them. He would be back.

Bell didn't know it when he left, but it would be close to three years before he would return to his destiny of Africa. Again denied the money to outfit himself properly, he got stale news of the Alaskan Klondike gold rush and decided to give it a go. With a .360 Fraser and 160 cartridges, he caught a steamer for Canada and then a train cross-country in the company of a fellow highlander named Mickey, a huge man with a gentle disposition. Mickey had been sent for by his brother, who had a paying claim in the Klondike. When Mickey suggested that the rifleman join him in working for the brother, Bell accepted, the pair paddling down the Yukon River and hiking overland to the claim. During the whole trip downriver, not a head of game was to be seen, the demand for food, particularly meat, having driven all the moose and caribou far from any area of human activity.

At the claim site, Bell was welcomed and paid ten dollars a day to work in the "placer" mining operation. With the thick permafrost, every grain of gold-bearing dirt had to be melted free before being washed for its yellow treasure, a task requiring the tedious heating of rocks in fires to melt the frozen soil, which was then shoveled into boxes and hoisted to the surface by muscle power. Despite the good pay, Bell rapidly decided that he was a shooter, not a shoveler. His thoughts shifted to the food shortage and the potential profit in meat hunting. At two dollars per pound when rarely available, it seemed a lucrative project, provided that he could find some way to freight the meat from the remote game areas back to Dawson.

Leaving the placer mine, Bell went to Dawson and formed a very casual partnership with a dog-sled-and-team owner who, as was the custom of the gold camps, used only his first name, Bill. The two men found a good hunting area in the mountains some 200 miles from Dawson and got there before the freeze. The arrangement was that Bell would do the hunting and prepare the carcasses, while Bill freighted the meat back to Dawson on the dog sled. Killing a grizzly bear and two moose one day, they let the meat freeze solid and built a large hut nearby. As the larder was growing toward the first shipment, Bell learned much American bushcraft from his partner, including how to make and use snowshoes. As he carried on hunting, Bell also found reinforcement for his precision-bullet-placement theory. With only 103 rounds left for the all-important and modestly powered .360, each shot had to count. And so it did. With Bill off with the first load of meat, leaving the youngster alone for twenty-seven days, the meat continued to pile up, although much was lost to wolves because Bell had only two dogs to help him drag back the manageable pieces to the hut. Delighted by the size of the stockpile on his return, partner Bill made ready to sled another load back, claiming to have deposited the proceeds of the first in a bank, having gotten a dollar seventy-five a pound for the whole works, including the bones.

The partnership went on until early spring, Bell even killing moose with Bill's borrowed Colt single-action revolver, a .45 caliber seven and a half-inch barreled "big iron" sixshooter, by chasing them into deep snow and brain-shooting them from close range. A trusting soul despite his experience with the "explorer," Bell never insisted on a division or accounting of the money that was supposed to be piling up back at the Dawson bank. Nor was he suspicious when, leaving one day with another sled of meat, Bill asked for the return of the Colt on the grounds that the wolves were becoming very bold on the trail. Taking an extralarge cargo of frozen meat which he said he could sell to some new claims on the way to Dawson, Bill mushed his huskies and was gone. For good.

Bell stuck around, continuing to hunt until the spring thaw began to spoil his stockpile, worrying more and more as Bill became increasingly overdue. At last, with three dogs,

Bell hiked the 200 miles back to Dawson, hearing no word of Bill from any claim he passed. Of course, it was the same story when he got to town; nobody could tell him of the whereabouts of this particular "Bill," the confusion compounded with the fact that Bell didn't even know the man's last name! He had completely conned the Scottish kid and disappeared without a trace. Whatever the case, Bell was back in the old spot of being stranded in the middle of East Nowhere with nothing to show for a lot of hard work. Fortunately, a handy little war came along that bailed him out. To put the frosting on his salvation, it was even in Africa!

Arriving at the recruiting office in Calgary, having sold his rifle for passage through Nome and the Aleutian Islands, Bell found 5,000 men competing for the quota of just 500 recruits to go to South Africa to fight the Boers. Nobody had much of an idea who these Boers might be, or what the war was all about, and cared less. The lure of travel and adventure was irresistible for most of the motley crew trying to join the Canadian Mounted Rifles, a rowdy crowd of hunters, trappers, cowboys and backwoodsmen of indeterminate profession. Although the competition was fierce, Bell shot a perfect score and passed his physical exam to be accepted, then spent what he had left—forty dollars—on a horse which the government would immediately buy back from him for his use.

Bell's participation in the Boer War is quite fuzzy, mostly left blank by him in his later writings. Of the conduct of the campaigns, he calls them merely a series of marches that killed a lot of horses, climaxed with distant and largely ineffective exchanges of rifle fire with the enemy. In one instance, though, a chance bullet killed his horse from under him, and, caught in the open, he was taken prisoner. The Boers couldn't make head or tail out of why a "colonial" Scot would be fighting on the English side and, on the presumption that he was young and misguided, treated him well. One night, instead of going to the wagon where he and a fellow prisoner were supposed to sleep, the two ducked into a stand of corn and escaped to the British command with little trouble. With the assumption that the two ex-prisoners had gained a personal knowledge of the enemy and his ways during their captivity, they were both posted as scouts to headquarters.

Eventually, and without further comment from Bell, the war was over, and he managed to take discharge and shipment back to Britain. Since he had left school, he had been a sailor, a bodyguard and meat hunter on two continents, a miner, a laborer in Tasmania and a front-line soldier and scout. But now, after fifteen years of frustration, he could at last do what he had dreamed of. At twenty-one Bell had come into his inheritance and immediately commenced outfitting for his third trip to Africa. He was going to be a professional ivory hunter. He had made it!

Although to this date (1901) Bell had not yet seen his first elephant in the wild, his selection of weapons for the coming venture remained in line with his experiences. His friendship with the master gunsmith of Edinburgh, Daniel Fraser, gave him plenty of exposure to try the heavy doubles; from the beating he took in testing them from the bench, entirely too much exposure. As Bell observed, the gunmakers' catalogs of this period were "marvellous" and exciting publications, carefully designed and illustrated, not to quite frighten a sportsman into canceling his shooting trip to Africa or India, but to convince him that he would be placing himself in mortal peril without the immense shocking power of the firm's fine double-express rifles at his disposal. The laws of physics being no different in 1901 than they are now, little mention was made of the fact that for every action there is an equal and opposite reaction. If tons of bullet energy were blasting from the muzzles of these shoulder cannons, then there was a likewise brain-rattling recoil slammed into the shoulder of the shooter. Bell would stick with a pair of sporter .303s converted from military rifles, each with ten-shot clips. He doesn't specifically mention purchasing it from Fraser, but Bell also bought a mean little Mauser pistol with a detachable shoulder stock that, in effect, turned it into a semiautomatic carbine. It wasn't meant for elephants but turned out to be mighty handy in some circumstances.

The "Lunatic Line" having snaked its bloody way to the end of the line at Kisumu on Lake Victoria by now, Bell rode the train through his old haunts until reaching the lake. Undecided where to mount his first trip, he determined to scout around a bit. Based on the advice of a steamer-captain friend, Uganda seemed a good area to try, and he proceeded to Entebbe, where the explorer had left from so long ago. Near here, he had a chance to try the .303s with their solid bullets, killing a buffalo with a single shot, which broke the hip and raked all the way through the bull's rear to his front, to catch the chest vitals. For sure, no penetration problems here!

Pushing farther up-country in search of elephant, heading for and reaching Unyoro (more commonly known as Bunyoro), Bell found the area reputed to have large and fine ivory. There was a problem even then of considerable crop damage to the native *shambas*, or cultivation areas, by raiding jumbo, and the local people were extremely well disposed toward anybody who professed to want to kill elephants. Not only would the locals get the meat, but shooting would also drive the herds away from their crops. Before Bell could begin hunting, however, he came down with a rousing dose of dysentery and was forced to call upon a man named Ormsby to whom he had a letter of introduction from a mutual pal in Entebbe.

Something of a character, Ormsby took Bell in and cured him with quinine and liberal draughts of Epsom salts. In spite of not being a hunter himself (Ormsby *was* involved in gunrunning with an ex-missionary named Stokes, who was later hanged by the Belgians), nevertheless he had been in the Unyoro region long enough to confirm to Bell that elephant were all over the place, their ivory long, heavy and of the most valuable "soft" texture. A price would have to be paid for them, however, as this was the rainy season, and the whole country was smothered in high grass. It would be hard, miserable going, but at least the large native population would not be underfoot, as the rains confined their activities to the villages. Using Ormsby's place as headquarters, Bell started off on his first elephant hunt.

One point that Bell's detractors frequently make is that many of the elephant he killed were unsophisticated and found right out in the open, particularly in Uganda. This is true and unquestionably did give him an edge; modern hunting is generally in heavy cover, making it much harder. On the other hand, these elephants had to be handled as perfectly in the stalk and kill as any others today, or the sounds of a dying tusker would invariably panic the survivors and any other elephants in hearing. For example, consider the first elephants Bell ever saw. . . .

Eight big bulls were lounging around a mud hole, quite a sight even for the time. Today, a pair of shootable bulls found together would be a rarity. As Bell made his approach, he remembered what a soldier from a nearby garrison had told him of the soldier's own great experience with the brain shot, having claimed to have killed two with this method. According to the man, the brain was located very high up in the top of the skull where, as Bell put it, "a man would have a bowler hat three sizes too small for him." Secure in the reliability of this piece of intelligence, Bell attacked the eight elephants, blazing away at the tops of their heads. After six "perfectly" placed bullets to this region, he began to wonder if the soldier had shot a couple of elephants with freak brain placements, as it was for damned sure that wasn't where *these* tuskers carried their brains. So ineffectual were the tiny bullets through the spongy, honeycomb bone of the top of the head that, although they moved off, the animals were absolutely unconcerned with the wounds. Catching up with several of the bulls, Bell was amazed to see that they had even returned to feeding as they ambled along.

When one stopped at a small puddle to squirt water over his back, Bell shot him with the little .303 just behind the shoulder, where he thought the heart should be. This, at least, brought a reaction from the tusker—and what a reaction! He instantly bolted away at top speed, trumpeting and roaring, then stopped and staggered, falling to the ground. His dying sounds electrified the rest of the bulls and probably every other elephant within earshot, clearing the whole area before Bell could get away another shot. He would never forget the effect of the sounds and swore to himself to learn the brain shot or die trying (which was a distinct possibility with such light rifles).

The next thing, he thought, smoking by the carcass of his first bull, was to find out for a fact the brain's location. But how? Leaving a couple of men, he hiked off back to Ormsby's and got a long, two-man logging saw. Having had his men skin the skull and remove it from the body, he had it cut exactly in two on a line between the tusks, down from front to back, no easy job in the damp heat and growing swarms of flies. Of course, the brain was nowhere near where the soldier had said it was, being in the center, rear portion of the skull, just forward of and slightly higher than the ear holes, depending, of course, upon the relative position of the animal's head in life. With his sketchbook, Bell—who was later to have one of his amateur paintings hung by the Royal Academy—drew careful "before" and "after" pictures of the anatomy. At last he really knew where to aim, starting his career of becoming probably the finest technician of brain shooting elephant who ever lived. True, some other hunters employed a brain shot sometimes, but it was literally a hit-or-miss proposition. Bell even learned to hit the brain from a rear angle, drilling his long, slender little bullets through the massive neck muscles and the back of the head. No one else I have ever heard of, even in modern times, has mastered this almost impossible angle.

In this particular bull, his first, the brain measured twelve inches by six inches, and the tusks scaled a fine eighty-one and seventy-eight pounds. As Bell does not mention any one elephant being especially better toothed than the others, we can presume that the bachelor herd may have represented as much as 1,200 or more pounds of ivory.

Over the following months in Unyoro, Bell began to perfect his hunting style as he gained more and more practical experience. The day after bisecting the elephant's skull, he applied what he had learned and killed several more tuskers with perfect brain shots, and was well on his way to the perfection of that art. Still, there was a lot more to successful commercial ivory hunting than that.

The next trick that he had to learn was the art of shooting elephants in a group without having the entire herd scatter in fear. Even with the instant death brought by a brain shot, should a falling bull bump into another, the whole group will panic. For whatever reason, possibly because they think it is a thunderclap, elephants do not necessarily take alarm at the close sound of a rifle shot if the brained animal just rolls over or falls into the kneeling position, remaining balanced, the head swinging from side to side on the big, elastic neck muscles. This phenomenon was common when I was conducting hunting safaris in Zambia and Botswana. After a careful stalk resulting in the death of the best tusker with a brain shot, the accompanying animals would normally ignore the old boy, figuring he had just decided to have a snooze. We would retreat carefully until the remaining elephants naturally drifted away rather than try to scare them off and risk a charge. Bell, of course, would regularly knock them off, one by one.

Although famous for his brain shooting, Bell was by no means against the application of the heart shot, particularly on lone bulls or those already disturbed. He preferred to place his small bullets into the thick network of arteries just over the heart, where even the diminutive .256 was a sure killer. The arteries are more vulnerable to the tiny hole left by the small bore than the massive heart itself; the great Jim Sutherland once reported that he had shot an elephant through the heart with a .303, only to have the bull travel more than a mile and live twelve hours! The problem, I believe, lies in the springy heart muscle itself, which tends to seal up the bullet hole, keeping leaking to a minimum.

Curiously, Bell later somewhat modified the position he had always maintained as the most effective way to kill animals other than elephant. Whereas he unequivocably stated in earlier works that the solid was the most deadly missile, even on light-skinned game such as lion—of which he killed sixteen alone with the .256 and .275 using solid bullets, all one-shot kills—he wrote, towards the end of his life in the early 1950s, that the neck shot was equally effective with the soft-point bullet at high velocities, perhaps even more so. His logic in singling out the neck as the only vital area close to the skin's surface is irrefutable. Yet any student of this great hunter must question Bell's own African experience in this area.

For one thing, he himself writes that he never carried anything but solids. Further, the really high-velocity calibers he refers to as being so effective against the neck were not developed—by his own observation—until the 1940s, and by that time he had long since stopped hunting in Africa. We know his home in the highlands was cleverly built between two famous "deer forests," with Bell located in the middle. He would happily shoot his neighbors' red deer when they strayed onto his property, quite legally. Undoubtedly, he used the neck shot on many of these animals with excellent results, but I cannot see where he could have tested this shot on Cape buffalo and rhino, both of which would seem to have large neck areas. Further, I am all the more positive that he never experienced high-velocity soft-point neck shots in Africa. He would have quickly observed that *nyika* or *miombo* scrub-bush conditions tend to preclude the use of light, fast bullets, because intervening brush frequently deflects or even ruptures them en route to the target. Also, the heavy neck skin of both these animals would almost certainly cause cratering of very light soft-points. Bell was undoubtedly influenced by American friends, such as the late Colonel Townsend Whelen, often called the "dean of American riflemen," who edited and assembled the manuscript of his last book, *Bell of Africa*. It's worth noting that Whelen, a great cartridge developer and fond of high velocities, never hunted in Africa himself.

While Bell was hunting in Unyoro, there was a bloody outbreak of mutiny among Sudanese troops, who, denied permanent female companionship at their posts, promptly whipped and killed every white officer they could find. It was quite an affair, the Sudanese grabbing all government property and arms, and paralyzing the countryside with the reintroduction of open slavery. When the mutiny was at last put down, the British became much more strict with their laws, which put a severe crimp in the caravan trading business. Clearly, some place out of reach of the bothersome authorities and their laws was required by the Muhammadan ivory/slave circuit, and it appeared to lie in the northeast of Uganda, an untouched land of savagery and raiding known ominously as Karamojo, today called Karamoj*a*. It was also reputed to have large numbers of huge-tusked elephants. Bell packed his bag.

In 1902, the town of Mumias at the foot of snow-capped Mt. Elgon was the last vestige of law and order, there being a government post with troops located there. Beyond Mumias, the starting point for caravans bound for the whole Lake Rudolph Basin, only the strength of one's party provided the least bit of safety. The laws of supply and demand being what they are and were, the first traders got much of the ivory already stockpiled at very low prices, the value of the commodity rising steadily as demand held and supply fell. As the natives had no guns at all, the only supply of new trade ivory was from snaring elephant, which was only marginally effective. Still, these relatively few tusks fetched extraordinary prices. When competition grew beyond reason for this ivory, some of the more enterprising traders decided it would be eminently more practical to steal and raid than pay, and so developed a massive campaign of intertribal warfare, assuring the outcome of these campaigns with their muskets. This caused the entire Karamojo region to become a segmented armed camp, nobody trusting anybody, particularly not strangers. This state of affairs also created the old problem Bell had encountered when trying to join an expedition in Kenya. As he was white and slaving was the order of the day in Karamojo, no trader would sell him donkeys, no Muhammadan would work for him and information about the interior was either a collection of straight lies or a casual shrug.

At first, Bell couldn't figure out why he was being treated with such difficulty. Later, upon crossing the Turkwell River, which flowed from Mt. Elgon and marked the limit of white law, he realized the atrocities being conducted on the other side of this aquatic "border." As the traders were an extremely rubbery batch of cookies who understood that the whites could often reach far beyond what seemed to be their jurisdiction in lightning punitive raids, the very presence of one of them in the traders' own backyard could spell trouble. Bell admits to being surprised that, considering the stakes, the trading community wasn't firmer in its resistance to his expedition, such as poisoning him or having his throat cut.

You may have noticed, however, that Bell was not easily dissuaded from anything he set his mind to. He got up a safari of non-Islamics: native Baganda, Kavirondo and WaNyamwezi men, using bullocks as heavy transport. The government agent at Mumias was a good sort and arranged for eight .577 Snider carbines for Bell's *askaris* to fight off possible trouble and "instill confidence" in his porters. What was really interesting about the agent's offer of the carbines was that there was no ammunition for them. Digging through the loose cartridges at the only store in Mumias, looking for .577s, Bell noticed that the Martini-Henry .450 cartridges had the same size base as the .577s and would fit in the chambers of the rifles, although the bore size was far too big. The effect would be like trying to blow a small marble through a sewage pipe; it could be done but would hardly be very effective or accurate. Or so Bell thought. In actuality, the *askaris* were such god-awful shots, anyway, that the odds of hitting something they were firing at were actually improved as the bullet, careening down the larger barrel, was guaranteed to fly just about anywhere except where aimed. This turned out to be precisely the effect, and Bell records that, during the trip, both hyenas and jackals were regularly killed in very poor light by his intrepid marksmen!

For his own battery, Bell now had a .303 Lee Enfield bolt-action repeater, a .275 Rigby Mauser (the British nonmetric designation for the 7 × 57 mm. Mauser caliber), a double-barreled .450–.400 and the Mauser pistol with the detachable stock. Leaving Mumias with a notable lack of enthusiasm

on the part of the populace, who normally put on a big send-
off for departing caravans, Bell and his men marched for
seven days to the Turkwell River. Injun country clearly lay
ahead.

The first Karamojong people were met immediately after
crossing the Turkwell. (Bell in his books calls them "Ka-
ramojans," although this is an incorrect anglicization from
the correct term "Karamojong.") Between the river and the
nearest sizable village were about 150 miles of scattered
settlements of "poor" or non-cattle-owning Karamojong,
who scratched out a living by snare hunting. This tribe
enjoyed a ferocious reputation among the traders, and with
very good reason. As is the common custom with several
African groups, manhood was achieved by proving one's
worth by murder. If you hadn't killed somebody—man or
woman, asleep or awake, armed or defenseless—you were
regarded as something of an underachiever and denied the
status of full manhood, along with all the goodies attached to
this lofty station.

It's difficult for the outside mind to comprehend the
seeming lack of logic among the Karamojong in not stipulat-
ing that the victim had to be vanquished in armed combat,
or some other situation that might get the dusky knight-
errant hurt or dead himself, thereby proving the bravery of
the deed. Even among the related Masai of Tanzania and
southern Kenya, fierce blood-and-milk-drinking lion hunters who gained manhood in the old days by spearing a lion
or an enemy single-handed, it was the degree of danger
associated with the act that brought the greatest glory,
similar to the American Plains Indian "counting coup" by
striking an armed enemy with his hand or a ceremonial stick
or bow. Not the Karamojong. A woman murdered by a knife
thrust in her sleep was as great a trophy as another warrior
killed in a spear fight. The only sign given of the sex of the
victim was the customary commemoration of the deed by
tattooing the right side of the killer if the prey had been a
man and the left if female. Obviously, due to this custom,
there was never any shortage of young Karamojong on the
prowl for strangers, particularly stragglers from a caravan.

While Bell was hunting in Karamojo, there were three attacks on entire large and heavily armed trading caravans by this tribe of very tall, lanky spearmen, whose women were strangely short and squat. To suggest that these ambushes were successful would be a masterpiece of understatement. The first two outfits were wiped out, slaughtered to the last defender *without the Karamojong attackers losing a man*! The third assault must have been a touch sloppy; although again there were no native casualties, one trader did survive and escape. Obviously, the traders could not have been very pleased with the loss of three complete caravans, along with all their men and goods, but strangely enough they did not overly object to the Karamojong brazenly picking off stragglers, and anybody caught at a disadvantage in that country was almost actuarily dead. The reason for this apathy over the murders of their own men was simple: desertion. As most of the personnel of these caravans were themselves slaves, the certainty of achieving increased ventilation at the hands of the Karamojong while escaping greatly dampened any smoldering ideas of running off. Also, this effectively provided a way to keep nonslaves separated from their wages for years. After all, if they couldn't get back to Mumias to complain to the government, how could they force payment?

Bell got off to rather a flat start with the first two spearmen on the banks of the Turkwell; they were generally surly but did come to advise him the next morning of the location of four big bull elephant that had passed near their sleeping place during the night. Unimpressed with his puny rifles, they wanted to see the white man make a fool of himself. Bell shot two of the bulls over the heart after a long walk, one of them a single-tusker with one extremely fine tooth. The two Karamojong, who were suspected by the safari of setting up an ambush, had an obvious change in their attitude toward the Scot, and word quickly got around the scrub country that watching the "red man" with his little guns was good fun and provided lots of free meat.

Hunting his way with good results, Bell arrived at the first large village, a headquarters for the traders called Mani-

Mani, some 150 miles from the Turkwell. Along the way, he had his first confrontation with the Karamojong of several to come and began to make the reputation that would eventually lead, over the next five years he hunted the large area, to a good relationship with the people, despite a series of potentially deadly showdowns.

The first of these confrontations was not really the fault of the Karamojong, but a misunderstanding. Knowing the custom of casual murder that pervaded the land, Bell was furious when told by his interpreter that five of his men were missing among the clusters of small villages. Suspecting foul play, he took five of his *askaris* and quickly cut out a large part of the Karamojong cattle herd. As might have been anticipated, this was not much appreciated by the natives, and in a few minutes Bell and his men were facing a good 400 highly motivated spearmen. The defiant little group of outsiders stood their ground, their leader ready with his ten-shot rifle and his Mauser pistol charged with the same number of rounds. Bell was not bluffing—he thought there was a good chance that if he killed the first few Karamojong, the rest would run before his new rapid-fire guns. He must have looked determined, because before it came to iron blades versus nickel-jacketed bullets, some elders, who had likely heard of him, lost their nerve, picking up and throwing grass in the traditional gesture for unconditional peace.

Not relaxing, Bell asked for his porters. He was told that the elders didn't know where they were but were certain that no harm had come to them. Telling them to go and bring the men back unharmed, the rifleman threatened to kill all the cattle (a very serious matter, as wealth was measured in cattle) and a generous assortment of the people, too. Almost immediately, the missing porters showed up, unhurt, having simply gotten lost in the maze of huts. The war was called off, but Bell always thought that his determination to protect any member of his party to the death probably carried far and wide that he was a "red man" best left alone.

The illegal slave and ivory traders were not exactly dancing in the streets of Mani-Mani in celebration of Bell's arrival there, but the Scot was most interested to meet the chap in charge, a very unusual man named Shundi. This huge, intelligent chief of pirates had been sold into slavery in Mombasa or Zanzibar, after being captured as a child at his native Kavirondo village. With enough smarts to realize that (this being before the "adoption" dodge) the Koran forbade one Muhammadan from keeping another of the faithful as a slave, he adopted the religion and was freed, and his own natural aptitude for business and trading had carried him to the top. This sable Horatio Alger ruled over quite a nasty collection of Arab, Persian, Baluchi and Swahili traders, none of whom were at all pleased with Bell's presence, as he could well be an agent for the white man's law. Any trouble they could possibly stir up for the inter-loper and his safari would be served with the greatest relish.

The traders at Mani-Mani who were so anxious to put Bell into a jam did not wait very long to create a situation. As it was now the dry season and the livestock had to be watered from wells sunk into the groundwater of a nearby dry river bed, the elephant hunter came immediately when brought word of an incident brewing. At the wells, he found a gang of local Karamojong toughs driving his bullocks away from the water, not permitting them to drink from a canvas-lined depression into which the hauled water had been poured. Asking the forty-odd spearmen what was going on, they just laughed and refused to answer. When he told his men to take the beasts back to the water, three of the gang began to beat the animals in the face to drive them off.

Bell was never short on courage nor especially shy. Surrounded by forty armed men, he snatched a heavy war club from one of the nearest and, leaping at one of the bloods hitting the bullocks, struck him over the head as hard as he could. Bell was a big man and in top condition, as well as furious. His dumbfounded reaction on smashing the native hard enough to kill him can be imagined when the war club shattered into splinters and the warrior turned around with a smile on his face. What Bell had forgotten was that all male Karamojong wear a clay headdress into which is molded a feltlike mass of their own and even their ancestors' hair, with inset sockets to hold plumes erect. The headgear had absorbed the shock of the heavy blow like a slab of armor plate.

Africans love nothing better than the unexpected, and the whole group of troublemakers exploded with laughter. Bell was nonplussed, but the laughter was infectious, and he was about to join in when he noticed a brave methodically sticking his spear blade through the irreplaceable groundsheet. That *wasn't* funny. Bell drew the Mauser.

The crowd became very quiet as the carbine stock was attached to the rear of the pistol's grip; now it was finally recognized as a weapon, however weird-looking. At this time in Africa, the prevailing belief was that the power of guns lay in the fire that erupted from the muzzle loaders' black-powder charge. The bullet was considered completely inconsequential, merely opening the skin so that the fire could get in and kill. The notion was firmly entertained that all one had to do to avoid being harmed was to duck upon seeing the first smoke puff. Smugly, everybody got ready to duck, after which they would probably have speared Bell and his men until they looked like a fancy cheese platter full of toothpicks. The "red man" took quick aim and fired. At the flat, bullwhip bark of the Mauser, the warrior who had been piercing the sheet was looking with injured amazement at his ruined spear, shot almost in half. Uh-oh, the Karamojong minds were clearly reflecting on their faces. No smoke! No good. Confused, the spearmen began to move back as Bell tried to tackle the man whose weapon he had destroyed, barely able to hold the powerful native until his men helped secure the man. Some of the crowd were beginning to turn mean, but before anybody could throw a spear, the Scot opened up on them with fast semiautomatic fire from the Mauser. The warriors panicked and ran, the bullets peppering the ground around their feet. Quickly reloading, Bell kept them hopping and scattering out to 500 yards.

Taking custody of his prisoner, Bell put out word that he would be freed upon payment of a fine of ten goats and sheep, which arrived shortly thereafter. Undoubtedly, the Karamojong had been put up to their escapade by the traders, who hoped to have Bell intimidated or even killed. Quite the opposite was the result; rather than thinking of the "red man" as just some sort of poor Arab who couldn't afford a proper caravan, both he and the Mauser, which was dubbed "Bom-Bom," were treated with a new, healthy, vitamin-enriched respect.

To give an idea of the physical aspect of elephant hunting and the fitness required on the part of a hunter, let's go back to the day Bell found a medium-sized herd at eight one morning, having just killed a superb white rhino. The herd was moving along quite well, but, by running hard, Bell was able to catch up and pull alongside for the side brain shot. Each time he killed a tusker, he would lose his position and fall far behind, having to run for a mile or more to get a shot again. It was a fiercely hot day, and the lone man carried no water, despite the hard, almost constant running. When he found a puddle, he would suck at the moisture through clenched teeth to filter out the larval insects swarming in it. All day, without a break, Bell stuck with the herd, killing a total of only fifteen bulls. At sundown, he found himself still following them, when he noticed the body of the dead rhino shot ten long hours ago. They had inscribed a perfect circle! He had probably run and jogged close to thirty miles without food and little water, the dead elephants so widely scattered that it took his crew two days to locate and cut the tusks from the fifteen bulls. *That* was real elephant hunting!

At the death of the Belgian King Leopold II in 1910, a great ivory rush started with the reversion of the lush Lado Enclave to the Sudan. It was a wild time, with the Belgians gone and the Sudanese not yet in authority; murder and theft were common among the whites who swarmed in. From the new Belgian Congo border posts, the heavily armed safaris of freebooters were a threatening sight, and some commandants feared an actual invasion. It was during this period that Bell happened to be paddling his new galvanized canoe down the shore of Lake Albert, leading his men in dugouts by several miles. When a heavy breeze sprang up and created a severe chop, the supply canoes pulled into the shelter of the Belgian post at Port Mahagi, where they were arrested by the Belgian forces and forced to the fort above. Returning, Bell was told what happened by some natives and, figuring it was all some kind of mistake, sent a note up and paddled away. In bare feet, his shoes with his captured men's equipment, he wasn't about to walk four or five hundred yards over sharp rocks.

Bell was almost out of the bay when he was hailed by some Belgian *askaris*, waving a letter from the fort. Turning back, he remained a few yards off the beach with a black paddler while the men came down. The paddler was apprehensive, so Bell was on his guard. The *askaris* came up, and when the one with the letter jumped to hold the canoe, Bell smashed him over the head with his heavy paddle. The shout went up to seize the white man; Bell's man pushed off as the Belgian troops cocked their rifles and started to aim. Bell shot one of them through the arm; the rest fired a blast and ran. Although the range was no more than ten yards, they all missed.

Tempted to kill them, the Scot refrained and paddled hard to get out of range. From the fort, he could tell that somebody was using a sporter rifle, and he actually had the man in his sights but again declined. Shortly, out of rifle range, the fort opened fire with a Nordenfelt cannon, an accurate gun in poor hands that dropped its shells no closer than one hundred yards from the easy target of the canoe. Although Bell felt that even a pair of decent riflemen could have taken the place, he was not anxious for an international incident and so paddled to the British side. Two days later, his men arrived. When the firing had broken out on the beach, everybody in the place except for the prisoners had run to the parapets, including the guards. Bell's men had simply walked out and disappeared into the bush, with the exception of one idiot who had run for the beach and had been shot dead.

Reoutfitting his lost equipment, Bell stayed in the enclave for nine months, hunting largely in the area of Mt. Schwein-furth, where he completed his bag of 210 jumbos, which averaged twenty-seven pounds per tusk. Allowing for the usual 10 percent one-tuskers, this would indicate that the net result of the trip was better than five tons of ivory.

From the Lado Enclave, the growing legend that was now known as "Karamojo" Bell went to Liberia, where he hunted the year of 1911 with moderate success, moving the following year to French Equatoria, where he "jumped off" from Bangui on the Ubangi River. The whole river basin was excellent elephant country, although hitherto difficult to reach. But Bell had solved the problem by ordering a thirty-five-foot-long steam launch from England, which was assembled in sections of about 150 pounds each. It was the perfect boat for hunting the many islands in the Ubangi, as it burned abundant wood for fuel and had a very shallow draught. Bell developed a technique of driving the herds of elephant on the bigger islands into an ambush, using his men to push them ahead and into his rifle. It was immensely profitable shooting but dried up when the animals left the islands at the beginning of the rains. At this point, Bell calculated that he had walked more than 60,000 miles, entirely on foot, in actual elephant hunting and walking to and from hunting areas. This does not count mechanized or animal-back trips.

Heading to the Chari-Chad watershed, Bell continued to add to his bag from the convenience of the steamer, until, one day in 1914, a letter from the commandant of a nearby military outpost mentioned in postscript that war had broken out between Great Britain and her allies and Germany. At once, Bell went back to Bangui, where he sold everything and got passage to London via Bordeaux on a French ship.

Although a rather long-in-the-tooth thirty-four, the elephant hunter was anxious to join the infant Royal Flying Corps as a fighter pilot. He obtained an interview with an "expert" who was to determine his qualification, and when Bell assured him that he knew how to ride a bicycle, he was placed on a list for flight school. After quite a while, and such adventures as a dead-stick landing on a sewage farm (always the hunter, Bell noted the presence of a large number of snipe), he got his solo credentials, and then his official "wings" by landing without engine so short of the permitted mark that he almost hit his commanding officer.

Expecting to go to France, Bell was pleasantly surprised to find himself posted to East Africa under General Jan Smuts. Before he realized it, he was at an airfield nestled beneath Mt. Kilimanjaro, feeling very much at home. His squadron was equipped with B.E.2.C's and Henri Farman fighters, very early and tricky machines which had to be assembled at the field. When they were ready, Bell was chosen to test the first plane, which he did in direct violation of his orders by putting it through a full series of loops and spins that his superiors did not believe possible under unknown tropical air conditions. When he landed, the squadron commander was foaming at the mouth, and Bell found himself having achieved the distinction of being the first pilot to be grounded in the East African campaign.

Miffed, he applied to be posted to ground intelligence, who were delighted to have him with his knowledge of the bush and African languages. For some time, he operated behind enemy lines as a scout and on one occasion met P.J. Pretorius, Smuts's chief scout. The Boer and another man came into Bell's camp with all appearances of having been dropped from an airplane without a parachute—covered with bruises and blood, dirty and with torn clothes. Bell asked them in astonishment what the Hun had been doing to them. With a snort of disgust, Pretorius replied, "Hun, nothing. It was a bloody rhino!"

During this period, Bell was probably the only man in the campaign to have a semiautomatic rifle. A friend of the inventor, Colonel Farquharson, he had gotten one of the prototypes and was out scouting with it one day when he discovered a small detachment of native troops on a river. In perfect position to beat them up pretty badly with the semiauto, Bell was confused by their uniform, which was of a design different from any he had ever seen before. Tempted to open fire, he decided to let them go on the chance that there had been some kind of new uniform issued to friendly troops.

When he made his intelligence report, headquarters went into a mighty flap. The soldiers could not have been friendly. Also, the implication seemed to Second Lieutenant Bell, who was not consulted by the General Staff on the highest matters, that this meant that somehow fresh supplies had gotten through the Allied blockade. Air reconnaissance was indicated, but the R.F.C. had packed up for the rains and granted leave to its pilots. Bell's senior asked for his advice. Karamojo knew of a place nearby that would be a perfect field with a bit of alteration. Requesting an aircraft and four mechanics with a tender, Bell proposed to set himself up with his own private air force, volunteering to fly various intelligence missions. As might be expected, his old commander and the R.F.C. were universally furious, but General Smuts pushed the deal through. With his own personal airplane, ground crew and field, detached from control of his squadron with only Intelligence to answer to, Bell was having the time of his life. From here, he flew all over the front, until a big push was made. Much to his annoyance, his old squadron took over his field, and he was reattached. However, his superiors had now changed their mind about him, and he was welcomed back into the fold.

Bell had a lovely time the next few months, tearing along at a dizzy sixty to seventy miles per hour, dropping ineffective bombs on enemy columns and dodging very accurate return fire while not having either armor plate or a parachute. But even this began to dull in his mind. The Germans had no aircraft in East Africa, so there was no aerial fighting, just "recon" flights and the bombing. Anxious for some action, the hunter put in for a transfer, going first to Egypt and then to the Balkan front, where he was stationed at Salonika. Here, Bell and his observer had great fun strafing enemy airfields, pouring in a couple of drums of Lewis machine-gun bullets through the hangars and beating it for home.

Shortly after Bell had been issued a single-seat fighter, with a belt-fed Vickers gun firing through the propeller blades (using the interrupter gear developed by Dutch designer Anthony Fokker for the Germans), he had his first brush with the enemy in the sky. On his maiden flight with this fighter, he brought along a pair of twenty-five-pound bombs, more or less for the hell of it, and climbed to 10,000 feet over the enemy lines. Inaccurate puffs of antiaircraft flack began to appear, and Bell threw the bombs overboard. To his surprise, the firing stopped, and he wondered if, by some impossible chance, he had hit the battery of guns. The next moment, a brilliantly painted Albatross scout with black German crosses tore past him—the reason the enemy had stopped their antiaircraft fire. On some account, the Hun forward gun was not shooting, which indicated that the pilot had a jam or stoppage. Bell slipped his plane quickly into line and saw the rear observer open up with his Spandau, brown tracer rounds streaking smokily all about the British plane. The Scot had no sights and had to aim by looking down the engine housing and lining up a row of tappets. Hitting the firing cable, the Vickers erupted smoothly, and, after only twenty rounds, Bell saw that the Albatross seemed hit. To his speechless delight, the enemy ship turned over onto its back and both German aviators fell out, almost two miles over the battlefield below. Bell was now worried that his first victory might have gone unnoticed and that he would not receive credit for the kill. He needn't have been concerned. At least two men would never forget being unwilling witnesses.

At the time of the combat, 7,000 feet below the fight, a British pilot and his observer were registering heavy artillery fire from friendly lines. Showing up at the field just after Bell landed, they climbed down and demanded a drink. Quite shaken, they had been loafing along, spotting for the artillery battery and adjusting fire, when, without warning, two human bodies whizzed right past them, very close by. They had seen nothing of the planes above them and, convinced they were hallucinating, called off their mission, orders or no!

The combat had also been seen from the front-line trenches, and both the corpses and the enemy plane had fallen in no-man's-land, where there was a good fight over them that night, the British winning out. Each of the

Germans had been shot neatly through the head. Bell makes no comment on the reason for the dead men to have fallen suddenly out of their cockpits, and it seems a mystery to me. Surely they would not have gone into combat without their seat belts fastened. Perhaps the "G" forces of the plane turning over were sufficient to break them.

It had been bothering Bell that there was something about the fight that wasn't quite right. As he went over each second in his mind, he realized what it was: when he fired, his makeshift sights were not in proper position to hit the German, who was curving away as Bell fired at him. He remembered having to apply a lot of rudder, too much, in fact, to line up the gun correctly. There was only one conclusion he could reach. The enemy had been hit by accident, because the gun was not properly sighted in. He *couldn't* have hit the Albatross if the alignment had been correct. When he had the tail of the plane jacked up to test the machine gun, he found that it shot nowhere near the point of aim. His first kill had been sheer luck!

Following his victory, Karamojo, now a captain, decided to take two weeks' leave, as he had been flying steadily for two and a half years. Along with him went a friend who had gotten his plane cut in two by an enemy propeller while attacking a German scout. Amazingly, the Irish pilot, Pat, survived the 11,000-foot fall in one half of the plane, landing without injury in friendly territory, where he was picked up smoking a cigarette when the rescue car arrived. There was one odd aspect to him, though; probably through centrifugal force, blood had been forced completely through the whites of his eyes, giving him a demoniacal appearance with the contrast of the pale blue iris. Of course, it was unnerving for anybody looking at him, and he absolutely loved it.

Taking a navy ship for transport, Karamojo and Pat were torpedoed in the Aegean, their 10,000-ton vessel sinking on an even keel within five minutes of being hit. They, together with sixty-eight other men, had a tricky time of it in a small boat marked for forty-five people, until making land at an island where they were rescued. Shortly after this, Bell was transferred to flying combat in France, where he almost certainly became the first, if not the only, pilot credited with destroying an enemy plane with a single machine-gun bullet. It was quite an extraordinary affair, earning a reluctant Walter Bell a bar to his Military Cross, no small award.

Bell was patrolling over the front lines when he and a German Halberstadt fighter saw each other at the same time. Charging head-on like aerial knights, neither plane was able to get its guns to fire, despite the later sworn testimony of the troops below that they could hear the machine guns "roaring" at each other. After the first pass, it broke up into a dog fight, each trying to get into firing position on the other's tail, both working like mad to unjam their guns. Bell got his Vickers in order first and attacked the Halberstadt. In range, he opened up, only to have the gun fire a single shot and again jam. He thought he was seeing things when the German immediately started diving for a piece of flat ground between the lines, instead of heading for his own territory which was just as close. As Bell followed him down, the pilot landed, jumped out and ran hell-for-leather for his own lines, just getting clear before the French "75" cannons tore the German plane apart.

A baffled Bell flew home and filled out his combat report, to the effect that he had attacked an enemy aircraft which broke off the fight after Bell's gun jammed on the first shot. He thought no more about the matter, until later his commanding officer came up to him with a telegram from the French which offered congratulations on the gallant victory. Bell's superior had then telephoned the French battery that had shelled the Halberstadt on the ground, and they, too, insisted on having witnessed the fight, complete with the "roaring" machine guns.

Asked what he had to say to that information, Bell told the officer again what had happened, and the C.O. blew his top! "Claims" were very important for the prestige of a squadron, and he wasn't about to give away a confirmed kill. Bell would get the credit, whether he liked it or not. "What, with one shot, sir?" he asked incredulously.

"Yes, and be damned to you!" snapped back the officer, stalking away.

One must suspect that that single bullet may have gotten

the undivided attention of the enemy pilot, possibly even nicking him, or striking near enough to convince him that he was in a real spot with his own gun useless. Else, why would he not have flown to his own territory before putting down, instead of taking the terrible chance of landing in no-man's-land? Since he was not captured and the plane was destroyed, it's academic. Yet it still remains that he capitulated immediately after that one shot was fired, and, thus, Bell was the direct cause of the destruction of an enemy plane.

I have been unable to discover what number of enemy aircraft Bell shot down in World War I, and he only discusses unusual and "fluke" events in his writings. He does admit to having won the Military Cross twice, and one of his nephews advises that he was five times mentioned in dispatches, a great distinction among the British military establishment. With such recognition, he possibly might have made "ace," with five or more confirmed aerial victories, although in fact he did not. He did have one very interesting victory in the air though which, to Bell's great good luck, did not become part of his record. . . .

When he was stationed at Salonika, the Germans used to send over a daily reconnaissance flight to take pictures of the shipping movements in the harbor. Called the "Iron Cross" flight by the British, it was rumored that anybody making the trip three times was automatically awarded that decoration. Certainly, all the British and Allied flyers were hot to chew a chunk off the taunting machine, but nobody had managed to reach the 20,000-foot altitude at which the Hun invariably flew.

The French contingent was especially keen to knock down the "Iron Cross" plane and had especially brought over one of the newest of their fighters, the Spad. Tripling the firepower of the sharp little ship by jury-rigging an extra machine gun on each wing along with the Lewis gun that fired through the prop, they picked their best pilot and, under perfect conditions, sent him up to intercept the German flight. Bell and his pal, Wynne Eyton, who later hunted Africa with him, were already high above, hoping for a shot themselves, their planes moping sluggishly along at their ceiling of 15,000 feet.

From a seemingly clear sky, Bell was startled to hear a chatter of automatic fire behind him and saw a fighter streak by on the tail end of its firing pass. In a blink, he was after it, his Vickers smoothly spitting out short, accurate bursts, Eyton right along with him, also firing hard. It looked as if the "Iron Cross" flight was about to be canceled. As the Vickers slugs swarmed home, a piece of the target plane fell off, and the two R.F.C. men followed the crippled plane down. The fighter crash-landed inside Allied lines, and, knowing that the trophy would be stripped within minutes by foot soldiers, the two landed close by and ran over to the downed plane. As they got there, they were startled when a burst of machine-gun fire streamed from one of the wings. Behind the gun was "a fierce-looking little man, evidently in a state of great excitement." Hopping mad, the pilot jumped from the wreckage, screeching French. They had shot down the top French pilot in the supposedly invincible Spad! Retiring quickly, Bell and Eyton took off and feigned complete ignorance of the incident upon their return. Tongue in cheek, Bell remarked that his only souvenir was a cluster of bullet holes in his plane from the Frenchman's first pass.

I don't believe a poll has ever been conducted on the subject, but I suspect that such would show Bell, even today, enjoying the reputation as the greatest elephant hunter of all time. Even his detractors don't tend to minimize his success at collecting ivory but concentrate their attacks on his small-bore techniques. In the context that Bell was an adventurer second to being a commercial ivory hunter, the number of elephants he killed and the size of their ivory must be the primary consideration toward the term "great," as it would be in baseball for the man with the greatest number of hits and home runs. Bell killed over 1,000 bull elephants in his travels, perhaps a shade more. John "Pondoro" Taylor, an Irishman who died recently, was a professional hunter for thirty years, mostly in southeast Africa, and the author of some very authoritative books on rifles and African hunting. Probably the last actual ivory hunter, Taylor states that Bell killed 1,011 bull jumbo (not including the six or seven shot by his staff). I have no idea where this precise figure originated but suspect that it is low, because Taylor says that 800 of these were killed with the .275 Rigby and 200 with the .303 cartridge. In fact, some of Bell's bag was taken with the .256, and a large number with the .318, which was not developed until 1910.

There were two factors that contributed most directly to Bell's great accomplishments: his physical fitness and his superb mastery of the rifle. His body conditioning does not warrant further comment, other than to observe that any-body who walks 60,000 miles is likely to be in pretty fair shape. As far as his shooting is concerned, just how good he was is worth a couple of examples. One incident took place back in Karamojo. . . .

After leaving Mani-Mani, Bell marched to Bukora, an especially restless country where he was not known. Shortly after his arrival, a stream of Karamojong started trickling into his camp, which aroused the suspicion of his Swahili headman. The Swahili noticed a bad sign; there were no women in sight and he drew Bell's attention to the fact that each small group of warriors had nonchalantly picked out one of the safari, keeping in spear range wherever the target went. Clearly, on a given signal, the Karamojong would start spearing everybody to death.

Trying to think of a way to impress the Karamojong, Bell walked out of camp, announcing that he was going to kill meat. A few hundred yards away, he saw a herd of zebra running across his front at a full gallop. Up came the .303, and as fast as he could work the bolt action, he killed ten with ten shots, one right after another. The Karamojongs were dumbfounded, their eyes as wide as dinner plates.

Even to the nonhunter, the rapid-fire shooting of ten running zebras without a miss will sound like a fair example of marksmanship, but to the experienced African hand it's nothing short of a miracle! The zebra is one of the toughest of all "plains" game and impossible to kill instantly, unless hit exactly right. To knock off ten in a row, firing as fast as possible, is a feat I doubt one man in 10,000 could pull off. But then, Bell was one in several million.

Bell's muscle conditioning was almost a religion, especially in the training of those muscles used in holding the rifle. He nearly always had a gun in his hands, and constantly practiced aiming and holding it in different positions until it was almost part of him. Not only was he able to mount and fire his rifle quickly and accurately, but through long familiarity he developed a subconscious sense of aiming that produced what he called "automatic accuracy." It was his claim that, just as the rifle fired after being carefully aimed, the subconscious part of his brain took over and made an automatic correction of the barrel that invariably put the bullet dead on target. It sounds rather like a personal brand of Zen Buddhism, or perhaps today it would just be called confidence. Whatever, it sure worked for Bell.

Karamojo Bell was no chest thumper in his writings, usually going to pains to point out his poorer performances, rather than to emphasize his accomplishments. Yet he did pen a passage that gives an idea of how truly gifted he was with the rifle. Speaking of his personal preference for open-aperture rear sights, Bell tells of having the pleasant problem of shooting up some 6,000 rounds of .318 ammunition which had proved unreliable by misfiring about 30 percent of the time. He was at Jinja, where Lake Victoria forms a falls by pouring over a rock ledge, a place which hundreds of cormorants passed over on their way to roost each evening. They were high and fast, some 300 feet above the ground, which is nearly twice the effective range of a modern 12-gauge shotgun. Bell took to amusing himself here some evenings, shooting at the flying fish eaters with his elephant rifle, just to get rid of the bum cartridges. At one time, his average on these nearly impossible targets was 80 percent and his overall hits about six out of ten! Consider a target a foot long and half as high without feathers, traveling at forty to fifty miles per hour a hundred yards or more away, and you will appreciate the timing and "lead" calculation to hit it more than half the time, shooting offhand with open sights!

One of these evenings, Bell was shooting unusually well, and a pair of Goanese clerks from the town came over and asked to look at his "shotgun," as it was far superior to theirs, being able to kill at such distances. I would have loved to have seen their faces when they discovered it was a rifle!

After the Great War, Bell was laid up for a good while with a combination of malaria and African complications. And speaking of complications for an elephant hunter, he had gotten married. But his heart was still on the ivory trail, and he returned to hunt the Ivory Coast, the Niger and Benue rivers, this time traveling mostly by canoe with his safari and Wynne Eyton. Covering more than 3,000 miles, all the way up the Bahr Aouck, a good deal of ivory was taken. This journey probably aggregated more than 8,000 miles from the west coast until return.

Returning home to his wife, he stayed for several years, content with his memories now that he was well into his forties. His last visit to Africa was not to hunt ivory, but a mechanized affair in the company of American friends using automobiles. Bell had planned to return for a last ivory hunt in 1939, he told Bruce Kinloch, chief game warden of Uganda, during Kinloch's visit to Bell's home about 1951, but the war canceled the trip.

After his motorized journey, Bell settled down for good at an estate near Garve in Ross-shire, the Scottish highlands, calling the home Corriemoillie. Here Bell did his first writing, submitting a piece to the prestigious *Country Life* magazine, which clamored for more. His articles for this magazine were later collected in book form and published in 1923 by the magazine under the title *The Wanderings of an Elephant Hunter*. It became one of the great classics of elephant hunting and was followed much later by *Karamojo Safari*, which was shorter and dealt more specifically with the Karamojo region of Uganda. His life story, which incorporated much material from his first book, was assembled after Bell's death by Whelan under the title *Bell of Africa*.

Bell continued his interest in sailing in his later years, eventually building a yacht named for Richard Lion-Heart's *Trenchemere*. He does not presume to give us her length, but she was a steel-hulled beauty with a mast which towered a colossal eighty-five feet from the deck. The yacht became a second home for Bell and his wife Katie, who raced and sailed her up until World War II broke out and the *Trenchemere* was requisitioned for government war service. She was never used, as it turned out, spending the war years in a fresh-water lock in the Caledonian Canal.

Bell got his yacht back in 1946 and sailed her extensively the next two summers. Despite a mild heart attack in 1948, he continued to cruise her but in 1950 was forced by failing health to sell *Trenchemere*. Somewhat over a year later, still hunting deer and rabbits near home whenever he could, fate closed the door on him. Another heart attack in 1951 proved to be the last of Walter Dalrymple Maitland "Karamojo" Bell. The man was dead; the legend lives on.

BIBLIOGRAPHY

Bell, W. D. M. *The Wanderings of an Elephant Hunter*. London: Country Life, 1923.

———. *Karamojo Safari*. New York: Harcourt Brace, 1949.

———. *Bell of Africa*. London: Neville Spearman and The Holland Press, 1960.

Bulpin, T. V. *The Hunter Is Death*. Cape Town: Books of Africa, 1968.

Capstick, Peter Hathaway. *Death in the Long Grass*. New York: St. Martin's Press, 1977.

Foran, Major W. Robert. *Kill: Or Be Killed*. London: Hutchinson & Co., Ltd., 1933.

Kinloch, Bruce. *The Shamba Raiders*. London: Collins and Harville Press, 1972.

Neumann, Arthur H. *Elephant Hunting in East Equatorial Africa*. London: Rowland Ward Ltd., 1898.

Taylor, John. *Pondoro, Last of the Ivory Hunters*. New York: Simon and Schuster, Inc., 1955.

Colonel Edward James Corbett

THE GIRL'S LEG, still warm to the touch, lay on the sun-dappled trail, blood gently oozing from just below the knee where it had been severed as though by the stroke of a sword. At the edge of a small pool a few yards away, red splintered bone and great gouts of gore stained the jungled floor of the mountainous Indian watercourse, seeping into the splayed pug marks of a tigress, a man-eating tigress who now heard a small sound from the ravine from which she had carried the girl's body in order to eat it. Swiftly and firmly, the striped cat gripped the fresh corpse with long fangs, effortlessly bounding up and over a fifteen-foot-high bank, carrying the body for several more yards. Tucking the half-eaten girl under an overhanging rock past a thick stand of hill shrubbery, the tigress turned back, flattening herself low in the brush, inching up to the edge of the bank overlooking the pool. Silent as a shadow, her only motion the uncontrolled twitch of her hidden tail, she watched through the cover as a man-thing stepped slowly into view. The steel muscles of her hind legs bunched in anticipation, curved talons gripping the earth for a spring onto the hunter below.

Jim Corbett had been following for nearly a mile, carefully tracking from the coagulating pool of blood and broken blue beads that marked the place of the kill. He was alone, the hillman who had started with him on the blood trail now perching in petrified terror back up the mountain on the highest rock he could find. Corbett stopped at the blood-stains and carefully glanced all about him, unmindful of the hard eyes that watched him just out of range. Cautiously, he stepped forward, fascinated by the youthful severed leg at the water's edge, his eyes downcast, now almost in reach of the tigress' charge. But something raised the hackles on his sweat-wet neck. It was the old feeling. He was being watched. The tigress sensed his tension, seeing the hated stick that smelled of iron in his hands swing in her direction. He knew she was there. The ambush was ruined. As she turned and ghosted back from the bank to her kill, a small clod of earth trickled down the incline and splashed softly into the water. By the time the man could reach the top of the embankment, the Champawat Man-eater, the most successful feline human-killer of all time, had recovered her four hundred thirty-sixth victim and carried the body into a bewildering maze of rocks and ferns choked with thorn-hooked blackberry plants.

All afternoon, the lone man followed the pug marks and the heavy blood spoor marking the dozen places the tigress had stopped to feed, only to be forced on, growling in anger, by the hunter's approach. At last, the deadly game was forced to an end. Long shadows spiked the slanting rays of the sun, beginning to settle into a fiery nest somewhere past the snaggled teeth of the western horizon. Alone and in the dark, Corbett knew he was a dead man, an easy kill for the tigress the hill people of Kumaon called Shaitan, the dark spirit. Returning to the pool of water, he took time to bury the leg of the Hindu girl so that some part of her could be recovered and burned on the *Ghats,* to flow from the Ganga Mai—the Mother Ganges—to the sea. Reaching the tall rock to which the frightened Indian still clung, he found the hill man quite relieved. He had heard the tiger growl many times, but no shot had reached his ears. His main worry had been how he would return to his village if the *sahib* had gotten himself eaten. As the shadows settled deeper into the dead girl's village, the man sat smoking, planning for tomorrow. He knew the tigress would finish eating the girl during the night and lie up in the rocky ravine the next day. Perhaps a beat down the valley would give him a shot, forcing the man-eater into his ambush. Yes, perhaps it might.

There could be very little debate that the great subcontinent of India has suffered through the ages more than any other place on earth under the unrelenting horror of man-eating tigers and leopards. This is hardly to say that the African man-eaters were pussycats; quite to the contrary. Yet the psychological impact upon a dense population may be quickly realized by reading Peter Benchley's novel *Jaws*. At least when a man-eating shark is at large in an area, one can get out of the water. When, however, a region is under the threat of a man-eating cat, the mere presence of such a creature disrupts the entire culture. Human life cannot continue in a normal manner where a man-eater is operating; crops cannot be planted or harvested in a land already bleakly famous for starvation; wood and water may be gathered only at mortal risk. But to survive, these risks are taken, and whatever the man-eater may be, tiger or leopard, it thrives on the flesh of those made bold by desperation.

The great predator of Asia—particularly with concern to man, who populates this continent more densely than any other—is the tiger. To the Westerner, the impact of this animal over the past 400 years of closely recorded history is almost unimaginable. To quote Richard Perry, a recognized expert who wrote a definitive work on this animal, *The World of the Tiger,* the tiger is "the monster that for four centuries certainly, and no doubt for very much longer than that, has darkened with terror the lives of millions of Indian villagers . . . in terms of human misery it was the constant suspense of being defenseless against a sudden and horrible death by day and night, over a period of months or even years, that broke the spirit of the villagers, rather than the actual number of deaths among them, although the latter were terrible enough."

How many people have tigers eaten throughout their wide range of the last century? The best thinking on the matter, distilled from expert sources, indicates that tigers alone have eaten at least 500,000 Indians and certainly a minimum of one million people over the entire Asian continent in the last four centuries. In the 1800s, when man-eating was at its statistical peak, there may have been as many as 800 killer tigers in business at the same time! These conditions existed, particularly in India, until after World War II, when tiger population began to drop quickly, yet the list of victims up until nearly 1950 still numbered some 800 deaths by tiger per year. Even though the tiger is endangered for the usual reasons, incidents of man-eating are not especially rare even today.

Considering the vast amount of material written about the natural history of the tiger, I see little point in adding to it here beyond the basic consideration of the world's largest cat as a man-eater, a profession at which he is highly talented. As an organism of carnivorous persuasion, the physical qualities of the tiger are purely awesome. A big male may weigh 550 pounds, and several have been recorded at nearly 600 pounds. The biggest—presumably a Siberian snow tiger—was presented to Nikita Khrushchev in the 1960s. Are you sitting down? Good. It weighed 700 pounds. A tiger's claws may reach four inches in length—the better to grab you by—and whereas canine teeth probably average around three inches in length, there is one in existence that is five and one-half inches long and three and one-half inches around. Maybe the saber-tooth isn't extinct after all!

Unlike the more gregarious lion, the tiger is a loner except when mating or with cubs, which may themselves be undertaking on-the-job training under mom if she is a man-eater. According to the literature and experience of famous tiger hunters, tigers do not seem inclined toward man-eating unless injured and unable to pursue their usual table fare. Opinions vary, but, unlike the irrefutable evidence of lions and leopards just doing what comes naturally when they take to eating folks, the majority of Indian man-eating tigers (and, to some extent, leopards) have been injured and in some way disabled. A high percentage of these cats run afoul of porcupines and get a face- or a pawful of barbed quills, which are chewed off short and remain in the body to fester and cripple. Others have been wounded by trap guns or native hunters and escaped, forced, through reduced capacity, to people-eating. Obviously, some are just old and decrepit, although even a very broken-down tiger can turn fatal attention on one hell of a lot of people before cashing in.

Hunting man-eating cats is spooky and exacting business, I can personally assure you, and those that manage to pursue this most dangerous game over a period of years and survive are, by definition, both talented and unquestionably lucky. I am the only one I know who has managed a respectable career based upon the latter consideration alone. But when it comes to India and man-eating cats, there is one name that looms through the legends like an oil tanker in a bathtub: Jim Corbett.

Born in 1875 in the town of Naini-Tal in the region known as Kumaon in India's United Provinces, young Jim grew up in the six-thousand-foot-high mountain country a naturally gifted woodsman and hunter. His understanding and knowledge of the wooded *terai* and rocky jungle-choked ravines were rare even for a native *shikari,* or professional hunter. Matter of fact, if there was a white man who grew to know more about tigers, leopards, and the many antelopes of that corner of India tucked against the L-shaped western border of Nepal, I haven't heard of him.

Jim Corbett became an official of the Indian railways in his adulthood, a strong parallel with John Henry Patterson, who shared his occupation, rank and, of course, his man-eaters. Although he had hunted practically since he was old enough to walk and had killed a great number of tigers and leopards, Corbett was really almost more of a student of the great cats than a hunter of them. A single glance at a three-day-old tiger pug mark, and *Sahib* Corbett could conjure out of the smudged track the age, sex, condition, bank balance, middle name and possibly blood group of the cat. His passion for logic and progressively conclusive deductions make him seem very much a bush-going Sherlock Holmes (a character, incidentally, reputed by some to have been modeled after a remote relative of mine, Inspector Capstick, once head of Scotland Yard). Corbett's writings are studded with fascinating diagrammed *ergos,* usually stimulated by a mere bent blade of grass or misplaced drop of dew, and escalating into the damnedest collection of correct diagnoses east of the Mayo Clinic. He was a fine writer and obviously a most sensitive man, but the common theme of his many books is a feeling for absolute truth. Corbett's personal opinions are labeled as such, but his eye for detail leaves no question as to authenticity.

Over the length of his career, Jim Corbett killed man-eating tigers and leopards which, among them, accounted for over fifteen hundred human victims. What is rather statistically amazing but true is that he brought to bag both the highest-scoring tiger and the leopard with the largest recorded number of human kills: the Champawat Tigress and the Panar Leopard respectively. Between just these two animals there were 836 dead human beings. Try to guess the odds against both Corbett and the two cats being alive at the same time, let alone in the same country.

It's interesting that, for all the man-eating going on at the time, Jim Corbett's first experience of hunting a genuine man-eater was not until 1907, when he was thirty-two years old. Ominously, this particular animal, the Champawat Man-eater, was the first man-eating feline recorded in Kumaon, the tigress that to this day has never been surpassed in numbers of human victims. It had come from Nepal, driven out of that country by an army of Nepalese sent against it, and chased over into India in 1903 (thanks a lot, chaps, but we already have plenty). To its score of 200 people killed in Nepal, it added another 236 during the four years it lived in the Kumaon area of Corbett's homeland. Despite large rewards and heavy hunting pressure, nobody could stem the growing terror of the Champawat Man-eater's depredation, and hundreds of square miles were in a complete funk. After the man considered the best *shikari* in India had failed utterly to connect, Corbett, by virtue of his reputation as a sportsman, was asked to try his hand at killing her. He started his hunt at the village of Pali some fifteen miles from Champawat, the namesake of the man-eater.

Five days before his arrival, a woman gathering leaves

from an oak tree had been pulled out of it by the tigress, who grabbed her by the ankles and jerked so hard that the skin of her palms was still hanging shredded from the branch she had grasped. That night and the next two, the tigress had stayed near the village, roaring throughout the darkness, completely paralyzing the people with terror. On Corbett's arrival, it was all he could do to get them to open up for him, and the amount of human nightsoil around the doors showed that nobody had budged since the attack. Gaining the villagers' confidence with some fancy shooting of three mountain goats, Corbett talked a few of the braver men into showing him the scene of the kill, where some bone splinters—all that was left of the woman—were gathered to be cremated.

While at Pali, Corbett heard the tragic story of an incident that had taken place nearby about a year past. Two sisters were out cutting grass when the Champawat tigress, who had been stalking them, sprang and killed the elder of the women. Gripping her body in her jaws, the tigress ran off with the dead woman, the younger sister chasing after the man-eater with a sickle to try and save the older. Before witnesses, she ran screaming behind the tigress for more than one hundred yards before the man-eater, who was becoming distraught at such unlikely behavior, dropped the body and charged her pursuer. The younger sister sheered off and the tigress let her go, but when she recovered from her run back in the village, it was discovered that she had lost her power of speech. When Corbett met her, he was told she had not uttered a sound in a year—obviously, a classic case of hysterical shock.

Corbett's first night of what were to be thirty-two years of man-eater hunting was spent with his back to a tree on the road that ran past the village, which makes one wonder whether or not Mrs. Corbett raised any idiots. Apparently not, because as soon as it was dark, Jim realized just what a handy main course he offered, and, although he was too terrified to try to walk back to the village, he kept awake through the night listening to his own chattering teeth. To everybody's amazement, he was still alive at dawn. The next three days he spent chance hunting in the vicinity until it was clear that the tigress had moved off.

Walking to Champawat, the protection of his rifle drew a good crowd of Indian travelers, so that by the time Champawat was reached, Corbett's party had grown from eight to thirty men. Several of these hill men had been in another group of twenty men, walking together for mutual protection some two months before on this same road. As they told the *sahib,* the terrible sounds of a woman screaming had been heard from the valley below, moving toward them as they huddled on the dirt track. Closer and closer had come the agonized shrieks, until they gasped to see a tigress come into sight, carrying a naked woman by the small of her back, her hair trailing on the ground on one side of the cat and her feet in the dust on the other. In desperation, she had beaten her chest with her fists, wailing hopelessly for help from God or man. Ignoring the group of men, the tigress had calmly walked past, fifty yards away, the shocked people frozen as the poor woman's cries had slowly faded in the distance.

Since none of the men had been armed, none of them had shown any particular enthusiasm for taking the woman away from the man-eating tigress. Shortly thereafter, however, a rescue party with some guns had come along, and the forces joined. Their large numbers must have been enough to frighten the tigress, for, after a mile of noisy following, the woman had been found, uneaten, lying on a flat rock. She had been licked clean by the killer, yet was untouched but for the fang holes in her back. It was a piteous scene:

> Beyond licking off all the blood and making her body clean, the tiger had not touched her, and, there being no woman in our party, we men averted our faces as we wrapped her body in the loincloths which one and another gave, for she looked as she lay on her back as one who sleeps, and would awaken in shame when touched.

At Champawat, Corbett presented letters of introduction to the *tahsildar* (tax collector), who was more or less the highest authority of the village and environs. The next day, on the *tahsildar*'s advice, Corbett moved to a *dak* bungalow (a rest house for people traveling on official business) a few miles away, in an area where the man-eater had been most active. Bingo! As he stood talking to the tax collector on a hill, a man came running up from the village with news that a girl had just been taken by the tigress. Grabbing his rifle, Corbett ran down the slope and was shown the patch of fresh blood and broken beads where the teenager had been killed. He was amazed that she had been taken so silently, on open ground, from among a dozen people gathering kindling. The only hint that survivors had had of trouble was a small choking sound made by the girl in the tiger's jaws.

At once picking up the pug marks and blood spoor, Corbett tracked for half a mile, finding the young woman's clothes. As he observed, "Once again the tigress was carrying a naked woman, but mercifully on this occasion her burden was dead." The spoor ran over a hill and through a thicket, the thorns of which had snagged several long strands of the dead girl's blue-black hair. Beyond this was a nasty bed of nettles, and, as Corbett was trying to see if he could avoid them, he heard someone approaching from behind. It was a frightened old man with a gun, sent by the *tahsildar*, of whom he was even more afraid than the tigress. Not wanting to waste time arguing, Corbett had him take off his heavy, noisy boots, and they proceeded painfully through the stinging patch of nettles. As the trail took a hard left turn and the cover grew thicker, the Indian's fear began to interfere with Corbett's concentration. Every few feet the man would grab the *sahib*'s arm, swearing that he could hear the tigress but a few feet away. When the pair came to a stand of rocks thirty feet high, Corbett told the old man to climb it and wait while he went on alone.

Some distance ahead, he found the leg by the pool of water, detected the man-eater's presence through a sixth-sense warning and finally had to give up the chase through impending darkness.

Corbett thought it could work. As he sat smoking, he

examined the land below, carefully noting each feature, planning the feasibility of a beat. Below him lay a natural amphitheater between the hills, cut by a valley worn by a small stream over eons of patient time. On the far side of the depression, the stream had hit rock and turned from east to north, flowing out of the amphitheater through a narrow gorge. There were also two hills, one so steep it was unlikely to be climbed by anything less than a bird, the other some two thousand feet of slope with little cover. Slowly, the idea took shape. If he could form the line of beaters across the ridge that ran between the stream and the very steep slope, the tigress should be forced from what he guessed to be her present position, in a thick wood slightly more than a half-mile per side, to seek the most likely line of escape. This would, logically, be through the gorge. But how to get the terrified men to leave the safety of their homes to beat drums and throw rocks to drive a tiger? It would take a big party to beat the hillside effectively. But then, perhaps the *tahsildar* had powers of persuasion. . . .

The next morning at ten o'clock, the *tahsildar* and one other man showed up at Corbett's bungalow. The hunter's heart sank. Then, as he watched with growing admiration for the tax collector's "persuasion," a small army of men, armed with an astounding collection of derelict firearms, drums, horns and gongs, began to stream up the hill. By noon, they were only two short of three hundred beaters. Considering their abject fear of the tiger, it was a brave showing, indeed.

The *tahsildar* had declared a full amnesty on the highly illegal guns which had been dug up from hut floors and collected from hollow trees; he had gone even further by agreeing to supply ammunition for those who had none. Of course, the value of the guns was in their noise effect, and there was little doubt that they would finish the day doing far more harm to their owners and other beaters than they ever would to the tigress. For this reason, the *tahsildar* decided to go with Corbett, rather than risk picking a chunk of burst gunbarrel out of his skull from one of the old pieces. When at last the whole crew was assembled, Corbett addressed them, giving his instructions after walking them to the ridge where the dead girl's skirt was still fluttering with lonely pathos in the mountain breeze. The beaters should form a line across the top of the hill, giving Corbett and the *tahsildar* time to get across into position on the opposite hill. When Corbett waved his handkerchief from the slope well below a lightning-struck pine, they should start the beat with a burst of gunfire and all the noise they could manage. It was by no means a classic tiger beat, as the men were not to move down the valley but rely on their stationary racket at the head to move the man-eater. It would have to be enough; to enter the jungle valley would be suicide.

Corbett and the *tahsildar* started off, assured that everybody understood his instructions, skirting wide around the valley and descending to the pine tree. At this point, the Indian, who was getting blisters from his patent leather shoes, begged a halt to take them off. As he sat down to do so, the beaters took it for the signal, and the amphitheater rocked with gunfire, horn blasts, shouts and rolling, bouncing rocks crashing down the slopes into the jungle below.

Too much, too early.

Corbett was fully 150 yards from the place where he intended to ambush the tigress, a lunar landscape nightmare of steep broken rock and scree. Nonetheless, he took the run at full speed, desperate he would miss the chance. Only his hill breeding let him reach a patch of two-foot-high grass near the gorge, heaving for breath, his neck yet unbroken. The grass would have to do, he quickly concluded, sitting down and keeping absolutely still, with half his body hidden. As any experienced sportsman knows, it is motion that betrays, not color. He took a deep, steadying breath. If she was coming, it would be soon. . . .

At the head of the valley, the beaters were going absolutely mad, a good sign they had caught sight of the man-eater. Suddenly Corbett saw a flicker of tawny, striped motion as the Champawat tigress came into view, bounding down the slope to the hunter's right front, some 300 yards away. Corbett snicked the safety off his express rifle. It was going to work. She was headed for the gorge!

Two distinct shots boomed and echoed up the hillside. God! No! The damn fool *tahsildar* had emptied both barrels of his decrepit shotgun at the man-eater as she passed, far out of range. Instantly, the tiger swapped ends, racing back up the hill, straight for the unsuspecting line of beaters, a worthless long-range bullet of Corbett's whapping with sterile force into the rocks at the edge of the jungle. Jim Corbett felt sick to his stomach. It wasn't just a failure, it was a disaster. Any second he would hear the shrieks of agony and terror as the big tigress burst from cover and tore, mauling and biting, through the line of beaters. How many widows would there be tonight because of his bright ideas?

As he held his breath helplessly, he was stunned to hear a roar of guns and voices exploding in joy from the ridge, so loud they made the first seem like whispers. Having heard the two shotgun blasts shortly followed by one shot from the *sahib*'s big double gun, they were certain that the tiger had been killed. Startled by the terrific outburst of sound, the tigress again ran down the valley, breaking into the open to Corbett's left, heading straight for the mouth of the gorge. As she hurdled the stream in a single, fluid bound, the .500 modified cordite rifle came up, the front bead nestling coolly in the wide vee of the rear sights, Corbett holding low on her shoulder, as the rifle had been sighted in at sea level and would shoot high in this thin air. As he felt the sear slip and the crunch of recoil from the first barrel, the tigress stopped completely, apparently unhurt. Turning toward the patch of grass, she presented a perfect angle on a left shoulder at about thirty yards, staring straight at Corbett. As the big bullet smashed home, she flinched but did not go down. Her eyes blazing, ears laid back, the low moan of a snarl built in her throat, as Corbett watched her over the sights, trying to decide how he would handle the charge.

It was quite an interesting problem, because Corbett was completely out of ammunition. Never having thought he would have a chance of more than two shots, he had brought only three, including one extra for "an emergency." The first had been wasted on the long shot up the valley, and the last two spent at thirty yards. Now it looked as if he would have to pay the price of his indiscretion. For what must have seemed several weeks to Corbett, the most dangerous man-eating cat in the world and the unarmed man looked into each other's eyes across ninety feet of Indian hillside.

I know you're asking the same, rather obvious question that ran through my mind: Was this guy Corbett nuts? Was he a couple of bubbles off plumb? Who goes man-eating tiger hunting with only three cartridges? Not me, forever-loving, bloody damn sure! I wouldn't go to Sunday school without at least twenty rounds, two large knives, one handgun and a pocketful of grenades, if they'd let me. It's easy enough to get yourself a one-way ticket West with any cat, man-eater or not; but to get nailed because you brought only three cartridges would be just too much!

Despite the variety of opinions on the subject, there apparently is a God. Or, by a function either of the deity or a good London gunmaker, the Champawat Man-eater was harder hit than Corbett had expected. She did not charge the man. Instead, she slowly turned, waded the stream and, crossing a tangle of broken rocks, forced herself up a slanting narrow ledge that ran across the front of the very steep hill. Reaching a projecting flat slab, she pulled herself onto its surface and began clawing and biting at a small bush whose windblown seed had taken root in a crack of the slab.

His heart having restarted, Corbett shouted for the *tahsildar* under the big pine tree up the slope to bring his gun. Getting a rather involved answer out of which Corbett could only discern the word "feet," he figured the hell with it and ran up the hill, grabbing the slug-loaded shotgun away from the tax collector. As he tore back down the slope and across the stream, toward the tigress on the rock slab, the man-eater stopped ripping up the bush and came toward Corbett. Hardly having glanced at the gun, he went to within twenty feet of the growling tigress, who was making it pretty clear she did not like him. Lifting the old gun to his shoulder, Corbett was bound to have gotten some idea that it just wasn't his day. As he looked at the breech to be sure it was closed, he noticed a gapping crack some three-eighths of an inch between the barrels and the breech block. There was no easy way to know—other than firing it—if the gun would blow up in his face. If the separation had been caused by the two shots the *tahsildar* had pegged at the tigress a few minutes ago, it could well take off Corbett's head as he pulled the trigger. At the very least, he ran a grave risk of being permanently blinded by the blow-back of burning gases erupting through the gap. Nonetheless, he lined up the baked potato of a foresight on the center of the tigress's open mouth and squeezed the trigger.

With a great burp of black powder smoke, the old gun fired. Twenty feet away, the tigress swayed and jerked forward, falling in a heap with her head overhanging the edge of the rock. She had probably been dead before the shotgun slug ever hit her. The slug, which barely broke the skin of the right forepaw, had been so ineffective that Corbett later pulled it out with nothing more than his fingernails!

The men now came down from the ridge with swords, axes, spears and every other form of weapon, hot on the idea of whipping up a bunch of tigerburger. As there were many among the men who had lost wives and children to this same tigress, their enthusiasm could be understood, but Corbett got them calmed down before they could chop the cat into chunks. It would be important, Corbett knew, to show her body to as many of the hill people as possible, so that they would know it was the same tiger and that she, unlike the spirit she was supposed to be, was well and truly dead.

Examining the body, Corbett noticed that both canine teeth on the right side of the mouth had been broken off long ago, one all the way down to the socket. Unable to kill her natural prey, she had been forced to take up man-eating. Corbett says that the injury was the result of a bullet wound, but whether there was clear evidence of this or it was mere reasonable surmise is not recorded.

There is an interesting epilogue to the death of the Champawat Man-eater. After the skin was taken, the body was given to the people, who whacked it up into small pieces to carry in lockets as charms to protect the bearer from becoming tiger food. Shortly thereafter, Corbett received a curious little package from the *tahsildar* of Champawat. In it was a bottle of alcohol containing the fingers of the girl who had been the last victim of the tigress. They had been eaten whole. Corbett sank this pathetic package in a holy lake near a Hindu temple. The girl's head, which had been found severed when the beaters came down the hill, was burned on the exact spot where the tigress had fallen. Somebody, presumably, remembered to dig up the leg.

Leaving Champawat with the skin of the tigress tied over the back of his saddle, Corbett and his men happened to pass the small house just outside Pali village where the woman lived who had been struck dumb by her experience with the man-eater the year before. Thinking she would like to know that her sister's killer was dead, Corbett went up to the house and spread out the fresh skin on the ground. The dumb woman, hearing her children chattering excitedly, came to the door. The minute she saw the tiger skin, her impediment vanished, and she ran back and forth, shouting at the top of her lungs for the village people and her husband to come and see what the *sahib* had brought.

The Champawat tigress was the first of an amazing number of man-eaters Corbett would kill over his thirty-two-year career in Kumaon. Yet if he was lucky beyond the powers of reason not to have become her four hundred thirty-seventh victim, he would push that luck to the breaking point in his future hunting life, certainly with tigers but especially with the other great man-eater of India, the leopard.

In relatively modern times, there have been two individual man-eating leopards in India that, during the some eleven years of their combined activities, caused as much human misery and loss of life as any two man-killing animals in history. They operated in different areas as solitary creatures some years apart, and although one, the Panar Leopard, had more than three times the number of victims as the challenger—the Man-eating Leopard of Rudraprayag—on a numerical basis (officially 400 to 125 respectively), the latter was far and away the more notorious. The reason for this was the difference in their range of operations. The Panar Leopard's hunting grounds were well off the major trade routes, deep in the Himalayas in what is now Uttar Pradesh province. Thus, its depredations were limited to extremely rural areas where it did not achieve the psychological impact upon the population that the less successful but far more terrifying Rudraprayag Leopard did, which stalked the 500 square miles of mountainous terrain surrounding the 25,645-feet-high Nanda Devi peak, keeping more than 60,000 pilgrims and local villagers in a state of terror for more than eight years.

In the entire history of the confrontation betwen man and the animals that eat him, there has probably never been a feline of any kind that displayed the intelligence and pure, sinister talent of the Rudraprayag Leopard. For more than eight years, killing people all the while, he survived every imaginable device employed against him, including hunters, set-guns, steel traps, baited bombs, ingestions of double and triple lethal doses of cyanide, strychnine and arsenic. He was even walled up in a cave for five days without food or water, breaking through a crowd of 500 armed men to make good his escape. At one time, more than 4,300 men armed with licensed guns (not counting probably four times that number of illegal arms), as well as hundreds of off-duty soldiers, spent most of their time trying to collect the 10,000-rupee cash reward and the income of two villages, which would be the bounty of collecting this leopard's hide. The combined results of this massive campaign amounted to one bullet crease on the left hind paw, the loss of a small piece of skin and a claw from one toe and the observation of the deputy commissioner of Garhwal, the province in which the man-eater operated, that the Rudraprayag man-eater actually thrived on the deadly poison he ingested from the bodies of his victims that had been laced with the stuff.

The first official recognition of the Rudraprayag Leopard—who was known by other names, as well—was after a kill on June 9, 1918, at a remote place called Banji. His last

kill was April 14, 1926; his formal tally laid at 125 victims. In fact, the Rudraprayag man-eater killed substantially more than this figure, which, consistent with the records of most bureaucracies, were misfiled or simply unrecorded. Corbett states that several people consumed by this man-eater while he was actually hunting it do not appear on the roster of the dead, although what the precise figure might be will never be known. Corbett says that had the leopard been killed during an early attempt, "several hundred" people it ate would have lived.

It had been fifteen years since Jim Corbett had hunted down and destroyed the Panar Leopard and eighteen years from his—shall we say—memorable meeting with the Champawat Tigress before he set his sights on the great leopard of Rudraprayag. For roughly seven years, the heavily traveled pilgrim route of torture from the lowlands to the south through the freezing mountains, the trail splattered with the blood and skin of the barefooted devout, had been a path of the purest terror. The man-eating leopard who prowled and ghosted through the blackness of the night around the resting places and native inns had caused the strictest of curfews; yet this deterred him hardly at all. Although past his prime, he was apparently supernaturally strong and equally determined, breaking into rural huts with ease and keeping the 50,000 inhabitants living between the Mandakin and Alaknanda rivers in as great a state of horrified expectation as the 10,000 pilgrims who annually tried to visit the shrines at Kedarnath and Badrinath.

Like most of the big cats, leopards are not bashful about scavenging, and this trait is probably how the Rudraprayag cat took up man-eating. We discussed the peculiar characteristics of man-eating leopards and the factors that make them so hard to hunt down in *Death in the Long Grass,* so that it does not bear repeating here, except to say that they are casual hunters who go right on eating livestock and game, as well as men. Unlike the tiger, man-eating leopards rarely carry injuries that force them into a career of people purloining; thus, they are far less predictable than tigers or lions, who have developed a sweet tooth for thee and me.

After the great influenza epidemic of 1918, which killed more than a million Indians, the dead were so profuse that the normal Hindu cremation ceremony of the Garhwal hills could not logistically be carried out, and a lip service literally was paid by the ritual placing of a live coal in each corpse's mouth. Left to rot in the bush, these bodies almost surely taught the neophyte man-eater that he had been missing a good thing, and the transition between dead bodies and live ones could have been no great adjustment to an enterprising leopard like him.

By the time Jim Corbett began hunting the Man-eater of Rudraprayag in 1925, there was quite a store of historical data on the cat on which to draw. Already, the leopard had become one of the most highly publicized man-eaters in history (with the possible exception of the African Tsavo lions), having been featured in the newspapers of at least ten major countries. Reams of government reports existed on the cat's activities, detailing not only the circumstances of attacks, but those attempts made at retribution.

The closest call the leopard had survived after three years of marauding was when he had been hunted by two young British officers in 1921. Somehow determining that the leopard at times used a suspension rope bridge across the Alaknanda River to hunt both banks, they set up an ambush at each end, hoping to catch the man-eater crossing at night. For two long months the men waited, shivering away the nights, one sitting on each suspension cable tower on the left and right banks. Then one night, the man in the left tower was astonished to see the leopard casually walk out onto the bridge and begin to cross. With admirable presence of mind, the hunter did not fire, waiting until the man-eater was well out on the bridge, so that if he missed the first shot he would have another if the cat ran back toward him. Taking careful aim in the murky darkness, he fired. Like a bolt of spotted lightning, the leopard flickered away, across the bridge straight toward the second officer. Whether this man did not have a rifle—which would be hard to believe—or was somehow caught off balance by his partner's bullet with his rifle out of reach is not known. He did, however, pull his service revolver and cranked out six shots at the cat as it ran by.

The next morning, although the leopard was nowhere in sight, some blood was found on the bridge. Through whatever logic it was they chose to apply, it was concluded that the leopard had been hit both in the head and the body. Corbett, who later spoke with one of the native trackers who helped to search for the wounded cat, disagreed with Garhwali's analysis of the blood spoor, convinced that it could have only been a foot wound. Of course, the leopard was not found, but Corbett was later proven to have been precisely correct; the first bullet had creased the left rear paw and clipped off a small piece of toe. The *pistolero* missed with all six shots. According to other government reports, a leopard whose description matched that of the man-eater to a tee was caught in a drop-door live trap. The Hindus, who were scared to death of the man-eater, wanted no part of killing the trapped animal, for fear that the spirits of his victims would come back to haunt them. What the logic of this was, I'm sure I couldn't tell you, but finally it was agreed to send for a Christian Garhwali to come and do the caged critter in. As might be expected, the Garhwal region of the Himalayas is not overrun with Christians, the nearest living some thirty miles away from the trap site. By the time the executioner was sent for and arrived at the scene, the man-eater—if indeed it had been the Rudraprayag Leopard—had dug a hole under the bars and was long gone.

Shortly thereafter, after killing and eating most of a man, a leopard was seen by a search party sneaking out of a small patch of jungle where he had been lying up and feeding. When the party chased the cat, it ducked into a cave with a small mouth, which was promptly plugged with thick thorn branches and heavy boulders. Word spread around the countryside of the leopard trapped inside the cave while five days went by.

By this time, a crowd reported at about 500 men had gathered outside, amazed that the leopard had not been heard to make the smallest sound in all this time. Inevitably, there arrived a man of considerable local influence, who got it into his head that there was no way for a leopard to be in the cave so long without some sign of its presence. Scoffing at the credulity of the crowd, he marched up to the cave, rolled away the stones and pulled off the thorns. Instantly, the leopard rocketed from the darkness, dashed straight through the mass of people and disappeared.

If it had had three miraculous escapes in the first few years of man-eating, this was just a simple drill in elusiveness, compared to the weird quirks of fate that saved its life time and again from the bullets of Jim Corbett.

Corbett was called to hunt the Rudraprayag Leopard in 1925 by William Ibbotson, later Sir William, who had been posted to Garhwal province as deputy commissioner. A famed big-game hunter in his own right, Ibbotson had himself been trying to kill the leopard without success and begged Corbett, his good friend, to lend a hand. Corbett's first attempt lasted ten weeks, beginning shortly after the leopard had dined on a *sadhu*, or holy man, who had overestimated the power of his faith by sleeping on an open platform with some other pilgrims outside a store along the road. Unfortunately, this kill had placed the leopard outside a well-organized beat going on at that time, set up by Ibbotson, who was combing the cat's regular lying-up place with 2,000 men, while the man-eater was sleepily digesting the *sadhu* several miles away.

With his usual analytical approach, Corbett set himself to making a plan that would enable him to guess where the leopard might be at a given time in the rugged 500 square miles of mountains. Quickly, he realized the key to the area lay with the rivers, both tributaries of the Ganges. The leopard had never crossed the barrier of the Mandakin River to the west but regularly killed on both sides of the Alaknanda, which ran west, forming a right angle with the Mandakin at Rudraprayag—"Prayag" meaning a confluence of rivers. Obviously, if he could determine which side of the Alaknanda the leopard was on, the area for the search would be cut roughly in half. Since there were only two points at which the Alaknanda's icy rushing current could be crossed—both suspension bridges—it should not be difficult to figure out which side of the river the leopard was on.

As the holy man had been taken a few miles from the easternmost bridge at Chatwapipal on the north side of the river, Corbett felt certain that, after abandoning the remains of the man, the leopard had crossed this bridge to make its next kill. After a death, the entire region closed up like a clam, making the securing of another victim in the same neighborhood difficult for a while, so the leopard would tend to move along. Despite the caution, though, over the eight years he was active, the Rudraprayag Leopard did take six people from one village, five each from two others, four from one more and three each from eight other villages.

A few days after arriving in the area, Corbett started to acquire an idea of the fascinating combination of boldness and elusiveness that marked the Rudraprayag Leopard as nearly unique among killer cats. Since it was well known that the leopard killed livestock along with men, a pair of goats were tied up as bait on either side of the Alaknanda, one on the pilgrim path and the other in a patch of very likely-looking scrub jungle. The next day, one had been killed by a male leopard, which, for some reason, had not eaten it. That afternoon and evening, Corbett sat in a tree over the carcass, but the lack of warning bird and animal calls indicated that the man-eater had abandoned the goat and was not in the vicinity.

From his experiences of man-eating tigers, Corbett was careful leaving the tree and walking back to his government bungalow, even though there had been no sign of the leopard. It didn't work both ways. The next morning, directly outside the rest house were the pug marks of the man-eater squarely in his shoe tracks. By following the spoor backward, Corbett learned with a chill that the big cat had shadowed him every foot of the way through the dark. There was no longer any question of on what side of the river the leopard was.

That night, in a small village on a hilly ridge 4,000 feet above the bungalow, a couple sat finishing their evening meal by the light of the hearth fire. In a very few days, the wife would give birth to the first son of the house. Great with child, she waddled to the doorstep to clean the few metal pots used in cooking. As the husband sat smoking, he heard the pans clatter to the ground and, curious, called out to the woman. Again, more sharply. No answer. What did that brave and devoted soul do? He ran across the room and slammed the door, bolting it from the inside. It was clearly not an Indian version of *Love Story*, especially as Corbett tells us as delicately as possible that the husband's greatest grief came when, after examining the mother's body, the exposed fetus in the dead woman's torn-open belly was a male heir.

Down the narrow lane between the houses, the Man-eater of Rudraprayag dragged his pathetic victim, all doors shut tight at the husband's first cries. Caught by the throat, she was still alive and probably conscious for the first fifty yards, until the spoor clearly indicated that the leopard had paused to kill her. The body in his jaws, the big leopard had carried her easily another one hundred yards into a little ravine along some fields and had eaten much of her at his leisure.

When Corbett arrived at the village after a long, hot climb the next day, he saw that the remains of the mother were still in the ravine where the leopard had left her, at the edge of a field which, forty yards from the corpse, had a hayrick or stack built into a stunted walnut tree. This would make an excellent blind. On the dirt of a tiny footpath running down to the body were the pug marks of the same leopard that had followed him two nights before, a huge male whose print showed the old bullet wound received on the suspension bridge four years earlier. Very likely, Corbett knew, the leopard would come back up this path if he returned at all. A most inhospitable reception would be waiting. With cut bamboo staves, he rigged gun traps using both his extra rifle and shotgun, slender lengths of fishing line acting as trip wires across the path. Even if the leopard came from another direction, if Corbett missed him at the kill, the leopard would probably run down the ravine anyway and shoot himself on the way out. The body of the woman was naked and, in the shadows of the ravine, the leopard would be nearly invisible, so Corbett placed a white rock a foot from the near side of the remains as a relative aiming point that would show up through the blackness. Comfortably settled into the walnut tree, hidden by the hay, Corbett sat back to wait.

There are three terms used here that bear some explanation. First, the hayrick wasn't a haystack as seen in the West, but rather a pile of hay formed around the branches of the walnut tree, leaving a space beneath the hay of some four vertical feet and rising to a height of ten feet from the ground. Also, the "fields" were actually terraces cut into the hillsides to take cultivation, some as narrow as two feet, as was the space under the tree. The last term, as Corbett points out, is the relativity of darkness to night. Complete blackness is rare, especially in tall mountains where snow-fields glare a diffused light even in mere starshine. When the eyes of a hunter are accustomed to it, visibility is often surprisingly good. Not, however, always . . . In fact, my personal dictum has become, "It's always darkest just before it's totally black."

Night had come down like a shroud. No sooner had the last feeble illumination of the sun faded in the west than a ripple of lightning flashed across the blackening sky, and fat, stinging drops of gale-born rain pelted the hunter, the downpour increasing to a wild deluge. The stars, suffocated by storm clouds, went out, and true blackness lapped up over the terraced ravine. At the height of the ferocious storm, Corbett heard a stone slide down the cut and, a few seconds later, the light rustle of straw, four feet directly below his feet. The man-eater had taken shelter from the rain under the hayrick and was lying dry, patient and unaware less than five feet below the hunter!

With the cat invisible, Corbett sat motionless in the wet, freezing wind, until the storm began to move on and gaps appeared between the rumbling, complaining clouds. Trying to keep his teeth from chattering, Corbett listened hard, staring as best he could through the remaining gloom. After a few minutes, his white marker rock disappeared as the leopard passed in front of it, and the awful sound of teeth crushing bone and ripping flesh was heard. Corbett had placed the rock on the wrong side of the corpse, as now that the rain had left puddles in the ravine, the leopard was feeding on the near side of the body. Ten very long minutes went by, until again the rock shone dully through the night. Corbett covered it with his foresight, only to hear a very strange rustling sound and to see the yellow form of the man-eater drifting like a patch of pale fog back under the hayrick. The cat's unusually light color could be accounted for by age, but Corbett remarked that he had never heard anything like the soft, silklike sound of his movement. The leopard was dividing his time between eating the woman and resting for a breather under the rick; Corbett kept the rock covered and was ready to fire the instant the cat passed in front of it again.

The next two hours are properly a monument to Corbett's skill at concealment and patience. Every time his muscles holding the heavy express rifle would give out and he'd be forced to rest for a moment, the rock would disappear. Three times this happened, the cat going back and forth between the body and the tree, until at last Corbett knew that, sooner or later, the leopard would detect him. How he managed to stay unnoticed at a range of a few feet for so long, considering the supersenses of a leopard, was miraculous enough. A chance would have to be taken. As the man-eater padded his rustling, unnerving way back for a fourth rest under the hayrick, Corbett leaned over and fired at a range of six feet.

At dawn, his bullet hole was found precisely in the center of the two-foot-wide terrace where the leopard was passing below, but there was no dead man-eater. Only a few clipped and scorched hairs marked the light bullet crease. Fate had decreed that fourteen more people must die before the great Rudraprayag Leopard met a reckoning, and, in a frightening number of incidents, Jim Corbett was very nearly added to the list.

Upon determining that the leopard had not crossed the suspension bridge as Corbett thought he might have, the hunter had them closed off at night, this being no inconvenience to anybody but the leopard, as nobody dared travel anyway. Those nights he was looking for the leopard elsewhere, the bridges were firmly plugged with wicked thorn bushes; the blockage to the bridge at Rudraprayag proper being left open when Corbett was free to keep a vigil. His perch was not one to inspire confidence to any other than a member of the Flying Wallenda family, being a slippery, flat rock atop a twenty-foot platform supporting the cables. With no handholds, merely reaching his hiding place was a venture of the first order, as the rickety bamboo ladder pressed into service was four feet short of the top. If getting there was all the fun, staying atop the rock in gale-force mountain night wind—the *dadu*—practically guaranteed to keep one in stitches. Several times, roaring gusts of glacier-frozen air almost blew Corbett from the platform onto the broken, jagged fangs of rock sixty feet below, from which his crushed body would neatly bounce into the wild torrent of the Alaknanda. For twenty nights, he sat alert and freezing on the platform above the river gorge, waiting for the leopard he had missed from six feet away. The only animal he ever saw was a lone jackal.

If one thing has struck me in researching and compiling the extraordinary events recorded in this book, it must be the truly strange quirks of fate that seem to surround the principal characters, both human and animal. The remarkable nature of close calls on both parts, largely due to the tiniest of factors, almost set one to wondering whether or not things really *are* "written" somewhere. Take the case, a few weeks later, when Corbett decided to reblock the Rudraprayag bridge and join forces with William Ibbotson and his men. . . .

As there wasn't enough room for the whole party in the bungalow, Corbett and his men moved out in favor of Ibbotson and his wife Jean. Erecting his forty-pound canvas tent on a small hill overlooking the pilgrim road, for some unaccountable reason the shelter was pitched under a huge prickly-pear tree that overhung the thorn shelter or fence around the tent, meant to keep out the leopard. Corbett originally had had it cut halfway through but changed his mind in the middle of the operation, appreciating that the tree would provide shade during the hot part of the day when he was resting from his night hunts. He must have had a lot on his mind, because by the time he figured out that he had provided a perfect bridge for the cat to get into the enclosure, it was so late at night that he decided to let it go. With six Garhwalis from his staff and a local cook, Corbett went to bed with the top of the tent left open, the bright moonlight bathing the interior of the fence in a soft eerie light.

About midnight, Corbett woke suddenly to the sound of hooked claws digging into the bark of the tree. Grabbing the loaded rifle on the bed at his side, he swung his feet down and into his slippers just as the prickly-pear tree creaked and cracked. There was a howl from the cook who had been sleeping, snoring on his back, of *"Sahib, bagh, bagh!"* Corbett didn't need to be told it was the leopard. Running out of the tent, he just missed getting off a shot as the man-eater scampered away up a hill. Corbett followed for a short distance, but it was clear that the leopard had kept going, out of range. The terrified cook, who had awakened at the cracking of the partially cut-through tree, had opened his eyes to stare smack into the leopard's face as it was gathering itself to drop down on the sleeping men. What if Corbett hadn't heard the claws? What if the tree hadn't cracked and unnerved the leopard into running, instead of charging? What if? In any case, the tree was cut down at dawn, heat be damned.

The next kills of the Rudraprayag Leopard were cows, people tending to be very hard to procure. Corbett and Ibbotson sat up over the first ill without success, shifting to a very ingenious blind built inside a large hayrick, when the leopard struck again, clearly having abandoned the first cow. Again, the most fantastic luck pervaded the scene. All bad.

Corbett and Ibbotson had built a double-decked blind in

the tall hayrick, using planks and wire mesh to create a hay-covered structure identical to the original but containing two platforms, one above the other, for the two hunters to sit upon. Corbett took the lower seat, with Ibbotson above him. About ten o'clock on a brilliantly moonlit night, Corbett heard the man-eater coming down a hill behind the blind and the now familiar rustle of hay as the leopard once more slipped under the blind to look over the kill. He was literally the thickness of one plank away from Corbett. A slow minute oozed by as the hunter waited, his breath held. Then the big, pale cat began to crawl out from under the rick, directly in front of Corbett's gun port, offering a simple shot at about one yard's distance. Just as the leopard's moonlit form started to come into view, there was a squeak. Instantly, the cat ran off to the right and up a hill, past the angle where he offered a shot. Ibbotson, who was probably unaware of the cat's presence, had gotten cramps in both legs and had shifted position at the critical second. Kismet? Makes one wonder.

Two more days passed before the leopard killed another cow, but not before scaring its owner nearly to death. The man lived alone in a small hut of one room, divided by a rather ramshackle partition of rough planks. One area was for sleeping, and the other contained a kitchen—which had been left open. The Garhwali was awakened by a sound across the divider and, sitting up, clearly saw the leopard in shafts of moonlight as it tried to find a way into the bedroom. Pacing the kitchen, for over an hour the man-eater tested each board, trying to tear it loose as the man cowered, soaked in cold sweat, watching helplessly from a few feet away. Unable at last to reach the juicy morsel blubbering in terror so near, the leopard walked out of the kitchen and killed the man's cow, which was tethered against the side of the hut.

In an effort to assist the hunters, the government had sent a shooting lamp and a massive double-spring gin trap, the same sort of affair that would have been used for bears in America. A full five feet long, this brute weighed eighty pounds and had springs so powerful that two men were needed to set the jaws—studded with three-inch teeth—in position. Figuring this would be a very good chance to use it, Corbett and Ibbotson carefully set it on a natural approach to the dead cow, pegging down the chain. That night, the hunters, neither of whom apparently suffered from hay-fever, settled down in another rick, twenty yards from the cow, and began to wait as thick clouds slid in, covering the sky like a manhole cover closing above their heads.

An hour slipped by without event, when suddenly both men were startled by a terrific eruption of furious roars near the cow. Aha! At last! Corbett flicked on the shooting light, a heavy battery-operated rig, and saw the leopard jumping madly around, both forelegs caught in the trap. Firing the first barrel of his .450 Express, his bullet neatly cut the half-inch chain, freeing the leopard. As it ran off at phenomenal speed—considering that both front legs had been pinioned by the heavy trap—Corbett fired and missed; so did Ibbotson with both his barrels. As might have been expected, while reloading, Corbett managed to screw up the electric light so it would not work.

This scenario was unfolding in what was practically downtown Rudraprayag. As the villagers heard the four shots, they assumed that the leopard had been killed and poured out of their houses shouting their joy, swarming toward the place where the trapped cat had disappeared. No good yelling at them; they were making too much noise to hear anything. Corbett scrambled down from his blind which, incidentally, was in a tree at the edge of a chasm hundreds of feet deep. Ibbotson got a second lamp—a gasoline type—working and lowered it to Corbett. When Ibbotson got down, they went after the man-eater, Corbett with his rifle to his shoulder and Ibbotson carrying a lamp above his head. A very superior way to get killed, if not especially imaginative. Cursing his luck for having shot away the restraining chain, Corbett tried to find some sign of the cat on the rocky, boulder-strewn terrace by the feeble glow of the lantern. A low growl drew his attention to an outcrop of rock and a small depression behind it. There, crouched and snarling, was the leopard. Corbett shot it instantly through the head. The Man-eating Leopard of Rudraprayag was dead!

Wasn't he?

The field went wild with exulting Garhwalis as Corbett examined the body. He didn't know why, but something just wasn't kosher here. It was a huge male leopard, presumably the one that had tried to break into the man's bedroom the night before; it had been shot in the center of an area where scores of people had been killed and eaten. It *had* to be the Rudraprayag Leopard. The hill people said they clearly recognized it. Ibbotson was convinced that it could be no other. So why the feeling of doubt? Only that Corbett had seen the man-eater the night he creased its neck with a bullet, and, despite the poor light, he simply wasn't convinced this was the same animal. Persuading Ibbotson not to notify the government for a few days, Corbett tried to get the Garhwalis to keep up their precautions in case he was right. The more people who came from distant villages to see the body, swearing they recognized it, the more positive Ibbotson was. But not Corbett.

That night, as Corbett lay doubting on his pillow, a pale yellow form slipped from shadow to shadow, icy amber eyes locked on the throat of a young mother squatting outside her hut. In a soft rush of motion without the slightest sound, four great fangs crunched home. Crossing the Chatwapipal bridge—which unaccountably had been left open—the Man-eater of Rudraprayag had hunted and killed at the first village he found.

When the girl's husband called to her, the leopard displayed an almost unbelievable show of strength. Carrying the body of the 150-pound girl—she was unusually large for a Garhwali woman—the leopard took her across two fields and made a jump straight down a twelve-foot ledge to a path. From the clear spoor, despite the fact that the impact of the jump would have increased the gravity of the body by two or three times, he did not let one part of her body touch the ground!

Carrying her another half-mile, the leopard tore off her clothes and ate a few pounds of flesh from both her upper and lower body, leaving the corpse in a patch of brilliant green grass beneath a vine-covered jungle tree. It was here, guarded by twenty men beating drums, that Corbett and Ibbotson were shown her remains the next day. They began to wait for the man-eater to return late that afternoon, under the distinct impression that *they* were hunting *him*. Man-eaters have a most disconcerting way of turning this relationship around. . . .

It was not a setup as easily hunted as on the other side of the river. The heavy vegetation of the jungle ravines allowed too much cover for the leopard to approach, so the men elected to place Ibbotson—who had a telescopic sight on his rifle that not only improved accuracy but by magnification gathered twilight long after a rifleman with ordinary sights would have been unable to see—in a tree overlooking a distant patch of forest where the leopard was believed to be lying up. If the man-eater came this way, it would be an easy shot. Corbett would cover the rear in case of an approach from that side.

The darkness slipped in quietly, broken only by the alarm of a frightened barking deer. The leopard was moving. But where? Darkness yielded to night, with only a few minutes' shooting light left, even for the 'scope sight. From his tree perch, Corbett started when a pinecone came rolling down the hill behind him from only thirty yards away. Instantly, he knew *he* was the hunted. As he listened to his heart pound, the light dropped away altogether, and he sat, helpless, listening to the leopard creeping closer. The fact that the heavy electric shooting lamp refused to work was not a source of great relief, so Corbett called to Ibbotson to cover him while he climbed down and lit the backup lamp, a gasoline mantle type called a "petromax." Getting it lit, he felt a good deal better, although the brilliant light did not project well, tending to blind the carrier. But still, it was one hell of a lot better than trying to climb the jungled hill by braille.

Ibbotson carried the lamp, while Corbett walked "shot-gun," and the pair started up the rugged ridge, hearing the whisper from close behind. They had only covered fifty yards when it happened: Ibbotson slipped on a rock, smashing the base of the lantern, the ash mantle disintegrating with the impact. If the small blue flame pumped by pressure from the fuel reservoir was not extinguished in three minutes, the heat would cause the bloody thing to explode. A half-mile of impossible terrain to cover in three minutes, closely followed by a man-eating leopard in complete night blindness, was the prospect. Oh, for the outdoor life!

Corbett wrote that he had never experienced a more terrifying trip than the eternity, scrambling by feel alone, up that black ridge. By some small miracle, they made it to the footpath that ran along the ridge's lip, but they were far from home free. The path, such as it was, ran through a series of buffalo wallows and patches of broken stone, at last reaching a series of rock steps. Climbing these, they found a small courtyard and a door. Fetching the door a hell of a kick, Corbett demanded that it be opened. No answer. Taking a box of matches from his pocket (one wonders why these were not judiciously used to get up the slope), Corbett swore to set the roof on fire. The door opened.

Inside were more than a dozen Garhwalis of various ages and both sexes, apologetic at having kept the *sahibs* waiting. Surely, though, they understood the people's fear that it could have been the demon leopard speaking to them in a man's voice. Corbett appreciated their terror very well. He hadn't expected to be alive at this moment himself. Borrowing a broken-down old lamp from this house, Corbett and Ibbotson got directions to the place where their men were housed. It took no little nerve to go back out into the night, but with the dim light, they managed to find the courtyard and flanking two-story houses where they were told their men would be. When they called out, a door opened, and they climbed the stairs to the second floor. Just as they reached safety, a village pye-dog came over, wagging his tail in friendship. After sniffing the hunters, the dog trotted over to the head of the stairs they had just climbed. Looking down them, he gave a panicked scream of fear and, barking insanely, backed away with his hair on end as if his tail had been plugged into an electrical outlet. The dog, with its better night vision, could clearly see the leopard in the courtyard below. Corbett lit another lamp and tried to shine it downward, but it just wasn't strong enough. Although the leopard was no more than ten feet away, he remained invisible. Looking at the dog as it watched the leopard, it was simple to follow the cat's movements as it circled about, finally moving off.

The next dawn—one Corbett had been convinced he would never see—the body proved to be untouched. Still, Corbett placed the gin trap and poisoned the corpse with arsenic, despite the fact that the leopard had already ingested large amounts of strychnine and cyanide with no apparent effects. But the leopard never did return to the dead girl.

When a cow was killed shortly thereafter, Corbett again placed the trap between the carcass' feet. The leopard ate the cow with his forepaws resting on the trap's springs the second night, then abandoned the body. To be doubly sure, the hunter poisoned the remains and was later surprised to find that they had been eaten by a leopard. But it was an ordinary leopard, not the man-eater, a wanderer who had happened on the cow by chance.

Ten weeks was enough. Frustrated, a nervous, thoroughly frightened wreck, the exhausted Corbett decided to quit, at least for a while. The press was hard on him, but the strain was just too much. If he kept at it without a rest, he'd be killed, and he knew it.

Jim Corbett abandoned the hunt in December of 1925 until March of the next year, during which time ten people were added as confirmed kills to the man-eater's scorecard. The last victim before Corbett's return was a small boy who was eaten completely, leaving nothing to draw the leopard for another meal. Back to square one. Ibbotson, who was not about to share Corbett's rock platform at the Rudraprayag bridge, had a platform constructed in an archway of the suspension tower, where the two men sat for five nights with no result. Ibbotson, who had to attend to urgent government business, left Jim Corbett to hunt alone. Over the span of a week or so, the leopard killed four goats, two cows and a dog, one of the cow carcasses offering Corbett another missed chance. Just as the leopard was approaching, a woman in a nearby house made a loud noise and spooked the man-eater. Another woman and her child had a very lucky but painful escape during this same time. While they were asleep in their house, the leopard tore open the front door and gripped the woman's arm in his jaws, dragging her across the floor to the opened exit. As the cat backed out the opening, the woman had the presence to slam the door on him—and her arm—enabling her to keep him out. Her arm was horribly mutilated and she had been clawed in the breast, but the child was unhurt, except for a head wound. They both recovered, charter members of the most exclusive of clubs—those who had escaped from the very jaws of the Rudraprayag Leopard. Corbett waited in this house for two nights, but there was no hint of the cat's return.

Corbett and Ibbotson continued their maddening game of hide-and-seek with the man-eater every night, somehow always missing what should have been "an easy shot." And the leopard, on several occasions, followed the hunters, waiting patiently for that one lapse of alertness that would bring a flashing attack. Recovering the body of a man named Gawiya, the hunters heavily dosed the corpse with cyanide which was unquestionably eaten by the leopard, who was then tracked to a hill cave. It was sealed off for ten days but proved to be empty of the cat, dead or alive. Apparently, he had been able to withstand the poison and also escape the cave through some unseen opening which led out to another part of the hill.

That he was still alive changed from conjecture to fact when he killed and ate a seventy-year-old woman, leaving enough of the body to provide a focal point for the continued efforts of the two frustrated hunters. It's difficult to say conclusively that any one episode in the incredible saga of the Man-eating Leopard of Rudraprayag was more exceptional than another, but the events surrounding the ambush set up over the old woman's body were so weird that even Corbett swears that he would not have told them had he not had witnesses.

After chasing the leopard around the rock slopes for a day with the usual results, it was concluded that, as the body was not in a proper location for the erection of a *machan,* or tree platform, a combination of set-guns, poison and the gin trap would be used. As both men were getting pretty tired of continually missing chance after chance, they really pulled the plug in this instance.

The body was lying at the edge of a ravine, on a small piece of flat ground against a high bank. After the vile business of cutting incisions in the corpse for the insertion of cyanide capsules, a .256 rifle of Ibbotson's and Corbett's extra .450 rifle were most carefully arranged, sighted and set with trip lines cut from Corbett's fishing reel. In addition to giving the leopard the chance to touch the trip lines as he came or went to or from the kill, the ends of the lines were also attached to the corpse's waist, so that the slightest tug would cause both guns to fire. As the .256 had a hair-set trigger, a distant sneeze would be enough to jar it off. Particular care was taken with the setting of the gin trap. Even though the leopard theoretically could come from any direction, there was one place which offered a natural approach to the kill, across a strip of flat ground some fifteen feet long. Here the earth was removed bit by bit, until a recess had been made which perfectly fitted the height and outline of the big trap. When the dirt had been carried away to an unsuspicious distance and scattered, every dead leaf, twig or other bit of natural debris was painstakingly replaced over a cover of green leaves and a layer of thin dirt. So perfect was the camouflage that even Corbett couldn't pick out the trap from the surrounding ground. As a final touch, a series of wild, thorny bushes was transplanted from the hillside to form a subtle funnel into the trap jaws. When the men left to take up their wait in a *machan* some distance away, they were absolutely convinced that nothing "bigger than a rat" could conceivably get to the body without meeting death in one of three forms.

The late afternoon began to chill off as the sun eased lower, and the hunters relaxed on the comfortable *machan*. Although they were more than two hundred yards from the dead woman's body, there was always a chance the leopard would show on his way from the thick mountain jungle where Corbett had been trying to get a shot that morning, and both men watched carefully without any hint of the cat until darkness. As the blackness settled in the hollows, leaving the ridge tops capped with golden light, the hunters put down their rifles. Too dark for a shot, but they were not depressed. Three chances remained for this to be the last night of the man-eater's life: the trap, the rifles and the poison.

When the sun was completely gone, something happened that neither Corbett nor Ibbotson had thought of: It began to rain. A sense of despair drained Corbett as he whispered his fears to his companion. The mere weight of the rain on the earth over the trip pan of the trap might set it off, so lightly was it cocked. And what of the hair-trigger .256? Would the rain cause the silk fishing line to shrink? The smallest increase in tension would fire the rifle, ruining the whole ambush. Worried, the two lay on the *machan*, staring into the blackness, the continuous rain soaking them through with an icy, night chill. Ibbotson had just asked Corbett for the time. "A quarter to eight," had been the whispered answer, the low words no sooner out of his mouth when the blackness was shattered with a terrible series of snarls and roars, coming directly from the kill. Could it be? Yes! The Man-eater of Rudraprayag was finally caught. Nothing could escape the grip of that savage trap. Risking their necks, Corbett and Ibbotson leaped blindly off the edge of the *machan* to the ground, Corbett at least breaking his fall by grasping a branch on his way down. Frantically, they scrambled to get to the petromax lamp hidden nearby, and, while Ibbotson was trying to light it, the commotion of the leopard suddenly stopped. Corbett made some negative remark—which, after his continuing experience with the man-eater, might be forgiven—and Ibbotson read him the Riot Act about being a confirmed pessimist. Ibbotson soon had the lamp working, and the pair made for the trap as fast as they could go, circling around to approach from the top of the bank, above the body. Working their way up to the edge, both were thrilled to see that the place where the trap had been hidden was now just an empty hole. But the higher their hopes rose, the deeper they plummeted when the bright sweep of the lamp showed the dull, steel outline of the sprung trap ten yards farther down the slope. It was mournfully empty.

Bitterly dejected, the hunters went back to the *machan* and settled down to sleep away their frustration, unable to imagine how the leopard had escaped all three of their traps. At the first hint of dawn, they found out, spelled clearly in the tracks on the rain-softened earth. What they discovered was a vivid, if not especially rare, example of the extraordinary intelligence of an experienced man-eating cat.

The man-eater had approached the place in exactly the manner Corbett thought he would, but that was the leopard's last predictable action. Instead of crossing the little flat spot hiding the trap, he had circled below it and come for the body on the side protected by the thorn bushes planted there. With no hesitation, he had then ripped three of the bushes out by their roots to make a hole and, on the safe side of the trip lines, had figured out how they worked. Disengaging them, he had gently pulled the body in such a direction as to create slack, relieving the tension of the triggers. Having defused the setup, he began to feed, starting with the two parts of the body without poison embedded in them, the head and neck, which he ate completely. Finishing his meal, he had worked on down the corpse, neatly eating between the poison incisions, until they and the small islands of flesh around them were all that was left of the dead woman.

Pleasantly satiated—and probably feeling deservedly smug—the leopard had then decided to leave and take shelter from the rain. By the craziest twist of luck, just as he was stepping over the hidden gin trap, the additional weight of the wet covering of dirt (possibly combined with the tiniest disturbance of his passing) caused the trigger pan of the trap to release the exact moment he was over it. With a snap like a gunshot, the vicious steel jaws had clashed over the knee joint of the man-eater's left hind leg. By all rights in heaven or hell, he *should* have died there, but he didn't. Impossible to believe under even the most liberal application of the laws of chance, it happened that, while the trap had been carried there from Rudraprayag, somebody had dropped it, the impact against a rock having broken off one of the three-inch intermeshing steel teeth. Just one lousy, goddamn tooth. But which one? The one located precisely, exactly, where the jaws had closed on the leopard's leg. After his initial roars of fear and surprise, the cat had simply pulled his leg free through the gap caused by the missing tooth and walked away. Even a couple of inches on either side of the gap would have held the leopard so firmly he would have needed a locksmith to get free. But no. Get out your calculator, professor, and tell me the odds on *that*!

Corbett continued to hunt the leopard, despite the growing sense of helplessness that gripped him. Several days after the trap incident, he tried enticing the man-eater into range by imitating the mating call. Everything went fine as Corbett sat in a high pine tree, the leopard steadily approaching to within sixty yards. What happened? Another leopard—a genuine female—started calling from the mountain past Corbett, and the man-eater chose her. As an *ersatz* Jezebel, Corbett was a complete failure.

That Corbett was getting desperate is evidenced by the fact that one night he talked himself into the suicidally dangerous idea of waiting on the ground near a dead cow killed by a leopard. It looked like a good chance, a snug place in the hollow at the base of a big rock to shelter him, a bush directly in front for cover, where he was sure he could kill the leopard easily as it came back for the cow, which had been undisturbed.

Slowly, the evening wore on without any sign of the cat. As the darkness thickened, Corbett took relief in the dense scattering of very dry leaves all over the area, which would clearly indicate the position of the man-eater for the shooting light taped to his rifle. As the hours dragged by, Corbett became more and more uneasy at the thought that the leopard had seen him settle in at the base of the rock and was waiting for a chance to attack. Moment by moment, he struggled to beat back the rising fear that threatened to burst into unreasoning terror. Blacker and blacker became the sky as clouds moved in and he was forced to rely entirely on the dry leaves to hear the approach of the cat. And then the last defense was gone. Heavy rain sluiced down, dampening the leaves and covering any small sound with wet noise. Badly frightened, Corbett knew that now would be the time the leopard would choose to come for him. He took off his coat and wrapped it tightly around his neck as protection from the terrible fangs, tying it securely with the sleeves. The rifle was useless now, and Corbett knew it. With grim determination, he shifted it to his left hand and drew his knife, a wicked-looking Afridi stabbing dagger he had bought as a curiosity from a deputy commissioner in the north. With three notches in the handle, it had been the killing weapon in a triple murder, an old evidence tag attached to the hilt at the time of the purchase.

Corbett's mind raced. Should he stay here, blind and deaf, for another six hours until light? What would his chances be to cover the five hundred yards to the nearest hut? In the end, he realized that, with his nerves already frayed from months of flirting with death, he might well be either dead or insane if he stayed. Shouldering the rifle, afraid to use the light for fear of drawing the man-eater, he stumbled his way through the rainy blackness, the knife tight in his white-knuckled fist. To his unspeakable relief, he made it. The next day, the kill proved to be untouched. Crisp, clear pug marks showed over his own footprints on the road. Corbett had survived the most terrifying night of his venturesome career with the most dangerous of animals, a night he would admittedly relive in cold, sweating nightmares the rest of his days.

The last human victim of the Man-eater of Rudraprayag was killed on April 14, 1926, a final and classic example of the skill and daring of the animal that had survived for more than eight years of steady man-eating.

Walking from the small spring at Bhainswara village that April evening were a widow, her twelve-year-old son, her daughter of eight and a neighbor's boy the same age. Carrying water back to the common-walled two-storied home, the widow was preceded by the neighbor's son and her daughter, and followed by her own son, who brought up the rear. In single file, a few feet apart, they proceeded up a long, flagstoned courtyard to one of a set of short steps used in common by these two families. It was broad daylight still, and when the neighbor boy happened to look into one of the ground-floor storage rooms of one of the houses, he was not surprised to see what he thought was a large dog lying there. Paying no attention, he said nothing.

The woman was halfway up the steps when she heard the clang of a brass water vessel dropping behind her. Putting down her own pot, she turned around to see what had happened. At the bottom of the stairs was her son's water jug, overturned, but no sight of the child himself. Going back down the steps the woman picked the jug up, looking around for her son. When he did not appear, she thought he had run off to escape punishment for his clumsiness, and she started to call after him. The rest of the neighbors had heard the crash and came out to see what was going on. As it was now starting to get dark, one old man lit a lantern and began to look around the many storage rooms on the first floors, presuming that was where the boy had gone to hide. In the dull glow of his lamp, he noticed something shiny on the flagstones and bent down next to the widowed mother. His fingers came up red and slick. At the old man's yell of horror, the rest of the village piled into the courtyard, one of them an experienced hunter. Borrowing the lantern, he followed the blood trail out the courtyard, over a low wall and into the edge of a yam field. Here in the soft dirt were the big tracks of the man-eater. Panic swept the village, although clearly the boy was dead, and nobody among the armed men attempted a rescue.

That a huge leopard could and did enter a village of more than one hundred persons, in full daylight, cross a completely open courtyard without being seen or scented by any of the village dogs, make a kill so quickly and silently in the open that a woman mere feet away did not detect the slightest struggle, carry off the body of the boy, again without the smallest sound, and escape cleanly merely serves to illustrate the unbelievable and uncanny skill of a practiced man-eater.

It seems almost an axiomatic observation that fate would again intervene to prevent Corbett from being able to kill the leopard over the body of the boy. While the hunter was waiting for the Rudraprayag Man-eater to return to his kill—which he was in the actual act of doing—another male leopard crossed the man-eater's path and attacked him, in defense of the local cat's territory. As Corbett sat waiting in the dark, he listened to a fantastic battle between the two big males, hoping that somehow the strange leopard would be able to kill the man-eater. No such luck. Although the fight lasted through various stages for quite a long time, the man-eater was driven off and never returned to the body of the boy.

Time was growing short for Corbett, now back with Ibbotson. In addition to the sensation-frenzied press which demanded the death of the man-eater and the removal of Corbett in favor of some other hunter, he was scheduled to be sent on temporary assignment by the railway to Africa in a short time. After the months of unrelenting frustration, Jim Corbett had decided that the Man-eater of Rudraprayag was either too smart, too lucky, or both, to be killed in ambush over one of his victims and that some other method of hunting, less vulnerable to the quirks of outrageous chance, would have to be adopted.

One thing had caught his attention during his long stay in Garhwal—the formation of a pattern. Since established patterns are more or less predictable by definition, it was exactly what he had been looking for. In this case, it was the fact that the man-eater had the habit of walking down the pilgrim road between Rudraprayag and the village of Gola-brai, just south of Rudraprayag, the location of a pilgrim shelter where three persons had been killed over the years and the proprietor himself badly mauled in the summer of

1921. He was the only other person beside the woman with the clawed arm who had been caught by the leopard and survived. On the average of once every five days, the pug marks of the cat could be seen on this road. So, reasoned Corbett, spending ten nights in ambush along the path might very well provide a shot.

Ibbotson, who had noticed how shaky Corbett's nerves were, was against it, but Corbett was adamant. If, at the end of ten consecutive nights the leopard had not been killed, he would pack it in and give up, going home for good.

Those ten long, dark nights seemed like ten centuries to Jim Corbett, perched in a *machan* built in a roadside mango tree, a small goat tied below his only companion. The first night, despite constant vigilance, the only sound he heard was the warning bark of a *kakar*, a barking deer. The next nine nights he heard or saw nothing at all. It looked like the end of the campaign; the man-eater was clearly the winner. Meeting with Ibbotson on the eleventh day, Corbett was reluctant to abandon the hunt, leaving an untold number of Indians to certain death. But facts had to be faced. In his government position, Ibbotson simply had to get back to important duties elsewhere. As for Corbett, he was already three months late for his African assignment and could not delay further. Still, no other hunter in India wanted any part of a leopard who had already eaten more than 125 people, so there was no replacement forthcoming. As a last resort, Corbett considered canceling his passage to Africa, and Ibbotson gave thought to taking a leave of absence to continue the hunt. Yet there were important matters affecting the entire business careers of both. It was left that they would take that night to think about the matter and make their decisions in the morning. As for Corbett, he would at least go down swinging, spending his last night back in the mango tree along the Golabrai Road.

That the leopard was still in the close vicinity was without question; over the past ten days he had three times broken into houses, killing a goat, a sheep and, on the last try, nearly a man whose interior door was just too strong for the cat. To Corbett's dismay, a party of 150 pilgrims had arrived at the nearby shelter that day. Although he could do nothing about it, Corbett told the innkeeper to keep them from moving around and to make them stay quiet, as there was no way such a big group could fit into the shelter.

As he took up his position in the mango tree in the late afternoon, Corbett noticed that a packman with a flock of sheep and goats and two noisy dogs had penned the animals in a heavy thorn enclosure some one hundred yards from his *machan*. Ibbotson had left for the bungalow nearby, and Corbett was alone with the bait goat when evening fell. Several days past full, the moon would not rise for some hours, and it would be much longer before the deep recesses of the mountainous terrain would be reached by its beams. Corbett was in his practiced ready position, enabling him to flip on his small flashlight and shoot with a minimum of movement and disturbance, when, around nine o'clock, he noticed a light carried by somebody leave the pilgrim shelter and go across a road, a foolhardy errand, whatever its purpose. In a minute, it was carried back to the shelter and blown out. Once again, complete gloom settled over Gola-brai.

A few seconds after the light was extinguished, the two big dogs at the packman's thorn enclosure began to bark insanely. Corbett flinched. It had to be the leopard they had seen, and from the direction of their barking, the man-eater was coming down the dark road. The cat had likely seen the lantern and was on its way to the shelter to make a kill. Then, as he listened through the night, the dogs shifted the direction of their attention toward Corbett. Had the leopard seen the goat? He must have, and was using the mango tree as cover to get closer. But would he kill the bait or just slip past and attack the pilgrim shelter? By the dogs having stopped their clamor, Corbett knew the cat had lain down to look the area over carefully, his widely dilated eyes seeing clearly, while the man's were useless. Shutting his eyes to concentrate better on his hearing, Corbett listened as the slow minutes dragged by without a giveaway sound.

Just when he was almost sure that the leopard had skirted around him and gone for a human kill, the goat's bell tinkled abruptly. As a reflex action, Corbett flipped on the small flashlight taped to his barrel and saw with disbelief that the sights were perfectly aligned on the shoulder of a huge leopard only twenty feet away. A twitch of Corbett's finger touched off the shot just as the light flickered out. The battery, on its last legs, had died. With no idea of the result of his shot, Corbett was left sitting alone in the dark, with several hours to wait for the moon. Across the road, a crack of light showed as the innkeeper opened his door and called out, asking if Corbett needed a hand. Listening too hard for the leopard to answer the man, Corbett kept quiet, and the Indian hurriedly slammed the door.

When, at 3 A.M., five hours after his shot, the moon was bright enough to give some visibility, Corbett climbed to the top of the tree but was disappointed that he could not make out anything in the direction of the hill, where he had had the impression the leopard had leapt at the shot. By five in the morning, dawn was close enough for him to descend finally, greeted by a cheerful bleat from the uninjured goat. With thumping heart and sweating palms, he approached the road, thrilled by a thick smear of blood, now dried, on a rock at the side. Following the blood trail for fifty yards down the hillside, Corbett was startled to see the leopard's head projecting from a hole in the rocks, staring straight ahead. He was as dead as a load of hamburger.

Strangely, there was no elation for Corbett, merely a draining sense of relief. Here, the enemy that had stalked his tracks so many dark nights, the devil-leopard that had slaughtered so many men, women and children, a *shaitan* that was now just a very big, whiskerless, straw-colored old cat, stiff and dead, looking rather shabby, considering his reputation. Nobody else seemed to feel this way.

A party of rescuers arrived at the *machan* at dawn and, seeing the blood trail and Corbett nowhere in sight, concluded that the leopard had killed and probably by now had eaten the *sahib*. When they discovered him and the perforated pussy, they went completely off their collective nut with joy, as did the gathering crowd of pilgrims. The relief of seeing their great enemy dead after eight years of terror released a fast-traveling mass paroxysm of euphoria. Even Ibbotson was beside himself with happiness as he sent cables and messages to the government and the press by the dozens. Corbett? He wanted a cup of tea, a hot bath and a rest, in that order. He could skin the leopard later. It wasn't going anywhere. . . .

From the physical standpoint of being an outstanding people processor, the Man-eating Leopard of Rudraprayag was very well qualified for his work. Twelve hours after he died, he was measured at seven feet six inches between pegs driven into the ground at nose and tail tip, seven feet ten inches over natural body curves. Considering that a leopard of just seven feet will place a sportsman's name forever in the record book of Mr. Rowland Ward of London, who keeps track of such matters, the man-eater was truly gigantic. He was very old, his hair pale and short with a tendency to be brittle. Interestingly, he had no whiskers at all. One very strange aspect of the leopard was that he had a completely black mouth and tongue, a condition I have never heard of before. Corbett speculated that it might have been the result of so many doses of various poisons, but this has never been confirmed.

The man-eater's teeth, consistent with his age, were quite worn, and one canine was broken. This, however, is not evidence of a reason for starting his man-eating eight years before, as he clearly demonstrated over his career that he had no trouble killing animals as big as cows and, if anything, was much more powerful and fit than a normal leopard.

That he was, indeed, *the* Rudraprayag Man-eater was testified to by his wounds. In addition to the killing shot by Corbett through the right shoulder, there was the clear mark of a bullet fired at him on the bridge by the young officer back in 1921, the scar on the left rear pad and the missing claw shot away by the same bullet. His recent territorial battle while Corbett was waiting for him at Bhainswara village must have been a real donnybrook, as he was covered with cuts on his head, tail and two legs. Corbett also found a single pellet of buckshot embedded just under the skin of the chest which, years later, was claimed to have been shot there by a Christian Indian the first year the man-eater opened for business.

After word of the man-eater's death was spread throughout Garhwal and beyond, great crowds gathered at Rudraprayag to see the "devil." Corbett was truly touched by the gratitude of the thousands, which was shown traditionally by the gift of a flower dropped at the feet. As he stood, listening to the tearful thanks and terrible stories of death in the night from survivors who had lost children, husbands, wives and parents, E. James Corbett's last recollection of the Man-eater of Rudraprayag was standing in a growing pile of tear-dewed flowers.

When India received her independence from Great Britain, Jim Corbett left his beloved hills and moved to the then crown colony of Kenya, in East Africa. With the army rank of colonel, he had played a recruiting role in both world wars and taught jungle warfare in the second. The ten man-eating tigers and leopards he personally destroyed under the most difficult of conditions without doubt saved thousands of lives, despite the more than fifteen hundred already lost to these cats.

Corbett, one of the only two men ever given "Freedom of the Forests" by the Indian government, died in Kenya on April 21, 1955, a bit short of his eighty-first birthday, an incredibly long life for a man who risked it so often and so willingly. Anyone who knew him, or followed his life through his books, cannot other than agree with the comment of Joseph Wood Krutch, quoted by the publishers of a posthumous omnibus of Corbett's work. He will always be remembered as a "fine writer and an admirable man—simple, kindly and courageous."

BIBLIOGRAPHY

Corbett, Jim (E. James). *Man-Eaters of Kumaon.* New York: Oxford University Press, 1946.

———. *The Man-Eating Leopard of Rudraprayag.* Oxford: Oxford University Press, 1948.

————. *Jungle Lore*. New York: Oxford University Press, 1953.

————. *The Temple Tiger and More Man-eaters of Kumaon*. New York and London: Oxford University Press, 1954.

————. *Man-Eaters of India* (A Corbett Omnibus). New York: Oxford University Press, 1957.

Perry, Richard. *The World of the Tiger*. New York: Atheneum, 1966.

And Furthermore . . .

IF YOU HAVE EVER HAD an extended lapse of sanity during which, between imitating birdcalls and drooling, you have written a book, I don't have to tell you that chapters are large, hopelessly blank stacks of square paper intended to be covered with characters and deeds which are invariably round. So much for any pending theories of literary geometry. I prefer to write about people who are safely dead and who, therefore, tend to come along quietly. But there are some whose ghosts and adventures are downright uncooperative and don't fit those fifty-odd typewritten pages, no matter how nasty you get with them. Worse, these people and events happen to be favorites of mine, the exclusion of which would leave this book something less than I mean it to be—whatever *that* is. Getting down to it, I suppose I'm saying that I'm writing this chapter as much to humor myself as you.

As a one-man wave of gargoyle-festooned romanticism posing as a professional small boy, it's been hard enough for me to leave out quite a few jolly chaps who have gotten the chop in one or another of the silent places, particularly since their stories could—and, in many cases, have—filled volumes. But there are still a couple of "hairies" that belong here, and thus this maverick chapter, a potpourri of peril, a trilogy of terror, maybe even a crate of—well, never mind. Enough. Rather than create a chapter by telling you why this one is different, let's get on with the goodies. They are events of great wonder and delight to me—the last one very close to my heart, not to mention my tail.

One of the greatest and best known of the "Victorian lions" during the tumultuous period of British Nile exploration was Samuel White Baker. As a sportsman and traveler, he practically foamed at the mouth with enthusiasm for the most dangerous escapade, fame and knighthood coming as a result of his journeys of discovery to Lake Albert and Murchison Falls, both of which he named in company with his "woman," later wife, Florence. Unparalleled as paragon of bravery, resilience and resourcefulness, Lady Baker had a most interesting and, by Victorian standards, shocking background: Sam had purchased her as a slave in the Balkans when she was still in her teens. No kidding. She was at his side virtually the rest of his life, even through the bloody battles later fought to suppresss the slave trade in East Africa, when Sam became Baker *Pasha* under the khedive of the Ottoman Empire.

Certainly, Baker's African experiences were interesting, yet the early part of his life, from a hunting standpoint, was even more so. Well known in England for running down stags on foot and killing them with a cut-down sword while his hounds bayed them, Sam Baker spent much of his young manhood in Ceylon (Sri Lanka), where, at one time, he probably had killed more Asian elephants than any man alive. Yet, for all his brushes with elephants, one of the closest calls he ever had occurred shortly after making the acquaintance of that terror of southern Asia, the water buffalo (*Bubalius bubalis*). The incident was immortalized in his book *The Rifle and the Hound in Ceylon* as "The Charge of Sixpences."

Not named by accident, the water buff is one of the most dangerous game animals not only by virtue of his tremendous strength and tendency to charge, but because of the wet, open terrain he loves, which prohibits stalking and the safety of trees when needed. With horns much larger and more swept back than his African Cape counterpart, he is every bit as resistant to bullet damage as a Mark IV Tiger tank. That's a major consideration for reviewing one's codicils before beginning a slogging hunt for water buff, even today with modern, heavy-caliber, smokeless-cartridge rifles. Imagine what the risks were back in the days when only muzzle-loading black-powder guns were available!

To appreciate the chances the early hunters took with dangerous game, let's have a quick review of the problems inherent in using the front-end charcoal burners. The main snag was the lack of firepower because of the intricate reloading process, difficult under laboratory conditions, let alone in a misty, jungle swamp or aboard a racing horse. The first part of the operation was the measuring and pouring down the barrel of a charge of black powder. Since the stuff wasn't as powerful as modern smokeless propellants, considerably larger ratios of powder quantity to caliber were the rule. When hunting really big game, the size and weight of the bullets or balls and the amount of black powder that powered them were enough to give a strong man sweaty palms in anticipation of the pummeling from the recoil of these shoulder-fired cannons. For them to be effective on animals the size of buffalo and elephant, such guns as found in Baker's Ceylonese battery were typical: He used a 4-gauge single-barrel rifle weighing a handy twenty-one pounds, powered by a ferocious sixteen drams of powder behind a *quarter-pound* bullet; a sixteen-pound 8-gauge; and four matching double-barreled rifles of 10-gauge which handled a two-and-a-half-ounce conical bullet from a fifteen-pound frame. "Gauge," incidentally, means the number of pure lead round balls required to total one pound; therefore, a 4-gauge fires a four-ounce ball, a 12-gauge a ball of one-twelfth of a pound and a 1-gauge, theoretically, would shoot a ball of one pound.

To give some idea of what was waiting for anything on the receiving end of one of these maulers, Baker tells of having shot a big bull buffalo in a shallow lake at about 150 yards' distance with a "light" load of only twelve drams of powder in his 4-bore. The ball slammed into the bull, passed through the near shoulder, on through the lungs, out the far shoulder and thick skin and skipped along the surface of the water for a full mile! That the buffalo, by the way, did not even flinch at the terrible wound and ran for more than 300 yards may give some idea of the vitality of the species.

Once the powder was measured and poured, the bullet or ball was "seated" just inside the muzzle of the gun on a leather or cloth patch meant to take the impression of the rifling of the bore. If the patch had not been lubricated and precut to size, it would have to be trimmed with a sharp knife before being driven down the barrel. On many guns which had tight-fitting bores or which were "fouled" by burned powder residue from previous shots, a "bullet starter" might have to be used, a short rod with a palm cushion to slam the bullet far enough down the barrel to get it to take the tight fit of the rifling. Then it was rammed full length down the barrel, tightly against the powder charge at the breech. The ramrod withdrawn and replaced, the gun now had to be primed.

In a flintlock action, a layer of fine powder was spread on a grooved pan connected by a flash hole to the main charge in the breech. A frizzen, or striking plate, was swung into position over the pan; when the trigger was pulled, the cocked hammer, gripping a piece of flint, would strike the frizzen in a shower of sparks that would ignite the layer in the pan and, thereby, touch off the main charge, firing the ball up the barrel. If only the powder in the pan ignited, it was called "a flash in the pan," still a common expression. If this happened while the hunter was trying to stop something that was trying to eat him, it was called "big trouble."

From the early 1800s, the improvement of a percussion-cap ignition system speeded up the operation somewhat, as well as giving better reliability. As in Baker's guns, this style used a hollow steel nipple, over which was seated a tiny, cup-shaped percussion cap, usually of copper, which had a shock-sensitive mercuric fulminate in it, waterproofed by a layer of dried lacquer. When struck by the hammer face when the trigger was pulled, this transmitted the ignition spark directly to the powder charge . . . at least most of the time.

If you reckon this takes rather a long time to explain, give some thought to the sensation of performing this process with something large and angry bearing down on your quaking carcass. Legion were the pioneer hunters whose last thought must have been, "Now, just a couple more minutes, buffalo, [substitute elephant, lion, tiger, rhino, etc., as

necessary for geographic accuracy] and I'll have this thing
relo—"

One of the most beautiful places in mid-nineteenth-
century Ceylon was called Minneria Lake, a vast wetland of
verdant grass and fingers of jungle projecting into the
shallow water for the entire twenty-mile circumference of
the lake. Sam Baker's first view of it was breathtaking on a
clear, late afternoon in 1846 (when he was still in his
twenties), after having ridden the whole day through a
dense tropical forest with natives cutting a path ahead. In
company with his brother, whom Sam identifies only by the
initial "B" but is probably James Baker—why "B," when he
had no brother whose name began with that initial?—both
men noted the incredible concentrations of wildlife: herds of
deer grazing peacefully on the plains along the shore;
swarms of ducks and geese; snipe flushing at every step.
And what were those black patches here and there in the
grass? Buffalo! Hundreds of them.

Sam Baker looked at the sun, at four o'clock inexorably
sinking from its position toward the horizon. Damn it all!
Where were the bearers with the heavy rifles? Somewhere
behind on the trail, there was no way to guess when they
might come up with the baggage. After a progressively
irritating twenty-minute wait for the column of coolies,
Baker happened to feel around in his pockets to find a few
solid lead balls that would fit the two shotguns he and his
brother carried for potting birds along the trail. Why not?
Loading the smoothbores, they left their horses and started
walking toward the nearest herd of buffalo, about a hundred in the closest bunch, with several mountainous old bulls
out to the sides.

With no cover to mask their stalk, the Bakers were seen
immediately, the herd coming to its feet and staring at them
in astonishment. Forming a close rank studded with seven
huge herd bulls in the forefront, the buffalo stood watching
nervously as the brothers ran forward. When the men got to
within thirty yards, one of the bulls feinted a charge, then
angled off, exposing his shoulder twenty paces away. Twin

shots rocked the tranquil plain as both men fired together, the old bull dropping to his knees with a smashed shoulder blade. In a moment, however, he was back up, hobbling out into the lake on three legs.

As the Bakers were lining up the wounded bull for a second broadside, a very odd thing happened. With a ferocious grunt, one of the other bulls began a full charge at the crippled one, catching him squarely on the side with awful force. The wounded animal was knocked into a heap and lay there, unable to get up, while his attacker wandered nonchalantly off across the plain.

Leaving James to finish off the dying buff, Sam took after the second. It was exasperating. At an easy canter, the bull would cover a hundred yards and haul up, letting Baker come just to the edge of the smoothbore's range before repeating the performance. For a mile, this continued, the hunter muttering anatomical impossibilities at the buffalo as he panted along behind until firing a long, missed shot in sheer disgust. Loading his last spare solid ball, he took up the frustrating chase again.

At the juncture of the lake and a creek flowing onto the plain, the bull turned at an angle and permitted Baker to "cut the corner" on him. Running as fast as he could, Sam was within thirty yards before the bull walked into the creek and started to swim across its sixty-yard width. Skirting around the mouth of the stream, Baker made it to the point on the opposite shore where the buff would emerge, and he waded out into the knee-deep shallows to intercept him. Just as he got there, the big, wide-horned bull swam out of the main channel and, surprised, stood looking at Baker from fifteen yards away.

Chuckling to himself, absolutely certain he could obliterate the bull with his first shot, Sam Baker permitted himself a mental pat on the back. With a steady aim at the point where the deep chest met the massive neck, he squeezed off the first barrel, the white burst of powder smoke drifting to the side so he could see the ball impact on the wet, rubbery hide. It was spot-on, and a thick stream of blood started to run from the wound and drip into the water. But there seemed to be some sort of misunderstanding; instead of crumpling up and falling in an explosion of watery spray, the buffalo did absolutely nothing. There was not a sound, not even a twitch of pig-iron muscle from the shot. The only difference Baker noticed, with an uneasy feeling, was in the bull's eyes. Previously dull and sullen, they had almost magically taken on a gleaming glow of pure fury. Better play it again, Sam. Shaken by the lack of effect of the first shot, Baker squinted down the twin tubes of the shotgun and loosed another ball at the bleeding wound. The thumping echo of the report rolled across the lake, but, except for a heavier blood flow and a darker glint in the bull's eyes, the results were the same. Astounded and now frightened, Samuel White Baker stood knee-high in bloody water with an empty gun and no more ammunition. With a ridiculous gesture, he drew his sheath knife. It would be about as effective on the more than a ton of horned fury as a pair of cuticle scissors. It was now the buffalo's turn, and, knowing that to retreat would bring a sure charge, Baker started giving some thought to what he had better do next.

James was roughly a mile away, back at the body of the first bull, but possibly Sam could get his attention with a whistle. Putting his fingers to his tongue, he cut loose with a piercing warble used to call his staghounds home in Scotland. The irate buffalo did not appear partial to the serenade, because, having rumbled to within ten yards of Baker, he now reduced this distance to less than twenty feet. Pawing the pink water with cloven hooves the size of mattock heads while grunting lustily, the bull had the definite, undivided attention of Sam Baker.

An idea began to take shape in Baker's numbed brain. If he was out of lead balls, why not use something else? But what? With his eyes still on the bull, willing him to delay his charge, he tore off a scrap of his shirt and, blindly digging through his pouch, discovered a half-dozen sixpence coins and two smaller *anna* pieces (local money for paying coolies). As fast as his fumbling fingers could manage it, he poured a *double* charge of powder down the right-hand barrel of the shotgun and, wrapping the coins tightly in the cloth, rammed them down the bore. As he was doing this, the bull sprang forward again so quickly that Baker only had time to jerk out the ramrod and let it fall into the water before he got a cap on the nipple and cocked the hammer. The bull stopped again, practically close enough to touch.

It was a different Sam Baker awaiting the charge he knew must come; not properly armed, but at least with some possible defense. He knew that he would have to wait until literally the last foot, perhaps even placing the muzzle of the gun on the buffalo's forehead for the improvised load to be effective. As the weird confrontation continued, Baker was startled to hear the splash of water behind him and a gasping of breath that proved to be his brother. He had heard the whistle and run the mile as fast as he could. Sam dared not look away from the buff but listened as James explained that he had only one loaded barrel and no more ammo. Sam gave instructions that James should hold his fire until the buffalo was almost on him and then shoot for the head. The words had barely cleared his lips when the exhausting tension came to an abrupt end. The bull lowered his massive head and charged straight at Sam.

James fired. His bullet had no effect as the bull hurtled onto his brother. In the second the buffalo was about to make contact, the horn tips actually on either side of Sam's body, Sam pulled the trigger with the muzzle almost touching the bull's head. With a deafening crash, the double-powder charge careened the package of small change down the smooth barrel and onto the bull's skull, knocking him cold, stopping him in his tracks as if he'd come up short at the end of a steamship hawser. The Baker brothers didn't hang around to see how badly he was hit. All vestige of Victorian reserve by now forgotten, they ran for their lives across the plain for the only cover, a big fallen tree about a half-mile away. After a very active first hundred yards, they turned to see what had happened to the bull. With a thrill of fright, the Bakers saw that he had regained his feet and was coming after them; not fast, but in a most determined manner. He was game, but nothing less than an elephant could have withstood the impact of such a violent collision with Victoria Regina's profile at point-blank range without developing a very advanced migraine. As obvious waves of dizziness swept the bull, he would lose his balance and fall, only to get back up and keep coming. The brothers reached the tree just as the bull collapsed two hundred yards behind them, seemingly unable to regain its feet. Sneaking into the jungle, Sam and James were able to make their way back to their horses.

Continuing on to Minneria village, three miles from the lake, the hunters met their porters and set up camp for the night. At dawn, Sam Baker was back on the plain with his trusty quarter-pounder 4-bore, but of the buffalo, nothing was ever found.

I would have to admit that I stand corrected with reference to my observation in *Death in the Long Grass* that "the *only* sure way to stop a charging buffalo is to take away his credit card." Sam Baker clearly proved that there are times when cash is definitely preferable.

Of all the groups of men who have contributed to the land and wildlife of Africa, none come to mind more deserving of praise, or having received less, than those—black and white—who have devoted their careers and often their actual lives to serving the many game departments. As they have found—these wardens of one rank or another, scouts, rangers, control and cropping officers—there are few jobs less financially rewarding on the one hand; on the other, few more frustrating microcosms of bureaucratic pecking order and red tape. As an ex-cropping officer, thinning over-populated elephant and buffalo herds in central Africa, I believe I know of what I speak. But then, most will tell you that there are a lot of ways to get paid. . . .

The early game officers—to generalize a title—were an especially harassed little band, dealing as they had to with an ecologically ignorant public, poachers, low-priority status from the governments and even lower budgets. Many of their lives were tragic existences marked by malaria, heat, cold, drought, locusts and tsetse fly, endless petty reports, loneliness, alcoholism and broken marriages. And, too, there were the animals.

A record of the close calls and fatalities that have befallen game officers in Africa could likely fill several books this size, yet it is not arbitrarily that the incredible story of a night in the life of Harry Wolhuter, a South African game ranger, has been selected. As a classic tale of man the *hunted,* it has few equals.

Wolhuter was a veteran of one of the most colorful British regular outfits of the Boer War, a crackpot command known as Steinacker's Horse for its feisty, bantam-cock leader. Shortly after the war, the Sabi Game Reserve—now the Kruger National Park—came under the wardenship of the well-known administrator, naturalist and author, Major J. Stevenson-Hamilton. Needing help from someone qualified as a hunter, as well as familiar with the terrain, the warden chose Harry Wolhuter as ranger, since much of Harry's time during the war had been spent in the area.

It was a cool winter day in August of 1903 in the Sabi Reserve, and Wolhuter was returning from a patrol on the Olifants River on horseback. With him were three black reserve police, some pack donkeys and three dogs, traveling to a water hole where Harry had planned on spending that night. Since the police were driving the donkeys and not mounted, Wolhuter decided to go ahead to the water hole while they followed behind. Although dusk was falling quickly, the ranger gave no particular thought to making the trip at night; he had often done so during the war to escape the summer heat. With him went one of the dogs, a big male named Bull, trotting alongside the horse as the path led over burned ground studded with occasional patches of tall, dried grass.

After six miles, as he rode through one of these patches of grass, Wolhuter heard two animals jump up in the darkness ahead of his horse. Supposing them to be reedbuck, which were common here, he expected them to run up the path and away, and was surprised when the rustling sounds seemed to be coming nearer. Still not alarmed, he kept riding slowly along until he could see two forms looming through the blackness ten feet away. They were not reed-buck. They were two male lions, and they were crouched to spring.

With no time to raise his rifle, Wolhuter jerked his horse around and gave him the spurs. Too late; there was a terrific shock as a lion jumped onto the horse's rump, hitting the ranger a strong blow on the back. Rearing up in pain and terror, the horse dislodged both the lion and Harry, the latter falling over his mount's right shoulder and almost on top of the second cat, which was rushing in to grab the horse by the throat. This hardly sounds like a marvelous piece of luck, but, in fact, it was; instead of closing his jaws on the man's head, the lion instead sank his teeth into Harry's right shoulder and started to haul him off, his legs and back dragging on the ground under the lion's body. The horse clattered away, chased by the first lion, who was himself chased by the dog.

Harry Wolhuter had plenty to think about as the cat straddled him, dragging him along easily, each step cutting his arms deeply with the lion's dew-claws. Wearing stout spurs, Harry tried to dig them into the ground to act as brakes, but at the resistance, the man-eater just jerked his head, causing pain so unbearable that Wolhuter gave up trying to slow him down. As has been discussed, reports vary widely from survivors of lion or other big cat attacks as to the pain experienced at the actual time of the mauling. David Livingstone wrote at considerable length of his sensa-tions while being chewed by a wounded lion, saying that there was no pain at all, just a kind of numb shock. Other men I have known who have come out on the tattered but alive side of a lion encounter say the agony was excruciating. Wolhuter not only claimed great physical pain, but a horrible, growing terror that the lion would begin to eat him without bothering to kill him first. In any case, he had given himself up for dead, although not necessarily without a fight.

As the lion continued to pull him in agony across the rough ground toward a nearby *spruit,* Harry suddenly happened to think of his belt knife, kept in a sheath on his right hip. His right arm and shoulder gripped in the savage vice of fangs, his face pulled tightly into the lion's rank-smelling mane, he listened to the rumble of the animal's purring as he tried to figure out a way to reach the blade. Slipping his left arm awkwardly behind his back, he didn't really expect to find the knife in its sheath; it was loose-fitting and had dropped out several times when he had been thrown from his horse during the war. Despite the aerobatics he had been through, to his intense joy his fingers touched the cool, hard-wood of the hilt, and he withdrew it. Great! But what the hell does he do now?

Wolhuter remembered having read somewhere (rather an esoteric bit of information, considering that he was actually in a lion's mouth on his way to dinner!) that if a cat is punched in the nose, he is forced to sneeze before doing anything else. What would happen were he to stick the lion in the snoot with the knife? Even though the theory is not correct, he dismissed the notion on the sound reasoning that if the lion did drop him, he would probably pick him up again, possibly with a fatal bite. On the basis that he couldn't very well be worse off, he decided to go for the heart.

Easier decided than done. The blade being an ordinary butcher-type "sticking" knife, with a six-inch cutting edge and no quillion, or guard, Harry reckoned that he would have to stab the left shoulder to be able to reach the heart, although it would have been a cinch to stick the cat through the right side, which was directly above his left hand. Without the use of his right hand or arm, he had to reach *very* carefully across his own chest and feel for the spot where the heart lay. He found it. With a quick backhand thrust, he struck, driving the blade as deeply as he could through the tawny hide. A second time the bloody blade flickered in the starlight. A terrible roar erupted as the cat dropped him, and Harry slashed for the throat above. A torrent of hot, sticky blood poured over Wolhuter as the steel flashed and bit, the lion slinking away into the surrounding blackness.

Not having any idea how badly the man-eater was hurt,

Harry staggered to his feet and, in hopes of frightening him off, shouted some very uncomplimentary things at the nearby location of a series of moans. And then he remembered. There were *two* lions! The first one would be unlikely to catch the horse and would return any second to find him hurt and helpless, except for the knife. His rifle had been lost when he fell and was invisible in the long grass. With his good hand, he fished out his matchbox with the idea of lighting the grass to keep away the other lion. Because of the tooth wounds, as well as several tendons in his right wrist severed by the talons like broken rubber bands, he had to hold the blood-spattered box in his teeth and strike with his left hand. I believe it safe to surmise he was not overly concerned about striking without closing cover. . . . But the grass was too damp with dew to burn anyway, and Harry gave it up, looking for a tree he could climb.

With the use of only one arm and weak with blood loss, this posed quite a project. But at last he found one with a low fork and managed to climb in agony about twelve feet up to a thick branch. In worse shape from the chilling effect of the night wind over his dew- and gore-soaked clothing, he was desperately cold and dizzy, the continuous heavy bleeding from his ripped shoulder making him fear he would pass out and fall. Somehow he strapped himself to the branch with his belt and, suffering from pain and a raging, burning thirst, began the vigil for his three men with the donkeys, who should be passing soon. The lion, which had been grunting and growling nearby all this time, at last gave a long, drawn-out gargle and was still.

Harry's satisfaction at having killed the lion lasted only a few moments; he heard the grass rustle with the approach of the other big male. Unable to catch the horse, the lion was smelling at the place where Wolhuter had stabbed his pal and was now padding along the blood trail, sniffing his way loudly to Harry's tree. With mounting terror, Wolhuter listened to him closer and closer, until the lion stopped at the base of the tree. A jolt of terror welled up over his pain when Harry felt the tree shake with the weight of the big cat. He was coming up! If it was so easy to climb that a weakened, one-armed man could manage it, then what impediment would it be for a determined, healthy maneating lion? With the starlight glimmering in the lion's eyes only a few feet away, Wolhuter shouted at it as loudly as he could.

At this crucial moment, there was another sound in the grass, and Harry was overjoyed to hear the harsh bark of the dog, Bull. Having discovered his master was not aboard the horse, he had returned to find the man. Harry sicked him on the lion, and the big Boer dog harried the cat from the tree, only to have him return again and again, each time more determined.

This went on for about an hour, until Wolhuter heard the sound of tin dishes rattling in the head bundle of one of his men some way down the path. Wolhuter shouted a warning to the native and heard the pack crash to the ground. When asked if he was in a tall tree, the African replied that it wasn't so tall, but he didn't think he would come down and look for a better one. A while later, the other men and the animals came up, Wolhuter calling to them to fire some shots and build a fire to keep off the lion, which they did. The maneater stayed in the shadows but did not run away. Getting their *Baas* down from the tree in his stiffened, painful condition wasn't easy but was finally accomplished.

Even more than the pain of his wounds, Wolhuter suffered from the growing torture of thirst. His men had no water with them, and, since the next pool—for which they had been headed originally—was still six miles away, they began walking at once. Arriving exhausted, Harry was distressed to find that it, too, was dry. There were some old huts at the water hole, left over from the war, and he determined to wait there while his men went to find water anywhere they could. Without a good drink soon, not having had a drop since the day before, Wolhuter knew he would die. At last, after several hours, two of his men returned with a horse's nosebag half-full of a filthy, stinking mixture which was, at least, wet. Harry drank almost all of it, leaving just a bit for his men to clean off his wounds. This process, however, was so unbearably painful that he simply couldn't stand it, and he lay awake all night, much of it with his mangled arm strapped to a hut pole in hope of relieving the agony. It was to no avail.

The next morning, the film of rotting meat on the lion's claws and teeth had done its work. The wounds—the largest of which was actually on Harry's back and not seen by him until reaching a hospital several days later—had turned septic, leaving him with a bonfire of a fever and unable even to stand. Staying in camp that day, he sent his men to skin the lion he had knifed, although not having seen the event they were understandably skeptical. Some time later, they returned with the skin, the skull and the heart, which clearly showed that the knife point had reached the vital organ with both stabs. Wolhuter also believed that he had cut the cat's jugular as it released him, but the manner in which it was skinned apparently left this undecided. The reserve police also had Harry's horse with them, none the worse for physical wear once salt had been rubbed into the claw marks on its rump but left totally neurotic from the attack. It would bolt at the sight of any game animal and Harry later had to sell him. The dead lion's stomach was completely empty, which tends to confirm my own experience and conclusions that a lion will eat a man any time he is hungry enough and one is available.

After another terrible half-delirious night, Harry sent off to a village for some men to carry him on the long journey to the nearest help at a town called Komatipoort, five days away on the Komati River. Dying by inches in his hammocklike *machila*, a litter made of a blanket swung from poles, Wolhuter suffered hell on earth. By now, the bites and claw marks were so septic and rotten, swollen enormously, that the stench of his own decomposing flesh forced him to lie with his face turned away. Somehow, he was still alive at Komatipoort, but the doctor there could do nothing for his pain, as he was flat out of morphia. The following day, a friend went on the train with him to Barberton and the hospital, where he lay near death for weeks. Although several times not expected to last the night, he did survive, and his arm was also saved. For the rest of his life, though, he could only with difficulty lift it high enough to reach the trigger of his shouldered rifle. At that, it was a cheap enough price to pay for escape after being dragged a measured sixty yards through the dark by a man-eating lion.

Harry Wolhuter served the South African government for another forty-two years, retiring at last in 1946. Although he is the only white man I can find on record who killed a lion with a knife in single combat, he is surely the only man in history to have killed *two* lions with that weapon! Stevenson-Hamilton, his boss, wrote that Harry killed a second badly wounded lion by stabbing it in 1945, or perhaps the year before. The reason given by Harry was "to save a cartridge." There may have been a war on, but that is true frugality!

The story of Harry Wolhuter and his knife fight with a lion would not be complete without a short consideration of the weapon itself. It was a standard wedge-shaped blade (sometimes used for the professional slaughtering of sheep and pigs), bearing the trade-mark "Pipe Brand," manufactured by T. Williams of London, a specialist in butcher knives of various styles. This brand was very well thought of at the time, and how Wolhuter had obtained his knife is an interesting sidelight: he had stolen it!

Visiting a cheese shop owned by a friend in Komatipoort years before, he noticed a big wheel of Dutch cheese on the counter and idly picked up the knife left alongside to cut it. When he saw that it was one of the highly regarded and hard-to-find "Pipe Brand" blades, he was horrified that such a fine instrument should be condemned to an existence of cutting cheese. Removing his own knife from its sheath, he switched the two. The owner never noticed, as the two knives were nearly identical in size and shape, unaware of the change having been made until years afterward when Wolhuter told him, explaining the dark deed by saying that "fair exchange was no robbery."

Some years after the stabbing incident, Harry was in London and dropped by the Williams shop to buy a dozen more of the good knives. Remarking to a young salesman that he had once killed a lion with the excellent Williams "sticking" model, the clerk thought he had never heard such an outrageous liar. Mr. Williams, who had heard of the feat, sent Harry an early version of what is today generally known as the "Swiss army knife," a multibladed pocket model with all manner of doodads and gimmicks built into it. A pal of Harry's once commented that it lacked only a small forge and an anvil to be complete.

The skin of Wolhuter's lion and the knife that killed it were on Harry's wall until his death some years ago and are now kept on display in South Africa by a relative, where they were inspected last year by a good friend of mine.

A man doesn't have to be crazy to want to hunt big, dangerous game under the most challenging circumstances possible, but then, it wouldn't be much of a disadvantage, either. Since I mentioned elsewhere in this book that I once killed a Cape buffalo with a spear—two of them, actually, but the first had been badly wounded by a deflected .375 H&H Magnum bullet and was not in much shape to contest the issue—I suppose the tale would bear repetition here. It is not offered as any particular example of the hairiness of my chest and is most certainly not to be construed as the most remote attempt to include myself as a member of the elite company of gentlemen between these pages. You will find no lingering legends in any African barrooms concerning *my* enthusiasm for deeds of derring-do, nor are you likely to unearth any in the future. I tell you this story because it happened and because I found the events quite nearly of fatal interest at the time.

The plane had stirred huge billows of henna Zambian dust as it raced down the little bush strip and sprang like a startled grasshopper into the heat of the colorless, vulture-punctuated central African sky. Piet, the Africaans pilot, swung the Cessna back over us and waggled the wings, showing the white hand flashes of the clients waving good-bye.

Ian and I both gave a sigh of relief. It had been a good safari we had shared, and we both felt the lovely warm lump of traveler's checks wadded in our bush shorts, an unrequired but appreciated gesture of gratitude for eleven new additions to the Rowland Ward record book. It had been five safaris in a row for us both, five months of bone-bruising hunting and thousands of miles of wrestling the long-wheelbase Land Rovers over the bush tracks and spring-snapping dried-mud elephant prints left over from the rainy season; up at four every morning, readying equipment, last to bed after the thirstiest client; five bloody months without a single break. We were ready for a rest, and now we had one. At the time, I didn't realize how permanent mine might become.

Ian walked to the back of his battered Rover and fished under the tarp for the cool white jug. When he placed it on a fender and pressed the button at the base, a long, sparkling stream of his homemade giant killer splashed into the scratched, pebbled plastic "glasses."

"I give you, *Bwana*," he said with a sweeping bow, "our temporary emancipation." He raised the glass. "One full week—seven days, count and savor each one—of the glory of gin and the character-building celibacy of the Natural Life. We are, had you not noticed, somewhat short of the gentle gender."

I lifted my drink to match his salute, trying to keep my eyes from crossing as the clear liquid slid into my stomach like Maury Wills stealing home plate with a shiny new set of cleats. He swung the jug back to Silent, my old gunbearer, who stowed it under the worn dust cover of the hunting car. "Westward, ho, the wagons, Yank!" proclaimed Ian, who has something of a sense for the dramatic. He slid behind the English-drive steering wheel, and we began the fifty-mile bash back to camp, my kidneys feeling as if they'd been through a Cuisinart by the time we pulled up at our joint semipermanent hunting headquarters.

The bush around the little group of grass-thatched *kaias* was blacker than a hanging judge's heart as we finished the platter of fried venison filets and fresh, hot bread. The campfire gleamed greenly through the glass carcasses of two dead bottles of Château Lafite Rothschild—'53, I believe—

leftovers of the clients, while Martin, my majordomo, materialized with two snifters of Fundador and a box of Havana Claros Ian had picked up from a Congolese border guard.

We settled down in the canvas camp chairs and watched the blue-white of the *mopane* wood fire weave its eternal mystery on the soul of all hunters since man first learned to sharpen the stick. A hyena's giggle floated up from the lagoon across the Luangwa River, and a baboon grumbled in his sleep in a nearby fig grove. The distant grunt of a lion blended with the watery adenoidal honk of hippos upstream. Ian held the snifter with both hands, slowly swirling the golden-colored liquid inside. I watched him from across the fire.

"I've got an idea for a few grins," I said tentatively. "We can't just sit around camp all week listening to our cuticles grow, you know."

"We can't?"

"Nope. Listen, chum, you remember my telling you about that pig-sticking down in Argentina?" He nodded and allowed that he recalled some such verbal chest-beating, dismissing it as just another of my usual postsundowner reveries. "Well, we've got a week off, so why not see if we can take a buff with a spear?" He looked at me as if I'd just announced I had found religion.

"Oh, Pedro, you *have* been working too hard! Have you put anything odd into the campfire or been tracking without your hat again?" I could tell he didn't seem to like the idea. "You mean a *Cape* buffalo? With a spear? Who do you think you are, St. George?" He shook his head and took a big bite of the brandy. Speaking slowly, as if to a clear case of diminished capacity, he went on. "Thankee kindly, old boy, but no thanks. I don't know about you, but my clients work hard enough at getting me recycled without any professional help from you. Anyway," he sniffed, "I have a tendency to be biodegradable."

"Now, just hang on a minute," I countered. "I think it can be done, and without getting hashed in the process, either." I topped up the snifters. "You don't have to do anything but cover me, anyway. I'm positive, if I can get up close enough to a bull in enough bush for a good approach, I can nail him. How about it?"

Ian does not sway easily. "Look," he explained with the same weary patience, "if you can get close enough to get *him,* then he will be close enough to get *you.* Try sticking some economy-size hatpin into one of those babies, and he'll be all over you before you can say whiskey soda, please. Remember what happened to our old buddy Karl?"

I remembered, indeed. Karl (which is not his real name) was a professional in a neighboring country who had started believing his own publicity, which is a no-no if you wish to finish your career with the same general bilateral symmetry you were issued. After a wealthy client had missed a close, easy shot, Karl had made the usual comment concerning being close enough to hit the buff with a ten-foot pole. Angry at the unflattering observation, the client had bet Karl a large sum at excellent odds that the professional didn't have the nerve to try just that. Karl did win the bet, but I don't believe it came close to covering his hospital and doctor bills over the next couple of years he spent in traction and on crutches.

"Just the same, chum," I continued undaunted, "I'd like to give it a go, anyway. If you'll back me up with that self-propelled gun of yours, that is."

Ian looked into the fire for a long time, then shrugged. "Okay, mate," he said finally. "I don't know where you got your Tarzan complex, but if you get mailed back to the land of the free in a manila envelope, remember who told you so."

Two days later, I remembered who told me so and wished I had listened.

All my life I had been fascinated by spear hunting, which I believe is the absolute apogee of sport. Before this particular exercise with Ian, my experience had been quite limited, totaling one Peter's gazelle in Ethiopia, two wild boar in Argentina and the aforementioned wounded and mostly incapacitated buffalo I stuck on safari in Zambia in 1969 with a client from New York. True, I was able to kill the

Chabunkwa man-eating lion while he was mauling Silent by cutting his spinal column with the edge of my gunbearer's broken-shafted spear, but that was sheer good luck and not true spear hunting.

Now the choice of Cape buffalo as my prey was really a matter of elimination, since this was the only species of really big game permitted on my professional hunter's "pot," or ration license, which permitted me, over a full season, to kill ten for food for myself and my native staff. Except for buffalo, impala and wildebeest, no other species may be taken by a licensed pro hunter in Zambia, and these only for food.

I see no need at this point to get into the awesome stature, temperament and reputation of the African Cape buffalo, because, unless you just learned to read this morning, you are aware that he can be one of the toughest, nastiest and trickiest animals ever placed on earth to keep strains of lunacy from spreading through the genes of big-game hunters. (I also suspect that motorcycle racing and hang gliding will, sure as nature, take over where polio and the black plague left off.) Still, no matter how tough he may be, if you can stick a razor-sharp piece of steel two and three-quarter inches wide and seventeen inches long into his boiler room and through the lungs, you're going to get his fatal attention. If great archer Fred Bear managed it with just one arrow in Mozambique, then the much wider wound channel of the spear would just *have* to be as effective. The only (and considerable) difference would be that old Fred can shoot an arrow a mite farther than I can throw a three-pound spear, and with a great deal more accuracy. I would have to be within ten yards. Ten yards is much closer in spearhunting Cape buffalo than it is at the goal line of the Super Bowl. . . .

A very bleary-looking Ian was already at the breakfast table of the dining hut with its wall-less vista of the Luangwa below. I ordered up scrambles and impala liver as the gaudy sunrise began to flood across the sparkling dewdrops of the African bushveldt. After breakfast, we drove over to the local village with a piece of broken spring from my Land Rover for the blacksmith to fashion into what I considered to be a proper spearhead. The style used locally was not to my liking: a tang formed at the base of the head which was set into a hollow at the head of the shaft male/female, and sweated tight with wrappings of native copper or a section of straightened bicycle handlebar. This prevented the spearhead from penetrating past the joint, and, brother, I wanted every inch of depth into that rocklike muscle I could beg, borrow or ransom. That afternoon, the smithy's son came trotting into camp with it. Perfect! It was five feet, ten inches overall, the blade wide and tapering with a central ridge for strength and an eight-inch female socket fitted exactly to the shaft of tough, knobby, seasoned thornwood. A counterweight was shod to the butt in a similar manner. I praised the boy and gave him the extravagant fee of fifty *Ngwee,* roughly thirty-five cents in U.S. money. I went off to practice with it, using the pithy portion of an elephant-damaged *baobab,* or cream-of-tartar tree, as a target.

Remembering that by some freak I had hit the wounded buff exactly in the heart (which had done nothing to depress the value of my stock locally) and the heart had continued to beat for a mighty long time, I knew I would have to be able to hit an eight-inch circle without fail. My eye still being "in," I found I could do this just about every throw from twelve yards; but *baobab* trees do not move or have long, sharp horns, so I decided not to try to throw from over ten yards, as I had previously calculated. Satisfied that I was up to my end of things and that the spear would do the job if I did mine, I went back to camp and sat down with Ian to cook up a plan of action.

We knew that there were several groups of buffalo bulls along this stretch of river fairly near camp, who watered at night and then retreated to the thickets a mile back from the water to feed and rest. In particular, there was one very large old boy with a boss corrugated like ancient oak bark that covered his head like a helmet. His once-long, immensely thick horns were now so worn with age they had lost their beauty, but if they now lacked the classic sweep of the mature bull, they were made even more impressive by the short, tent-peg points that looped low and deadly. Ian and I had both seen him many times but never let a client take him because the measurement was no longer there, yet we knew where he spent the hot afternoons, dodging the tsetse, and decided that, on the basis of one barrel of trouble at a time being sufficient, we would try him, rather than fool around with a small herd of bulls.

In cover of this thick type, I knew I was risking the shaft glancing off a branch or twig and had determined not to risk a throw unless I had a clear, broadside angle where I could be fairly certain of getting the long spearhead past the barrel-stave ribs and into heart, lungs or major arteries. I would go first, with the spear, and Ian would follow ten to fifteen yards behind and to my left, always keeping me in sight. If he was directly behind me, I would be in his line of fire in case of a frontal charge. "Of course," he mused, "doesn't really matter if I shoot you or that buff catches up with you. Dead's dead." Nice guy, Ian.

The next afternoon, right after lunch, we piled into my Rover and drove for the heavy bush about two miles from camp, cutting the engine halfway there. Ian fed four ugly, blunt-snouted, full-jacket rounds into his .458 Winchester Magnum Model 70 and slipped the bolt home with an oily snick.

We picked up the early-morning spoor of the bull and followed it across an open *dambo* into a patch of scrub and thorn. The big bull had moved slowly, casually, pausing frequently to graze from the fresh clumps of green grass sprouting from the black patches of a bush fire some weeks old. Once, he had stopped to rub against a sapling, the core of dried mud from his morning wallowing still slightly damp, despite the midday heat.

Ahead was a tallish *mopane* tree with some lower branches. I lay the spear on the ground and silently climbed fifteen feet up the tree. I could see about one hundred yards, probing the mottled tangles for movement. At first, he was invisible in the shadows, although I realized with a start that I had been looking right at him forty yards away. Then he flicked a thorn-torn, ragged ear to dislodge a fly, and his black-gray bulk began to take shape. I hand-signaled to Ian and slithered down the tree. We planned the stalk by scratching with sticks on a clear spot of ground, and I indicated to him the tops of the bushes where the bull was standing.

I crawled through the cover an inch at a time, sliding the spear quietly ahead, laying it down, then creeping up to it for another move forward. I kept my eyes on the bush where the bull stood, trying to picture him, listening for any possible change in his position—such as directly at me in a flat-out charge. After twenty-five yards, I could make out his hind quarters and his rear legs, the dung-matted tail flipping only a few feet from where I had first seen him. He was fifteen yards away now, still facing three-quarters away from me.

There was one light screen of bush between us as I slowly rose into a crouch. My legs ached from the slow-motion change of my position, and the spear felt tiny in my wet hand. I struggled to fight down that odd choking sensation, the mixture of terror and exhilaration that we all know who put ourselves in harm's way for the sake of the experience itself. I felt as if every drop of my strength had leaked out and soaked into the hard ground, positive I could have lit a blue-tip kitchen match on the dry surface of my tongue.

One more step, and I would be clear for the throw. I stole a glance at the curved beauty of the spearhead, the forge marks and tiny striations along the cutting edge where the whetstone had licked it. I gripped the knobby shaft tightly, mentally talking to myself. Easy, now . . . wait until the angle's right. He's coming a little more broadside. Take it cool. Wait. Wait. That's a nice moo-cow, one more little step. Okay. Raise the spear very slowly, or he'll see the movement. Very nice.

Now! I whipped the blade forward with every fiber of my body and saw it flash through a shaft of sun, winging dead-on into the center of that black, muscular shoulder, driving well past the point, almost a foot of the shaft slicing deep. There was a dull, meaty *thug!* and a *screek!* as the steel scraped on rib bone. A wild thrill of victory surged through me as I instantly turned to run for a tree to my right. It turned to numb fear as I caught my foot on something, and the ground came up to belt me in the face.

The bull gave a screaming, wet bawl and spun toward me, a gush of claret blood pouring from his nostrils and open mouth. In an instant, I was back on my feet, running faster than I had ever thought possible, the dirt and leaves flashing away beneath me, the steady thudding of the hooves louder and louder just behind my back. In that second, I knew I wasn't going to make it.

There was a deafening bang and the whock of a big bullet slapping meat, but the hooves were still there, even closer. I jinked to one side as the .458 slammed again, and there was a crashing sound like a tree falling. Ian had gotten the bull before it had gotten me.

The buffalo lay on his right side, the spear shaft jutting stiffly from his lung area. Six inches above the spear wound was a white-edged hole where Ian's second shot had broken the bull's spine, dropping him as dead as chastity in his tracks, which were at the time about one yard short of *my* tracks when my feet were still in them. He was dead, and I was alive. That seemed a pretty pleasant proposition at the time, and still is.

Ian walked up, his hands fumbling for a cigarette. He started to say something but gave up on the second try, just shaking his head. After examining the bull in silence and tying my bush jacket (having wrung it out) to the carcass to keep off vultures until the staff could come and butcher it, we went back to the Rover and drove home. Back at camp, Martin had a couple of tall ones waiting, with several to follow.

Drawing a reasonably normal breath, I looked at Ian and said, "Guess you know that it really doesn't count." He looked at me incredulously.

Gaping, he managed, "What the bloody hell do you mean it bloody well doesn't *count*? You got him, didn't you?"

"Nope. You did. It's against the rules, old chappie, though I'm mighty glad you broke them. Same as in archery; you have to make your kill unaided. Same thing should apply to spear hunting, seems to me. Rules, you know. Playing fields of Eton and all that."

Although I had made the stalk successfully and gotten in a throw that would obviously have killed the buff in a matter of a few minutes at most, I still couldn't claim that I had killed a Cape buffalo with a spear single-handedly. In fact, if Ian hadn't dropped him cold with that spine shot, my hash would have been rather thoroughly settled in about another half-second.

"What the hell," Ian snorted. "You did what you wanted to do—prove that a man *could* kill a buff with a spear. As it is, you're bloody lucky I was able to spine him, or we'd be grooming your receding hairline with a shovel right about now. Whaddya want? An egg in your beer?"

I took another long pull at the frosty mug and thought about it. No, I did not want an egg in my beer.

BIBLIOGRAPHY

Baker, S. W. Esq. *The Rifle and the Hound in Ceylon.* London: Longman, Brown, Green, and Longmans, 1854.

Wolhuter, Harry. *Memories of a Game Ranger.* Johannesburg: The Wildlife Protection Society of South Africa, 1948.